The Urbana Free Library

To renew materials call
217-367-4057

Valhalla Rising

Valhalla Rising

Clive Cussler

Thorndike Press • Chivers Press
Waterville, Maine USA   Bath, England

This Large Print edition is published by Thorndike Press, USA and by Chivers Press, England.

Published in 2002 in the U.S. by arrangement with
G. P. Putnam's Sons, a member of Penguin Putnam Inc.

Published in 2002 in the U.K. by arrangement with
Penguin Books.

U.S. Hardcover 0-7862-3813-5 (Basic Series Edition)
U.S. Softcover 0-7862-3818-6
U.K. Hardcover 0-7540-1746-X (Windsor Large Print)
U.K. Softcover 0-7540-9141-4 (Paragon Large Print)

The text of this Large Print edition is unabridged.
Other aspects of the book may vary from the original edition.

Set in 16 pt. Plantin by Elena Picard.

Printed in the United States on permanent paper.

British Library Cataloguing-in-Publication Data available

Library of Congress Cataloging-in-Publication Data

Cussler, Clive.
    Valhalla rising / Clive Cussler.
        p.   cm.
    ISBN 0-7862-3813-5 (lg. print : hc : alk. paper) —
    ISBN 0-7862-3818-6 (lg. print : sc : alk. paper)
    1. Pitt, Dirk (Fictitious character) — Fiction.
2. Shipwrecks — Fiction. 3. Large type books.   I. Title.
PS3553.U75 V3 2002
    813'.54—dc21   2001054419

*I'm enormously grateful to
Penn Stohr, Gloria Farley, Richard DeRosset,
Tim Firme, U.S. Submarines and
my local fire department
for their guidance and expertise.*

Into Oblivion

VIKINGS IN THE FJORD

They moved through the morning mist like ghosts, silent and eerie in phantom ships. Tall, serpentine prows arched gracefully on bow and stern, crowned with intricately carved dragons, teeth bared menacingly in a growl as if their eyes were piercing the vapor in search of victims. Meant to incite fear into the crew's enemies, the dragons were also believed to be protection against the evil spirits that lived in the sea.

The little band of immigrants had come across a hostile sea in long, elegantly shaped black hulls that skimmed the waves with the ease and stability of trout in a peaceful brook. Long oars reached from holes in the hulls and dipped into the dark water, pulling the ships through the waves. Their square red-and-white striped sails hung limp in the listless air. Small lapstrake boats twenty feet long and carrying extra cargo were tied to the sterns and towed behind.

These people were the precursors of those who would come much later: men, women and children, along with their meager possessions, including livestock. Of the paths Norsemen had blazed across the oceans, none was more dangerous than the great voyage across the North Atlantic. Despite the perils of the unknown, they'd boldly sailed through the ice floes, struggled under the gale-force winds, fought monstrous waves and endured vicious storms that surged out of the southwest. Most had survived, but the sea had exacted its cost. Two of the eight ships that had set out from Norway were lost and never seen again.

Finally, the storm-worn colonists reached the west coast of Newfoundland, but instead of landing at L'Anse aux Meadows, the site of Leif Eriksson's earlier settlement, they were determined to explore farther south in the hope of finding a warmer climate for their new colony. After skirting a very large island, they steered a southwesterly course until they reached a long arm of land that curved northward from the mainland. Continuing around two lower islands, they sailed for another two days past a vast white sandy beach, a great source of wonder to people who had lived all their lives on unending coastlines of jagged rock.

Rounding the tip of the seemingly unending stretch of sand, they encountered a wide bay. Without hesitation, the little fleet of ships entered the calmer waters and sailed west, helped along by an incoming tide. A fog bank rolled over them, casting a damp blanket of moisture over the water. Later in the day, the sun became a dim orange ball as it began to set over an unseen western horizon. A conference was shouted among the commanders of the ships and it was agreed to anchor until morning, in hopes the fog would lift.

When first light came, the fog had been replaced with a light mist, and it could be seen that the bay narrowed into a fjord that flowed into the sea. Setting out the oars, the men rowed into the current as their women and children stared quietly at the high palisades that emerged from the dying mist on the west bank of the river, rising ominously above the masts of the ships. What seemed to them to be incredibly giant trees forested the rolling land behind the crest. Though they saw no sign of life, they suspected they were being watched by human eyes hidden among the trees. Every time they had come ashore for water, they had been harassed by the Skraelings, their term for any foreign-born natives that lived in the alien country they hoped to colonize. The Skraelings had not proven friendly, and on more than one occasion had unleashed clouds of arrows against the ships.

Keeping their usual warlike nature under firm control, the expedition leader, Bjarne Sigvatson, had not allowed his warriors to fight back. He knew well that other colonists from Vinland and Greenland had been plagued by the Skraelings, too, a situation caused by the Vikings who had murdered several of the innocent inhabitants purely out of a barbaric love of killing. This trip Sigvatson would demand that the native inhabitants be treated in a friendly manner. He felt it vital for the survival of the colony to trade cheap goods for furs and other necessities, without the bloodshed. And, unlike Thorfinn Karlsefni and Leif Eriksson, whose earlier expeditions were eventually driven off by the Skraelings, this one was armed to the teeth by men who were blood-hardened Norwegian veterans of many battles with their archenemies, the Saxons. Swords slung over their shoulders, one hand clutching a long spear, the other a huge axe, they were the finest fighting men of their time.

The incoming tide could be felt far up the river and helped the rowers make headway into the current, which was mild due to the low gradient. The river's mouth was only three-quarters of a mile wide, but it soon broadened to almost two miles. The land on the sloping shore to the east was green with lush vegetation.

Sigvatson, who was standing with his arm around the great dragon prow of the lead ship, gazing through the dying mist into the distance, pointed to a shadow in the steep rock palisades looming around a slight bend. "Pull toward the left bank," he ordered the rowers. "There looks to be an opening in the cliffs where we can shelter for the night."

As they drew closer, the dark, forbidding entrance of a flooded cavern grew in size until it broadened wide enough for a ship to enter. Sigvatson peered into the gloomy interior and saw that the passage traveled deep under the sheer walls of the cliff. He ordered the other ships to drift while the mast on his ship was unstepped and laid flat to permit entry beneath the low arch at the cavern's mouth. The fjord's stream swirled around the entrance, but the hardy rowers easily drove the ship inside, shipping the oars only slightly to keep them from striking the flanks of the opening.

As they passed through, the women and children leaned over the bulwarks and stared down through water of startling clarity, schools of fish clearly visible swimming over the rocky bottom nearly fifty feet below. It was with no little trepidation that they found themselves in a high-ceilinged grotto easily large enough to hold a fleet of ships three times the size of the little Viking fleet. Though their ancestors had embraced Christianity, old pagan traditions died hard. Naturally formed grottos were regarded as the dwelling places of the gods.

The walls on the interior of the grotto, formed by the cooling of molten rock 200,000 million years earlier, had been sculpted and worn smooth by the waves of an ancient sea against the volcanic rock layers that were an extension of nearby mountains. They arched upward into a domed ceiling that was bare of moss or hanging growth. Surprisingly, it was also free of bats. The chamber was mostly dry. The water level stopped at a ledge that ascended three feet and stretched into the inner reaches of the cavern for a distance of nearly two hundred feet.

Sigvatson shouted through the grotto entrance for the other ships to follow. Then his rowers eased off their strokes and let the ship drift until its stem post bumped lightly against the edge of the second cavern's floor. As the other ships approached the landing, long gangplanks were run out and everyone scurried onto dry land, happy to stretch their legs for the first time in days. The foremost matter of business was to serve the first hot meal they'd eaten since an earlier landing hundreds of miles to the north. The children spread out throughout the caverns to gather driftwood, running along the shelves that eons of water erosion had carved in the rock. Soon the women had fires going and were baking bread, while cooking porridge and fish stew in large iron pots. Some of the men began repairing the wear and tear on the ships from the rugged voyage, while others threw out nets and caught schools of fish teeming in the fjord. The women were only too happy to find such comfortable shelter from the elements. The men, on the other hand, were big, tousle-haired outdoorsmen and sailors who found it unpleasant to exist in rockbound confinement.

After eating and just before settling in for the night in their leather sleeping bags, two of Sigvatson's young children, an eleven-year-old boy and ten-year-old girl, came running up to him, shouting excitedly. They grabbed his big hands and began dragging him into the deepest part of the cavern. Lighting torches, they led him into a long tunnel barely large enough to stand in. It was a tube passage, a rounded cave system originally formed when underwater.

After climbing over and around fallen rock, they ascended upward for two hundred feet. Then the children stopped and motioned to a small crevice. "Father, look, look!" cried the girl. "There is a hole leading outside. You can see the stars."

Sigvatson saw that the hole was too small and narrow even for the children to crawl through, but he could clearly see the night-time sky. The next day, he put several men to work smoothing the tunnel floor to ease access and widening the exit hole. When the opening was expended so a man could walk through while standing straight, they found themselves stepping into a large meadow bordered by stout trees. No barren, Greenland timberless land here. The supply of lumber to build houses was limitless. The ground was thick with wildflowers and grass to graze their livestock. It was on this generous land high above the beautiful, blue fjord bountiful with fish that Sigvatson would build his colony.

The gods had shown the way to the children, who led the grown-ups to what they all hoped was their newly found paradise.

The Norsemen had a lust for life. They worked hard, lived hard and they died hard. The sea was their element. To them, a man without a boat was a man in chains. Though feared throughout the Middle Ages for their barbarian instincts, they re-shaped Europe. The hardy immigrants fought and settled in Russia, Spain and France and became merchants and merce-naries, renowned for their courage and ability with the sword and battle-ax. Hrolf the Gange won Normandy, which was named after the Norsemen. His descendant William conquered England.

Bjarne Sigvatson was the image of a golden Viking. His hair was blond with a beard to match. He was not a tall man, but broad in the shoulders, with the strength of an ox. Bjarne was born in 980 on his father's farm in Norway, and like most young Viking men grew up with a restless yearning to see what was over the next horizon. Inquisitive and bold, yet deliberate, he joined expeditions that raided Ireland when he was only fifteen. By the time he was twenty, Bjarne was a battle-ripened, seaborne raider with enough pillaged treasure to build a fine ship and mount his own raiding expeditions. He married Freydis, a sturdy self-reliant beauty with long golden hair and blue eyes. It was a fortunate match. They blended together like sun and sky.

After amassing a vast fortune from plundering towns and villages up and down Britain and sporting numerous scars from battle, Bjarne retired from raiding and became a merchant, trading in amber, the diamond of its time. But after a few years, he became restless, especially after hearing the sagas about the epic explorations of Erik the Red and his son Leif Eriksson. The lure of strange lands far to the west beckoned, and he became determined to mount his own voyage into the unknown to found a colony. He soon put together a fleet of ten ships to carry 350 people with their families, livestock and farming tools. One ship alone was loaded with Bjarne's fortune in amber and plundered treasure, to be used for future exchange with ships transporting goods from Norway and Iceland.

The cavern made an ideal boat and storage house as well as a fortress against any attack by the Skraelings. The sleek craft were pulled from the water onto trees cut into rollers and placed in hewn cradles on the hard rock shelf. The Vikings constructed beautiful ships that were the marvel of their age. They were not only incredibly efficient sailing machines but also masterworks of sculpture, magnificently proportioned and lavishly decorated with elaborate carvings on stem and stern. Few vessels before or since have matched their lines for pure elegance.

The long ship was the vessel used for raiding around Europe. She was extremely fast and versatile, with ports for fifty oars. But it was the *knarr* that was the workhorse of the Viking explorers. Fifty to sixty feet long with a broad fifteen-foot beam, the *knarr* could carry fifteen tons of cargo over great distances at sea. She relied mostly on her big square sail for the open sea, but mounted as many as ten oars for cruising in shallow water near shorelines.

Her fore and aft decks were planked with a spacious open deck amidships that could be loaded with cargo or livestock. The crew and passengers suffered in the open, protected only by ox hides. There were no special quarters for chieftains such as Sigvatson; Vikings sailed as ordinary seamen, all equal to one another, their leader assuming command for important decisions. The *knarr* was at home in rough seas. Under gale winds and towering swells, she could barrel through the worst the gods could throw at her and still plunge ahead at five to seven knots, covering over 150 miles a day.

Built of sturdy oak by superb Viking shipwrights who shaped by hand and eye and used only axes to work the wood, the keel was cut from a single piece of oak into a T-shaped beam that increased stabilization in heavy seas. Next came oak planks that were hewn into thin strakes running with the grain and which curved gracefully before being joined at the stern and stem posts. Known as a clinker-type hull, the planks above overlapped the ones below. Then they were caulked with tarred hair from the animals. Except for the crossbeams that braced the hull and supported the decks, there wasn't another piece of wood on the ship that lay in a straight line. The whole thing looked too fragile for the storms that swept the North Atlantic, but there was a method to the seeming madness. The keel could flex and the hull warp, enabling the ship to glide effortlessly with less resistance from the water, making her the most stable ship of the middle centuries. And her shallow draft allowed her to slip over huge waves like a shingle.

The rudder was also a masterwork of engineering. A stout steering oar attached to the starboard quarter, its vertical shaft was turned by the helmsman using a horizontal tiller. The rudder was always mounted on the right side of the hull and was called a *stjornbordi* — the word came to mean starboard. The helmsman kept one eye on the sea and the other on a bronze, intricately designed weathervane that was mounted on either the stem post or mast. By studying the whims of the wind, he could steer the most favorable tack.

A large oak block served as the keelson where the foot of the mast was set. The mast measured thirty feet tall and held a sail that spread nearly twelve hundred square feet cut in a rectangle only slightly wider than a square. The sails were woven from coarse wool in two layers for added strength. Then they were dyed in shades of red and white, usually in designs of simple stripes or diamonds.

Not only were the Vikings master ship-builders and sailors; they were exceptional navigators as well. They were born with a genius for seamanship. A Viking could read the currents, the clouds, the water temperature, wind and waves. He studied the migrations of fish and birds. At night he steered by the stars. During the day he used a sun shadow board, a disklike sundial with a center shaft that was slipped up and down to measure the sun's declination by tracing its shadow on notched lines on the board's surface. Viking latitude calculations were amazingly accurate. It wasn't often that a Viking ship became hopelessly lost. Their mastery of the sea was complete and never challenged.

In the following months the colonists built thick wooden longhouses with massive beams to support a sod roof. They raised a great communal hall with a huge hearth for cooking and socializing that also served for storage and as a livestock shelter. Hungry for rich land, the Norsemen wasted no time in planting crops. They harvested berries and netted fish in great abundance from the fjord. The Skraelings proved curious yet reasonably friendly. Trinkets, cloth and cows' milk were traded for valuable furs and game. Sigvatson wisely ordered his men to keep their metal swords, axes and spears out of sight. The Skraelings possessed the bow and arrow, but their hand weapons were still crudely made of stone. Sigvatson correctly took it for granted that before long the Norseman's superior weapons would either be stolen or demanded in trade.

By fall they were fully prepared for a harsh winter. But this year the weather was mild, with little snow and few frigid days. The settlers marveled at the sunny days that were longer than they'd been used to in Norway and during their short stay in Iceland. With spring, Sigvatson prepared to send out a large scouting expedition to explore the new and strange land. He chose to remain behind to assume the duties and responsibilities of running the now-thriving little community. He picked his younger brother, Magnus, to lead the expedition.

A hundred men were selected by Sigvatson for the journey he expected would be long and arduous. After weeks of preparation, sails were raised on six of the smallest boats while the men, women and children who remained behind waved farewell to the little armada as it set off up the river to find its headwaters. What was to have been a two-month scouting expedition, however, turned into an epic journey of fourteen months. Sailing and rowing except when they had to haul their boats overland to the next waterway, the men traveled on wide rivers and across enormous lakes that seemed as vast as the great northern sea. They sailed on a river that was far larger than any of them had seen in Europe or around the Mediterranean. Three hundred miles down the great waterway, they came ashore and camped in a thickly wooded forest. Here they covered and hid the boats. Then they launched a year-long trek through rolling hills and endless grasslands.

The Norsemen found strange animals they'd never seen before. Small doglike creatures that howled in the night. Large cats with short tails, and huge furry beasts with horns and enormous heads. These they killed with spears and found the flesh as delectable as beef.

Because they did not linger in one place, the Skraelings did not consider them a threat and caused no trouble. The explorers were fascinated and amused by the differences in the Skraeling tribes. Some stood proudly and possessed noble bearing, but others looked little better than filthy animals.

Many months later, they came to a halt when they saw the peaks of enormous mountains rising in the distance. In awe of the great land that seemed to go on forever, they decided it was time to turn back and reach the colony before the first snows of winter. But when the weary travelers finally reached the settlement in midsummer expecting a joyous welcome, they found only devastation and tragedy. The entire colony had been burned to the ground and all that was left of their comrades, wives and children were scattered bones. What terrible friction had caused the Skraelings to go on a rampage and slaughter the Vikings? What had caused the break of peaceful relations? There were no answers from the dead.

Magnus and the enraged and grieving surviving Norseman discovered that the opening to the tunnel leading down to the cavern where the ships were stored had been covered over with rocks and brush by the late inhabitants and hidden from the Skraelings. Somehow the settlers had managed to hide the treasures and sacred relics Sigvatson had plundered in his younger days, along with their most cherished personal possessions, concealing them in the ships during the Skraelings' attack.

The anguished warriors might have turned their backs on the carnage and sailed away, but it was not in their genes. They lusted for revenge, knowing it would most likely end in death. But to a Viking, dying while fighting an enemy was a spiritual and glorious death. And then there was the terrible possibility that their wives and daughters might have been carried away as slaves by the Skraelings.

Wild with grief and rage, they collected the remains of their friends and families and carried them down the tunnel to the cavern, where they placed them in the ships. It was part of their traditional ceremony to send the dead to a glorious hereafter in Valhalla. They identified the mutilated remains of Bjarne Sigvatson and laid him in his ship, wrapping him in a cloak and surrounding his body with the remains of his two children and his treasures from life and buckets of food for the journey. They longed to place his wife, Freydis, beside him, but her body could not be found, nor were there any livestock left to sacrifice. All had been taken by the Skraelings.

Traditionally, the ships and their dead would have been buried, but that was not possible. They feared that the Skraelings would dig up and plunder the dead. So the saddened warriors hammered and chiseled at a huge rock above the grotto's entrance until it dropped in a massive spill along with tons of smaller boulders, effectively sealing off the cavern from the surface of the river. The rock jammed together in a chute several feet below the waterline, leaving a large unseen opening underwater.

The ceremony completed, the Norsemen prepared themselves for battle.

Honor and courage were qualities they held sacred. They were in a state of euphoria, knowing they would soon see battle. Deep within their souls, they had longed for combat, the clash of arms, the smell of blood. It was part of their culture, and they had grown up and were trained by their fathers to be warriors, expert in the art of killing. They sharpened their long swords and battle-axes that were forged from fine steel by German craftsmen — treasured objects, highly prized and worshiped. Both sword and axe were given names as if they lived and breathed.

They donned their magnificent chainmail shirts to protect their upper bodies and their simple conical helmets, some with nosepieces but none with horns. They took up their shields made of wood painted in bright colors, a large metal rivet in the front attached to arm straps in the rear. All carried spears with extremely long, sharp points. Some wielded broad double-edged swords three feet in length, while others preferred the big battle-ax.

When ready, Magnus Sigvatson led his force of a hundred Vikings toward the large village of the Skraelings, three miles distant from the horrible massacre. The village was actually more of a primitive city containing hundreds of huts housing nearly two thousand Skraelings. There was no attempt at guile or stealth. The Vikings stormed out of the trees, howling like mad dogs, and rushed through the short stake fence that surrounded the village, built more to keep animals out than attacking humans.

The smashing onset wrought great havoc among the Skraelings, who stood stunned and were cut down like cattle. Nearly two hundred were slaughtered by the ferocious savagery of the unexpected assault before they could grasp what was happening. Quickly, in groups of five and ten men, they began to fight back. Though they were familiar with the spear and had formed crude stone axes, their favorite weapon of war was the bow and arrow, and soon a hail of arrows filled the sky. The women joined in the chaos, throwing a shower of stones that did little but dent the Vikings' helmets and shields.

Magnus charged ahead of his warriors, fighting two-handed with spear in one hand, gigantic battle-ax in the other, both drenched and dripping crimson. He was what the Vikings called a *beserkr*, a word that would pass down the centuries as berserk — a seemingly crazed man intent on striking terror in the minds of his enemies. He shrieked like a maniac as he hurled himself at the Skraelings, felling many with his flailing axe.

The brutal ferocity overawed the Skraelings. Those who tried to fight the Norsemen hand-to-hand were beaten off with terrible casualties. Though they were decimated, however, their numbers never diminished. Runners scattered to nearby villages and soon returned with reinforcements, and the Skraelings fell back to regroup as their losses were replaced.

In the first hour, the avengers had worked their deadly way through the village, searching for any sign of their women, but none could be found. Only bits and pieces of cloth from their dresses, worn as adornment by the Skraeling women, were ferreted out. Beyond wrath there is rage, and beyond rage is hysteria. In a frenzy the Vikings assumed that their women had been cannibalized, and their fury turned to ice-cold madness. They did not know that the five women who had survived the slaughter at the settlement had not been harmed but passed on to chiefs of other villages as tribute. Instead, their ferocity mushroomed and the earth inside the Skraeling village became soaked in blood. But still the Skraeling replacements kept coming, and eventually the tide began to turn.

Overwhelmingly outnumbered and severely weakened from wounds and exhaustion, the Vikings were whittled down until only ten were still left standing around Magnus Sigvatson. The Skraelings no longer made frontal assaults against the deadly swords and axes. They no longer feared the Norsemen's spears that had been either thrown or shattered. A growing army, now outnumbering the dwindling Vikings by fifty to one, stood out of range and shot great flights of arrows into the small cluster of survivors who crouched under their shields as the arrows struck and protruded like quills from a porcupine. Still the Vikings fought on, attacking, ever attacking.

Then the Skraelings rose up as one, and with reckless abandon smashed against the Viking shields. The great tide engulfed the small band of Norsemen and swirled around the warriors making their final stand. The few who were left stood back to back and fought to the brutal end, enduring an avalanche of vicious blows by hatchets made of stone, until they could endure no more.

Their last thoughts were of their lost loved ones and the glorious death that was waiting. To a man they perished, sword and axe in hand. Magnus Sigvatson was the last to fall, his death the most tragic. He died as the last hope for colonizing North America for the next five hundred years. And he left a legacy that would dearly cost those who would eventually follow. Before the sun fell, all one hundred of the brave Norsemen found death, along with more than a thousand Skraeling men, women and children they had slaughtered. In a most horrible manner, the Skraelings had come to recognize that the white-skinned strangers from across the sea were a marauding threat that could only be stopped by savage force.

A pall of shock spread over the Skraeling nations. No blood battle between tribes had ever matched the pure ghastly death toll, nor the horrible wounds and mutilation. The great battle was only an ancient prelude to the horrendous wars that were yet to come.

To the Vikings living in Iceland and Norway, the fate of Bjarne Sigvatson's colony became a mystery. No one was left alive to tell their story, and no other immigrant-explorers followed in their path across the truculent seas. The colonists became a forgotten footnote in the sagas passed down through the ages.

Monster from the Deep

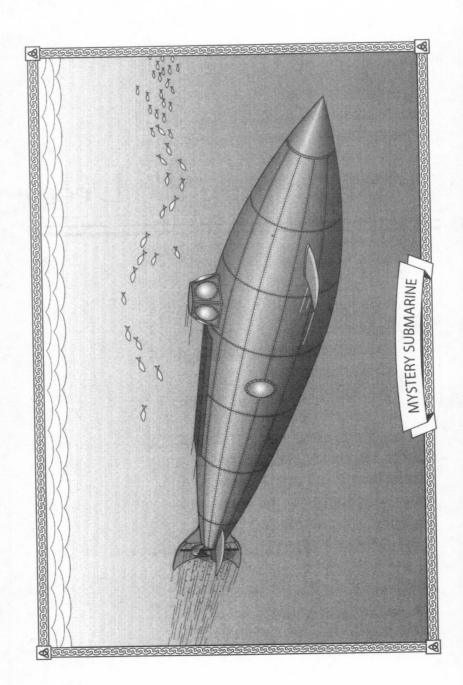

MYSTERY SUBMARINE

FEBRUARY 2, 1894
THE CARIBBEAN SEA

No one on board the old wooden-hulled war-ship *Kearsarge* could have foreseen the catastrophe that was about to strike. Displaying the flag and protecting United States' interests in the West Indies, she was on a voyage from Haiti to Nicaragua when her lookouts spotted a strange shape in the water a mile off the starboard bow. Visibility under clear skies stretched to the surrounding horizons and the sea was calm, the swells rising no more than two feet from trough to crest. The black-humped back of a strange species of sea monster could clearly be seen with the naked eye.

"What do you make of it?" Captain Leigh Hunt asked his first officer, Lieutenant James Ellis, as he stared through a pair of brass binoculars.

Ellis squinted through a telescope, braced against the railing to keep it steady, at the object in the distance. "My first guess is that it's a whale, but I've never seen one move so steadily through the water without showing its tail or diving beneath the surface. Also, there's a strange mound protruding forward of its center."

"It must be some type of rare sea serpent," said Hunt.

"No beast I'm aware of," murmured Ellis in awe.

"I can't believe it's a man-made vessel."

Hunt was a thin man with graying hair. His leathery face and deep-set brown eyes were those of a man who spent many long hours in the sun and wind. He clutched a pipe between his lips that was very seldom lit. Hunt was a navy professional with a quarter century of oceangoing experience and a fine record of efficient conduct behind him. He had been given command of the most famous ship in the navy as an honor before his retirement. Too young to have served in the Civil War, Hunt graduated from the naval academy in 1869 and served on eight different warships, rising through the ranks until he was offered command of the *Kearsarge*.

The venerable ship had earned her fame after an epic sea battle thirty years earlier in which she'd battered and sunk the infamous Confederate raider, *Alabama*, off Cherbourg, France. Though evenly matched,

Kearsarge had reduced *Alabama* to a foundering wreck in less than an hour after the start of the battle. Her captain and crew were feted as heros by a grateful Union after their return to home port.

In later years she had served on cruises around the world. With a length of 198 feet, a beam of 33 feet and a fifteen-foot draft, her two engines and one screw could propel her through the water at eleven knots. Her guns had been replaced ten years after the war with a newer battery consisting of two eleven-inch smoothbores, four nine-inch smoothbores and two twenty-pound rifled barrels. She carried a crew of 160 men. Ancient though she was, she still packed a powerful punch.

Ellis put down the telescope and turned to Hunt. "Shall we investigate, sir?"

Hunt nodded. "Order a ten-degree turn to starboard. Request Chief Engineer Gribble to increase our speed to Full, turn out the crew for gun station two and double the lookouts. I don't want to lose sight of that monster, whatever it is."

"Aye, sir." Ellis, a tall balding man with an expansive, neatly trimmed beard, carried out his orders and soon the time-honored ship began to increase her speed, the waves splitting her bow with sheets of foam as she swung against the wind. A plume of heavy black smoke poured from her funnel along with a spray of sparks. The decks of the old warhorse trembled with anticipation as she took up the chase.

Soon the *Kearsarge* began to close with the strange object that neither increased nor decreased its speed. A gun crew assembled, rammed a power charge and a projectile down the barrel of a twenty-pound rifled gun and stood back. The gunnery officer stared up at Hunt, who stood next to the helmsman.

"Number two gun loaded and ready to fire, sir."

"Put a shot fifty yards ahead of the monster's nose, Mr. Merryman," Hunt shouted through his megaphone.

Merryman simply acknowledged with a wave of one hand and nodded at the man standing next to the gun with the lanyard in his hand and another man who was aiming the elevation screw on the breech. "You heard the captain. Lay your shot fifty yards ahead of the beast."

The adjustment was made, the lanyard was pulled, the big gun roared and leaped back against the thick stay rope running through the eye ring on its butt. It was a near-perfect shot, and the shell splashed directly in front of the giant hump that effortlessly slipped through the water. Animal or machine, it ignored the intrusion and maintained its speed and course without the slightest deviation.

"It doesn't appear impressed with our gunnery," Ellis said with a slight grin.

Hunt peered through his glasses. "I judge her speed at ten knots against our twelve."

"We should be alongside in another ten minutes."

"When we've closed to three hundred yards, fire another shot. This time, lay it within thirty yards."

All hands except the engine-room crew were lining the rails now, gazing at the monster that was closer to the bow of the ship with every passing minute. There was only a ripple on the surface, but white froth could be seen swirling in its wake below. Then the mound on its back flashed and glinted.

"If I didn't know better," said Hunt, "I'd say the sun is reflecting off some kind of window or port."

"No sea monster has glass built into it," Ellis muttered.

The gun crew reloaded and fired another shot that struck with a great splash between fifteen and twenty yards forward of the monster. Still no reaction. It continued as if the *Kearsarge* was little more than a passing annoyance. It was near enough now that Captain Hunt and his crew could make out a triangular housing atop the monster, with large round quartz ports.

"She's a man-built vessel," gasped Hunt in amazement.

"I can't believe it's possible," Ellis said vaguely. "Who could have built such an incredible contraption?"

"If not the United States, it has to be of British or German origin."

"Who can say? She flies no flag."

As they watched, the strange object slowly slid beneath the waves until it vanished from view. The *Kearsarge* passed directly over the spot where it sank, but the crew could detect no sign of it in the depths.

"She's gone, Captain," one of the seamen called to Hunt.

"Keep a sharp eye out for it," Hunt shouted back. "Some of you men take to the rigging for a better view."

"What do we do if she reappears?" asked Ellis.

"If she won't heave to and identify herself, we'll pour a broadside into her."

The hours passed and sunset came, as the *Kearsarge* cruised in ever-widening circles in a fading hope of finding the monster again. Captain Hunt was about to break off the pursuit when a lookout in the rigging shouted down to the deck.

"Monster off the port beam about a thousand yards, heading our way."

The officers and crew rushed to the port railing and stared out over the water. There was still enough light to see it clearly. It appeared to be coming directly toward the

Kearsarge at a very rapid rate of speed.

During the search, the gun crews had stood patiently, their great muzzle-loaders primed and ready to fire. The gunners on the port side quickly ran out their guns and sighted on the approaching apparition. "Allow for her speed and aim at that projection aft of her bow," Merryman instructed them.

Adjustments were made and the gun muzzles depressed as the monster loomed in the sights. Then Hunt yelled, "Fire!"

Six of the *Kearsarge*'s eight guns roared, their explosive blasts shattering the air as fire and smoke spouted from their muzzles. Staring through his binoculars, Hunt could see the shells from the two big eleven-inch pivot guns smash the water on each side of the baffling thing. The nine-inch smoothbores added to the geysers erupting around the target. Then he saw the shell from the twenty-pounder rifled gun strike the monster's back, bounce into the air and ricochet across the water like a skipping stone.

"She's armored," he said, stunned. "Our shot glanced off her hull without making a dent."

Unfazed, their nemesis aimed its bow unerringly amidships of the *Kearsarge*'s hull, increasing its speed and gathering momentum for the blow.

The gun crews frantically reloaded, but

by the time they were ready for another broadside, the thing was too close and they could not depress their muzzles low enough to strike it. The detachment of Marines aboard the ship began firing their rifles at the assailant. Several of the officers stood on the railing, grasping the rigging with one hand while firing their revolvers with the other. A typhoon of bullets merely glanced off the armored hull.

Hunt and his crew stared in disbelief at the nightmare that was about to ram the ship. Transfixed by the long cigar-shaped vessel, he gripped the railing to brace himself for the inescapable collision.

But the expected shock never came. All any of the crew felt was a slight shudder beneath decks. The impact seemed little different from a slight bump against a dock. The only sound was the faint crunch of shredding wood. In that frozen moment of time, the unearthly thing had slashed between the *Kearsarge*'s great oak ribs as cleanly as a murderer's knife thrust, penetrating deep inside the hull just aft of the engine room.

Hunt gaped in shock. He could see a face through the large transparent view port on the pyramid-shaped housing on top the underwater ram. The bearded face had what seemed to Hunt to be a sad and melancholy expression, as if the man inside felt remorse for the disaster his strange and bizarre vessel had caused.

Then the mysterious vessel quickly backed off and fell away into the depths.

Hunt knew the *Kearsarge* was doomed. Down below, seawater poured into the *Kearsarge*'s aft cargo hold and galley. The gaping wound was almost a perfect concave hole through the hull planking six feet below the waterline. The torrent increased as the warship slowly began to list on her port side. The only thing that saved her from immediately foundering was the bulkheads. In keeping with naval regulations, Hunt had ordered them sealed as if the ship were going into battle. The inrush of water was contained, but only until the bulkheads gave way to the crush of tremendous pressure.

Hunt swung around and stared at a low coral island not two miles away. He turned to the helmsman and shouted. "Steer for that reef off the starboard beam." Then he called down to the engine room for full speed. His main concern was for how long the bulkheads could hold back the flood of water from gushing into the engine room. While the boilers were still able to make steam, he just might have time to run his ship aground before she sank.

Slowly, the bow came around, as the ship picked up speed and set a course for shallow water. First Officer Ellis did not need a command from Hunt to prepare the boats and the captain's gig to be lowered. Except for the engine-room gang, all crew members were assembled on deck. To a man, they focused their eyes on the low, barren coral reef that was nearing with agonizing slowness. The propeller thrashed the water as the boilers were fired by the stokers in a near frenzy. They shoveled coal with one eye on the open grate and the other aimed at the creaking bulkhead, all that stood between them and a horrible death.

The single screw thrashed the water, driving the ship toward what everyone hoped was salvation. The helmsman called for help in fighting the wheel as the ship became sluggish with the escalating weight from the incoming flood and the list to port that had increased to six degrees.

The crew stood at the boats, ready to board them and abandon ship at Hunt's expected command. They shifted uneasily as the deck sloped ominously beneath their feet. A leadsman was sent to the bow to throw out a lead weight and sound the bottom. He called out the depth in fathoms.

"Twenty fathoms and rising," he yelled out with the barest trace of optimism.

They needed another hundred-foot rise in depth before the *Kearsarge*'s keel would strike bottom. It seemed to Hunt that they were approaching that tiny strip of coral with the pace of a drunken snail.

Kearsarge was settling deeper in the water with each passing minute. Her list was nearly ten degrees, and it was becoming almost impossible to sustain a straight course. The reef was coming closer. They could see the waves striking the coral and bursting in a glistening spray under the sun.

"Five fathoms," the leadsman called out, "and rising fast."

Hunt wasn't going to risk the lives of his crew. He was about to give the order to abandon ship when the *Kearsarge* drove onto the coral bottom, her keel and hull gouging a path through the reef until she came to an abrupt stop and rolled over until she rested on a list of fifteen degrees.

"Praise the Lord, we're saved," murmured the helmsman, still gripping the spokes of the wheel, his face red from the effort, his arms numb with exhaustion.

"She's hard aground," Ellis said to Hunt. "The tide is ebbing, so the old girl won't be going anywhere."

"True," Hunt acknowledged sadly. "A pity if she can't be saved."

"Salvage tugs might pull her off the reef, providing the bottom isn't torn out of her."

"That damnable monster is responsible. If there's a God, it will pay for this travesty."

"Maybe she has," Ellis said quietly. "She sank pretty fast after the collision. She must have damaged her bow and opened it to the sea."

"I can't help but wonder why she didn't simply heave to and explain her presence."

Ellis stared thoughtfully over the turquoise Caribbean water. "I seem to remember reading something once, about one of our warships, the *Abraham Lincoln*, encountering a mysterious metal monster about thirty years ago. It tore her rudder off."

"Where was this?" asked Hunt.

"I believe it was the Sea of Japan. And at least four British warships have disappeared under mysterious circumstances over the past twenty years."

"The Navy Department will never believe what happened here," said Hunt, looking around his wrecked ship with growing anger. "I'll be lucky if I don't get court-martialed and drummed out of the service."

"You've got a hundred and sixty witnesses who will back you up," Ellis assured him.

"No captain wishes to lose his ship, certainly not to some unidentifiable mechanical monstrosity." He paused to look down into the sea, his mind turning to the job at hand. "Start loading supplies into the boats. We'll move ashore and wait for rescue on firm ground."

"I've checked the charts, sir. It's called Roncador Reef."

"A sorry place and a sorry end for such an illustrious ship," he said wistfully.

Ellis threw an informal salute and began directing the crew to shuttle food, canvas for tents and personal belongings onto the low coral cay. Under the light of a half-moon, they labored all night and into the next day, setting up camp and cooking the first of their meals ashore.

Hunt was the last man to leave the *Kearsarge*. Just before he climbed down the ladder to a waiting boat, he paused to stare down into the restless water. He would take to his death the sight of the bearded man staring out of the black monster at him. "Who are you?" he murmured under his breath. "Did you survive? And if so, who will be your next victim?"

In the next several years, until he died, whenever a report reached him of a warship that had vanished with all hands, Hunt could not help but wonder if the man in the monster was responsible.

Kearsarge's officers and men existed without hardship ashore for two weeks before a trail of smoke was sighted on the horizon. Hunt sent out a boat with First Officer Ellis, who stopped a passing steamer that took Hunt and his men off the cay and carried them to Panama.

Strangely, when Hunt and his crew returned to the United States, there was no board of inquiry, a very unusual circumstance. It was as if the secretary of the Navy and the admirals wanted to sweep the incident quietly under the carpet. To Captain Hunt's surprise, he was elevated in rank to full captain before his honorable retirement. First Officer Ellis was also promoted and given command of the Navy's newest gunboat, *Helena,* and saw service during the Spanish-American War in Cuban waters.

Congress authorized $45,000 to raise the *Kearsarge* from Roncador Reef and tow her home to a shipyard. But it was found that natives from nearby islands had set her on fire to salvage her brass, copper and iron. Her guns were removed, and the salvagers returned to port, leaving her hulk to disintegrate in a coral tomb.

Part One

INFERNO

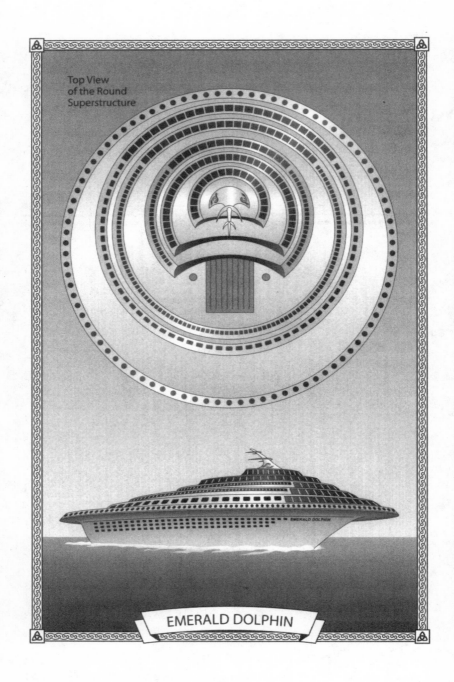

Top View
of the Round
Superstructure

EMERALD DOLPHIN

1

JULY 15, 2003
THE SOUTH PACIFIC OCEAN

If the disaster had been planned months in advance with meticulous insight and judgment, it could not have been more catastrophic. Everything that could go wrong did so beyond imagination. The luxurious cruise ship *Emerald Dolphin* was on fire and no one on board had an omen, a premonition, not even the slightest trace of suspicion of the danger. Yet flames were slowly devouring the interior of the ship's wedding chapel, located amidships just forward of the sumptuous shopping village.

On the bridge, the officers went about their watch, oblivious to the pending disaster. None of the ship's automatic fire-warning systems, nor their backups, hinted at a problem. The console, with its schematic profile of the entire ship that displayed every fire-warning indicator aboard, was a sea of green lights. The one light that should have revealed a fire in the chapel failed to blink red.

At 4 A.M., the passengers were all asleep in their staterooms. The bars and lounges, magnificent casino, nightclub and dance ballroom were empty, as the *Emerald Dolphin* plowed the South Seas at twenty-four knots on a cruise from Sydney, Australia, to the islands of Tahiti. Launched only the year before and then fitted out, *Emerald Dolphin* was on her maiden voyage. She did not have the flowing, elegant lines of other cruise ships. Her hull looked more like a giant hiking boot with a huge disk in the center. The entire superstructure of six decks was round and circled 150 feet beyond and above both sides of the hull, and fifty feet over the bow and stern. If anything, her superstructure resembled that of the Starship *Enterprise*. There was no funnel.

The pride of the Blue Seas Cruise Lines, the new ship would unquestionably receive a six-star rating and was expected to become a very popular vessel, especially with her interior, which resembled that of an ornate Las Vegas hotel. She sailed on her maiden voyage with every stateroom booked. At 750 feet in length and a gross tonnage of 50,000, she carried 1,600 passengers in opulent style, served by 900 crew members.

The marine architects of the *Emerald Dolphin* had gone over the top creating ultra-modern glitz in the five dining rooms, three bar and lounge areas, the casino, ballroom, theater and staterooms. Glass in wildly different colors abounded throughout the ship. Chrome, brass and copper swirled on the walls and ceilings. All the furniture was created by contemporary artists and celebrity interior designers. Unique lighting created a heavenly atmosphere, or at least the designer's conception of heaven as described by those who'd died, gone there and were then revived. Except for the outside promenade decks, there was little demand for walking. Escalators, moving ramps and walkways spread throughout the interior of the ship. Glass-enclosed elevators were spaced throughout the decks within a short stroll.

The sports deck featured a short four-hole golf course, Olympic-sized swimming pool, basketball court and a huge workout gym. A shopping avenue two city blocks long rose three decks high, and might have been taken from the Emerald City of Oz.

The ship was also a floating museum of Abstract Expressionist art. Paintings by artists Jackson Pollock, Paul Klee, Willem de Kooning and other notables were on view throughout the ship. Bronze sculptures by Henry Moore stood in niches on platinum pedestals in the main dining room. The collection alone cost seventy-eight million dollars.

The staterooms were circular, with no sharp corners. They were all spacious and exactly alike — there were no small inside staterooms or penthouse suites on the *Emerald Dolphin*. The designers did not believe in class distinction. The furniture and decor looked like something out of a science-fiction movie. The beds were raised, with extremely soft mattresses, beamed with soft overhead lights. For those on a first or second honeymoon, mirrors were mounted inconspicuously in the ceiling. The bathrooms had built-in chambers that dispersed mist, spray, rain or steam amid a jungle of flowering tropical plants that looked as though they'd been grown on an alien planet. Sailing on the *Emerald Dolphin* was an experience unique among cruise ships.

The ship designers also understood where their future passengers would be coming from, and fashioned the ship in the image of the affluent young. Many were well-off doctors, attorneys and entrepreneurs of small and large businesses. Most brought their families. The single passengers were in the minority. There was a fair-sized group of senior citizens who looked like they could well afford the finest money could buy.

After dinner, while most young couples danced in the ballroom to a band playing whatever popular music was on the charts, hung out in the nightclub with its floor show or gambled in the casino, those families with children attended the theater and watched the ship's troupe perform the latest Broadway smash success, *Sonofagun from Arizona*. By 3 A.M., the decks and lounges were empty. No passengers who went to bed that night would have thought that the old grim reaper was about to swing his scythe at the *Emerald Dolphin*.

Captain Jack Waitkus made a brief inspection of the upper decks before retiring to his cabin. Old by most cruise ship standards, Waitkus was only five days away from his sixty-fifth birthday. He had no illusions about remaining at sea after this voyage. The directors of the company had notified him that he would be on the beach as soon as the ship returned to its home port in Fort Lauderdale after its maiden voyage to Sydney and back. Actually, Waitkus looked forward to retirement. He and his wife lived on a beautiful forty-two-foot sailing yacht. For years they had planned to take a leisurely cruise around the world. Waitkus's mind was already charting a course across the Atlantic to the Mediterranean.

He had been named commander of the *Emerald Dolphin*'s maiden voyage in honor of his distinguished service to the company. He was a stout man with the jolly appearance of a Falstaff without the beard. His blue eyes had a leprechaun look to them, and his lips seemed always turned up in a warm smile. Unlike many cruise ship captains who did not care to mingle with the passengers, Captain Waitkus enjoyed circulating among them. At his table in the dining salon, he regaled his guests with stories of how he had run away to sea when he was a young boy in Liverpool, sailed on tramp steamers in the Orient, and worked his way up through the ranks. He'd studied hard and passed the ships' officers' tests until finally receiving his master's papers. He'd then served for ten years with the Blue Seas Cruise Lines, as second and first officer until he was named master of the *Emerald Dolphin*. He was very popular and the directors of the Line were reluctant to let him go, but it was company policy and they felt they could make no exceptions.

He was tired, but never dropped off to sleep until he'd read a few pages of one of his books on underwater treasure. He had one shipwreck in mind that had carried a cargo of gold and gone down off the coast of Morocco that he especially wanted to search for during his retirement journey. He made one final call to the bridge and was told all was normal before he drifted off to sleep.

At 4:10 A.M., Second Officer Charles McFerrin thought he caught a distinct whiff of smoke as he made a routine tour of the ship. Sniffing the air, he gauged the smell to be strongest at one end of the shopping avenue where the boutiques and gift shops were located. Mystified, because no alarm had been sounded, he followed the acrid scent along the avenue until he stood in front of the wedding chapel. Sensing heat on the other side, he pulled the door open.

The interior of the chapel was a raging mass of flames. Stunned, McFerrin stumbled backward away from the intense heat, tripped and fell to the deck. He quickly recovered and called the bridge on his radio communicator and shouted a series of commands. "Wake up Captain Waitkus. We have a fire in the chapel. Sound the alarm, program the damage-control computer and engage the fire-control systems."

First Officer Vince Sheffield automatically turned to the fire-systems console. All the lights were green. "McFerrin, are you sure? We have no indication here."

"Trust me," McFerrin shouted into the mouthpiece. "It's an inferno, and it's out of control."

"Are the sprinklers activated?" Sheffield demanded.

"No, something is radically wrong. The fire-extinguishing system is not operating, and there was no heat alarm."

Sheffield was at a loss. The *Emerald Dolphin* had the most advanced fire-alarm and -control system of any ship at sea. Without it, there were no options. Staring at the console that showed all was well, he wasted precious seconds vacillating while standing in frozen disbelief. He turned to the junior officer on the bridge, Carl Harding. "McFerrin is reporting a fire in the chapel. Nothing shows on the fire-control console. Go down and check it out."

More time was lost while McFerrin frantically fought the growing conflagration with extinguishers, but he might just as well have tried stopping a major forest fire by beating it out with a burlap sack. The flames were spreading beyond the chapel as he fought them alone. He simply could not believe that the automatic sprinklers were not operating. The flames were unstoppable unless crew members appeared and turned on the water valves and attacked the fire with hoses, but only Harding appeared, walking leisurely down the shopping avenue.

Harding was stunned when he saw the extent of the holocaust, more so when he found McFerrin fighting a losing battle by himself. He called up to the bridge. "Sheffield, for God's sake! We've got a raging firestorm down here and have nothing to fight it with but portable extinguishers. Call out the fire crew and engage the fire-control systems!"

Still wallowing in disbelief, Sheffield hesitated before switching on the manual override on the extinguishing system in the chapel. "System is on," he called to the men at the chapel.

"Nothing is happening!" McFerrin cried. "Hurry, man. We can't stop this alone."

As if in a daze, Sheffield finally called and reported the blaze to the fire-crew officer and then woke Captain Waitkus.

"Sir, I have a reported fire in the chapel."

Waitkus came instantly awake. "Are the fire-control systems taking care of it?"

"Officers McFerrin and Harding, who are on the scene, report the systems as inoperative. They're attempting to contain the fire with extinguishers."

"Call out the fire crew to man the fire hoses."

"I've seen to that, sir."

"Have the lifeboat crews man their stations."

"Yes, sir. Right away."

As he hurriedly dressed, Waitkus could not conceive of an emergency that would call for him ordering 2,500 passengers and crew to board the lifeboats and abandon ship, but he was determined to take all precautions. He rushed to the bridge and immediately studied the fire-control console. It was still awash with green lights. If there was a fire, none of the sophisticated systems was detecting it, nor were they automatically engaging to put it out.

"Are you sure about this?" he asked Sheffield skeptically.

"McFerrin and Harding swear there is a fire raging in the chapel."

"This is impossible." Waitkus picked up the phone and called the engine room.

Assistant Chief Engineer Joseph Barnum answered. "Engine room. This is Barnum."

"This is the captain. Do your fire-control and detection systems show any indication of a fire anywhere on the ship?"

"One moment." Barnum turned and peered at a large panel. "No, sir, I've got green lights across the board. No indication of a fire on this end."

"Stand by to activate your fire-control system manually," ordered Waitkus.

At that moment a crewman came running onto the bridge. He rushed up to Sheffield. "Sir, I thought you should know, I smelled smoke when I came around the port promenade deck."

Waitkus picked up the phone. "McFerrin?"

The second officer barely heard the phone buzz over the crackle of the fire. "What is it?" he snapped harshly.

"This is Captain Waitkus. You and Harding get out of the chapel. I'm going to close the steel fire doors and seal off the chapel."

"Make it fast, sir," said McFerrin loudly. "I fear the fire is about to burst through into the avenue."

Waitkus pressed the switch that would send the concealed fire doors around the chapel area, sealing it off. He stood bewildered when the activation light failed to illuminate. He called McFerrin again. "Have the fire doors closed?"

"No, sir. There is no movement."

"This is impossible," Waitkus muttered for the second time in the past two minutes. "I can't believe the entire system has shut down." He rang the engine room again. "Barnum," he barked, "use your manual override and close the fire doors around the chapel."

"Closing the fire door," Barnum acknowledged. Then, "My board shows no movement. I don't understand. The fire-door control system is not functioning."

"Damn!" Waitkus gasped. He gave a curt nod to Sheffield. "I'm going down to check out the situation for myself."

The first officer never saw the captain

again. Waitkus entered the bridge elevator, rode down to A Deck and approached the wedding chapel from the side opposite the crew fighting the fire. Unthinkingly, unaware of the enormity of the danger, he jerked open the door behind the altar. A storm of flame burst through the doorway and engulfed him. Almost instantly, his lungs were seared and he was turned into a walking torch. He reeled backward and fell dead in a fireball before he struck the deck.

Captain Jack Waitkus died horribly, never knowing that his ship was about to die, too.

Kelly Egan awoke from a nightmare. It was a kind she often dreamed, in which she was being chased by some sort of indescribable animal or insect. In this one, she was swimming and a huge fish brushed up against her. She moaned in her sleep and popped her eyes open, seeing only the glow from the night-light in the bathroom.

She wrinkled her nose and sat up, slowly becoming aware of the faint smell of smoke. She inhaled, trying to trace its origin, but it was barely a whiff. Satisfied that it was not coming from inside her stateroom, she lay back down and sleepily wondered if it was only her imagination. But after a few minutes, the scent seemed to become stronger. She also sensed that the temperature in her stateroom had risen. She threw back the covers and set her bare feet on the carpet. The carpet seemed abnormally warm. The heat seemed to be emanating from the deck below. Kelly stood on a chair and placed her hand on the ornate copper ceiling above. It felt cool.

Concerned, she pulled a robe over her shoulders and padded across the floor to the door leading to the adjoining stateroom occupied by her father. Dr. Elmore Egan was in a deep sleep, as evidenced by his snoring. A Nobel Prize–winning mechanical genius, he was traveling on the *Emerald Dolphin* because she carried the revolutionary new engines that he had designed and developed, and he was making a study on how they were performing on their first voyage. He was so engrossed in his state-of-the-art creation that he seldom came up from the engine room, and Kelly had hardly seen him since departing Sydney. The previous night was the first time they had sat down and had dinner together. Egan had finally begun to relax after satisfying himself that his huge magnetic water jet propulsion engines were operating efficiently and without problems.

Kelly leaned across his bed and shook him lightly by the shoulder. "Dad, wake up."

A light sleeper, Egan came instantly awake.

"What is it?" he asked, staring up at the

shadowy form of his daughter. "Are you ill?"

"I smell smoke," Kelly answered. "And the floor feels hot."

"Are you sure? I don't hear any alarms."

"See for yourself."

Fully awake, Egan leaned out of bed and placed both palms on the carpet. His brow raised, and then he sniffed the air. After a moment's deliberation, he looked up at Kelly and said, "Get dressed. We're going out on deck."

By the time they had left their staterooms and reached the elevator, the smell of smoke had become more pronounced and distinct.

On the A Deck shopping avenue outside the wedding chapel, the crew was retreating in its battle against the fire. The portable extinguishers were used up. All the fire-control systems were inoperative, and to add to their desperation, the hoses could not be attached because the valve caps were frozen closed and could not be removed by hand. McFerrin sent a man down to the engine room to bring back pipe wrenches, but it was an exercise in futility. Two men using their combined strength still could not untwist the caps from their threads. It was as if they had been welded shut.

To the men fighting the fire, frustration turned to terror as the situation worsened.

With the fire doors unable to close, there was no way to isolate the blaze. McFerrin hailed the bridge. "Tell the captain we're losing control down here. The fire has burned through onto the salon deck into the casino."

"Can't you keep the fire from spreading?" asked Sheffield.

"How!" McFerrin yelled back. "Nothing works. We're running out of extinguishers, we can't connect the hoses and the sprinkler systems won't flow. Is there any way the engine room can override the systems and close the fire doors?"

"Negative," answered Sheffield, anxiety obvious in his voice. "The entire fire-control program is down. Computers, fire doors, sprinklers, the works — they've all failed."

"Why haven't you sounded the alarm?"

"I can't alarm the passengers without the captain's authority."

"Where is he?"

"He went down to judge the situation for himself. Haven't you seen him?"

Surprised, McFerrin searched the area but saw no sign of Waitkus. "He's not here."

"Then he must be on his way back to the bridge," replied Sheffield, becoming uneasy.

"For the safety of the passengers, give the alarm and send them to their lifeboat stations in preparation for abandoning the ship."

Sheffield was aghast. "Order sixteen hundred passengers to abandon the *Emerald Dolphin*? You're overreacting."

"You don't know what it's like down here," McFerrin said urgently. "Just get the show on the road before it's too late."

"Only Captain Waitkus can give such a command."

"Then for the love of God, man, give the alarm and warn the passengers before the fire breaks onto the stateroom decks."

Sheffield was swept by indecision. He'd never faced an emergency like this in his eighteen years at sea. It was why he'd never wanted to be a captain. He'd never wanted the responsibility. What should he *do?* "You're absolutely certain the situation warrants such drastic action?"

"Unless you can get the fire control systems operational in the next *five minutes,* this ship and everybody on it is doomed," McFerrin shouted.

Sheffield was becoming disoriented now. All he could think about was: His career at sea was in jeopardy. If he made the wrong decision now . . .

And the seconds ticked away.

His inaction would ultimately cost over a hundred lives.

2

The men struggling to contain the inferno were well trained in fighting shipboard fires, but they were working with both hands tied behind their backs. Dressed in their fire-proof suits with full helmets and oxygen tanks on their backs, each of them was becoming increasingly frustrated. With all the fire-fighting systems and equipment inoperative or useless, they could do nothing but stand helplessly and watch the blaze burn unchecked. Within fifteen minutes, A Deck was a holocaust. Flames consumed the shopping avenue and spilled out on the nearby boat decks. Crew members preparing to launch the lifeboats scattered for their lives as a torrent of fire surged over the port and starboard lifeboats.

And still no alarm had sounded.

First Officer Sheffield appeared to be in denial. It was with fearful reluctance that he took over command of the ship, still unable to accept the possibility that Captain Waitkus was dead, or that they were all in mortal danger. Like all modern cruise ships, the *Emerald Dolphin* had been constructed to be fireproof. That flames could have spread with such lightning speed went against all the marine architect's safety designs.

He wasted valuable time by sending men to find the captain, and waiting until they all reported back that he was nowhere to be found. Sheffield entered the chartroom and studied the course line across a large chart. The last marking from the Global Positioning System, laid by the ship's fourth officer less than thirty minutes previously, showed the nearest landfall to be the island of Tonga, more than two hundred miles northeast. He returned to the bridge and stepped out onto the bridge wing. A rain squall was sweeping down upon the ship and the wind had risen, increasing the height of the waves marching against the bow to five feet.

He turned and looked back, aghast to see smoke erupting from amidships and flames eating at the lifeboats. The conflagration seemed to be devouring everything in its path. Why had all the fire-control systems failed? *Emerald Dolphin* was one of the safest ships in the world. It was unthinkable that she might end up at the bottom of the sea. As if immersed in a nightmare, he finally set off the ship's fire-alarm system.

By now the casino had been turned into a fiery Hades. The incredible intensity of the heat, combined with the total lack of fire-fighting systems and equipment to slow it down, melted any object it met or consumed it within seconds. The fire tore through the theater and quickly turned it into an incinerator, the stage curtains exploding in a flaming shower of fireworks, before the flames moved on, leaving a blackened and smoldering shell. The fire was now only two decks below the first of the lower staterooms.

Bells clanged and sirens whooped throughout the ship, the only warning system that had functioned on command. Drugged by sleep, 1,600 passengers came awake, confused and questioning the harsh interruption. They reacted slowly, mystified by the emergency alarm going off at 4:25 in the morning. At first, most were calm and went about the business of pulling on comfortable, casual clothes. They also put on their life vests as they had been instructed to do during the drills before moving to their lifeboat stations. Only those few who stepped out on their verandas to see what the fuss was all about were confronted with reality.

Illuminated by the ocean of lights from the ship, they saw billowing clouds of thick smoke and tongues of flame gushing through melted and smashed ports and windows on the decks below. The sight was dazzling as well as terrifying. Only then did panic begin to mushroom. It became total when the first of the passengers to reach the boat deck found themselves facing a wall of fire.

Dr. Egan had led his daughter into the nearest elevator and taken it to the observation deck on the upper section of the superstructure where they could get an overall view of the ship. His worst fears were confirmed when he saw the conflagration rolling from amidships seven decks below. From his vantage point, he could also see the blaze eating along both decks where the lifeboats were mounted in their davits. On the stern, the crew was feverishly throwing canisters containing life rafts into the sea, where they were ejected and automatically inflated. The scene struck Egan as something from a Monty Python sketch. The crew did not seem to consider that the ship was still moving at cruise speed, and the empty rafts were soon left floating far in the wake of the ship.

Ashen-faced and stunned at what he'd seen, he spoke sharply to Kelly. "Go down to the open cafe on B Deck and wait there."

Dressed only in a halter and shorts, Kelly asked, "Aren't you coming?"

"I must retrieve my papers from my stateroom. You go ahead. I'll be along in a few minutes."

The elevators were jammed, overloaded with people from the decks below. There was no way they could descend from the observation deck, so Kelly and her father had to fight their way down the stairwells among hordes of frightened passengers. The mob poured into every passage and companionway, every elevator, like termites in a mound under attack by an aardvark. People who lived responsible and disciplined lives had suddenly become pitiful rabble overcome with the fear of death. Some stumbled blindly, without knowing where they were going. Many walked in a daze, bewildered by the pandemonium. Men cursed, women screamed. The drama was rapidly turning into a scene from Dante's *Inferno*.

The crew, the officers, stewards and stateroom stewardesses, all did their best to control the general chaos. But it was a lost cause. Without the haven of the lifeboats, there was no place for anyone to go but over the side into the water. The crew and officers moved about the frightened throng, checking that their life vests were worn properly and assuring them that rescue ships were on the way.

It was a forlorn hope. Still in paralysis, Sheffield had yet to send out a Mayday call. The chief radio operator had run from the radio room three times and asked him if he should send a Mayday and contact all ships in the area, but Sheffield had failed to act.

In a few minutes, it would be too late. The flames were less than fifty feet from the radio room.

Kelly Egan struggled through the madness to the open cafe on B Deck at the stern of the *Emerald Dolphin*, and found it already crowded with passengers milling around. They looked lost and dazed. Here, there were no ship's officers to maintain calm. People were coughing from the smoke that was swirling around the ship, blown by the wind that fanned over the stern while the ship still forged ahead at twenty-four knots.

Miraculously, most of the passengers had escaped death in their staterooms, having calmly left before the flames had closed off the corridors, stairways and elevators. At first they'd refused to take the disaster seriously, but anxiety had soon run high after they found the lifeboats unapproachable. The officers and crew had showed exceptional courage by herding everyone to the stern decks where they could congregate temporarily free of the flames.

Entire families were there: fathers, mothers and children, many still in their pajamas. A few of the children were whining in terror, while others enjoyed it as a big game until they saw the fear in their parents' eyes. Women with disheveled hair in bathrobes stood amid others who had refused to be rushed and had put on makeup, dressed stylishly and carried handbags. Men were in a variety of casual dress. Several wore sport coats over Bermuda shorts. Only one young couple came prepared to jump. They were wearing their swimsuits. But the one thing they all had in common was a fear of death.

Kelly pushed her way through the throng until she reached the railing, then hung on to it in a death grip. It was still dark as she stared down at the whirling foam churned by the ship's propellers. In the predawn darkness under the ship's floodlights, the wake was visible for two hundred yards. Beyond, the black sea blended into the black horizon still quilted with stars. She wondered why the ship did not stop.

A woman was moaning hysterically, "We'll be burned alive. I don't want to die in a fire." Before anyone could stop her, she climbed over the rail and jumped into the sea. Stunned faces watched as she sank. All they caught was a fleeting glimpse of her head when it bobbed to the surface before she became lost in the darkness.

Kelly began to fear for her father. She was contemplating going back to their state-rooms to look for him when he reappeared, carrying a brown leather case. "Oh, Dad," she cried. "I was afraid I'd lost you."

"It's bedlam, absolute bedlam," he gasped, short of breath, his face flushed. "It's like a herd of cattle stampeding around in circles."

"What can we do?" she asked anxiously. "Where can we go?"

"In the water," answered Egan. "It's our only hope to stay alive as long as we can." He looked solemnly into his daughter's eyes. They sparkled like blue sapphires when the light hit them just right. He could never help marveling at how much she looked like her mother, Lana, at the same age. Their height and weight and body shapes were identical: both tall, finely con-toured, with the near-perfect proportions of models. Kelly's long, straight, maple-sugar brown hair framing a strong face with high cheekbones, sculptured lips and perfect nose were a mirror image, too. The only dif-ference between mother and daughter was the suppleness of their arms and legs. Kelly was the more athletic, while her mother had been soft and graceful. Both Kelly and her father had been devastated when Lana had died after a long battle with breast cancer. Now, as he stood there on the burning ship, his heart felt an indescribable heaviness at realizing that Kelly's own life was in dire jeopardy of being cut short.

She smiled at him gamely. "At least we're in the tropics and the water will be warm enough for a swim."

He squeezed her shoulders, and then looked down into the sea that was rushing past the great hull nearly fifty feet below. "There's no reason to jump until the ship stops," he said. "We'll wait until the absolute last minute before we go over. There are bound to be ships coming to rescue us."

On the bridge, First Officer Sheffield gripped the bridge rail and stared at the red glow reflecting on the waves like a kaleidoscope. The whole midships were ablaze, with flames pouring out like fiery rivers through the ports and windows that had burst open from the intense heat. He could hear the groan of protest from the mighty cruise ship as she succumbed. It seemed inconceivable that before another hour would pass, the *Emerald Dolphin*, the pride of the Blue Seas Cruise Lines, would be a burned-out hulk, drifting dead and aimless on a turquoise sea. His mind had long ago shut down to any thoughts concerning the lives of the 2,500 passengers and crew.

He gazed unseeing over the darkened sea. If there were lights from other ships, he was blind to them. He was still standing there when McFerrin burst onto the bridge. The second officer's face was blackened, his uniform scorched, his eyebrows and much of his hair singed away. He grabbed Sheffield by the shoulder and roughly swung him around.

"The ship is maintaining cruising speed directly into the wind. The fire's being fed like a giant bellows. Why haven't you given orders for her to stop?"

"That's the captain's prerogative."

"Where *is* Captain Waitkus?"

"I don't know," Sheffield said vaguely. "He went away and never came back."

"Then he must have died in the fire." McFerrin saw that it was useless trying to communicate with his superior. He grabbed the phone and called down to the chief engineer. "Chief, this is McFerrin. Captain Waitkus is dead. The fire is beyond our control. Shut down the engines and get your men topside. You can't exit amidships, so you'll have to make your way to either the bow or the stern. Do you understand?"

"The fire is really that bad?" asked Chief Engineer Raymond Garcia dumbly.

"It's worse."

"Why don't we just head for the lifeboats?"

This was crazy, McFerrin thought. No one on the bridge had alerted the engine

74

room crew that the fire had already destroyed half the ship. "All the lifeboats have been destroyed by the fire. The *Emerald Dolphin* is doomed. Get out while you can. Keep the generators going. We'll need light to abandon the ship and guide any rescue vessels."

No more wasted words came from Chief Engineer Garcia. He instantly gave the order for the engines to shut down. Soon afterward, his crew abandoned the engine room and made their way through the cargo and baggage compartments to the bow.

Garcia was the last to leave. He made certain that the generators were operating smoothly before he ducked into the nearest passageway.

"Have any ships responded to our Mayday call?" McFerrin asked Sheffield.

Sheffield stared blankly. "Mayday?"

"Didn't you give our position and request immediate assistance?"

"Yes, we must send out a call for help. . . ." Sheffield muttered vaguely.

McFerrin immediately read the incoherence in Sheffield's tone and eyes and was horrified. "Oh God, it's probably too late. The flames must have reached the radio room."

He snatched up a phone and called the radio room, but heard only static. Exhausted and in pain from his burns,

McFerrin sagged despairingly against the ship's control counter. "More than two thousand people are about to burn to death or die in the water with no hope of a rescue," he murmured in solemn frustration. "And we can do nothing but join them."

3

Twelve miles to the south, a pair of opaline green eyes gazed into the brightening sky to the east before turning and examining the red glow on the northern horizon. Absorbed, the man stepped from the bridge wing into the pilothouse of the NUMA oceanographic survey vessel, *Deep Encounter*, picked up a pair of strong binoculars that were sitting on the bridge counter and returned. Slowly, deliberately, he focused the glasses and stared into the distance.

He was a tall man, three inches more than six feet, and a lean 185 pounds. His every movement seemed consciously planned. The black hair was wavy, almost shaggy, with a touch of gray beginning to show at the temples. The face was a face that knew the sea above and below. The tanned skin and the craggy features revealed a love of the outdoors. He was obviously someone who spent far more time under sun and sky than under the fluorescent lights of an office.

The early-morning tropical air was warm and humid. He wore blue denim shorts under a colorfully flowered Hawaiian aloha shirt. His narrow feet that stepped straight as a spear were strapped into sandals. It was the uniform of the day for Dirk Pitt when he was on a deep-water research project, especially when he was working within a thousand miles of the equator. As special projects director for the National Underwater and Marine Agency, he spent nine months out of each year at sea. On this expedition, the NUMA scientists were conducting a deep-water geological survey in the Tonga Trench.

After studying the glow for three minutes, he retraced his path into the pilothouse and leaned into the radio room. The radio operator on the graveyard shift looked up sleepily and said automatically, "Latest satellite weather forecast reports heavy squalls headed our way with thirty-mile-an-hour winds and ten-foot seas."

"Perfect for flying a kite," Pitt said, smiling. Then his expression turned serious. "Have you picked up any distress signals in the last hour?"

The operator shook his head. "I had a

short conversation with the radioman on board a British containership around one o'clock. But no distress signal."

"A large ship off to the north looks like it's on fire. See if you can make contact with her."

Pitt turned and touched Leo Delgado, the officer on duty, on the shoulder. "Leo, I'd like you to turn the ship north and proceed at full speed. I believe we have a ship on fire. Wake Captain Burch and ask him to come to the pilothouse."

Though Pitt was head of the project and outranked Burch, the captain still commanded the ship. Kermit Burch came almost immediately, wearing only a pair of polka-dot shorts. "What's this about a ship on fire?" he asked Pitt, suppressing a yawn.

Pitt motioned out on the bridge wing and handed him the binoculars. Burch peered at the horizon, paused, rubbed the lenses on his shorts and peered again. "You're right. She's blazing like a torch. I make her out to be a cruise ship. A big one."

"Odd that she hasn't sent out a Mayday."

"That *is* curious. Her radio must be disabled."

"I requested Delgado to turn from our course and head toward her at full speed. I hope you don't mind my stepping in your territory. I thought it would save a few minutes."

Burch grinned. "You gave the same order I would have given." Then he stepped over to the ship's phone. "Engine room, roust Marvin out of bed. I want every revolution he can get out of the engines." He paused to listen to the voice on the other end. "Why? Because we're going to a fire. That's why."

After the news went out, the survey ship came alive, as crew and scientists were assigned special duties. The ship's two thirty-five-foot hydrographic survey launches were made ready to drop in the water. Slings were attached to the two telescoping deck cranes used to raise and lower submersibles and survey equipment, so that groups of people could be pulled from the water. Every ladder and rope on the ship was coiled to be thrown over the sides, along with cradles to lift children and the elderly on board.

The ship's doctor, with the assistance of the marine scientists, prepared the hospital and a casualty station in the mess room. The cook and his galley help began setting out bottles of water, pots of coffee and vats of soup. Everyone chipped in to provide clothing for those who might be rescued without any. Officers instructed selected crewmen to channel survivors onto different parts of the ship, to be cared for as well as act as ballast. With an overall length of 230 feet and a 50-foot beam, the *Deep Encounter* was not designed to support, much less float, with two thousand passengers. If the horde that was expected to come on board was not placed strategically to balance the ship, it could roll over and capsize.

The *Deep Encounter* was only rated at a top speed of sixteen knots, but Chief Engineer Marvin House pulled every ounce of power from his two big 3,000-horsepower diesel electric propulsion engines. Seventeen knots became eighteen, then nineteen, until the bow was thrusting through the sea at twenty knots. Her bow almost leaped clear of the water as she burst through the crest of the rolling waves. No one knew the *Deep Encounter* could drive so hard.

Fully dressed, Captain Burch paced the deck, giving orders for the hundred and one details to carry out in readiness for the expected invasion of survivors. He ordered the radio operator to contact the other ships in the area, give them a sketchy report on the fire, request their position and estimated time of arrival. There were only two within a hundred miles. One was the *Earl of Wattlesfield*, the British containership the radio operator had contacted earlier. Her captain had quickly responded and was coming at full speed, but he was thirty-seven miles to the east. The second vessel was an Australian missile cruiser that had changed course and was charging toward the position given by Burch from the south. But she had sixty-three miles to go.

Satisfied there was nothing left to consider, Burch joined Pitt on the bridge wing. Every soul that did not have a duty to perform lined the rails of the *Deep Encounter*, staring at the red glow lighting up the sky. Closer and closer, the survey ship pounded toward the burning cruise liner. Loud talk trailed off into murmurs as the extent of the disaster became more shocking with each passing mile. Fifteen minutes later, they all stood as if put in a trance by the incredible drama unfolding before them. What had once been a luxurious floating palace filled with laughing, happy people was now a fiery funeral pyre.

Seventy percent of the once-beautiful ship was a vortex of flames. Already, her superstructure was a twisted, seething tangle of red-hot steel that virtually divided the ship in two. Her once-emerald-and-white color scheme was blackened and charred. The interior support bulkheads had contorted into an indescribable mass of melted and scorched metal. The lifeboats, or what was left of them, hung in their davits, barely recognizable.

It was a grotesque monster beyond the imagining of the most demented horror writer.

Studying the *Emerald Dolphin* as she drifted broadside to the rising wind and building sea, Pitt and Burch stood stunned, uncertain that the survey ship, its scientists and crew could cope with the enormity of the tragedy.

"Good lord," mumbled Burch. "No one got away in the boats."

"Looks as if they were all burned before they could be launched," Pitt said grimly.

Flames roared and towered into the sky, reflecting like terrible demons in the water around the ship. She looked like a ghastly torch, dead in the water, waiting to be put out of her misery by slipping beneath the sea. There came a screeching roar, more like a wail, as the interior decks collapsed. For anyone within two hundred yards, it would have felt as if someone had opened the door of a blast furnace. It was light enough now to observe the charred debris littered around the burning liner, floating on a blanket of gray and white ash. Burning bits of paint and shards of fiberglass filled the air in swirling clouds. Their first impression was that nobody could have been left alive in such a holocaust, but then the great mob of people became visible, choked together on five of the liner's open stern decks. At the sight of the *Deep Encounter*, a steady stream of them begin to leap into the water and swim toward her.

Burch trained his binoculars on the water around the *Emerald Dolphin*'s stern. "People are jumping off the lower decks like lemmings," he exclaimed. "Those crammed higher up on the stern seem frozen."

"Can't really blame them," said Pitt. "The upper decks are nine to ten stories high. From their viewpoint, the water must look like it's a mile away."

Burch leaned over the railing and shouted an order to his crew. "Away the boats. Get to those people swimming in the water before they float out of sight."

"Can you bring *Deep Encounter* under the stern?" asked Pitt.

"You mean put our ship alongside?"

"Yes."

Burch looked skeptical. "I won't be able to get close enough for them to jump on board."

"The nearer the fire gets to them, the more will leap over the side. Hundreds will die before we can pick them all out of the water. If we tie up to the stern, her crew can throw lines for the passengers to slide down to our deck."

Burch looked at Pitt. "In this sea, we'll beat hell out of *Deep Encounter* against that monster. Our hull plates will be crushed and open to the sea. We could easily sink ourselves as well."

"Better to try to sink alongside than never

84

to try at all," Pitt said philosophically. "I'll take full responsibility for the ship from my end."

"You're right, of course," Burch agreed. He took over the helm and began orchestrating the controls of the two omnidirectional Z-drives and jet bow thrusters of the survey ship, gently nudging her starboard hull sideways against the massive stern of the *Emerald Dolphin*.

As the passengers reached tentative relief from the fire on the afterdecks, the terror and panic subsided to common fear and apprehension. The officers and crew, especially the women, circulated through the milling crowds, calming the most overwrought and reassuring the children. Until the *Deep Encounter* seemingly appeared out of nowhere, almost all of them had conditioned themselves to the thought of going in the water rather than being burned alive.

When the slightest degree of hope had seemed all but destroyed, however, the sight of the turquoise-painted NUMA survey ship plowing through the water in the light of the new dawn came like a divine miracle. The more than two thousand people crammed on the afterdecks cheered madly and waved their arms frantically. They saw salvation close at hand. It was to prove an optimistic assessment. The ship's officers quickly realized that the little ship was too small to take aboard even half the people still clinging to life.

Not yet realizing Pitt and Burch's intent, Second Officer McFerrin, who had struggled down from the bridge and reached the stern with a bullhorn to help in calming the passengers, called out across the water. "To the ship off our stern. Do not come any closer. There are people in the water."

In the mass of bodies crammed on the stern decks, Pitt could not see who was hailing him. He snatched his own bullhorn and shouted back. "Understood. Our boats will pick them up as fast as possible. Stand by, we're going to approach and tie next to you. Please have your crew ready to take aboard our lines."

McFerrin was astonished. He couldn't believe the NUMA captain and crew were willing to risk their own lives and ship in a rescue attempt. "How many can you take on board?" he inquired.

"How many have you got?" Pitt asked back.

"Over two thousand. Up to twenty-five hundred."

"Two thousand," Burch groaned. "We'll sink like a rock with two thousand people piled on the decks."

Discovering the officer on the upper deck who was hailing him, Pitt shouted back.

"Other rescue ships are on the way. We'll take all if we can. Have your crew drop lines so your passengers can descend to our deck."

Burch smoothly worked the propulsion controls, moving his ship slowly forward, then manipulating the bow thrusters with a deft hand, swinging his ship toward the liner inches at a time. Everyone on board *Deep Encounter* stared up in awe at the great stern soaring over them. Then came the scraping sound of steel against steel. Thirty seconds later, the two ships were firmly lashed together.

Hawsers were passed over by the survey ship's crew, while the cruise liner's crew uncoiled lines and threw them over the sides, their ends trailing into the waiting hands of the scientists, who hurriedly tied them to any object that held firm. The instant all lines were secure, Pitt shouted for the *Emerald Dolphin*'s crew to begin lowering the passengers.

"Families with children first," McFerrin shouted through his bullhorn to the crew. The old tradition of women and children first was now commonly ignored by modern seamen in favor of keeping families intact. After the sinking of the *Titanic*, when most of the men had gone down with the ship, leaving widows with fatherless small children, practical minds had felt that families should either live as one or die as one. With few exceptions, the younger, single passengers and the senior citizens stood back bravely and watched as crewmen lowered husbands, their wives and young children down to the *Deep Encounter*, where they found themselves safe on the work deck amid the submersibles, robotic underwater vehicles and hydrographic survey equipment. Next came the elderly who had to be forced to drop over the side, not because they were afraid but because they believed the younger people, with their lives ahead of them, should go first.

Surprisingly, little fear was shown by the children descending down the lines. The cruise director and members of the ship's band and theatrical troupe began playing and singing songs from Broadway shows. For a while, some people even began to sing along as the evacuation seemed to be going efficiently, without bottlenecks, but as the fire came closer, the heat intensified and the fumes made it difficult to breathe, the crowd turned back into a frightened mob. Suddenly, there was a mad rush by those who decided to take their chances in the water rather than wait their turn to shimmy down the lines to safety. The ones who jumped were mostly younger people who went over the railing from the lower decks. They fell like rain, colliding with those already floating in the water. Several miscalculated and dropped onto the deck of the *Deep Encounter*, sustaining major injuries or dying horribly on impact. Others fell between the ships and were crushed to death when the wave action pushed the hulls together.

The *Emerald Dolphin*'s crew did their best to instruct the passengers on how to jump. To strike the water with their arms over their heads meant the impact would tear the life vest over their heads, leaving them to stay afloat on their own. Those who did not grasp the collar of the life vest and pull down upon impact ran the risk of breaking their necks.

Before long, a small sea of dead bodies was drifting in the debris alongside the two ships.

Kelly was scared. The little survey ship looked so close, yet seemed so far. There were only ten people ahead of them on one of the lines attached to the vessel below. Dr. Egan was determined that he and his daughter would endure the heat and smoke and climb down to safety when their turn came. But the undisciplined rush by the choking, coughing mob forced Egan against the railing. Suddenly, a heavy man with red hair and a mustache that stretched across his cheeks to his sideburns emerged from the human surge and tried to snatch Egan's leather case from his hands. Initially stunned, the engineer managed to hold on to the case in a death grip and refused to release it.

In horror, Kelly watched the struggle between the two men. An officer in an immaculate and unwrinkled uniform stood watching with what seemed total indifference. He was a black man with a face of hardened obsidian, his features chiseled and sharp.

"Do something!" Kelly screamed at him. "Don't stand there! Help my father!"

But the black officer simply ignored her, stepped forward and, to Kelly's astonishment, began to help the red-haired man in his struggle for the leather case.

Pushed by the combined physical force of the two men, Egan lost his balance and stumbled backward against the railing. His feet lifted free of the deck and the momentum pitched him overboard headfirst. Startled by the unexpected movement, the black officer and red-haired man froze, then melted back into the crowd. Kelly screamed and rushed to the railing and looked down just in time to see her father strike the water with a huge splash.

She held her breath, waiting for what seemed like an hour but was less than twenty seconds, before his head rose to the surface. His life vest was gone, having been torn from his body by the impact. She was distressed to see that he looked unconscious. His head dipped forward and rolled listlessly.

Suddenly, without warning, Kelly felt hands around her throat, and fingers squeezing relentlessly. Dazed and in shock, Kelly frantically kicked backward while attempting futilely to pull the hands from her throat. In what was a lucky thrust, her foot caught the attacker in the groin. There was a sudden intake of breath and the pressure on her throat relaxed. She spun around, and saw that it was the black officer again.

Then the red-haired man pushed the black man out of the way and launched himself at Kelly, but she clutched the collar of her life vest and leaped clear of the railing and dropped into the void, just as the red-haired man reached out for her.

Everything around her became a blur during the fall. In what seemed the wink of an eye, she splashed into the water, the impact knocking the breath out of her. Saltwater flowed up her nose, and she fought off the urge to open her mouth to exhale a breath to purge the flow.

Down she plunged in an explosion of bubbles, as the sea closed over her. When her impetus slowed, she looked up and saw the surface shimmering under the lights of the two ships. She stroked upward, helped by her life vest, before she finally burst into the air. She sucked in several deep breaths as she looked around for her father, and saw him floating limply about thirty feet away from the scorched hull of the cruise ship.

Then a wave swept over him and she lost him. Unnerved, she frantically swam to the spot where she had last seen him. A wave raised her on its crest and she spotted her father again, no more than twenty feet away. She reached him, put one arm around his shoulders and pulled back his head by the hair. "Dad!" she cried.

Egan's eyes fluttered open and he stared at her. His face was twisted, as though he was in great pain. "Kelly, save yourself," he said haltingly. "I can't make it."

"Hold on, Dad," she encouraged him. "A boat will pick us up soon."

Still clutching the brown case, he pushed it toward her. "When I fell in the water, I struck this. I must have broken my back. I'm paralyzed and can't swim."

A body floating facedown drifted against Kelly, and she fought to keep from gagging as she pushed it away. "I'll hold on to you, Dad. I won't let you go. We can use your hand case as a float."

"Take it," he muttered, forcing her to grab the case. "Keep it safe until the proper time."

"I don't understand."

"You'll know . . ." He barely got the words out. His face contorted in agony and he sagged.

Kelly was shocked at his defeatism until she realized that her father was dying before her eyes. As for Egan, he knew he was dying. But there was no panic, no terror. He accepted his fate. His biggest regret was not the loss of his daughter — he knew she would be all right. It was not knowing if the discovery he had created on paper would work. He looked into Kelly's blue eyes and smiled faintly.

"Your mother is waiting for me," he whispered.

Kelly looked around desperately for a rescue boat. The nearest was less than two hundred feet away. She released her father, swam several yards, waved her hands and shouted. "Over here! Come this way!"

A woman, weakened by smoke inhalation and foundering in the waves, saw Kelly just as she herself was plucked from the water, and pointed her out to a seaman, but the rescuers were too engrossed in pulling others from the sea, and they failed to see her. Kelly rolled over and backstroked back to her father, but he was not to be seen. Only the leather case floated there.

Egan had released his grip on the case and slipped beneath the waves. She grabbed for it and cried out for him, but at that instant a young teenager, jumping from the upper deck, splashed in the water nearly on top of her, his knee striking her on the back of the head and sending her into a pool of blackness.

4

At first the survivors streamed onto the *Deep Encounter*, but the stream soon became a flood of humanity that inundated the crew and scientists. There were not enough of them to handle it. The fifty-one men and eight women aboard the *Deep Encounter* could not work hard or fast enough.

Despite their feelings of frustration and anguish at seeing so many dead and dying in the water, the rescuers refused to slacken their efforts. Several of the oceanographic scientists and systems engineers, ignoring the risks, tied ropes around their waists and leaped into the churning waters to grab two survivors at a time, while their shipmates towed them back to the *Deep Encounter* and hauled them aboard. Their fervor to save lives would become legend in the annals of sea history.

The crew of the survey vessel manned the

boats and frantically fished people out of the water as more and more of them threw themselves into the sea. The water under the stern soon became alive with screaming men and women, hands reaching out for the boats, afraid they might be missed.

The crew on board the ship also operated the crane equipment, which dropped rafts and nets over the side for swimmers to clamber onto before lifting them up to the work deck. They even threw over hoses and tied stepladders to the railings for swimmers to climb. As unwavering in their efforts as they were, however, they were simply overwhelmed by the sheer numbers of people struggling in the water. Later, they would agonize over those who drowned and were lost before the boats could reach them.

The women scientists took over once the passengers came on board, greeting and cheering them up before tending to the burned and injured. A great number had been blinded by the smoke and fumes and had to be led to the hospital or the aid station in the mess room. None of the scientists were trained in treating smoke inhalation, but they all learned fast and it would never be known how many lives were spared by their dedicated efforts.

They guided the unhurt down to designated interior staterooms and compartments, spacing them out to maintain the ship's stability and balance. They also set up a passenger assembly area to list the survivors and to help them find friends and relatives that had become missing or lost in the confusion.

During the first thirty minutes, more than five hundred people were pulled out of the water by the boats. Another two hundred made it to the rafts alongside the *Deep Encounter* and were lifted on board by the slings attached to winches. The rescuers concentrated only on the living. Any bodies found to be dead when pulled into the boats were returned to the sea to make room for those who still clung to life.

Retrieving and carrying twice the capacity of passengers allowed under maritime regulations, the boats came around to the stern, where they were quickly lifted on board by one of the boom cranes. The survivors were then able to step on deck without climbing the side, and those who were injured were immediately laid onto stretchers before being carried to the ship's hospital and medical station. This system, devised by Pitt, was far more efficient and actually emptied the boats and put them back in the water in half the time it would have taken to unload the exhausted survivors from the boats and heave them over the sides one at a time.

Burch could not allow his mind to stray to

the rescue operation. He concentrated on keeping the *Deep Encounter* from bashing in her hull. He felt it was his task, and his task only, to try to keep his ship from destroying itself against the great cruise liner. He'd have given his left arm to have engaged the ship's dynamic positioning system, but with both ships drifting under wind and current, it proved futile.

With a wary eye on the increasing height of the swells sweeping against the port side of his ship, he boosted the power to the thrusters and Z-drives every time one threatened to shove *Deep Encounter* crashing against the massive stern of *Emerald Dolphin*. It was a battle that he did not always win. He'd wince, knowing that hull plates were being crushed and buckled. He didn't have to be a psychic to know that water was beginning to spurt through the ruptures. A few feet away in the pilothouse, Leo Delgado computed weight and list factors as literally tons of survivors poured on the survey ship like an unending tidal wave. Already, the Plimsoll marks, indicating the maximum load level on the hull, were eighteen inches below the surface.

Pitt took on the job of masterminding and directing the rescue operation. To those working frantically to save more than two thousand people, it seemed he was everywhere, giving orders over his portable radio, pulling survivors from the water, directing the boats to where those in the water had drifted away, helping work the cranes as the boats were brought on board and unloaded. He shepherded survivors descending down the lines into the waiting arms of the scientists who then guided or carried them below. He caught children in midair whose arms and hands had gone numb from the effort and let go of the last ten feet of line. With no small apprehension, he saw that the ship was becoming dangerously overloaded with another one thousand passengers yet to save.

He ran up to the pilothouse to check with Delgado on the weight distribution. "How bad is it?"

Delgado looked up from his computer and gave a gloomy shake of his head. "Not good. Add another three feet to our draft and we'll become a submarine."

"We've still another thousand bodies to go."

"In this sea, the waves will start surging over the gunnels if we take on another five hundred. Tell your scientists they've got to spread more survivors toward the bow. We're getting too heavy in the stern."

Absorbing the bad news, Pitt gazed up at the multitude of people sliding or being lowered on the lines. Then he looked down to the work deck as a rescue boat unloaded another sixty survivors. There was no way he could condemn hundreds of people to their deaths by refusing to save them aboard the little survey ship. A solution, although partial, formed in his mind. He hurried to the work deck and assembled several of the ship's crew.

"We've got to lighten the ship," he said. "Cut the anchors and chain and drop free. Hoist the submersibles over the side and let them drift in the water. We can pick them up later. Every piece of equipment that weighs over ten pounds, toss it overboard."

After the submersibles were swung over and released to float away, the huge A-frame on the stern of the ship that was used to launch and recover oceanographic equipment was unmounted and dropped over the sides as well. Except that *it* didn't float. It went straight to the bottom of the sea, followed by several winches and their miles of heavy cable. He was cheered to see that the hull rose out of the water by nearly six inches.

Next, as another weight-saving measure, he instructed the men in the boats as they came alongside, "Our load problem has become critical. After you pick up your final haul of survivors, remain adrift next to the ship, but do not send anyone aboard."

The message was acknowledged by a wave of the hand as the helmsmen steered the boats back toward the mass of people struggling in the water.

Pitt looked up as McFerrin hailed him from above. From his vantage point, the second officer could see that the survey ship, despite the equipment that was jettisoned, was still dangerously low in the water. "How many more can you take on board?"

"How many people are still left up there?"

"Four hundred, give or take. Mostly crew now that the passengers have fled."

"Send them down," Pitt instructed him. "Is that the lot?"

"No," answered McFerrin. "Half the crew escaped to the bow."

"Can you give me a number?"

"Another four hundred and fifty." McFerrin looked at the big man on the *Deep Encounter* who seemed to be running the evacuation with incredible efficiency. "May I have your name, sir?"

"Dirk Pitt, special projects director for NUMA. And you?"

"Second Officer Charles McFerrin."

"Where is your captain?"

"Captain Waitkus is missing," McFerrin replied, "and believed dead."

Pitt could see that McFerrin had suffered burns. "Hurry down, Charlie. I've got a bottle of tequila waiting for you."

"I prefer scotch."

101

"I'll distill a bottle especially for you."

Pitt turned away and raised his hands to snatch a little girl off a line and pass her into the waiting arms of Misty Graham, one of the *Deep Encounter*'s three marine biologists. The mother and father followed and were quickly guided below. Moments later, Pitt was lifting swimmers onto the work deck who were too exhausted to climb from the rescue boats on their own.

"Circle around to the cruise ship's port side," he ordered the boat's helmsman, "and pick up the people who were carried away by the current and waves."

The helmsman looked up at Pitt, exhaustion straining his face, and managed a faint grin. "I've yet to receive one tip."

"I'll see they put it on the tab later," Pitt said, grinning back. "Now get going before —"

The piercing cry of a child seemed to come from beneath his feet. He ran to the rail and looked down. A young girl, no more than eight years old, was hanging on to a rope that dangled over the side. Somehow she had fallen overboard after coming on board and been overlooked in the confusion. Pitt lay on his stomach and reached down, gripping her by the wrists as she crested on a wave. Then he pulled her free of the water and onto the deck.

"Did you have a nice swim?" he asked,

trying to diminish her shock.

"It's too rough," she said, rubbing her eyes, which were swollen from smoke.

"Do you know if your parents came with you?"

She nodded. "They climbed out of the boat with my two brothers and sister. I fell in the water and nobody saw me."

"Don't blame them," he said softly, carrying her over to Misty. "I'll bet they're worried sick about you."

Misty smiled and took the little girl by the hand. "Come along and we'll find your mommy and daddy."

In that instant, a glimmer of light brown hair caught Pitt's eye, spread on the blue-green water like lace filaments on a satin sheet. The face could not be seen, but a hand made a slight gesture, as if trying to paddle through the water, or was it simply movement caused by the waves? Pitt ran twenty feet down the deck for a closer look, hoping against hope that the woman — the hair had to be that of a woman — had not drowned. The head rose slightly above the water, far enough for him to see two large beautiful blue eyes that appeared languid and dazed.

"Pick her up!" Pitt yelled to the rescue boat's helmsman, motioning to the woman. But the rescue boat was already halfway around the stern of the *Emerald Dolphin*, and the helmsman failed to hear him. "Swim toward me!" he shouted to the woman. He could see that she was staring in his direction without seeing him.

Without another second's hesitation, Pitt climbed on top of the railing, balanced for a moment and then dove into the water. He did not immediately rise to the surface but stroked mightily underwater, like an Olympic swimmer after leaping from a platform. As his hands and head broke clear, he barely spotted the head sinking below the surface. Twenty feet and he was there, pulling her head from under the water by her hair. Despite her drowned-rat appearance, he could see that she was a very attractive young woman. Only then did he notice that she was gripping the handle of some sort of small suitcase that had filled with water and was dragging her down.

"You fool!" he snapped. "Let loose of it!"

"I can't!" she abruptly hissed, with a determination that surprised him. "And I won't!"

Elated that she wasn't on death's doorstep, he didn't argue the matter but grabbed her by the halter and began towing her to the *Deep Encounter*. When he reached the side of the hull, willing hands reached down, clutched her by the wrists and pulled her on board. Released from his burden, Pitt climbed up a rope ladder. One of the female scientists threw a blanket around the woman and was about to guide her down a companionway when Pitt stopped her.

He looked into those blue eyes and asked, "What's so important in that briefcase that you almost died trying to save it?"

She gave him an exhausted look. "My father's lifework."

Pitt looked at the case with new respect. "Do you know if your father was saved?"

She slowly shook her head and looked forlornly into the ash-coated water with its many floating bodies. "He's down there," she whispered.

Then she abruptly turned and disappeared down the companionway.

Finally, the boats had retrieved as many of the living as could be found. They transferred those who were badly in need of medical attention onto the survey ship, and then pulled away a short distance, carrying as many survivors as they could hold without endangering them and helping to relieve the tightly packed conditions aboard.

Pitt contacted the boat crews through his portable radio. "We're heading around to the bow to look for more survivors. Follow in our wake."

No anthill could have been more congested than the *Deep Encounter* when the final living survivor was taken on board.

Bodies were crammed in the engine room, the scientific storerooms, the laboratories and the crew and scientists' quarters. They were sitting or stretched out in the lounge, the galley, staterooms and mess room. Every passageway was full. Five families were crowded in Captain Burch's cabin. The pilothouse, chart room and radio room were filled with people. The 3,400-square-foot main work deck was like an unseen street, a sea of souls packed on top of it.

The *Deep Encounter* was sitting so low that water sloshed over the gunnels onto the work deck whenever the hull was struck by waves higher than four feet. Meanwhile, the crew of the *Emerald Dolphin* did themselves proud. Only when the cruise ship's stern was free of the last passenger did they begin to drop down the lines themselves and board the crowded survey ship. Many had suffered burns, having waited until the last moment to see the passengers off before fleeing the consuming flames and abandoning the ship.

No sooner had they stepped on deck than those of them who were able to began assisting the overworked scientists to make the passengers' congested situation more comfortable. Death also came aboard the *Deep Encounter*. Several of the badly burned and those injured from the fall into the water succumbed and died amid the low murmur of prayers and weeping, as the bodies of loved ones were carried out and put over the side. Space for the living was too valuable.

Pitt sent the ship's officers up to the pilothouse to report to Captain Burch. To a man, they offered their services, which were gracefully accepted.

McFerrin was the last man down.

Pitt was waiting for him and caught his arm to keep the burned and exhausted man from stumbling and falling. He looked at the seared flesh on McFerrin's fingers and said, "A pity I can't shake the hand of a brave man."

McFerrin studied his burned hands as if they belonged to someone else. "Yes, I think it will be awhile." Then his face clouded. "I have no idea how many, if any, of the poor devils who made their way to the bow are still alive."

"We'll know soon," Pitt replied.

McFerrin looked around the survey ship, seeing the waves slosh over the work deck. "It would seem," he said calmly, "that you are in an extremely perilous situation."

"We do what we can," Pitt joked with a grim smile.

He sent McFerrin to the hospital, then turned and shouted to Burch up on the bridge wing. "That's the last of them on the stern, Skipper. The rest went for the bow."

Burch simply nodded and closed down

the thruster control console. Then he moved into the pilothouse. "The helm is yours," he said to the helmsman. "Take us around to her bow nice and easy. We don't want to aggravate whatever damage there is to our hull."

"I'll treat her as gently as a butterfly," the young man at the helm assured him.

Burch was greatly relieved to move his ship away from the cruise liner. He sent Leo Delgado down to sound the hull for buckled plates and leaks due to the battering. While he waited for the report, he called down to Chief Engineer Marvin House. "Marvin, how does it look in your neighborhood?"

Down in the engine room, Chief House stood on the walkway between the engines and eyed the thin stream of water that was pooling around their mountings. "My guess is we have major structural damage somewhere up forward, probably in one of the storerooms. I've got the main pumps working at full capacity."

"Can you keep ahead of the flow?"

"I've ordered my crew to set up auxiliary pumps and hoses to help stem the flood." House paused, and then as he looked around at the cruise ship survivors who were jammed in every open inch of his beloved engine room, he asked, "What does it look like topside?"

"Packed like Times Square on New

Year's Eve," answered Burch.

Delgado returned to the pilothouse, and Burch knew by the grim look on the officer's face the report was far from pleasant.

"Several of the plates are crushed and sprung," Delgado gasped, out of breath from running up from below. "Water is coming in at an alarming rate. The pumps are keeping ahead of the flow, but they won't be able to cope if the sea gets much worse. If the waves rise over eight feet, all bets are off."

"Chief House says he's going on auxiliary pumps in an attempt to stay ahead of the flow."

"I only hope it's enough," said Delgado.

"Round up the damage-control crew and go to work on the hull. Shore up and reinforce the plates the best you can. Report to me any change in the leakage, good or bad, immediately."

"Yes, sir."

Burch was staring apprehensively at the sullen gray clouds that were building to the southwest when Pitt returned to the pilothouse. Pitt followed the captain's gaze. "What's the latest on the weather?" he asked.

Burch smiled and pointed through a skylight at the twelve-foot-diameter dome that held a Doppler radar system. "I don't need up-to-the-minute meteorological predictions of storm dynamics by a state-of-the-art computer to tell me that we're in for a blow within the next two hours."

Pitt gazed at the gathering clouds no more than ten miles away. It was full daylight now, but the dawn sun was hidden by the menacing clouds. "Maybe it will pass us by."

Burch licked an index finger and held it in the air. He shook his head. "Not according to *this* computer." Then he added ominously, "There is no way we're going to stay afloat."

Pitt wearily wiped his brow with his bare arm. "Figuring the average weight of the men, women and children at one hundred twenty pounds, *Deep Encounter* is transporting an extra one hundred twenty tons, not counting her crew and scientific team. Our only salvation is in staying afloat long enough to transport most of the survivors to another vessel."

"No way we can make for port," Burch added. "We'd sink before sailing a mile."

Pitt stepped into the radio room. "Any word from the Aussies and the tanker?"

"According to radar, the *Earl of Wattlesfield* is only ten miles away. The Aussie frigate is coming on strong, but she still has thirty miles to go."

"Tell them to push hard," Pitt said gravely. "If that storm strikes before they get here, they may not find anyone left to rescue."

5

The interior of the *Emerald Dolphin* was disintegrating, bulkhead toppling against bulkhead, deck falling on deck. In less than two hours after it had burst into flames, the ship's grand interior had been consumed. The entire superstructure was collapsing into a fiery hellpit. The ornate decor, the elegant shopping avenue with its stylish shops, the seventy-eight-million-dollar art collection, the lavish casino, dining rooms and lounges, the luxurious staterooms and opulent entertainment and sporting facilities, all had been reduced to smoldering ashes.

Everyone crowded on the open decks of the *Deep Encounter*, former passengers and crew, the men and women working feverishly on the NUMA survey ship, all stopped whatever they were doing and gazed at the holocaust with a mixture of grief and fascination as Captain Burch steered around the stern of the gigantic ship toward the bow.

No longer a ball of raging flame, she was melting down into a dying furnace. The frenzied fire having attacked and consumed every flammable material, every combustible object, now found nothing left to destroy. The fiberglass-hull lifeboats hung grotesquely and contorted, having melted into unrecognizable shapes. The great circular decks were drooping down around the hull like the decayed wings of a dead vulture. The high observation lounge and most of the bridge had fallen inward and all but disappeared, as if swallowed in an immense chasm. Much of the glass that had melted was cooling and rehardening into unnatural configurations.

Consumed by the holocaust, the entire circular superstructure caved in upon itself under a great billowing pall of smoke. Fresh flames suddenly leaped through the open sides of the hull from explosions deep below. The *Emerald Dolphin* shuddered like a great tortured beast. Yet she refused to die and slip beneath the waves. She drifted doggedly on a sea that was turning gray and nastier by the minute. Soon she would be little more than a gutted hulk. Never again would she hear the footsteps, conversation and laughter of cheerful and excited passengers. Never would she majestically sail into exotic ports throughout the world as proud a ship as ever sailed the seas. If she remained afloat after the fires cooled, and her hull plates did not buckle from the intense heat, she would be towed to her final harbor and to a shipyard, where she would be cut down into scrap.

Pitt stared at her with deep sadness, watching a fabulous ship reduced to a ruin. He could feel the heat of the flames reach across the water and touch him. He wondered why such beautiful vessels had to die, why some sailed the oceans for thirty years without incident before heading for the scrappers, while others, like the *Titanic* on her maiden voyage or the *Emerald Dolphin* on hers, came to early grief. There were lucky ships and there were those that sailed into oblivion.

He stood hunched over the rail, lost in his thoughts, when McFerrin came and stood next to him. The cruise ship's second officer remained strangely silent as the *Deep Encounter* moved slowly past the macabre drama. The rescue boats with their overloaded cargo of survivors followed in the wake.

"How are your hands?" asked Pitt solicitously.

McFerrin held them up and displayed bandages that looked like white mittens. His face, with burned and reddened skin, was smeared with antiseptic lotion and looked like an unsightly Halloween mask. "Not easy going to the bathroom, let me tell you."

Pitt smiled. "I can imagine."

McFerrin, on the verge of tearful rage, gazed entranced at the ghastly sepulcher. "It should never have happened," he said, his voice quavering with emotion.

"What do you think caused it?"

McFerrin turned from the glowing, twisted hulk. His face strained in anger. "It was not an act of God. I can tell you that."

"You think it was terrorism?" Pitt asked incredulously.

"There is no doubt in my mind. The fire spread too quickly for it to have been accidental. None of the automated fire-warning or fire-control systems went into operation. And when they were manually engaged, they refused to function."

"What mystifies me is why your captain failed to send off a distress signal. We turned toward you only after we saw the glow of your fire on the horizon. Our radio inquiries regarding your situation went unanswered."

"First Officer Sheffield!" McFerrin fairly spat out the name. "He was incapable of command decisions. When I found that no message had been sent, I immediately contacted the radio room, but it was too late.

The fire had already reached it and the operators had fled."

Pitt gestured up at the high-angled bow of the cruise ship. "I see life up there."

A large group of human figures could be seen waving excitedly on the forepeak of the ship. Unlike those who had run for the stern, fifty or more passengers and large numbers of the crew had made their way to the open forepeak above the bow. Fortunately for them, the bow was a good two hundred feet away from the forward bulkheads of the superstructure and upwind from the fire and acrid smoke that had streaked toward the stern.

McFerrin straightened, held a hand over his eyes to shield them from the rising sun and peered up at the tiny figures wildly gesturing above the bow. "Mostly crew, with a sprinkling of passengers. Actually, they look like they might be okay for a little while. The fire's going the other way."

Pitt took a pair of binoculars and scanned the waters around the bow. "None appear to have jumped. I see no sign of floating bodies or swimmers."

"So long as they're safe from the fire for the moment," said Burch, approaching from inside the pilothouse, "it's better we leave them until another ship arrives or the weather settles down."

"It's obvious we can't stay afloat in rough

seas with another four hundred people on board," Pitt agreed. "We're just a hair away from capsizing and sinking as it is."

The wind was beginning to fling itself at them, rising from ten miles an hour to thirty. The sea was tossing whitecapped foam in the breeze, and the swells came marching in like an irresistible force, now rising nearly ten feet high. It was only a warning of the fury that was yet to come.

Pitt rushed off the bridge and shouted for the crew and scientists to get as many people as possible off the work deck and to secure those who were left before the waves smashed over the sides and swept them away. The crush on the lower decks was quickly becoming unbearable, but there was no alternative. To leave hundreds of people exposed to the elements during a tempest would be signing their death warrants.

Pitt studied the crews of the two boats trailing in the wake. He was gravely concerned about their situation. The sea was too chaotic for them to come alongside and unload their passengers. Pitt looked at Burch. "I suggest, Skipper, that we turn and come around on the lee side of the cruise ship and use her for a shelter from the storm's battering. If we can't get the boat crews and the survivors on board, we've got to move them to calmer water in the next few minutes or it will be too late for them."

Burch nodded. "A sound recommendation. It may be our only salvation as well."

"Can't you bring them on board?" asked McFerrin.

"Another hundred people on this vessel will be the straw that broke the camel's back," said Burch soberly.

McFerrin looked at him. "We can't play God."

The expression on Burch's face was one of torment. "We can if it means the lives of all the passengers already aboard."

"I agree," Pitt said firmly. "They're better off sheltered from the worst of the storm on the *Emerald Dolphin* than coming on board the *Deep Encounter*."

Burch stared down at the deck for several moments, considering every option. Finally, he nodded wearily. "We'll keep the boats tied close to our stern in case their situation becomes critical and they have to come on board." Then he turned and looked at the wall of dark clouds that were rushing across the water like a thick swarm of locusts. "I can only hope God gives us a fighting chance."

The storm roared toward the little ship and its mass of humanity. Another few minutes and it would enshroud them. The sun had long disappeared, taking any hint of blue sky. The crests of the waves swirled like dervishes and threw off billows of froth and spray. Warm green water sloshed over the work deck, drenching those who were unable to find room below. As many as humanly possible had been shoved through the hatches, jammed into the passageways like commuters on a rush-hour bus.

Pulled close to the burning ship, those in the boats suffered more from the heat that radiated from the fire than from the wind and waves that tossed them about the stormy sea. Both Pitt and Burch kept a sharp eye on their condition, ready to haul them on board at the first sign of trouble.

If help did not come quickly and the *Deep Encounter* sank, taking its precious cargo with her, there would be few survivors.

"Do you know if anyone up there has a radio?" Pitt asked McFerrin.

"All officers carry portable radios."

"Their frequency?"

"Twenty-two."

Pitt held the radio close to his mouth and covered it with one side of his coat to cut down the sound of the wind that was building to a howl. "*Emerald Dolphin*, this is *Deep Encounter*. Is there an officer on board who can read me? Over." He repeated the request three times through heavy static before a voice came back.

"I hear you, *Deep Encounter*," a woman's

voice replied. "Not well, but enough to understand you."

"I have a woman," said Pitt, looking at McFerrin.

"It sounds like Amelia May, our chief purser."

"The fire is causing interference. I can barely make her out."

"Ask how many people are on the forepeak," ordered Burch.

"Am I speaking to Amelia May?" Pitt inquired.

"Yes, how do you know my name?"

"Your second officer is standing beside me."

"Charles McFerrin?" she exclaimed. "Praise God. I thought Charlie died in the fire."

"Can you estimate the number of passengers and crew left on board?"

"My best guess is four hundred and fifty crew, with about sixty passengers. When can we begin to abandon the ship?"

Burch was looking up at the bow with an intense look of dismay. "No way we can take them aboard," he said again, with a sad shake of his head.

"Either way you look at it," said Pitt, "it's a no-win situation. The wind and sea are rising at an alarming rate. Our boats can't pick them up, and it would be suicide for them to jump into the water and attempt to swim to our ship."

Burch nodded in agreement. "Our only hope is for the British containership to get here in the next half hour. After that we're in God's hands."

"Ms. May," called Pitt. "Please listen to me. Our ship is loaded far beyond capacity. We are also in danger of sinking, due to a crushed hull. You must hold out until the weather slackens or a rescue ship arrives. Do you understand?"

"Yes, I understand," she echoed. "The wind is blowing the fire aft and the heat is not unbearable."

"Not for long," Pitt warned her. "The *Dolphin* is swinging around and will begin drifting broadside against the wind and current. The fire and smoke will move closer and pour off to your starboard."

There was a pause, then Amelia said resolutely, "I guess we'll have to break out the marshmallows."

Pitt looked up to the bow, squinting against the spray thrown by the wind. "You're a very intrepid lady. I hope we can meet when this is over. Dinner is on me."

"Maybe . . ." There was a hesitation. "You'll have to tell me your name first."

"My name is Dirk Pitt."

"A strong name. I like that. Over and out."

McFerrin grinned wearily. "She's a gorgeous creature, Pitt. And quite independent

120

when it comes to men."

Pitt grinned back. "I wouldn't want it any other way."

The rains came like a glistening solid wall, not gradually, but in a sudden deluge. And still the *Emerald Dolphin* burned. Her sides were glowing red as the rain struck the ferocious heat, quickly covering the flaming ship in a vast cloud of steam.

"Bring her within two hundred feet of the hull slow and easy," Burch ordered the helmsman. He was troubled at the pitching and rolling of his ship as she was pounded by the rising waves. He became even more troubled when Chief Engineer House called the bridge.

"The old girl is being hammered down here," he reported. "The leaks are getting worse. I can't guarantee how much longer the pumps can keep up, even with the auxiliaries adding to the discharge."

"We've come under the hull of the cruise ship," replied Burch. "I'm hoping her bulk will protect us from the worst of the storm."

"Every little bit helps."

"Do the best you can."

"It's not easy," grumbled House. "Not when you're climbing over bodies packed tighter than an anchovy jar."

Burch turned to Pitt, who was peering into the wet gloom with the binoculars.

"Any sign of the containership or the Aussie frigate?"

"The heavy rain has cut visibility to a bare minimum, but radar has the containership closing within a thousand yards."

Burch took out an old bandanna and wiped the moisture from his brow and neck. "I hope the captain is a good seaman, because he's going to need all the experience he's got."

Captain Malcolm Nevins, master of the Collins and West Shipping Lines containership *Earl of Wattlesfield*, sat in an elevated swivel chair with his feet propped on the bridge counter and contemplated the radar screen. Just ten minutes earlier, the burning ship was in visual contact, but then the storm closed in with phenomenal swiftness and the accompanying deluge had curtained off all view. With an air of practiced indifference, he eased a platinum cigarette case from his pants pocket, lifted out a Dunhill and placed it between his lips. Incongruously, he lit the expensive cigarette with an old scratched and dented Zippo lighter that he had carried since serving in the Royal Navy during the war of the Falklands.

Nevins's ruddy features, usually humorous and pleated, were set in concentration; his limpid gray eyes squinting and uneasy. He wondered what kind of hell he was about to find. The radio reports from the American survey vessel were morbid with descriptions of over two thousand people trying to escape the blazing cruise ship. In all his thirty years at sea, he could not recall a disaster of such magnitude.

"There," shouted his first officer, Arthur Thorndyke, pointing ahead off the starboard bow through the bridge windshield.

The falling sheets of rain parted for a minute, as though they were drapes, revealing the blazing cruise ship enshrouded by smoke and steam. "Engines on SLOW," Nevins ordered.

"Aye, sir."

"Are the boat crews standing by?" asked Nevins, as the huge liner materialized out of the downpour.

"Boat crews standing by and ready to lower away," answered Thorndyke. "I must say, I don't envy them floating on a sea with twelve-foot swells."

"We'll lay to as close as we can to save them time and distance between ships." He picked up a pair of binoculars and peered at the water around the cruise ship. "I don't see anyone swimming, and there is no sign of lifeboats."

Thorndyke nodded at the torched remains of the ship's lifeboats. "Nobody left the ship in those."

Nevins stiffened, his mind picturing a blazing hulk carrying thousands of dead. "The loss of life must be horrendous," he said darkly.

"I don't see the American survey vessel." Nevins read the situation instantly. "Come around the ship. The Americans must be on her sheltered side."

The *Earl of Wattlesfield* lumbered steadily through the chaotic waters, as if disregarding all dire threats from the sea and daring the elements to throw their best at her. At 68,000 tons, she was more than a city block long and her decks were piled several stories high with boxed units filled with freight. For ten years she had sailed every ocean in the world through every kind of sea without losing one container or one life. She was considered a lucky ship, especially by her owners, who had profited millions of pounds from her reliable service.

After this day she would become as famous as the *Carpathia*, the ship that had rescued the *Titanic* survivors.

The wind was approaching gale force and the waves became steeper, but they had little effect on the big containership. Nevins held little hope of rescuing any passengers or crew. Those who had escaped burning to death, he thought, had jumped overboard and had surely drowned in the turbulent waters by now. As the *Earl of Wattlesfield* slowly rounded the high, sloping bow, he stared up at the raised, green painted letters, *Emerald Dolphin*. He felt despondent as he remembered seeing the beautiful cruise ship as she'd left port in Sydney. Then, abruptly, he was staring disbelievingly at an entirely unexpected spectacle.

The *Deep Encounter* was rolling heavily in waters reflecting the orange flames, her hull sunk almost to the gunnels, her decks overflowing with huddled figures. No more than twenty yards behind her stern, two launches bobbed up and down, their interiors also filled with human bodies. The ship looked as if she was about to plunge under the sea at any moment.

"Good lord!" muttered Thorndyke. "She looks like she's sinking."

The radio operator leaned from the radio room. "Sir, I have someone on the American ship."

"Put them on the speaker."

Within seconds, a voice boomed through the amplifiers. "To the captain and crew of the containership, are we ever glad to see you."

"This is Captain Nevins. Am I speaking to the ship's captain?"

"No, Captain Burch is down in the engine room examining the water flooding the ship."

"Then who are you?"

"Dirk Pitt, Special Projects Director for

the National Underwater and Marine Agency."

"What is your condition? You look like you are foundering."

"We're close to it," Pitt answered candidly. "We knocked in our hull plates when we tied to the cruise ship's stern to rescue her crew and passengers. We're taking on water faster than the pumps can handle it."

"How many survivors do you have on board?" asked Nevins, still astounded at the number of people struggling on the work deck to keep from being swept overboard.

"Somewhere in the neighborhood of nineteen hundred, with another hundred still in the boats."

"My word!" Nevin's voice was slow, stunned, almost a whisper. "Are you saying that you've rescued two thousand survivors?"

"Give or take fifty here and there."

"Where in the world have you put them?"

"You'd have to come over and see for yourself," said Pitt.

"No wonder you look like a goose who swallowed a barbell," Nevins muttered in wonderment.

"There are still close to five hundred crew and passengers waiting to be rescued on the forepeak of the cruise ship. We simply could not take them all without endangering everyone's life."

"Any chance they may be burned?"

"We're in contact with their ship's officers and they report that they're in no immediate peril," explained Pitt. "I respectfully suggest, Captain, that our first priority be to transport as many people as possible from our ship to yours while we're still afloat. We'd be grateful if you took those in our rescue boats on board first. They're having the worst of it."

"We will indeed. I'll lower my boats and begin ferrying the survivors on your vessel to mine. We certainly have more room for them over here. Once your boats are unloaded, that will leave them free to take on those still on the cruise ship's bow, who can lower themselves down on ropes."

"We have the routine down to a science by now."

"Then we had best get to it."

Then Pitt added, "Believe me, Captain Nevins, you'll never know what a blessing your timely arrival is."

"I'm thankful we were in the neighborhood."

Nevins turned to Thorndyke, his normally humorous expression incredulous.

"It's a miracle they put all those people on such a small ship."

"A miracle it is," murmured Thorndyke, equally astonished. "To paraphrase Churchill, Never have so many been saved by so few."

6

Kelly sat on the deck in one of the *Deep Encounter*'s storerooms, her knees pulled up to her chin. She felt as if she had been transported to the Black Hole of Calcutta. Survivors were so crammed in the small compartment that only the women could sit, while the men stood. No one seemed to pay any attention as she laid her head in her hands and cried. She felt a wave of sorrow over her father's death. To have watched him lose his life within an arm's reach left her achingly helpless and grief-stricken.

Why had it happened? Who was the red-haired man and why had he struggled with her father? And the black officer? Why hadn't he intervened instead of helping the attacker? They appeared to be attempting to snatch her father's case. She looked down at the leather case, stained with salt water, that she still held tightly against her breasts, wondering why its contents were so important that her father had died for them.

She fought off exhaustion and forced herself to stay awake in case the red-haired man reappeared and made another attempt to take it from her. But the hot, humid closeness of so many bodies, and the struggling air-conditioning system that made as much difference as an ice cube in an oven, combined to make her drowsy, and she finally drifted off in a fitful sleep.

She woke up suddenly, still sitting on the deck, her back against a locker, but remarkably the storeroom was now empty of people. A woman who'd introduced herself earlier as a marine biologist leaned down and gently brushed the damp hair from Kelly's eyes as if she were a child. The woman's face and eyes looked tired and drained, but she managed a sympathetic smile.

"Time to move along," she said softly. "A British containership has arrived and we're transferring everyone over to her."

"I'm so grateful to you and your crew, and especially the man who dove in the water and saved me from drowning."

"I don't know who that was," said the woman, a pretty redhead with brown eyes.

"Can't I stay aboard this ship?" asked Kelly.

"I'm afraid not. We're taking on water

and there is doubt whether we can stay afloat through the storm." She helped Kelly to her feet. "You'd better hurry or you'll miss your boat."

The woman left the storeroom to herd other passengers topside so they could board the containership's boats. Alone, Kelly stiffly rose to her feet, her back aching from sitting on the hard deck. She was almost to the doorway when suddenly she was stopped by a large man. She hesitated, looked up and found herself staring into the icy features of the red-haired man who had struggled with her father on the cruise ship. He stepped inside the storeroom and slowly closed the door.

"What do you want?" she whispered fearfully.

"Your father's case," he answered in a deep, quiet voice. "You won't be hurt if you hand it over. Otherwise, I will have to kill you."

Kelly could see resolve in the cold, dead, black eyes. And something else: The man was going to kill her whether she gave him the case or not.

"My father's papers? What do you want with them?"

He shrugged. "I'm only a hired man. My job is to deliver the case and its contents, that's all."

"Deliver to whom . . . ?"

"It doesn't matter," he said, his voice turning impatient.

"Are you going to shoot me?" Kelly asked, desperately stalling for every second of life.

"I don't use guns and I don't use knives." He held up his hands, huge and callused, and grinned. "These are all I need."

She felt panic stab her, and started to back away from him. He moved toward her and she could see the white teeth beneath the red mustache as his lips widened in a malevolent grin. His eyes had the smug gleam of an animal who has his quarry trapped and helpless. Her panic turned to terror, her heart began to pound, her breath to come in gasps. Her legs felt weak and they tottered beneath her. Her long hair streaked across her eyes and face, and the tears involuntarily began to flow.

His arms reached out, the hands like claws, and clutched her. She screamed, a high shrill cry that reverberated in the small storeroom with its steel bulkheads. She tore out of his grasp and spun around. It was as if he deliberately let her go so he could play with her as a cat toys with a mouse before devouring it. Unable to resist, she began to feel faint, and crumpled to the deck, crouched in one corner of the storeroom, shuddering uncontrollably.

She could only stare at him through huge,

131

glazed blue eyes as he stepped slowly toward her. He bent over, took her under the arms and lifted her up in one effortless motion. The cold, murderous expression had been replaced by a leer of lust. As if in slow motion, he pressed his lips against hers. Her eyes flew wide and she tried to scream again, but all that came out were muffled sobs. Then he pulled back and grinned again.

"Yes," he said, in a voice that was hard and indifferent. "Scream all you wish. No one can hear you above the storm outside. I like it when a woman screams. I find it exhilarating."

He lifted her off the floor as if she weighed no more than a mannequin stuffed with foam. Then he pinned her against a bulkhead and his hands began to move over her body, crudely, roughly, bruising her skin. Numb with terror, Kelly went limp and cried the age-old woman's cry.

"Please, you're hurting me."

His huge hands moved up to her throat and locked around it. "I promise," he said, with the emotion of a block of ice. "Death will come quick and painless."

He began to squeeze, and a black cloud fell over Kelly's eyes. "No, please," she pleaded, her voice becoming little more than a rasping whisper.

"Sweet dreams, dear heart."

Then a voice behind him said, "Your technique for romancing women leaves a lot to be desired."

The red-haired killer released Kelly's throat and spun around in a movement as quick as a cat's. A shadowy figure was standing in the doorway, one outstretched hand casually resting on the door latch, his face dark and silhouetted by the light behind him in the passageway. Quickly, the killer whipped into a martial-arts position, his hands poised in the air, and launched his foot at the intruder.

Unknown to the killer and Kelly, Pitt had heard the screams and silently opened the door, then stood there for a few brief seconds, appraising the situation and devising contingency tactics. There was no time to go for help. The girl would be dead before anyone arrived to back him up. He immediately sensed this was a dangerous man who was no stranger to killing. Men such as this had to have a concrete reason for coldly murdering a defenseless woman. He braced himself for the attack he knew would come.

In a violent corkscrew motion, he twisted out of the doorway into the passageway as the killer's leg and foot sliced through the air. The intended blow missed Pitt's head by an inch and impacted on the frame of the door. The ankle bone broke cleanly with an audible crack.

Any other man would have writhed in agony. Not this one, not this hunk thick with muscle and trained to ignore pain. The killer glanced up and down the passageway to make sure Pitt was alone and had no help, and then he came forward, arms and hands moving rhythmically in martial-arts motions. Then he leaped toward his prey, hands chopping the air like axes.

Pitt stood as if frozen, feigning fear, until the last microsecond. Then he dropped to the deck and rolled toward his assailant, whose momentum caught him off balance and carried him over and beyond Pitt, tripping on his body and crashing in a heap to the deck. Pitt was on the red-haired killer like lightning. Using every pound of his body, he pinned the man to the deck, digging one knee into an unprotected back and clapping his hands violently against the ears.

The man's eardrums burst as though an icepick had been jabbed from one side of his head to the other. The killer uttered a ghastly howl and convulsively wrenched to one side, hurling Pitt against a closed door. Pitt was stunned at the brutal strength of the man and his seeming immunity to pain. Half on his back, he lashed out with both feet, not into the killer's groin, but smashing down on the broken ankle.

No outcry this time, only a snarl and a hissing through clenched teeth. The face twisted into a hideous grimace, the eyes glinting with ferocity. He was hurt now, truly hurt. But he was still the aggressor, and he continued his advance toward Pitt, dragging his mangled foot behind him. Altering his strategy, he gathered himself for the next assault on Pitt.

It didn't take a wizard's gray matter for Pitt to realize that he was no match for a highly trained killer with a body like a demolition ball on a crane. Pitt backed away, knowing his only advantage was faster footwork, now that his adversary could only perform on one leg, eliminating any possibility of a vicious kick to the head.

Pitt had never taken a martial-arts course in his life. He had boxed during his years at the Air Force Academy, but his wins usually equaled his losses. He had learned the tactics of free-for-all fighting after having survived a number of barroom brawls. Lesson one, which he'd learned early on, was never fight close-in with your fists. Fight with your brain and any object that you can throw, shove or swing at your attacker — a bottle, chair or whatever. The survival rate without injuries was much higher among those who fought from the outside in.

Suddenly Kelly appeared in the doorway behind the killer. She was holding the leather case as though it were growing out of her chest. The red-haired executioner was so focused on Pitt that he didn't detect her presence.

Pitt saw an opportunity. "Run!" he shouted to Kelly. "Run up the stairs and out onto the deck!"

The killer hesitated, not certain whether Pitt was trying the age-old bluff. But he was a true professional, who studied his victims. He saw the tiny shift in Pitt's eyes and whirled around as Kelly ran toward the stairway leading up to the open work deck. Focusing on his main target, he took off after Kelly, half running, half hobbling, fighting the agony that erupted from his fractured ankle.

It was the move Pitt had hoped for.

Now it was his turn to attack. He sprinted forward and leaped on the back of the killer. It was a brutal football tackle, using the combined impetus of both their bodies to bring the runner down from behind, falling with all his weight on the other's body while ramming his face and head into the deck.

Pitt heard his attacker's head hit the thinly carpeted steel deck with a sickening thump and a crack and felt the body go limp. If not a fracture, the skull must have suffered a concussion, he thought. For a moment, Pitt lay on top of the man, breathing heavily, waiting for his heart to slow. He blinked his eyes as he felt the sting of sweat trickling into them and rubbed the sleeve of his coat across his face.

It was then he noticed the killer's head was twisted in an unnatural position and the eyes were open and unseeing.

Pitt reached down and pressed his fingers against the jugular vein. There was no hint of a pulse. The killer was dead. He must have struck his head at an angle, forcing it sideways and breaking the neck, Pitt concluded. He sat back on the deck and leaned against the closed door to the compartment where batteries were stored, and assessed the situation. None of it made sense. All Pitt knew for certain was that he happened to walk onto the scene of an attempted murder of a woman he had rescued from drowning. Now he was sitting there staring at a total stranger he had accidentally murdered. He looked into the man's unseeing eyes and murmured to himself, "I'm as rotten as you are."

Then he thought of the woman.

Pitt came to his feet, stepped over the sprawled body of the dead man and hurried up the stairs to the outer deck. The work deck was crowded with survivors who were holding on to safety ropes strung by the *Deep Encounter*'s crew. They stood uncomplaining as the rain lashed their heads and shoulders while they moved in line and climbed into the *Earl of Wattlesfield*'s rescue boats for the trip to the container ship.

Pitt rushed through the line searching for the woman with the leather case, but she was not in the group that was being transported across the water. It was as if she had vanished. One look at the boats having unloaded and on their way back to the survey ship told him that she could not have left the *Deep Encounter*. She must still be on board.

He had to find her. How else could he explain the dead body to Captain Burch? And how else would he ever find out what was going on?

7

Things were finally looking up for the *Deep Encounter*. By late afternoon, except for ten who were too injured to be moved, all but one hundred of the survivors from the *Emerald Dolphin* had been ferried over to the *Earl of Wattlesfield*. Without the horde of survivors on board, the battered survey ship rose five feet out of the water. The crew then went to work and shored up the badly damaged hull plates, which reduced the incoming flow and enabled the pumps to gain on the flooding.

The Australian guided-missile frigate arrived and added their boats to the ferry operation, taking the survivors who'd dropped down the ropes from the bow and relieving the exhausted boat crews from *Deep Encounter*. Thankfully, the storm passed almost as suddenly as it arrived and the sea settled down to a mild chop.

McFerrin was the last man off the survey vessel. Before he boarded the containership's boat, he personally thanked the entire crew and scientists. "Your rescue of so many souls will go down in the annals of sea history," he told them, to expressions of modest embarrassment.

"I regret we couldn't have saved them all," Burch said quietly.

"What you did was nothing short of miraculous." Then McFerrin turned and placed his bandaged hands on Pitt's shoulders. "Dirk, it has been a privilege. Your name will always be spoken with honor in the McFerrin home. I sincerely hope we meet again."

"We must," said Pitt jovially. "I owe you a bottle of scotch."

"Good-bye, ladies and gentlemen of NUMA. God bless you all."

"Good-bye, Charles. They don't come better than you."

McFerrin climbed down into the *Earl of Wattlesfield*'s boat and gave a final salute as it swung away.

"Now what?" Pitt asked Burch.

"First, we pick up the submersibles or Admiral Sandecker will behead us on the steps of the Capitol Building," he said, referring to the chief director of NUMA. "Then we set a course for Wellington, the nearest port with a shipyard and the dry-dock facilities to repair our damage."

"It's no great loss if we can't find the *Ancient Mariner* — she's an old workhorse that has more than paid for herself — but the *Abyss Navigator* is state-of-the-art, fresh from the factory and cost twelve million dollars. We can't afford to lose her."

"We'll find her. Her beacon signal is coming in loud and strong."

He almost had to shout to be heard above the sounds coming from the sky. The air above the ships swarmed with aircraft flown from New Zealand, Tonga, Fiji and Samoa, most of them chartered by the international news media, covering what would become known as the most magnificent rescue operation in the history of the seas. The radios on all three ships were inundated with messages from governments, anxious relatives of the survivors, corporate officials of the Blue Seas Cruise Lines, and representatives of the underwriters who had insured the *Emerald Dolphin*. The radio traffic was so heavy that all communication among the three rescue ships was conducted by handheld portable radios or blinkers.

Burch sighed as he relaxed in his elevated captain's chair and lit his pipe, then smiled faintly. "Do you think the admiral will turn the air blue when he hears what we did to his research ship?"

"Under the circumstances, the old sea dog will milk the publicity to the last drop."

"Have you thought of how you're going to explain that body lying below to the officials?" asked Burch.

"I can only tell what I know."

"Pity the girl can't act as a witness."

"I can't believe I missed her during the evacuation."

"Actually, your problem has been solved," Burch said, with a devious grin.

Pitt looked at the captain for a long moment. "Solved?"

"I like to run a tight, clean ship," explained Burch. "I personally threw your friend over the side. He's joined the other poor souls from the *Emerald Dolphin* who died during the tragedy. As far as I'm concerned, the matter is closed."

"Skipper," Pitt said, with a twinkle in his eye, "you're okay. I don't care *what* they say about you."

The harried radio operator came from the radio room. "Sir, a message from Captain Harlow of the Australian missile frigate. If you wish to leave station, he will stand by to pick up bodies and stay with the cruise liner until tugs arrive to tow her to port."

"Acknowledge and express my deepest gratitude to the captain and his crew for their gallant assistance."

A minute later, the operator returned. "Captain Harlow wishes you Godspeed and calm seas."

"I imagine it has to be the first time in history a guided-missile frigate took on five hundred civilian passengers," said Pitt.

"Yes," said Burch slowly, as he turned and gazed at the burned-out leviathan.

The downpour of rain had done little to alleviate the fire. Flames still flickered and smoke spiraled into the sky. Except for a small space around the bow, the entire ship was blackened and scorched. The steel plates were buckled and her superstructure was little more than a labyrinth of charred, twisted and contorted frameworks. Nothing organic was left. Everything that could burn had been reduced to ugly piles of ashes. It had been a ship that its architects and builders swore could never burn. Fire-retardant materials had been used throughout. But they'd never counted on the dynamic heat that had fanned itself into a firestorm that could melt metal.

"Another one of the great mysteries of the sea," Pitt said, his voice distant.

"Ship fires occur with alarming frequency around the world every year." Burch spoke as if he were lecturing to a class. "But I've never heard of one more baffling than the blaze on board the *Emerald Dolphin*. No fire on a ship that large should have spread so fast."

"Second Officer McFerrin suggested that it spread out of control because the fire-warning and control systems were inoperative."

"An act of treachery, do you think?"

Pitt nodded at the smoldering, gutted hulk. "It defies logic that it was a series of unfortunate circumstances."

"Captain," the radio operator interrupted again, "Captain Nevins of the *Earl of Wattlesfield* would like a word with you."

"Put him on the speaker."

"Go ahead, sir."

"Captain Burch here."

"Captain Nevins here. I say, if you chaps are going to try for Wellington, I'll be most happy to shepherd you along the way, since that's the closest major port to disembark the survivors."

"That's very kind of you, Captain," replied Burch. "I accept your offer. We've set a course for Wellington, too. I hope we don't slow you down too much."

"Wouldn't do for the heroes and heroines of the hour to sink along the way."

"Our pumps are keeping ahead of the flooding. Barring a major typhoon, we should make Wellington in good shape."

"As soon as you get under way, we'll follow."

"How are you managing with eighteen hundred people on your ship?" asked Pitt.

"We have most of them in two of our empty cargo holds. The rest are scattered throughout, some in half-empty containers. We have enough food in the galley for one proper meal. After that, everyone, including my crew and I, will go on a rigid diet until we reach Wellington." Nevins paused for a moment. "And, oh yes, if you could pass between my ship and the Aussie frigate, we'd like to give you a send-off. Over and out."

Burch looked bemused. "Send-off?"

"Maybe they want to say aloha and throw streamers." Pitt laughed.

Burch picked up the ship's phone. "Chief, are you ready and able to get under way?"

"I'll let you have eight knots, no more," answered House. "Any more speed and she'll leak like a rusty bucket."

"Eight knots it is."

To the ship's crew and the NUMA scientists, haggard and dead-tired from twelve hours of nonstop physical and mental exertion, it was an ordeal just to stand on their two feet, but stand they did, straight and proud as Pitt lined them up on the work deck. The ship's crew was grouped on one end of the deck while the scientists, men and women intermingled, stood opposite. Everyone was there. Burch insisted that the entire engine room crew turn out. Chief Engineer House balked at leaving the pumps unattended, but the captain prevailed. Only the helmsman stood alone in the pilothouse, steering the survey vessel between the *Earl of Wattlesfield* and the Australian guided-missile frigate that lay to no more than two hundred yards apart.

The little survey ship seemed dwarfed between the two much larger ships. She sailed proudly, the NUMA flag flying on her radar mast and a huge stars-and-stripes streaming stiffly on the stern jack staff.

Pitt and Burch, standing beside each other, stared up, startled to see the crew of the frigate turn out as if for a formal military review. Then suddenly, as the *Deep Encounter* entered the gap between the two ships, the silent tropical air was shattered by the whoops of the ships' air horns and the cheers of the more than two thousand survivors who lined the rails of the containership and frigate. Pandemonium broke out across the water. Men, women and children all waved wildly and shouted words that went unheard in the din. Shredded newspaper and magazines were thrown in the air like confetti. Only at that moment did everyone on board the *Deep Encounter* fully realize what their magnificent exploit had achieved.

They had gone far beyond the rescue of over two thousand people; they had proven that they were willing to sacrifice their lives to save other humans. Tears flowed unashamedly from the eyes of everyone.

Long afterward, the men and women of the survey ship could never describe it accurately. They were too moved to fully absorb the event. Even the tremendous rescue effort seemed like a nightmarish dream in a distant past. They might never forget it, but they could never do it justice with mere words.

Then, almost as one, each head turned and gazed for the last time at the lamentable image that only twenty-four hours before had been one of the most beautiful ships ever to sail the seas. Pitt stared, too. No man of the sea likes to see a ship die dreadfully. He could not help but wonder who had been responsible for such a hideous act. What was the motive?

"What is it worth to read your thoughts?" asked Burch.

Pitt looked at him blankly. "My thoughts?"

"I'll bet my grandmother's rosary beads that curiosity is eating you alive."

"I don't follow you."

"The same question that's on all our minds," explained Burch. "What motive would a madman have for murdering twenty-five hundred helpless men, women and children?"

"As soon as she's towed into Sydney Harbor, an army of marine fire insurance company investigators will sift through the

147

ashes and find the answers."

"They won't find much to sift."

"Don't underestimate them," said Burch. "Those guys are good. If anyone can ferret out the cause, they can."

Pitt turned and smiled at Burch. "I hope you're right, Skipper. I'm just glad it's not on my shoulders."

By the end of the week, Pitt would be proved wrong. Never would he have predicted that he would be the one called upon to solve the mystery.

8

The first tug to reach the *Emerald Dolphin* was the Quest Marine Offshore Company's *Audacious*. At 190 feet in length, with a beam of 58 feet, she was one of the largest tugs in the world. Her twin Hunnewell diesel engines provided a total of 9,800 horsepower to drive her propulsion units. Since she'd had the advantage of being stationed in Wellington, the closest port, she had beat out two other big tugs from Brisbane.

The *Audacious'* master had run her hard, like an overweight greyhound after the rabbit, homing in on the position updates provided by the Aussie missile cruiser. He'd kept radio silence during the race across the South Pacific, a routine ploy among tugboat captains racing toward the same wreck, because the winner received the Lloyds Open Form for salvage and 25 percent of the stricken vessel's value.

Now that Captain Jock McDermott was in sight of the smoldering cruise liner and the Australian guided-missile cruiser, he opened contact with the Blue Seas Cruise Lines officials, who after half an hour of bargaining accepted the "no cure, no pay" contract, naming Quest Marine as the principal salvage contractor for what was left of the *Emerald Dolphin*.

Closing on the liner that still glowed red, McDermott and his crew were stunned at the devastation. A pile of incinerated rubble floating on a restless turquoise sea was all that was left of the once-beautiful cruise liner. She looked like a photo of Hiroshima after the horrendous firestorm from the atomic bomb: blackened, misshapen and shriveled.

"She ain't worth nothin' more than scrap," spat the *Audacious*' first officer, Herm Brown, a former professional rugby player who'd gone to sea when his knees gave out. He stood under a shaggy mane of blond hair, his beefy legs showing under his shorts and a hairy chest visible through the unbuttoned shirt pulled taut by his shoulders.

McDermott pulled his spectacles down over his nose and peered over the lenses. A sandy-haired Scotsman with a narrow beaklike nose and hazy green eyes, he had spent twenty years in oceangoing tugs. But for the jutting jaw, and eyes that seemed to focus like light beams, he might have passed for Bob Cratchit, Scrooge's bookkeeper. "The directors of the company won't be happy with this job, that's for sure. I never thought a ship that big could burn itself into nothing more than a heap of soot."

The ship's phone buzzed and McDermott picked up the receiver. "Captain of the tug, this is Captain Harlow of the cruiser off your port beam. Whom am I speaking to?"

"Captain Jock McDermott of the Quest Marine tug *Audacious*."

"Now that you've arrived, Captain McDermott, I can leave station and head for Wellington. I've got five hundred survivors on board who are anxious to set foot on land again."

"You've had a busy time of it, Captain," McDermott replied. "I'm surprised you didn't depart two days ago."

"We've been busy picking up the bodies of the cruise liner's victims who died in the water. I was also asked by the International Maritime Commission to remain nearby and report on the wreck's position after it became classed as a menace to navigation."

"She no longer resembles a ship."

"A pity," said Harlow. "She was one of the most beautiful vessels afloat." Then he added, "Is there anything we can do to help you get her under tow?"

"No, thank you," answered McDermott. "We can manage."

"She looks in a bad way. I hope she stays afloat until you reach safe harbor."

"Without knowing how badly her hull was damaged by the heat, I won't bet the farm on it."

"Burning her guts out considerably lightened her. Riding high out of the water should make her an easy tow."

"No tow is easy, Captain. Be prepared for a welcoming committee and a horde of reporters when you reach Wellington."

"I can't wait," Harlow responded dryly. "Good luck to you."

McDermott turned to his first mate, Arle Brown. "Well, I guess we'd best get to work."

"At least the sea is flat," said Brown, nodding through the windshield of the bridge.

McDermott stared for several seconds at the wreck. "I have a feeling a flat sea may be all we have going for us."

McDermott wasted no time. After circling the derelict and seeing that the rudder looked to be set in the flat zero-degree position, he brought the *Audacious* to within two hundred feet of the *Emerald Dolphin*'s bow. He could only hope the rudder was frozen in place. If it moved, the hulk would shear off to the side and become impossible to control.

The tug's motor launch was lowered into the water. Brown and four of the tug's crew motored toward the wreck until they were directly under the great overhanging bow. They had visitors. The waters around the hull were teeming with sharks. Through some primeval instinct, they knew that if the ship went down there might be some tasty edibles left floating on the surface.

Climbing aboard the hulk wasn't going to be easy. She was still too hot to come aboard amidships, but the bow remained free from the worst of the fire. There were at least thirty ropes hanging from the railings above. Luckily, two of them were Jacob's boarding ladders with wooden rungs. As the boat's helmsman angled the launch under one of the ladders hanging from above, he kept the bow aimed into the waves to maintain better control.

Brown went first. Keeping a wary eye on the sharks, he firmly planted his feet on the gunnels and balanced his body. He stretched out his arms, grabbed the ladder and pulled it toward him. As the launch rose on the crest of the wave, he stepped onto a rope rung and climbed steadily upward, covering the vertical height of nearly fifty feet in less than three minutes. At the top, he caught the railing and pulled himself over onto the forepeak. Next, he swung one of the lines the survivors had thrown off the bow until it was caught by one of the men in the boat. The line was then tied to the end of another line that the launch had towed from the tug.

After three of his crew had ascended the Jacob's ladder to the forepeak, the line was pulled up and slipped around an enormous round towing bollard whose designers never expected it to be used this way. Then the end was passed back down to a man in the launch, who tied it off. Brown watched the launch as it returned to the tug, where the heaving line was passed up and secured to the end of a cable wound around a huge winch. Before Brown gave the signal to engage the winch, he watched as one of his crew smeared grease around the bollard.

With no power on board the *Emerald Dolphin*, it was no small chore to lift aboard the tug's massive eight-inch-diameter tow cable that weighed one ton per hundred feet. By using the bollard as a pulley, the winch was engaged and began pulling the line running between the two ships around a small drum attached to the main winch. A two-inch cable that had been attached to one end of the line soon began winding itself around the bollard and back to the tug again. The other end of this cable was connected to the big eight-incher, which was then pulled up to the bow of the cruise ship and clamped with a series of U-bolts to the anchor chains because the big liner did not have a capstan on the foredeck. It was mounted below on a deck that was burned and unreachable.

"Cable secured," Brown notified McDermott over his portable radio. "We're coming back aboard."

"Acknowledged."

Ordinarily, a small crew would remain on board a derelict under tow, but without knowing to what extent the fire had ravaged the hull, there was too great a danger for the men to remain on board the *Emerald Dolphin*. If she should abruptly head for the sea floor, they might not have time to escape and would be sucked down with her.

Brown and his men dropped down the ladder into the launch. As soon as the launch and its crew were taken aboard the tug, McDermott gave the order for dead slow ahead. Brown, who was operating the gigantic tow winch, paid out the cable until the cruise ship was a good quarter of a mile astern. Then he set the brake, the slack went out of the cable and the winch took up the strain as the *Audacious* began to inch forward.

Every man on the tug held his breath to see how the *Emerald Dolphin* would act. Slowly, inch by inch, foot by foot, like an obedient elephant led by a mouse, her bow began to part the water. Nobody moved, still anxious, but the immense liner came arrow-straight into the tug's churning wake and stayed there. At seeing the still-burning hulk under way without shear, everyone on board the tug began to relax.

Ten hours later, the *Audacious'* big engines were towing the enormous hulk at a respectable two knots. Most of the fire was out. Only a few flickers of flame could still be seen amid the twisted wreckage of the superstructure. There was no moon, and overcast clouds covered the sky. The night was so black it was impossible to tell where sea left off and the sky began.

The tug's big searchlight was beamed on the *Emerald Dolphin*, illuminating her bow and gutted forward superstructure. The crew took turns on watch, making sure the big tow followed behind as planned. After midnight, the ship's cook took his turn. He settled in a folding deck chair he carried on board to enjoy the sun when he wasn't busy in the galley. It was too hot and humid for coffee, so he drank Diet Pepsi, the cans nestled in a small bucket of ice. With a soft drink in hand, he lit a cigarette and leaned back, gazing dutifully at the ponderous mass following astern.

Two hours later, he was barely awake, fighting off drowsiness with his tenth cigarette and third Pepsi. The *Emerald Dolphin* was still where she was supposed to be. The cook sat up and tilted his head when he heard what sounded like a deep rumble come from within the hulk. It reminded him of thunder over the distant horizon, not one but a series of booms, as if they were timed a few seconds apart. He sat up and squinted his eyes. He was about to write it off to his imagination when he noticed that something had changed. It took a moment for him to realize that the ship was sitting lower in the water.

The scorched cruise ship sheared her starboard slightly before wallowing back on a straight course. Under the searchlight, a huge billow of smoke issued from the wreckage forward of amidships before spiraling into the darkness outside the searchlight's beam. Then the cook's face froze in horror.

The *Emerald Dolphin* was foundering, and she looked to be going down fast.

In shock, the cook ran up onto the bridge to shout, "She's sinking. Holy mother, she's going under!"

McDermott heard the commotion and burst from his cabin. He asked no questions of the cook. One look was enough to tell him that if they didn't cut the tow cable, the sinking liner would take the *Audacious* and her crew down twenty thousand feet to the sea floor with her. He was joined by Brown, who also took in the situation with a glance. Together, they ran to the giant winch.

Frantically, they struggled to release the brake, paying out the massive cable, watching it unreel into the abyss, rapidly falling from a near-horizontal angle to vertical as the cruise ship buried her bow in the water. The great cable that was wound around the winch's drum began to unreel ever faster until it became a blur. McDermott and Brown could only hope that when the cable finally unwound, its end would rip from its connectors. If not, the *Audacious* would be pulled under by the stern.

The dead cruise ship was plunging deeper with uncanny speed. Already her bow was diving beneath the surface. She was sinking on a shallow fifteen-degree angle, but sinking fast. An awful groaning sound came from the battered hull as her fire-tortured bulkheads contorted and twisted apart from the strain. Her rudder and the great jet thrusters lifted out of the water into the night. The stern hung there for a few seconds, and then slowly it followed the bow into the black sea, faster and faster until the entire ship plummeted out of sight, leaving a great swelling of air bubbles.

Only one row of cable remained wound around the reel, but suddenly it became taut and the stern of the tug dipped abruptly, jerking the bow out of the water. Every man on board stood stock-still, staring at the unwinding drum, seeing the jaws of death close. Then the drum spun for the last time as the cable's entire length was yanked sharply into the abyss. The drama had reached its climax.

There came an earsplitting shriek, and then the end of the cable shot off the drum and whipped out of sight into the sea. Released from the strain, the tug's bow came down hard as she righted herself, rocking on her keel forward and aft before settling down. The crew stood in stunned silence at their narrow brush with death.

Finally, Brown muttered, as the trauma of the last minutes slowly faded, "I never believed a ship could sink in the blink of an eye."

"Nor I," McDermott agreed. "It's as though her entire bottom dropped out."

"There goes a million pounds' worth of cable. The company directors aren't going to be too happy."

"It was beyond our control. It all happened too fast." Then McDermott paused and held up a hand. "Listen!" he said sharply.

Everyone gazed at the spot where the *Emerald Dolphin* had vanished. Out of the night, a voice was shouting, "Help me!"

McDermott's first thought was that one of the crew had fallen overboard during the excitement, but a quick scan of the deck showed him they were all present. The shout came again, only this time it was weak and barely perceptible.

"Somebody's out there," said the cook, pointing in the direction of the voice.

Brown ran over to the searchlight, swung it around and played its beam on the water. The dark face of a man could barely be seen against the ebony of the sea less than a hundred feet off the stern. "Can you swim to the boat?" Brown yelled.

There was no answer, but the man did not appear exhausted. He stroked strongly and evenly toward the tug.

"Throw him a line," Brown ordered a crewman, "and haul him in before the sharks get him."

A rope was heaved over the side. The man caught it, and two crewmen pulled him to the stern and heaved him aboard.

"He's an aborigine," said Brown, a native Aussie.

"Not with curly hair," observed McDermott. "More like African."

"He's wearing a ship's officer's uniform."

Hardly expecting to see a survivor this late in the game, McDermott looked at the man questioningly. "May I ask where you came from?"

The stranger unleashed a wide-tooth smile. "I thought that was obvious. I am, or rather was, the *Emerald Dolphin*'s passenger relations officer."

"How come you remained on board after all the survivors were taken off?" asked Brown. He found it hard to believe the man was free of injuries, and except for his soaking-wet uniform he looked none the worse for his experience.

"I fell and struck my head while helping passengers abandon ship onto the research vessel. Everyone must have thought I was dead and left me. When I woke up, you had the ship under tow."

"You must have been unconscious for the better part of twenty-four hours," said McDermott skeptically.

"I must have."

"Seems incredible you weren't burned to death."

"I was extremely lucky. I fell into a companionway that was spared by the fire."

"You speak with an American accent."

"I'm from California."

"What's your name?" asked Brown.

"Sherman Nance."

"Well, Mr. Nance," said McDermott, "you'd better get out of that wet uniform. You're about the same size as Mr. Brown, my first officer. He can loan you dry clothes. Then go to the galley. You must be dehydrated and famished after your ordeal. I'll see that our cook gives you something to drink and fixes a hearty meal."

"Yes, thank you, Captain . . ."

"McDermott."

"I *am* pretty thirsty."

After Nance was escorted below by the cook, Brown peered at the captain. "Uncanny that he survived a fire of such magnitude without a singed eyebrow or a burned finger."

McDermott rubbed his chin doubtfully. "Yes, uncanny." Then he sighed. "It's not our concern. I now have the distasteful duty of notifying the directors that we lost our tow and their expensive cable."

"She shouldn't have done it," Brown growled absentmindedly.

"Done what?"

"One minute she's floating high in the water, the next she's on her way to the bottom. She shouldn't have gone and sunk so fast. It ain't natural."

"I agree," McDermott said with a shrug. "But it's out of our hands."

"The insurance underwriters won't be happy, with nothing left to investigate."

McDermott nodded wearily. "Without evidence, it will always have to remain another one of the sea's great mysteries."

Then he walked over to the big searchlight and switched it off, casting the lost cruise liner's watery burial shroud into stygian blackness.

As soon as the *Audacious* reached Wellington, the man that McDermott had pulled from the sea after the *Emerald Dolphin* sank disappeared. The dockside immigration officials swore that he hadn't left the ship down the gangway or they would have detained him for the inquiry proceedings into the cruise ship's fire and loss. McDermott decided the only way for Sherman Nance to have left the ship was over the side when they pulled into harbor.

After McDermott gave his report to insurance investigators, he was told that no crewman or officer named Sherman Nance was listed as having served on board the *Emerald Dolphin.*

9

While the *Earl of Wattlesfield* stood by, the crew of the *Deep Encounter* homed in on the signal beacons of the drifting submersibles and lifted them on board. Once they were secured, Captain Burch advised Captain Nevins, and the two ships resumed their course toward Wellington.

Dead tired after securing the submersibles, Pitt straightened up his cabin from the mess made by the forty people who had somehow managed to pack into the small enclosure during the cruise ship's evacuation. His muscles ached, a condition he noticed that was creeping up on him with age. He threw his clothes in a laundry bag and stepped into the small shower, turning on the hot water so it sprayed into one corner as he lay on his back on the floor with his long legs extending up to the soap dish. In that position, he promptly dozed off for twenty minutes. Coming awake fully refreshed, but still sore, he soaped and rinsed before toweling dry and stepping out of the shower and staring into the mirror above the brass sink.

The face and body on the other side were not what they were ten years ago. The hair had yet to show any indications of baldness. It was still thick, black and wavy, but gray was beginning to creep in along the temples. The piercing green eyes beneath dense eyebrows had yet to dim. They were eyes passed on by his mother, and they had a hypnotic quality about them that seemed to reach into the very soul of people who came into contact with him. Women were especially absorbed by his eyes. They sensed an aura about them, something that revealed him as a down-to-earth man who could be trusted.

The face, though, was beginning to show the unstoppable result of aging. Deepening mirth lines spread from the edges of his eyes. The skin did not have the elasticity of his younger years and was slowly achieving a weathered look to it. The craggy features around the cheeks and forehead seemed more pronounced. The nose still seemed reasonably straight and intact, considering that it had been broken on three different occasions. He was not Errol Flynn–handsome, but he still possessed a presence that made people turn and stare in his direction when he entered a room.

Yes, he thought, his facial features came from his mother's side of the family, while his humorous outlook on life and his tall, lean body had definitely been passed down by his father and his father's ancestors.

He lightly ran the fingers of one hand over the several scars spread across his body, reminders of his many adventures during his two decades of service with the National Underwater and Marine Agency. Though he had attended the Air Force Academy and still held a commission as a major in the Air Force, he had jumped at the chance to serve under Admiral James Sandecker and the newly formed oceanographic and marine science agency. Never married, he had come close during a long-running relationship with Congresswoman Loren Smith, but their lives were too complicated. His job at NUMA and hers in Congress were just too demanding for marriage.

Two of his former loves had died under tragic circumstances, Summer Moran in a devastating underwater earthquake off Hawaii, and Maeve Fletcher, shot by her sister off the coast of Tasmania.

It was Summer who never ceased to haunt his dreams. He always saw her swimming into the depths to find her father who was trapped in an underwater cavern, her lovely body and flowing red hair vanishing into the green water of the Pacific. When he'd reached the surface for air and found her gone, he'd tried to dive back, but the men in the boat that rescued him knew it was hopeless and physically restrained him from returning.

Since that time, he had lived only for his work on and under the water. The sea became his mistress. Except for his home in an old aircraft hangar on one corner of Washington's Ronald Reagan Airport, which contained his car and airplane collection, he was always happiest when on a research ship sailing the oceans of the world.

He sighed, put on a terry-cloth robe and lay down on his bed. He was about to drift off into a deserved sleep when he suddenly thought of something and sat up. The girl with her father's leather case jumped strangely into his mind. The more he thought about it, the less it made sense that she left in one of the containership's boats without his seeing her. Then it became obvious.

She hadn't left. She was still hiding somewhere on board the *Deep Encounter*.

Ignoring the allure of sleep, he came off the bed and quickly dressed. Five minutes later, he began his search at the stern end of the platform deck, peering into every nook and cranny in the generator room, winch room, propulsion motor room and scientific equipment storeroom. It was a slow process because there were so many places amid the stores and equipment where someone could hide.

He checked out the repair parts storeroom and almost missed it, that little something seemingly out of place. He noticed several gallon cans of various lubricating oils, all neatly stacked on a workbench. Nothing that at first glance looked out of the ordinary. But he knew they should have been stored in a wooden storage crate. He walked whisper-quiet over to the crate and eased open the lid.

Kelly Egan was sleeping an exhausted sleep so sound she did not perceive Pitt's presence. The leather case was sitting propped against the side of the crate, and one of her arms hung over it. He smiled, removed a clipboard from a bulkhead hanger, tore off a page from the pad and wrote a note.

Dear Lady,
When you wake, please come to my cabin on deck level two, number eight.
Dirk Pitt.

As an afterthought to entice her, he added,

Food and drink will be waiting.

He laid the note gently on her chest, softly closed the lid to the crate and quietly stepped from the parts room.

At slightly past seven in the evening, Kelly rapped lightly on Pitt's cabin door. He opened and found her, eyes lowered sheepishly, standing in the passageway, still clutching the handle of the leather case. He took her by the hand and led her inside. "You must be starved," he said, smiling to show he wasn't angry or annoyed.

"Are you Dirk Pitt?"

"Yes, and you're . . . ?"

"Kelly Egan. I'm so sorry to have caused you —"

"No trouble at all," he interrupted. He motioned to a desk with a tray of sandwiches and a pitcher of milk. "Not exactly a gourmet dinner, but about the best the cook could do with what's left of our food supply." He held up a woman's blouse and shorts. "One of our scientists guessed at your size and kindly loaned some clothes. Eat and then take a shower. I'll come back in half an hour. Then we'll talk."

When Pitt returned, Kelly had showered and already finished off a pile of ham-and-cheese sandwiches. The pitcher of milk was all but drained, too. He sat down in a chair opposite her. "Feeling like you belong to the human race again?"

She smiled and nodded, looking like a schoolgirl who had been caught at mischief. "You must be wondering why I didn't leave the ship?"

"The thought crossed my mind."

"I was afraid."

"Of what? The man who attacked you and your father? I'm happy to report that he joined the other victims of the ship who drowned."

"There was another one," she said hesitantly. "A ship's officer. He seemed to be an accomplice of the red-haired man who tried to kill me. Together, they attempted to steal my father's case, and I believe they meant to murder him. But something went wrong during the struggle, and all they succeeded in doing was push him over the railing into the water —"

"Taking the case with him," Pitt said, finishing the sentence.

"Yes." Tears came to Kelly's eyes as she relived her father's death. Pitt reached in a pocket and handed her a handkerchief. After wiping the tears, she stared at the cloth. "I didn't think men carried these anymore. I thought everyone used tissue."

"I come from the old school," he said quietly. "You never know when you may encounter a blue lady."

She gave him a very strange look and

smiled faintly. "I haven't met anyone quite like you."

"My type has never developed a herd instinct." He returned to the subject at hand. "Can you describe this officer?"

"Yes, he was a tall black man, African-American I suppose, since the ship belonged to a domestic shipping line and most of the crew were from the United States."

"Odd that they waited until a ship's fire to make their move."

"It wasn't the first time Dad was harassed," she said angrily. "He told me of being threatened on several different occasions."

"So what is so important that your father had to die for it?" said Pitt, gesturing at the case sitting on the deck at her feet.

"My father is" — she paused — "was Dr. Elmore Egan, a brilliant man. He was both a mechanical and a chemical engineer."

"I'm aware of the name," said Pitt. "Dr. Egan was a widely respected inventor, wasn't he? The creator of several different types of water propulsion engines? As I recall, he also formulated a highly efficient diesel fuel that is widely used in the transportation industry."

"You know that?" she asked, impressed.

"I'm a marine engineer," he admitted. "I'd get an F on the test if I hadn't heard of your father."

"Dad's latest project was the development of magnetohydrodynamic engines."

"Like the propulsion units in the *Emerald Dolphin*."

She nodded silently.

"I must confess my ignorance about magnetohydrodynamic engines. What little I've read suggested the technology was still thirty years away. That's why I was surprised to read they had been installed in the *Emerald Dolphin*."

"Everybody was surprised. But Dad created a breakthrough, a revolutionary design. He compounded the electricity found in seawater before running it through a highly magnetic core tube kept at absolute zero by liquid helium. The electrical current that is produced then sets up an energy force that pumps the water through thrusters for propulsion."

Pitt was listening attentively, and her words caused him to stiffen. "Are you saying that his engine's only outside fuel source is seawater?"

"Saline has a very small electrical field. My father discovered a method of intensifying it to an incredible degree to produce energy."

"It's hard to envision a means of propulsion with an inexhaustible source of fuel."

Kelly's face reflected pride in her father. "As he explained to me —"

"You don't work with him?" Pitt cut in.

"Hardly." She laughed for the first time. "He was terribly disappointed in me, I'm afraid. I can't think in abstract terms. I never had it in me to conquer algebra. Solving equations was a hopeless cause for me. I majored in business at Yale, where I received my master's. I work as a merchandise analyst for a firm of consultants — our clients are department stores and discount houses."

Pitt's lips spread slightly in a grin. "Not as exciting as creating new forms of energy."

"Perhaps not," she said, with a toss of the head that sent her light brown hair swirling in a cloud around her neck and shoulders, "but I make a good income."

"What breakthrough led your father to perfect the technology of magnetohydrodynamic engines?"

"Early in his research and development, he reached a roadblock when his experimental engine exceeded power and energy expectations but experienced extreme friction problems. The engines only had a life span of a few hours at high rpm before grinding to a halt. He and a close associate and family friend, Josh Thomas, a chemical engineer, then formulated a new oil that was a hundred times more efficient than any commercial oil available on the market today. Now Dad had a new power source that could run indefinitely without measurable wear for years."

"So the super oil was the element that advanced your father's magnetohydrodynamics engine from the drawing board to reality."

"True," she acknowledged. "After the pilot model's successful test program, the Blue Seas Cruise Lines directors approached Dad about constructing and installing his engines in the *Emerald Dolphin*, which was then under construction at the shipbuilders in Singapore. They were also building an underwater luxury submarine passenger liner, but I forget the name. They gave him an exclusive license to build the engines."

"Can't the oil formula be duplicated?"

"Formula, yes. Process, no. There is no way of repeating the exact production process."

"I assume he protected himself with patents."

Kelly nodded vigorously. "Oh, yes. He and Josh Thomas were awarded at least thirty-two patents on the engine design."

"What about the oil formula?"

She hesitated, then shook her head. "He preferred to keep that to himself. He didn't even trust the Patent Office."

"Dr. Egan could have become an enormously wealthy man by working out royalty agreements on his oil and engine."

Kelly shrugged. "Like you, Dad did not walk the same road as other men. He wanted the world to benefit from his discovery, and he was prepared to give it away. Besides, he was already busy on something else. He told me that he was working on an even greater project, something that would cause an unbelievable impact on the future."

"Did he ever tell you what it was?"

"No," she answered. "He was very secretive, and said it was better that I didn't know."

"A sobering thought," said Pitt. "He wanted to protect you from whoever was desperate to gain his secrets."

A sad, forlorn look came into Kelly's eyes. "Dad and I were never very close after Mom died. He was basically a good and caring father, but his work came first and he was always lost in it. I think he invited me along on the maiden voyage of the *Emerald Dolphin* as a way of bringing us closer together."

Pitt sat thoughtfully quiet for nearly a minute. Then he nodded toward the leather case. "Don't you think it's time you opened it?"

She held her hands over her face, hiding her confusion. "I want to," she said hesitantly, "but I'm afraid."

"Afraid of what?" he asked quietly.

She flushed, not from embarrassment, but more from an apprehension of what she might find inside. "I don't know."

"If you're afraid I'm an evildoer out to abscond with your father's precious papers, you can forget it. I'll sit comfortably across the room while you peek inside with the lid up so I won't see anything."

Suddenly, it all seemed so ludicrous to her. She held the leather case on her lap and giggled softly. "You know, I don't have the foggiest idea what's inside. For all I know, it's Dad's laundry or notepads of his undecipherable scribbles."

"Then it won't hurt to look."

She sat there hesitating for a long moment. Then very slowly, as if she were opening a canister holding one of those pop-up clowns, she clicked the latches and lifted the lid.

"Oh, good lord!" she gasped.

Pitt sat up. "What is it?"

As if in slow motion, she turned the case around and let it fall from her hands to the deck. "I don't understand," she whispered. "It's never been out of my hands."

Pitt leaned down and peered inside the leather case.

It was empty.

10

Two hundred miles out of Wellington, the meteorological instruments predicted calm seas and clear skies for the next four days. Now that *Deep Encounter* was no longer in any immediate danger of flooding and sinking, Captain Nevins ordered his containership to pass ahead and reach port as quickly as possible. The sooner the *Earl of Wattlesfield* reached Wellington, the better. With two thousand unexpected passengers on board, food supplies were critically low.

As the great ship surged past, the crew and passengers of the *Emerald Dolphin* waved good-bye. A voice began singing a Woody Guthrie song, and soon over a thousand voices picked it up and serenaded the men and women on board the little survey vessel with *So long, it's been good to know yuh.*

It was a moving moment as they sang the

last line of the chorus . . . *An' I've got to be driftin' along*. Before another hour passed by, the *Earl of Wattlesfield* was hull down over the horizon.

Captain Nevins sailed his ship into Wellington six hours ahead of *Deep Encounter* and met with a joyous, yet solemn, welcome. Thousands of people lined the waterfront, staring silently and talking softly as the containership slowly eased into a berth. New Zealand's heart went out to those who had miraculously survived the worst ship fire in maritime history.

A spontaneous outpouring of sympathy for the living and the dead swept the country. Homes were thrown open to the survivors. Food and clothing were passed out in abundance. Customs officials cleared them through with only a few questions, since almost all had lost their passports in the fire. Airlines put on extra aircraft to fly them to their home cities. High-ranking New Zealand government leaders and the United States ambassador formed a greeting committee. Members of the news media descended in swarms and besieged the survivors, who were eager to get ashore and notify friends and relatives of their rescue. It was the largest news event in the country's recent history, and the lead story was the heroic rescue by the crew and scientists of the *Deep Encounter*.

Already, an investigation was launched. Most of the passengers volunteered to answer questions and give statements regarding the crew's actions during the fire. The surviving crew members, required to remain silent by the cruise company attorneys, were provided with quarters for an indefinite stay until their examination and subsequent testimony could be heard and recorded during an inquiry.

If the arrival of the *Earl of Wattlesfield* was a melancholy affair, the welcome awaiting the *Deep Encounter* took on the atmosphere of a wild and crazy party. As the survey ship came through Cook Strait and headed for Wellington, it was met by a small fleet of private yachts that swelled to hundreds of vessels of every description by the time her bow nosed into the harbor. Fireboats escorted the ship to a dock, their hoses spraying a curtain of water high in the air that formed rainbows under the bright sun.

The crowds could easily see the scraped turquoise paint and mangled plates of the hull where she had beaten herself against the cruise ship during the incredible rescue of nearly two thousand people. Captain Burch had to use a bullhorn to shout his orders for the docking procedure because of the noise from all the shouting and cheers, backed by the blare of a thousand car horns, the ringing of church bells and the shriek of sirens, while a storm of streamers and confetti showered the decks of the ship.

The crew and scientists had no idea they had become instant international celebrities and acclaimed heroes. They stood amazed at the resounding reception, unable to believe that it was for them. They no longer looked like tired, bedraggled scientists and crew members. At seeing the welcoming armada, everyone had quickly prettied up and changed into their best clothes. Women wore dresses, the male scientists slacks and sport coats, the crew in NUMA uniforms. They all stood on the work deck, devoid of all oceanographic equipment except the two submersibles, and waved back.

Kelly perched next to Pitt on the bridge wing, elated yet saddened at the sight and wishing her father was with her to see it. She turned and looked into Pitt's eyes. "I guess this is good-bye."

"You'll be flying to the States?"

"Just as soon as I can make reservations on the first available flight home."

"Where do you call home?" he asked her.

"New York," she replied, catching a paper streamer that drifted down from above. "I have a brownstone on the Upper West Side."

"You live alone?"

"No." She smiled. "I have a tabby cat

called Zippy and a basset hound that answers to Shagnasty."

"I don't get to the city often, but next time I'm in town, I'll call you for dinner."

"I'd like that." She scribbled her phone number on a scrap of paper and gave it to him.

"I'll miss you, Kelly Egan."

She looked into those incredible eyes and saw that he was serious. The blood suddenly rushed to Kelly's face and she felt her knees weaken. She clutched the railing, wondering what was coming over her. Stunned at losing control, she stood on her toes, abruptly circled her arms around Pitt's head, pulled him down and kissed his lips long and hard. Her eyes were closed, but his widened in pleasurable surprise.

When she pulled back, she willed herself into a state of feminine composure. "Thank you, Dirk Pitt, for saving my life, and much, much more." She took a few steps and then turned. "My father's leather case."

"Yes?" he answered, unsure of her meaning.

"It's yours."

With that, Kelly turned and stepped down the companionway to the work deck. As soon as the gangway was lowered onto the dock, she stepped ashore and was swallowed up by a crowd of reporters.

★ ★ ★

Pitt left the glory to Burch and the others. While they were feted in the city at hastily thrown-together banquets, he remained aboard ship and gave a full report over his Globalstar satellite phone to Admiral Sandecker in the NUMA headquarters building in Washington.

"The *Encounter* took quite a beating," he explained. "I've made arrangements with the shipyard to take her into dry dock in the morning. The shipyard foreman estimated that the damage will take three days to repair."

"Newspapers and television have been running the rescue story all morning, noon and night," the Admiral replied. "The aircraft took fantastic photos of the burning cruise ship and the *Encounter*. NUMA phone lines have been jammed by calls congratulating us, and there's a hive of reporters swarming throughout the building. I owe you and everybody on board the *Encounter* a sincere vote of thanks on behalf of the agency."

Pitt could picture the admiral in his office, brimming with pride and loving every minute of the limelight. He could see the flaming red hair with all trace of gray tinted away, the matching Vandyke beard, trimmed to a sharp point, the blue eyes that had to be flashing like neon signs from heartfelt satisfaction. And, he could almost smell the acrid smoke of one of Sandecker's personalized cigars.

"Does that mean we all get a raise?" asked Pitt sarcastically.

"Don't let it go to your head," Sandecker snapped back. "Money can't buy glory."

"A bonus might be a nice gesture on your part."

"Don't push your luck. You're lucky I don't take the ship repairs out of your pay."

Pitt wasn't fooled for a second by the gruff attitude. Sandecker had a reputation for generosity among the employees of NUMA. Pitt would have bet the admiral was already computing bonus checks, and he would have been right. Not that Sandecker didn't have a mercenary streak when it came to his beloved NUMA. Pitt didn't need a crystal ball to know that Sandecker was already planning on how he would milk the rescue and its resulting publicity to obtain an extra fifty million dollars out of Congress for his next year's budget.

"That's not all you might want to deduct," said Pitt roguishly. "To stay afloat we had to jettison almost all our equipment into the sea."

"The submersibles, too?" Sandecker's voice took on a serious tone.

"We set them adrift but picked them up later."

"Good, you're going to need them."

"I don't follow you, Admiral. With half our underwater research gear lying on the seabed, there is no way we can carry out our original mission of mapping the Tonga Trench."

"I don't expect you to map the trench," he said slowly. "I expect you to dive on the *Emerald Dolphin*. Your job now is to survey what's left of her for evidence relating to the fire and the cause of her unexplained rapid sinking." He paused. "You *did* know she inexplicably sank while under tow."

"Yes, Captain Burch and I monitored communications between the tug and its home office."

"The *Deep Encounter* is the only vessel within a thousand miles that can do the job."

"Exploring a monstrous cruise ship from a submersible at twenty thousand or more feet is not the same as sifting through the ashes of a burned-out house. Besides, we had to deep-six the crane."

"Buy or rent a new one. Do the best you can and try to come back with something. The cruise ship industry is going to suffer regardless of what you find, and the insurance companies are more than willing to compensate NUMA for our efforts."

"I'm not a fire insurance investigator. Just what exactly am I supposed to look for?"

"Don't worry," said Sandecker. "I'm sending someone who has experience in marine disasters. He's also an expert in deep submergence vehicles."

"Anybody I know?" asked Pitt.

"You should," said Sandecker cagily. "He's your assistant special projects director."

"Al Giordino!" Pitt exclaimed happily. "I thought he was still working on the Atlantis Project in the Antarctic."

"Not anymore. He's in the air now and should be landing in Wellington tomorrow morning."

"You couldn't have sent a better man."

Sandecker relished toying with Pitt. "Yes," he said slyly. "I thought you'd think so."

11

Albert Giordino trudged across the gangway leading from the top of the dry dock to the deck of the *Deep Encounter*, lugging an old-fashioned steamer trunk over a burly shoulder. The sides were covered with colorful labels advertising hotels and countries around the world. One hand was clutched to a strap of the metal trunk, with its varnished wooden bands running across the top and bottom, while the other hand clutched an equally antique leather satchel. He paused at the top of the gangway and dropped his load on the deck. He gazed around the empty work deck and up at the vacant bridge wing. Except for shipyard workers repairing the exterior hull, the ship looked deserted.

Giordino's shoulders were almost as wide as his body was tall. At five feet four inches and a hundred and seventy-five pounds, he was all muscle. His Italian ancestry was apparent in his olive skin, black curly hair and walnut-colored eyes. Gregarious, sarcastic and jovial, his cutting humor often made those in his presence either laugh or cringe.

Friends since childhood, Pitt and Giordino had played on the same football teams in high school and at the Air Force Academy. Wherever one went, the other was sure to follow. Giordino didn't think twice about joining Pitt at the National Underwater and Marine Agency. Their adventures together above and under the sea had become legend. Unlike Pitt and his aircraft hangar full of antique cars, Giordino lived in a condo with decor that would incite an interior decorator to suicide. For transportation, he drove an old Corvette. Besides his work, Al's passion was women. He saw nothing wrong with playing the role of a gigolo.

"Ahoy the ship!" he shouted. He waited before shouting again, as a figure walked out onto the bridge from the pilothouse and a familiar face stared down at him.

"Can you restrain yourself?" Pitt said in mock seriousness. "We don't take kindly to barbarians coming aboard an elegant vessel."

"In that case, you're in luck," said Giordino, flashing a vast smile. "You could use a vulgar rowdy to liven up the place."

"Stay put," Pitt said. "I'll come down."

In a minute, they were unashamedly embracing like the old friends they were. Though Giordino was three times stronger, Pitt always delighted in lifting the shorter man off the ground.

"What kept you? Sandecker said to expect you yesterday morning."

"You know the admiral. He was too cheap to let me borrow a NUMA jet, so I came commercial. As was expected, all flights were late and I missed my connection in San Francisco."

Pitt slapped his friend on the back. "Good to see you, pal. I thought you were on the Atlantis Project in the Antarctic." Then he stood back and stared at Giordino with a questioning look. "The last I heard, you were engaged to be married?"

Giordino held up his hands in a helpless gesture. "Sandecker took me off the project, and my lover took off without me."

"What happened?"

"Neither one of us was about to quit our job and move to a house in the suburbs. And, she was offered a job to decipher ancient writings in China, which would have taken two years. She didn't want to turn down the opportunity, so she flew off in the first plane to Beijing."

"I'm happy to see you can cope with rejection."

"Oh well, it beats being beaten with a

whip, having your tongue nailed to a tree and thrown in the trunk of a 1951 Nash Rambler."

Pitt picked up the satchel, but made no effort to hoist the steamer trunk. "Come along, I'll show you to your suite."

"Suite? The last time I was aboard the *Encounter*, the cabins were the size of broom closets."

"Only the sheets have been changed to protect the innocent."

"The boat looks like a tomb," Giordino said, motioning around the deserted ship. "Where is everyone?"

"Only Chief Engineer House and I are aboard. The rest are staying in the finest hotel in the city, pampered and glamorized, giving interviews and accepting awards."

"From what I heard, you're the man of the hour."

Pitt gave a modest shrug. "Not my style."

Giordino gave him a look of genuine respect and admiration. "It figures. You always play Humble Herbert. That's what I like about you. You're the only guy I know who doesn't collect photos of himself standing next to celebrities and who hangs all his trophies and awards in his bathroom."

"Who'd see them? I rarely throw parties. Besides, who cares?"

Giordino gave a slight shake of his head.

Pitt never changes, he thought. If the president of the United States wanted to present him with the nation's highest award, Pitt would send his regrets and claim he'd developed a case of typhoid.

After Giordino had unpacked and settled in, he entered Pitt's cabin, to find his friend seated at a small desk studying deck plans of the *Emerald Dolphin*. He set a wooden box down on top of the plans.

"Here, I brought you a present."

"Is it Christmas already?" Pitt said, laughing. He opened the box and sighed. "You're a good man, Albert. A bottle of Don Julio Reserve blue agave anejo tequila."

Giordino held up two sterling-silver cups. "Shall we test it and make sure it meets our qualifications?"

"What would the admiral say? Are you dismissing his tenth commandment about no alcohol on board a NUMA vessel?"

"If I don't get medicinal spirits in my system soon, I may well expire."

Pitt pulled off the cork top and poured the light brown liquid into the silver cups. As they held them up and clicked the metal edges, Pitt toasted, "To a successful dive on the carcass of the *Emerald Dolphin*."

"And a successful return to the sunlight." After savoring a swallow of the tequila,

Giordino asked, "Where exactly did she go down?"

"On the west slope of the Tonga Trench."

Giordino's eyebrows lifted. "That's pretty deep."

"My best guess is that she lies in about nineteen thousand feet."

Giordino's eyes followed his brows. "What sub do you plan on using?"

"The *Abyss Navigator*. She's built for the job."

Giordino paused, and his face took on a dour expression. "You know, of course, that her specified depth is nineteen-five, and she has yet to be tested that deep."

"There's no better opportunity to see if her designers knew their stuff," said Pitt off-handedly.

Giordino passed his empty cup to Pitt. "I think you'd better pour me another drink. On second thought, I'd better have ten or twelve, or I won't sleep between here and the Tonga Trench while having nightmares about imploding submersibles."

They sat there in Pitt's cabin until midnight, sipping the reserve tequila, telling old war stories and reliving their adventures together throughout the years. Pitt told of finding the *Emerald Dolphin* on fire and the rescue, the timely arrival of the *Earl of Wattlesfield*, the report of the sinking by the captain of the *Audacious*, his rescue of Kelly and the killing of the assassin.

When he finished, Giordino rose to return to his cabin. "You've been a busy boy."

"I wouldn't want to go through it again."

"When does the shipyard expect to have the hull repaired?" he asked.

"Captain Burch and I hope to get under way the day after tomorrow and be on site four days later."

"Time enough for me to regain the tan I lost in the Antarctic." He noticed the leather bag sitting in the corner of the cabin. "Is that the case you mentioned that belonged to Dr. Egan?"

"The same."

"You say that after all that, it was empty?"

"As a bank vault after Butch Cassidy rode out of town."

Giordino picked it up and ran his fingers over the leather. "Fine grain. Quite old. German made. Egan had good taste."

"You want it? You can have it."

Giordino sat back down again and set the leather case on his lap. "I have a thing about old luggage."

"So I've noticed."

Giordino unlatched the catches and lifted open the lid — and nearly two quarts of oil flowed out into his lap and onto the carpet covering the deck. He sat there in mute surprise as it soaked his pants legs and pooled on the carpet. After the shock faded, he gave Pitt a very acidic look indeed.

"I never knew you had a thing for practical jokes."

Pitt's face reflected pure astonishment. "I don't." He jumped to his feet, rushed across the cabin and peered into the case. "Trust me. I had nothing to do with this. This case was empty when I checked it yesterday. No one but Chief Engineer House and I have been on board for the past twenty-four hours. I don't understand why somebody would bother to sneak in here and fill it with oil. What's the point?"

"Then where did it come from? It obviously didn't just materialize."

"I haven't the foggiest idea," said Pitt. There was a strange look in his eyes that hadn't been there before. "But I'm betting we'll find out before the voyage is over."

12

The mystery of who put the oil in Egan's leather case was set aside as Pitt and Giordino began checking and testing the equipment and electronic systems of the *Sea Sleuth*, the survey vessel's autonomous underwater vehicle (AUV). During the voyage to the grave of the *Emerald Dolphin*, they discussed the wreck probe procedure with Captain Burch and the ocean engineers on board. All agreed that for reasons of safety the autonomous vehicle should be sent down first rather than the manned submersible, *Abyss Navigator*.

There was nothing sleek or streamlined about the design of the *Sea Sleuth*. She was the extreme of functional design. Utilitarian and expedient, she made a Mars lander look artistic. Seven feet high by six feet wide by seven feet in length, she weighed in at slightly less than seven thousand pounds.

Her skin was a thick layer of titanium, and from a distance she looked like a huge elongated egg open on the sides, standing on sled runners. A circular protrusion on top housed her two variable-buoyancy tanks. Support tubes laced her inner construction beneath the variable-buoyancy tanks.

Mounted inside, almost as if they had been placed there by a child with his Lego set, were high-resolution video and still cameras, a computer housing and sensors that recorded salinity, water temperature and oxygen content. A pressure-balanced, direct-drive DC motor provided her propulsion and was energized by a powerful manganese-alkaline battery system. Highly sophisticated transducers transported signals and imagery through the watery depths to the mother ship far above on the surface, and it sent control signals in return. Her path was illuminated by an array of ten external lights.

Like some mechanical monster out of a science-fiction movie, a complicated robotic arm, or manipulator, as it was called, extended from one side of the vehicle. It had the muscle to lift a four-hundred-pound anchor and the sensitivity to pick up a teacup.

Unlike earlier robotic vehicles, *Sea Sleuth* was untethered and had no umbilical cord connected to controls in the pilothouse. She was completely autonomous; her propulsion and video cameras were operated from the command room of the *Deep Encounter* thousands of feet above.

A crewman came up to Pitt as he was helping Giordino adjust the robotic arm. "Captain Burch said to let you know that we're three miles from the target."

"Thank you," said Pitt. "Please tell the skipper that Al and I will join him shortly."

Giordino threw a pair of screwdrivers into a toolbox, stood up and stretched his back. "She's ready as she'll ever be."

"Let's head up to the bridge and see how the *Dolphin* looks on the side scan sonar."

Burch and several other NUMA engineers and scientists were in the command center compartment just aft of the pilothouse. Everyone's faces and hands were reflected in a weird purplish cast from the overhead lighting. Recent experiments had determined that instrumentation was easier to read for long elements of time under a red-blue wave band of light.

They were massed around the computer-enhanced screen on the Klein System 5000 recorder, watching the seabed twenty thousand feet below unreel as if on a scroll. The colored image showed a fairly smooth bottom that sloped off into the deep abyss. Burch turned as Pitt and Giordino entered and pointed at the Global Positioning System digital readout that showed the distance remaining to the target.

"She should be coming up in another mile," he commented.

"Is this the GPS position given by the tug?" asked Giordino.

Burch nodded. "Where the liner went down when the tow rope broke."

Every eye in the compartment in the command center focused on the Klein imagery screen. The seabed deep below the sensor that trailed far behind the *Deep Encounter* on a cable showed the flat, desertlike surface covered with dingy, gray-brown silt. No jagged rocks or hills were visible. No wasteland came close to being so desolate. Still, the image was mesmerizing because everyone was waiting expectantly for an object to materialize and creep across the screen.

"Five hundred yards," Burch announced.

The crew and the men and women of the scientific team went silent. The command center became as quiet as a crypt. To most, the wait would have been agonizing, but not to the men and women who searched the seas. These were patient people. They were used to spending weeks at a time staring at instruments, waiting for an interesting object, a sunken ship or an unusual geological formation to reveal itself, but usually seeing nothing other than a seemingly endless and sterile seabed.

"Something's coming," announced Burch,

who had the best view of the screen.

Slowly, the recorder showed a hard image that took on a man-constructed shape. The outline looked jagged and uneven. It looked too small, not at all the immense image of the cruise liner they were expecting.

"That's her," stated Pitt firmly.

Burch grinned like a happy bridegroom. "Got her on the first pass."

"The tug's position was right on the money."

"It's not the right size for the *Emerald Dolphin*," Giordino observed in a monotone.

Burch aimed a finger at the screen. "Al's right. We're only seeing part of her. Here comes another piece."

Pitt studied the images on the screen thoughtfully. "She broke up, either on the way down or on impact when she struck bottom."

A large section of what Burch identified as the stern crept across the screen. A vast debris field between the fragments of the wreck revealed hundreds of unidentifiable objects large and small, scattered as if hurled by a passing tornado.

Giordino made a quick sketch of the images on a notepad. "It appears to be broken in three pieces."

Pitt studied Giordino's sketches and compared them with images on the sonar screen. "They rest about a quarter of a mile from one another."

Burch said, "Because of the ship's weakened internal structure from the fire damage, she probably disintegrated on the way down."

"Not unheard of," said one of the scientific team. "The *Titanic* broke in half as she sank."

"But she pitched downward at an extreme angle," Burch clarified. "I talked to the tugboat captain who had the Dolphin under tow when she sank. He claimed that she plunged under rapidly on a very shallow angle of not more than fifteen degrees. The *Titanic* dove at a forty-five-degree angle."

Giordino stared through the forward window at the sea ahead. "The most logical scenario is that she sank intact and shattered when she struck bottom. Her speed was probably somewhere between thirty and forty miles an hour."

Pitt shook his head. "If that were the case, the wreckage would be more concentrated. As we can see, she's spread all over the landscape."

"Then what caused her to break up on the way down?" Burch asked no one in particular.

"With luck," Pitt said slowly, "we'll find the answers when and if *Sea Sleuth* lives up to her name."

★ ★ ★

A dazzling orange sun rose across the flat blue horizon in the east as the *Sea Sleuth* hung under a new crane that had replaced the one dumped overboard during the rescue. It had been installed at the shipyard, and the crew had finished connecting the winch and its cable only hours earlier. Anticipation reigned as the oblong AUV was swung over the stern. The sea was fairly smooth, with waves running no more than three feet.

The ship's second officer directed the launch, and signaled to the crewman operating the winch when the vehicle was free of the stern. Then he waved an all-clear, and *Sea Sleuth* was lowered until just above the surface. One final check of her electronic systems, and then she was slowly dropped into the blue Pacific. As soon as she was afloat, a switch was activated, the electronic snap released and the lifting cable came free.

Inside the command center, Giordino sat in front of a console with a series of knobs and switches mounted around a joystick. He would pilot the *Sea Sleuth* during its journey into the abyss. As one of the team who'd written the probe's computer software, he was also the chief engineer in charge of its production. Few men knew more about the eccentricities of piloting an AUV four and half miles deep under the ocean than Giordino. As he glanced at the monitor that showed the AUV floating free of the ship in the water, he activated the valves of the buoyancy tank and watched as she descended beneath the waves and disappeared.

Next to him, Pitt sat at the keyboard, entering a series of commands into the computer on board the AUV. While Giordino controlled the vehicle's propulsion and attitude systems, Pitt operated the cameras and lighting systems. In back of them and to their side, Misty Graham sat at a table studying a copy of the *Emerald Dolphin*'s construction plans that had been flown in from the architects. All other eyes were locked on the array of monitors that would relay images of what *Sea Sleuth* recorded in the depths.

Misty was a petite woman, full of fire and vinegar. Her black hair cropped short for easy maintenance on board ship, she might have looked boyish if she didn't have well-defined construction. With light brown eyes under a pert little nose and soft lips, Misty had never been married. A dedicated scientist and one of the best marine biologists with NUMA, she spent far more time at sea than she did in her condominium in Washington and seldom had time to date.

She looked up from the chart and spoke

to Burch. "If she's caved in on herself, *Sea Sleuth* won't have an easy time finding anything of interest."

"We won't know till we get there," he said slowly.

As with other underwater search projects, conversation filled the compartment. Now that the probe was under way, the three and a half hours it would take for the AUV to reach the bottom were simply a dreary routine. There was little to see unless one of the strange species of fish that lived in the deep oceans happened to pass in front of a camera lens.

It is generally thought by the public that underwater searches are exciting. The truth is, they are downright dull. Many hours are spent waiting for something to happen, or what is known in the trade as "an event." Yet everyone remains in optimistic anticipation for an anomaly to reveal itself on the sonar or camera monitors.

All too often the searchers fail to find anything. Still, the vision returned from the deep had a hypnotic effect, and the crew and scientists could never tear their eyes from the monitors. Fortunately, in this case, the whereabouts of the shipwreck, after its four-mile fall to the bottom as recorded by the tugboat's Global Positioning System, was accurately targeted within an area the size of a football stadium."

The progress of the *Sea Sleuth* was displayed on the guidance monitor with digital readings of direction and altitude on the bottom of the screen. Once the vehicle reached the bottom, Giordino had only to send her directly to the wreckage without the bother of a time-consuming search operation.

He read out the digital numbers relayed by the probe's altimeter. "Two thousand, five hundred feet."

He reported the depth readings every ten minutes as the *Sleuth* descended into the black void far beneath the keel of the survey ship. Finally, after two and a half hours, the sensors began to transmit a rapidly narrowing gap with the bottom.

"The bottom is at five hundred feet and rising."

"Turning on lower lights," Pitt responded.

Giordino slowed the descent rate of the *Sleuth* to two feet every second in the event she came down directly on top of the wreck. The last thing they needed was for it to become trapped in the twisted debris, and lost. Soon the drab silt of the sea floor came into view on the monitors. Giordino stopped the probe's descent, hovering it at 100 feet.

"What's the depth?" asked Burch.

"Nineteen thousand, seven hundred and

sixty," Giordino answered. "Visibility is extremely good. Almost two hundred feet."

Now Giordino took over actual control of the *Sea Sleuth*, staring at the monitors and operating the knobs and joystick as if he were flying an aircraft in a flight simulator computer game. The bottom passed beneath in what seemed like agonizing slowness. Because of the extreme water pressure, the *Sleuth*'s thrusters could only move her forward at slightly better than one knot.

Pitt pecked away at the keyboard of his computer, sending commands down to the computer on board *Sea Sleuth* to adjust and focus the cameras mounted on the bow and keel for viewing ahead and directly below. To his left, Burch sat at his guidance console, checking the AUV's position and keeping the *Deep Encounter* positioned directly above the wreck.

"Which way?" Giordino asked Burch.

"Move on a heading of eighteen degrees. You should run into her hull in another four hundred feet."

Giordino set the *Sleuth* on the course indicated. Ten minutes later, a phantom shape loomed ahead. The dark mass spread and rose beyond view of the monitors. "Target dead ahead," he called out.

Gradually, features of the wreck became distinguishable. They came on slightly off the starboard bow near the anchor. Unlike earlier passenger ships, the modern cruise ship's anchors were nestled farther back from the bow and not as far above the waterline.

Pitt switched on the powerful forward lights that cut through the gloom and illuminated most of the bow section. "Cameras in motion, and rolling tape."

Unlike other shipwreck discoveries, this one was not greeted with cheers and laughter. Everyone was as silent as if they were looking down at a coffin in a grave. Then, as though drawn and tightened by a giant rubber band, they moved closely around the monitors. They could see now that the *Emerald Dolphin* was not sitting entirely upright. She rested in the silt on a twenty-five-degree angle, exposing her lower hull almost to the keel.

Giordino eased the *Sea Sleuth* along the hull, watching for any obstructions the vehicle might encounter that could cause her to become caught and trapped. His calculated cautiousness paid off. He stopped the AUV ten feet away from a massive opening in the hull, the plates contoured into jagged unrecognizable shapes.

"Zoom in for a closer look," he said to Pitt.

The command was entered and the camera lenses aimed at the shattered hole from different perspectives. Meanwhile,

Giordino maneuvered the probe so that its bow faced the mangled destruction head-on.

"Hold station," Pitt instructed him. "This looks interesting."

"That wasn't caused by the fire," said one of the ship's crew.

"The wreckage is blown from the inside out," observed Pitt.

Burch rubbed his eyes and gazed at the monitors. "A fuel tank explosion maybe?"

Pitt shook his head. "The magnetohydrodynamic engines did not run on flammable fossil fuel." He turned to Giordino. "Al, take us along the hull until we reach where it broke off from the amidships section."

Giordino did as he was instructed and jockeyed the joystick, moving the *Sea Sleuth* on a parallel path with the hull. In another two hundred feet, they came on a second, even larger, hole. This one also indicated an interior blast that had ripped the hull plates outward.

"The section inside the hole is where the air-conditioning equipment was housed," Misty informed them. She examined the deck plans closely. "I see nothing here that would cause such damage."

"Nor I," Pitt agreed.

Giordino steered *Sea Sleuth* upward slightly until the boat deck came into view.

Several of the burned lifeboats had been torn out of their davits during the plunge to the bottom. The rest that remained with the ship were burned and melted beyond description. It didn't seem possible that the most technically advanced ship on the seas could have had all her boats rendered useless in so short a time.

The AUV then passed around the devastated part of the hull that had broken away from the rest of the ship. Pipes, twisted beams, shattered deck plating spread from the aft end like the remains of a burned-out oil refinery. It looked as though the *Emerald Dolphin* had been wrenched apart by some gargantuan force.

The amidships section was totally unrecognizable as part of a ship. It was nothing but a huge pile of blackened, twisted rubble. The abhorrent sight was left behind as the AUV passed over the bleak ocean landscape again.

"What course to the stern section?" Giordino asked Burch.

The captain examined the digital numbers on the bottom of his guidance monitor. "You should find it three hundred yards on a ninety-degree course west."

"Turning ninety degrees west," Giordino echoed.

Here, the bottom was littered with all kinds of debris, most of it burned beyond recognition. Only scattered heaps of ceramic seemed to have survived. Dishes, bowls and cups, many still in stacks unfolded in the silt like a deck of cards spread across a gray felt table. To the observers in the command center, it seemed macabre that objects so fragile had endured the terrible fire and a drop of almost twenty thousand feet into the abyss without being shattered into thousands of shards.

"Stern coming up," Giordino alerted them, as the debris field was left in the wake of the thrusters, and the final section of the sunken ship began to materialize under the AUV's penetrating lights. Now the horrible nightmare truly came home, as the men and women who had worked so courageously to rescue the passengers and crew from the burning wreck found themselves staring once again at the stern decks where survivors had abandoned the ship down the ropes or jumped into the sea before they were taken aboard the *Deep Encounter*.

"I never thought I'd have to look at that again," murmured one of the women.

"It's not something easily forgotten," said Pitt. "Come around to the forward section where it separated from amidships."

"Coming around."

"Descend down to five feet above the silt. I want to get a look at her keel."

The *Sea Sleuth* followed Giordino's commands and crawled around the bottom of the stern that sat nearly upright. Very cautiously, inching over and around debris, Giordino stopped the vehicle and hovered it at a point where the ship's stern section was ripped open. The massive steel keel was free of the silt. They could all plainly see that it was warped and curled downward where it had been torn in half.

"Only explosives could have done that," Pitt commented.

"It's beginning to look like her bottom was blasted out," said Giordino. "Her internal structure, weakened by the fire and the blast, broke apart from the increasing water pressure during her fall to the bottom."

"That would explain her abrupt sinking," added Burch. "According to the tugboat captain, she went down so fast she almost took his boat with it."

"Which leads to the conclusion that someone had a motive for setting the ship afire and then sinking her in the deepest part of the ocean so her wreckage couldn't be examined."

"A sound theory," said Jim Jakubek, the team's hydrographer. "But where is the hard evidence? How can it be proven in court?"

Pitt shrugged. "The simple answer is, it can't."

"So where does that leave us?" asked Misty.

Pitt stared thoughtfully at the monitors. "*Sea Sleuth* has done its job and has shown that the *Emerald Dolphin* did not destroy herself, nor was it an act of God. We have to dig deeper and come up with enough proof for an investigation, proof that will lead to the doorstep of the murderous slime who is responsible for the loss of a beautiful ship and more than a hundred lives."

"Dig deeper?" inquired Giordino, smiling as if knowing the answer. "How?"

Pitt looked at his friend through Machiavellian eyes. "You and I go down on the wreck ourselves in the *Abyss Navigator* and bring home the goods."

13

"We're free," said Giordino, as he waved to the diver outside his thick window who had released the hook and cable from the *Abyss Navigator*'s lifting eye. Then he waited for the diver to give the submersible a final inspection before flooding the buoyancy tanks for the slow fall to the sea bottom. After a few minutes, the diver's head and face mask appeared in one of the four view ports and gave a thumbs-up signal.

"All systems are go," Pitt notified the crew in the *Deep Encounter*'s command center who would monitor the journey from surface to bottom to surface again.

"Looking good on this end," replied Burch. "Ready anytime you are."

"Flooding tanks now," said Giordino.

The *Abyss Navigator* descended by filling her upper ballast tank with water. Once on the bottom, the extreme pressure was too much for pumps to expel, so weights on the vehicle's bottom were dropped, allowing it to float to the surface.

A four-man submersible, the *Abyss Navigator*'s nerve center was a round titanium alloy ball that housed the pilot and the technician who controlled the life-support systems, external lights, cameras and the two manipulator arms. The latter were mounted under the round hull and protruded like the special-effects arms of a robot in a science-fiction movie. A metal basket sat under the mechanical fingers to retrieve any artifacts picked off the bottom. Connected to the tubular framework around the manned ball were the pressure housings for the electronics, batteries and communications equipment. Though they served similar purposes and basically carried the same equipment, the *Navigator* and the *Sleuth* looked as much alike as a Saint Bernard and a mule. One carried a cask of brandy, the other one or more humans.

This trip the *Navigator* was carrying three people. Misty Graham had joined Dirk and Al for two reasons. One, whatever project Misty tackled, she threw herself into it with every ounce of her soul. After spending every free minute studying the deck plans of the *Emerald Dolphin*, she knew more about specific compartment locations than anyone on the survey ship. And, two, this was an opportunity for her to study the marine organisms of the deep.

Once Pitt had loaded the cameras and checked them out, he monitored the life-support system before positioning a small reclining seat for his lanky frame. He settled in for the long, boring trip to the seabed by working a crossword puzzle. He occasionally looked up and peered out one of the view ports as the light from the surface above began to lose reds, greens and yellows before turning a dark blue and finally pitch-black. He switched on one of the exterior lights, but there was nothing to see. No curious sea life bothered investigating the strange intruder falling into their liquid domain.

They entered the black, three-dimensional universe of the ocean's mid-zone, an eternal region extending from about five hundred feet beneath the surface to five hundred feet above the seabed. Here, they received their first visitor.

Pit laid down the puzzle and gazed through the port-side view port and found himself face-to-face with an anglerfish that was keeping up with the descent of the *Navigator*. There were few fish as ugly and grotesque as an anglerfish. With beady eyes the color of gray pearls, it bore a shaft that stuck up vertically from a hole in its nose. A little luminous light beaconed at its tip, a lure that attracted the anglerfish's dinner in the infinite blackness.

Scaleless, unlike its distant cousins nearer the surface, it was sheathed in wrinkly brown skin that looked like rotting parchment. A huge mouth, accommodating hundreds of tiny needlelike teeth, stretched across its lower head like a yawning cavern. Though equal in size — a few inches in length — a piranha encountering an anglerfish in a dark underwater alley would have turned tail and fled.

Pitt smiled. "A perfect example of the old cliché, a face only a mother could love."

"Compared to other denizens of the deep," said Misty, "the anglerfish is downright gorgeous."

The homely little carnivore's curiosity soon waned, and it swam out of the light back into the darkness.

Beyond two thousand feet, they encountered the world of bizarre sea life known as siphonophore, gelatinous predators that come in all shapes and sizes, some less than an inch long, others that stretch to more than 120 feet. They live in a realm that covers 95 percent of the Earth's waters, and yet they are a mystery to ocean scientists, seldom seen and rarely if ever captured.

Misty was in her element as she stared entranced at the remarkably beautiful, deepwater siphonophore. Like their jellyfish cousins that inhabit surface waters, they are delicately transparent and come in spectacularly luminescent colors, with different characteristic light displays. Their bodies are modular with multiple internal organs, sometimes with more than a hundred stomachs, usually visible through their diaphanous interior. Many varieties have long, ethereal tentacles that stream over one hundred feet. The tentacles of others are more feathery, while some are similar to a dust mop. Like a spider's web, their tentacles are deployed like nets to catch fish.

The heads of most siphonophore are called bells. They are devoid of eyes or mouths but function as a means of propulsion. In an incredibly efficient system, water is drawn in through a series of valves. Then it is expelled by muscular contractions, propelling the glutinous beast in whatever direction it decides to travel, depending on which valves in the bells are compressed.

"Siphonophore shy away from bright light," Misty said to Pitt. "Can you fade the lamps?"

Pitt complied and reduced the *Navigator*'s beams to a dim glow that also allowed the animals to show off their bioluminescent rainbows.

"An apolemia," Misty whispered reverently, as she watched the creature glide past, uncoiling its ninety-foot tentacles in a deadly net.

For the next several thousand feet, the show continued while Misty furiously recorded her observations in a notebook as Pitt recorded on the video and still cameras. As the number of creatures diminished, those that remained became much smaller. They existed in the depths under thousands of pounds of pressure because the interior of their bodies equaled the force from outside.

Pitt was so absorbed by the drama outside his view port that he never went back to his crossword puzzle. He turned from the port only when Giordino nudged him.

"Bottom coming up."

Outside, the water was becoming filled with falling *marine snow*, tiny light gray particles, consisting of dead organisms and waste produced by the sea creatures above. The men inside the submersible felt as though they were driving through a light blizzard. Pitt wondered what underwater phenomena caused the snow to look heavier now than it had under the lights and cameras of *Sea Sleuth* the day before.

He switched on all lights and stared down through the view port mounted on the floor of the *Navigator*. As if it were land materializing through a fog, the bottom took shape beneath the sled runners as the submersible's shadow appeared under the bottom lights on the silt.

"We have the bottom," he alerted Giordino.

Giordino slowed the ascent by dropping a pair of weights, neutralizing the buoyancy until their downward motion slowed to a crawl, and stopped only twenty feet above the bottom. Like an aircraft making a picture-perfect landing, Giordino had maneuvered the sub to a halt right on the mark with great skill.

"Well done," Pitt complimented him.

"Just another of my many accomplishments," Giordino replied grandiosely.

"We're on the bottom and need a direction," Pitt called Burch in the command center four miles upward.

"You'll find her two hundred yards southeast," the captain's voice came back through the depths. "Follow a course of one hundred forty degrees and you should come up on the aft end of the forward section where it tore away."

Giordino engaged the thruster motors and steered the *Navigator* with his control column along the compass direction given by Burch. Fourteen minutes later, the mangled wreckage where the ship had ripped apart came into view. Seeing the devastating effects of the holocaust fire firsthand rather than through an image on a video monitor was a shock. Nothing was recognizable. They felt as if they were gazing into a monstrous cavern piled with burned-out scrap. The only resemblance to what had once been a ship was the outline of her hull.

"Where to?" Giordino inquired.

Misty took several moments to study the interior deck plans of the *Emerald Dolphin* and get her bearings. Finally, she circled an area and passed it to Giordino.

"You want to go inside?" he asked Pitt, knowing he'd be less than pleased with the answer.

"As far as we can go," Pitt replied. "If at all possible, I'd like to penetrate into the chapel where the crew reported the fire started."

Giordino gave a doubtful stare inside the blackened and ominous-looking wreckage. "We could easily get trapped in there."

Pitt grinned. "Then I'll have time to finish my crossword puzzle."

"Yeah," Giordino grunted. "For all eternity." His sarcastic attitude was strictly for show. He would have leaped with Pitt off the Golden Gate Bridge if his friend had stood on the railing. He gripped the control column and gently placed his hand on the throttle. "Tell me where and say when."

Misty tried to ignore their sardonic humor, but the thought of dying alone, never to be found in the deepest reaches of the sea, was not a pretty one.

Before Pitt gave the word, he called up the *Deep Encounter* to report their situation. But there was no response. No voice replied over the speakerphone.

"Odd," he said, perplexed. "They're not answering."

"The communications equipment probably malfunctioned," Giordino said calmly.

Pitt wasted no more time in trying to raise the control center. He checked the oxygen gauges on the life-support system. They had an hour of bottom time left. "Go on in," he ordered. Giordino gave a faint nod and orchestrated the submersible's controls, very slowly steering her into the opening.

Already, sea life was probing the wreckage and setting up housekeeping. They spotted several rat-tailed fish, a species of shrimp and what could only be described as a sea slug that had somehow wiggled its way into the jagged ruins.

The burned-out interior of the shipwreck looked menacing. There was a mild current but not enough to cause Giordino a problem in keeping the *Navigator* steady. The dim outline of what was left of the decks and bulkheads came out of the gloom. Looking back and forth from the plans of the ship and the viewport, Pitt estimated which deck to enter to get to the chapel.

"Rise to the fourth deck," directed Misty.

"It leads through a shopping mall to the chapel."

"We'll try to gain entry there," said Pitt.

Slowly, Giordino maneuvered the sub upward without dropping any more weights, using only the thrusters. As soon as they reached the deck Misty had indicated, he hovered the *Navigator* for a minute while both men stared inside the wreckage, now illuminated by the four forward lights. Melted pipes and electrical wiring hung down like distorted tentacles. Pitt turned on the camera systems and began recording the mess.

"We'll never get around that," said Giordino.

"Not around," Pitt contradicted, "but through. Run our bow against those pipes dead ahead."

Without argument, Giordino eased the submersible into a maze of melted pipe that hung down from the ceiling of the deck above. The pipes parted and crumbled as if they were made out of poor-quality plaster of Paris, sending out a cloud of ashes that the sub easily slipped through.

"You called that right," muttered Giordino.

"I figured they'd be brittle after being subjected to the intense heat."

They soared though the charred wreckage of the shopping avenue. Nothing was left of the open three-deck avenue of stylish boutique shops. They had all burned to nothingness. Blackened and warped bulkheads were all that remained to indicate where they once stood. Giordino cautiously navigated around and over the piles of debris that rose like a range of hills covered with jagged black lava rock.

Misty felt an eerie feeling, more so than the men, knowing they were moving through space where men had strolled and relaxed while women shopped; where children had laughed and run ahead of their parents. She could almost imagine seeing the ghosts stalking the avenue. Most of the passengers had cheated death and were now on their way home, taking memories that would haunt them the rest of their lives.

"Not much to look at," said Giordino.

Pitt gazed at the desolation. "No shipwreck treasure hunter will ever waste his time and money on this ruin."

"I wouldn't bet on it. You know how it goes. Twenty years from now, someone will claim the ship went down with a million dollars in cash in the purser's safe. Fifty years later, it will be rumored as fifty million dollars in silver. Then in two hundred years, they'll say she went down with a billion in gold."

"Intriguing, when you consider more has been spent searching for gold under the seas during the last century than has ever been found."

"Only the *Edinburgh*, *Atocha* and *Central America* truly paid off."

"Exceptions to the rule," said Pitt.

"There's more treasure in the sea than mere gold," said Misty.

"Yes," Pitt replied, "treasures yet to be discovered that did not come from man."

They stopped talking as several fallen beams blocked their way. Carefully, Giordino threaded the *Navigator* through the maze, scraping the paint on the sled runners. "Too close," he sighed. "Now the trick is to get back out."

"Coming to the site of the chapel," Misty notified them.

"How can you tell in this mess?" asked Pitt.

"There are still a few features left that I can match on the plans," she said, her face set in concentration. "Come to a halt in another thirty feet."

Pitt lay on his stomach and peered through the bottom view port as Giordino covered the distance and then stopped the sub. It hung as if levitating over the space once occupied by the *Emerald Dolphin*'s nondenominational chapel. The only distinguishing evidence that indicated they were in the right area were melted floor mountings in rows that held the pews.

Pitt leaned over the small console that contained the controls for the manipulator arm. With a light touch of the knobs and levers, he began moving the articulated arm downward until it began probing and sifting through the charred debris with its mechanical fingers.

Clearing a ten-foot-square area and finding nothing of interest, he glanced at Giordino. "Move us five feet forward."

Giordino complied and sat patiently until Pitt asked him to maneuver the sub to another search grid. There was little conversation while each man became engrossed in his own tasks. Thirty minutes later, Pitt had sifted and examined most of the chapel area. As luck would have it, he found what he was looking for in the last grid. A strange-looking substance lay in a tiny twisted lump on the deck. The object or substance, less than six inches in length and two inches wide, did not have the usual heat-fused look to it, but rather it appeared smooth and rounded. Its colors were odd, too. Instead of black or scorched gray, it had a greenish tint to it.

"Time is up," Giordino warned. "We don't have much oxygen in reserve to reach the surface safely."

"I think we may have found what we came for," said Pitt. "Give me another five minutes."

Very tenderly, he worked the fingers of the manipulator and slowly eased them under the peculiar material half buried in the ashes. When the object was delicately gripped, Pitt fingered the controls and lifted it free of the incinerated debris. Next he pulled back the mechanical arm and cautiously set the payload into the artifact basket. Only then did he release the fingers and pull back the arm to its locked position.

"Let's head for home."

Giordino sent the submersible into a slow, gliding 180-degree turn and aimed it back through the shopping avenue area.

Abruptly, there was a clunk sound and the submersible jerked to a stop. For a moment, neither man spoke. Misty's hands came together against her breasts in sudden fear. Pitt and Giordino merely looked at each other and briefly dwelled on the possibility that they might be irreversibly trapped for eternity in this hideous place.

"I do believe you struck something," Pitt said casually.

"It would seem so," Giordino replied, about as agitated as a three-toed sloth who didn't like the taste of a leaf he was chewing on.

Pitt tilted his head and stared through the overhead viewport. "It looks like the ballast tank is hung up on a beam."

"I should have seen it."

"It wasn't here when we entered. I suspect it must have fallen after we passed."

Misty was frightened, and she couldn't understand how the two men could make light of such a deadly situation. She did not know that Pitt and Giordino had been in far tighter spots than this during their long friendship. Humor was a mechanism to keep their minds clear from creeping thoughts of fear and death.

Giordino gently eased the *Navigator* backward and down. There was a horrendous screeching noise. Then the sub broke free and the eerie void became silent again.

"The tank does not look good," reported Pitt stoically. "It's badly dented and looks to be caved in across the top."

"Since it's already full of seawater, at least it can't leak."

"Luckily, we won't need it for the trip home."

Outwardly, Giordino looked as serene as a millpond, but down deep he was greatly relieved when he evaded the maze of hanging debris and piloted the *Navigator* into open water again. As soon as they were clear of the wreck and Giordino dropped the weight for the ascent, Pitt called the surface again. When he received no reply, his eyes became pensive.

"I don't understand why the communications phone is inoperative," he said slowly.

"There is nothing wrong with the system on this end, and they're far better equipped to deal with any problem than we are."

"Murphy's Law can strike anywhere, anytime," Giordino said philosophically.

"I don't think the problem is serious," said Misty, vastly relieved that they were on their way to the surface and sunshine.

Pitt gave up trying to contact the *Deep Encounter*. He switched off the camera and external lighting systems to conserve battery power in case of an emergency. Then he relaxed in his seat and took up his crossword puzzle again. He soon finished it except for 22 across. Ring-necked Fuzzwort. Then he killed time by taking a nap.

Three hours later, the water began to turn from deep black to deep blue again as the colors of the spectrum returned. Looking through the overhead view port, they could see the sea's restless surface shimmering and sparkling above. Less than a minute later, the *Abyss Navigator* broke the surface. They were happy to find the swells rolling over at a mere two feet between crest and trough. The submersible, her mass still several feet below the surface, only slightly pitched and rolled.

There were still no communications with the survey ship on the surface. They could not see the ship because all but one of the view ports were below. The top port offered no horizontal vision; the sub's crew could only look straight up. They waited for the divers to come and attach the lifting cable, but after ten minutes, there was no sign of them. Something was not going according to plan.

"Still no contact," said Pitt. "No diving team. Have they all fallen asleep?"

"Maybe the ship sank," Giordino said jokingly between yawns.

"Don't say that," Misty scolded him.

Pitt grinned at her. "Not very likely. Certainly not in calm water."

"Since the waves aren't sloshing over the top, why not crack the hatch and have a look?"

"A sound proposal," said Misty. "I'm tired of breathing male body odor."

"You should have said something sooner," said Giordino cavalierly. He held up a bottle of new car odor spray and misted the submersible. "Foul air, begone."

Pitt could not help but laugh as he stood up in the narrow tunnel that traveled through the damaged buoyancy tank. He was concerned that the collision with the beam might have jammed the hatch, but after turning the wheel that snugged it down, it swung back on its hinge with little effort. He then crawled through and stood with his head and shoulders above the hatch, breathing in the fresh sea air and looking around for the survey ship and small boats with the dive recovery team. His eyes made a 360-degree sweep of the horizons.

It would be futile to describe the storm of incredulity and emotion that swept through him then. His reactions ranged from utter bewilderment to pure shock.

The seas were empty. *Deep Encounter* had vanished. It was as though she had never existed.

14

They came aboard at almost the same moment the *Abyss Navigator* reached the seabed and Pitt phoned in a status report. The crew was going about their routine duties while the scientific team was in the command center monitoring Pitt and Giordino's investigation of the *Emerald Dolphin*'s wreck. The hijacking came so suddenly and unexpectedly, no one on *Deep Encounter* realized it was happening.

Burch was leaning back in his chair, arms folded across his chest, eyeing the monitors, when Delgado, who was standing next to the radar equipment, noticed a fast-moving blip on the screen. "We have a visitor coming our way out of the northeast."

"Probably a warship," said Burch, without turning from the monitors. "We're a good two miles off the commercial shipping lanes."

"She doesn't have the look of a warship,"

answered Delgado. "But she appears to be moving at a fairly high rate of speed, and she's coming straight at us."

Burch's eyebrows rose. Without replying to Delgado, he picked up a pair of binoculars and walked out onto the bridge wing. As he stared into the distance through the 7-by-50 lenses, a bright orange-and-white boat increased in size as it cut the water toward *Deep Encounter*. Any hint of apprehension faded. The approaching vessel did not seem to suggest any threat.

"What do you make of her?" asked Delgado.

"An oil company utility work boat, a big one," replied Burch. "And fast, by the look of the spray flying over her bow. Good for at least thirty knots."

"I wonder where she came from. There are no oil rigs within a thousand miles."

"I'm more interested in why she's interested in us."

"Does she have a name or a company emblem on the hull?"

"Odd," Burch said slowly. "The name on her bow and any sign of whatever company owns her are covered over."

As if prompted, the radio operator joined them on the bridge wing. "I have the skipper of the oil company boat on the ship's phone," he said to Burch.

The captain opened a watertight box and

switched on the bridge wing speaker. "This is Captain Burch of the NUMA ship *Deep Encounter*. Go ahead."

"Captain Wheeler of the Mistral Oil Company boat *Pegasus*. Do you have a doctor on board?"

"Affirmative. What is your complication?"

"We have a badly injured man."

"Come alongside and I'll send over our ship's doctor."

"Better we bring him aboard your ship. We have no medical facilities or supplies."

Burch looked at Delgado. "You heard?"

"Most odd," said Delgado.

"My thoughts also," agreed Burch. "Having no doctor on a work boat is understandable, but no medical supplies? That doesn't figure."

Delgado began to step toward the companionway. "I'll have a crew standing by to hoist a stretcher on board."

The work boat came to a stop about fifty yards away from the survey ship. A few minutes later, a launch was lowered, with a man covered with blankets on a litter and laid across the seats. Four men also entered the launch, and it was soon rising and dropping in the waves next to the *Deep Encounter*'s hull. Unexpectedly, three of the work boat's crew jumped on board and helped lift the injured man onto the work deck, rudely pushing the *Deep Encounter*'s crew aside.

Suddenly, the visitors threw back the blankets and snatched up automatic weapons that had been hidden beneath them and turned them on Burch's survey crew. The man on the stretcher leaped to his feet, took an offered gun and ran toward the starboard stairway leading to the bridge.

Burch and Delgado realized immediately that it was a hijacking. On a commercial ship or private yacht, they'd have rushed to a gun locker and begun passing out weapons. But under international law, survey ships were not allowed to carry arms. They could do nothing but stand helpless until the intruder stepped onto the bridge deck.

The hijacker did not look like a pirate, no peg leg, parrot or eye patch. He had more of an executive air about him. The hair was prematurely gray, the face dark. He was of medium height with a stomach slightly larger than his waist. He wore the appearance of a man comfortable with authority, and he was smartly dressed in a golf shirt and Bermuda shorts. Almost as an act of courtesy, he did not aim the muzzle of his automatic rifle at either Burch or Delgado, but held it casually pointed toward the sky.

For a moment, they inspected one another warily. Then the intruder ignored Delgado and turned to Burch, speaking politely in American English. "Captain Burch, I presume."

"And you are?"

"My name is of no consequence," the pirate said in a tone that rasped like a file against iron. "I hope you will offer no resistance."

"What in hell are you doing on my ship?" Burch demanded.

"We are confiscating it," replied the intruder, with a hard edge in his tone. "No one will be harmed."

Burch stared at him incredulously. "This ship is the property of the United States government. You don't have the authority to simply walk on board and confiscate her."

"Oh, but we can." He held up the gun. "This is our authority."

As he spoke, the three armed gunmen on the work deck began rounding up the survey ship's crew. The work boat's launch soon returned with ten more armed men, who stationed themselves throughout the ship.

"This is madness," snarled Burch indignantly. "What do you hope to accomplish by this criminal act?"

The tall, dark man smiled deprecatingly. "You can't begin to comprehend the purpose."

An armed hijacker approached. "Sir, the ship is secure and all crew members and scientists are under guard in the dining area."

"The engine room?"

"Awaiting your orders."

"Then prepare to get under way. I want full speed."

"You won't get anywhere fast enough not to get caught," said Delgado. "She won't do more than ten knots."

The hijacker laughed. "Ten knots? You shame your ship, sir. I happen to know you made twice that in speeding to the *Emerald Dolphin*'s rescue. However, even twenty knots is too slow." He paused and motioned to the bow, where the work boat was moving into position in preparation for taking the survey ship in tow. "Between the two of us, we should be able to make over twenty-five knots."

"Where are you taking us?" demanded Delgado, as angry as Burch had ever seen him.

"It's not your concern," the man rasped carelessly. "Have I your word, Captain, that you and your crew will not attempt to resist or disobey my orders?"

"You have guns," Burch said simply. "We have no arms other than kitchen knives."

While they talked, the tow rope was brought aboard and looped over the *Deep Encounter*'s forward bollard. Burch's eyes suddenly took on a look of naked discomfort.

"We cannot leave!" he said sharply. "Not yet!"

The hijacker gazed at him, trying to read any sign of a crafty expression. He saw none. "Already you are questioning my orders."

"You don't understand," said Delgado. "We have a submersible down on the seabed with two men and a woman inside. We can't just leave them."

"A pity." The pirate shrugged indifferently. "They will have to make land on their own."

"Impossible. That would be murder."

"Don't they have communications with the outside world?"

"They have only a small portable radio and an underwater acoustic phone," explained Delgado. "They couldn't contact another vessel or aircraft unless they were within two miles of them."

"Good lord, man," pleaded Burch. "When they return to the surface and find us gone, they'll have no hope of rescue. Not this far off the shipping lanes. You'll be signing their death warrants."

"Not my problem."

Enraged, Burch took a step toward the hijacker, who swiftly raised his gun and shoved the muzzle against the captain's chest. "It would not be wise to antagonize me, Captain."

His fists clenched at his sides, Burch stood there staring at the black man as if he was mad, then turned and gazed vacantly at the area of the sea where he had last seen the *Abyss Navigator*. "God help you if those men die," he said, in a voice that could have cut steel. "Because you will surely pay."

"If there is retribution," said the pirate coldly, "you will not be the one to enforce it."

Defeated and heartsick thinking about Pitt, Giordino and Misty, with no course of action open to them and no ground to negotiate, Burch and Delgado could only allow themselves to be led away to the dining hall by an armed guard.

Before the *Abyss Navigator* had risen to the surface, the *Deep Encounter* had long disappeared beyond the northeastern horizon.

15

Sandecker was working at his desk, so intent that he did not immediately notice that Rudi Gunn had entered the office and sat down across from him. Gunn was a little man with a genial disposition. The remaining wisps of hair across the top of his head, the thick horn-rimmed glasses, the inexpensive watch on his wrist suggested a dull and colorless bureaucrat who slaved away unnoticed in a cubicle behind the water cooler.

Gunn was anything *but* colorless. Number one in his class at Annapolis, he'd served with distinction in the Navy before joining Sandecker at NUMA as assistant director and chief of operations. Known to possess a brilliant mind coupled with a pragmatic instinct, he ran the day-to-day operations of NUMA with an efficiency unknown in other government agencies. Gunn was a close friend of Pitt and Giordino. He often stood behind and backed their wild, adventurous schemes that ran counter to Sandecker's directives.

"Sorry to interrupt, Admiral, but we have a serious problem."

"What is it this time?" asked Sandecker, without looking up. "Another project running over budget?"

"I'm afraid it's far worse."

Only now did the admiral glance up from his paperwork. "What do you have?"

"The *Deep Encounter* and all on board have vanished."

There was no hint of surprise. No questioning expression. No automatic repeat of the word *vanished*. He sat with icy calm, waiting for Gunn to elaborate.

"All our radio and satellite phone inquiries have gone unanswered —" Gunn began to explain.

"There could be any one of a hundred reasons for a breakdown in communications," Sandecker cut in.

"There are backup systems," Gunn said patiently. "They can't all have failed."

"How long has it been since they last responded?"

"Ten hours." Gunn braced himself for the outburst he was sure would come.

This time, Sandecker reacted as expected. "Ten hours! My instructions are that all survey and research ships on station maintain status reports to our communications department every two hours."

"Your instructions were carried out to the letter. *Deep Encounter* responded as scheduled."

"You've lost me."

"Someone claiming to be Captain Burch made contact every two hours and gave updated reports on the project to investigate the wreckage of the *Emerald Dolphin*. We know it was not the captain, because the voice systems recording on all our communications did not accept the voice patterns. Someone was attempting to imitate him. Did a rather poor job of it, too."

Sandecker was taking in every word, his razor-sharp mind sorting out the consequences of what Gunn was telling him. "You are very sure of this, Rudy?"

"I can honestly say I am absolutely certain."

"I can't believe the ship and all on board vanished into thin air."

Gunn nodded. "When our communications department alerted me, I took the liberty of having a friend at the National Oceanic Atmospheric Agency analyze satellite weather photos of the area where *Deep Encounter* was working. Photo enhancement shows no sign of the ship within a hundred miles."

"What were weather conditions?"

239

"Clear skies, ten-mile-an-hour winds and calm seas."

Sandecker was trying to sift through confusing doubts. "The ship couldn't have just gone under for no reason. She carried no chemicals that might have destroyed her. There is no way she could have blown herself to pieces. A collision with another ship, perhaps?"

"She was out of regular shipping lanes and no other ships were close to her."

"A phony voice giving up-to-date reports." The admiral fixed Gunn with a piercing state. "What you're suggesting, Rudy, is that *Deep Encounter* was hijacked."

"It's beginning to look that way," acknowledged Gunn. "Short of her being sunk by an undetected submarine, a ridiculous theory at best, I see no alternative. She must have been seized and sailed out of range before the weather cameras on the satellite passed over."

"But if she was hijacked, where did they take her? How could she have disappeared in less than two hours? I know from experience that *Deep Encounter*'s best speed is barely over fifteen knots. She couldn't have sailed more than a hundred and fifty nautical miles since her last status report."

"My fault," said Gunn. "I should have asked for an extended camera range. But I made the request before I knew of the phony radio communications, and hijacking was the last thing on my mind."

Sandecker leaned back in his chair and buried his face in his hands for a moment. Then he stiffened. "Pitt and Giordino, they were on the project," he said, more as a statement than a question.

"The last report, given by Captain Burch himself, stated that Pitt and Giordino were aboard the *Abyss Navigator*. They were preparing to lower into the water for their descent onto the wreck."

"This is madness!" snapped Sandecker. "Who would dare to hijack a United States government ship in the South Pacific? There are no wars or revolutions going on in that part of the world. I fail to see a motive."

"Nor I."

"Have you contacted the Australian and New Zealand governments and requested an extensive search?"

Gunn nodded. "They assured me of their full cooperation. Any ships near the area, military or commercial, have offered to depart from their scheduled course and begin searching."

"Obtain from whatever source, NOAA or one of the security agencies, expanded satellite photos for a thousand-square-mile grid of that part of the Pacific. I don't want to miss an inch. The *Deep Encounter has* to be out there somewhere. I refuse to believe she went to the bottom."

Gunn rose from his chair and headed for the door. "I'll see to it."

Sandecker sat there for several moments, staring at a photo gallery that covered one wall. His eyes settled on a color picture of Pitt and Giordino standing next to a submersible, drinking from a bottle of champagne as they celebrated the discovery and salvage of a Chinese government treasure ship in Lake Michigan. He also noted that Giordino was smoking one of the admiral's private cigars.

There was a very close friendship among the three men. Pitt and Giordino were like the sons he'd never had. In his wildest imagination, Sandecker could not believe the two men had died. He swiveled his executive chair and gazed out the window of his office on the top floor of the NUMA building overlooking the Potomac River.

"What mischief," he muttered softly to himself under his breath, "have you two guys gotten yourself into this time?"

16

After accepting the disappearance of the *Deep Encounter* in the vast emptiness of the sea, Pitt, Giordino and Misty settled into the tight enclosure of their submersible and concentrated on staying alive. They found no trace of flotsam or an oil slick, so optimism overcame pessimism and they assumed that for whatever reason the survey ship had sailed away and would soon return.

But night passed. The sun rose and set twice more and still no sign of the mother ship. Worry unfolded, and they began to suspect the worst when, hour after hour, their eyes scanned the limitless horizon and saw nothing but green sea and blue sky. No ship or even a high-flying jetliner made an appearance. Their onboard GPS told them they had drifted over the international date line and were moving far south of the shipping lanes. Hope of a rescue dwindled.

They also didn't fool themselves. A passing ship would have to be almost on top of them to spot the tiny hatch of the *Abyss Navigator*. Their homing beacon reached out for twenty miles, but its signal was only programed to be received by a navigation computer on board the *Deep Encounter*. A passing ship or aircraft was not likely to detect it. Their only hope was if a rescue craft came within a two-mile range of their little radio.

Water was the first priority. Fortunately, rainsqualls were frequent. A vinyl mat that covered the floor of the sub was spread out and held over the hatch; it caught the rain and sent it down a crease into the water bottles they'd carried on the dive. After the sandwiches were consumed, they began a project for catching fish. Using tools carried on board for emergency repairs, Pitt fashioned a series of hooks, while Misty relied on her artistic talent for making colorful lures out of any material she could find. For fishing lines, Giordino disassembled electronic wiring and connected it to the hooks and lures. Not relying on one line, they cast out several and were rewarded with three small fish that Misty identified as frigate mackerel before they were quickly cut up, used for bait and chummed in the water to attract more fish. Within ten hours, they had a small stock of raw fish, expertly scaled and gutted by Misty. They ate sushi style, down to the last morsel. It had little taste, but no one complained so long as it supplied nourishment.

After endless conjecturing about the whereabouts of *Deep Encounter* and its crew and scientists, they finally gave up in frustration and discussed, debated and philosophized every subject from politics to food to ocean technology. Anything to take the edge off the tedium while one of them stood in the hatch to catch rain or scour the sea for a vessel while the others charted their drift and paid out the fishing lines.

The substance they had retrieved from the wreck had been carefully removed from the basket soon after breaking the surface and placed in a plastic bag. With nothing but time on their hands, they spent endless hours speculating about its chemical composition.

"How far have we drifted?" Misty asked for the hundredth time, shading her eyes from the glare as she spoke to Pitt at her feet below the hatch.

"Almost thirty-two miles southeast by east since this time yesterday," he answered.

"At that rate we should make the coast of South America in another six months," she said grimly.

"Either there or Antarctica," muttered Giordino.

"We've been there," said Pitt. "I've never developed a fondness for vacationing in the same place twice."

"I'll make your feelings known to the wind and currents."

"Maybe we could rig a sail with the floor mat," said Misty.

"With ninety-five percent of their mass underwater, submersibles aren't known for their ability to sail before the wind."

"I wonder if Admiral Sandecker is aware of our situation?" said Misty softly.

"Knowing him as we do," said Pitt confidently, "I'll bet he's moving heaven and hell to launch a search-and-rescue operation."

Giordino was curled up in his seat, dreaming of a thick porterhouse steak, medium rare. "I'd give a year's pay to know where *Deep Encounter* is at this moment."

"No sense in rehashing that mystery," said Pitt. "We won't have a clue until we're fished out of the sea."

The fourth day broke under gloomy skies. The routine never varied. Catch water if possible, catch fish if possible, and search the horizon. Conditions did not worsen, nor did they improve. Each person stood a two-hour watch. The hatch tower of the submersible only protruded four feet above the water, so the person on duty usually got soaked when the swells slapped over the top rim. Giordino dropped all the weights, but the heavy mass still tended to pull the craft under the crest of most waves. The little sub rolled sickeningly, but fortunately its crew had long ago become immune to *mal de mer,* all three having spent nearly half their lives at sea.

Pitt fashioned a spearhead by carving with his Swiss army knife on the plastic back of a clipboard that Misty had used to make notes. During Giordino's watch, he speared a three-foot white-tipped shark. A bland-tasting feast soon followed, washed down with their last pint of water.

During Misty's watch, an aircraft flew within a mile of the drifting submersible. Despite her frantic waving of the floor mat, the aircraft continued on. "It was a rescue plane," she cried, barely holding back her emotions. "He flew right over and didn't see us."

"We're awfully hard to spot," Pitt reminded her.

Giordino nodded in agreement. "They'll never detect us from an altitude much more than five hundred feet. Our hatch tower is too tiny. From the air we're as obvious as a flyspeck on a barn door."

"Or a penny on a golf course," Pitt added.

"Then how will they ever find us?" Misty asked, her resolve beginning to crack.

Pitt gave her a comforting smile and

hugged her. "The law of averages," he said. "They're bound to catch up."

"Besides," Giordino chimed in, "we're lucky. Aren't we, pal?"

"As lucky as they come."

Misty wiped a glistening eye, straightened her blouse and shorts and ran a hand through her cropped hair. "Forgive me. I'm not as tough as I thought I was."

In the next two days, Pitt and Giordino were hard-pressed to keep up their quixotic manner. Three more planes flew over and failed to spot them. Pitt tried to hail them over the portable radio, but they were out of range. Knowing that rescuers were raking the seas to find them and coming so close without discovering them was disheartening. Their only encouraging awareness was the certainty that Admiral Sandecker was using every influence at his command to conduct an extensive search operation.

The gray skies that had dogged them all day cleared at sunset. Twilight deepened from an orange sky in the west to the velvet blue of the east. Giordino was on watch, leaning over the rim of the hatch tower. He soon developed a flair for catnapping, dozing off and then coming awake fifteen minutes later almost to the minute. Sweeping the horizon and seeing no light for the tenth time that evening, he dropped off into his temporary dreamland.

When he returned to the reality of his ordeal, he woke up to music. Initially, he thought he must have been hallucinating. He reached over the side, scooped up a handful of seawater and splashed it on his face.

The music was still there.

He could make out the tune now. Out of the night came a Strauss waltz. He recognized it as "Tales from the Vienna Woods." Then he saw a light. It looked like another star, but it was moving back and forth in a small arc on the western horizon. It was almost impossible to estimate distance across the water at night, but Giordino swore the music and the moving light were no more than four hundred yards away.

He jumped down through the hatch, groped for a flashlight and climbed up again. Now he could see the vague outline of a small vessel, and dim lights showing through square windows. He switched the flashlight on and off as fast as his thumb could move the switch, and he yelled like a sick goat.

"Over here! Over here!"

"What is it?" Pitt called out below.

"Some kind of boat!" Giordino shouted back. "I think she's headed our way!"

"Fire off a flare," Misty said excitedly.

"We don't have flares on board, Misty. We only dive during the day and ascend to the surface within easy sight of the mother ship," Pitt explained in a steady voice. Calmly, he picked up the portable radio and began calling on five different frequencies.

Misty was aching to see what was happening, but there was room for only one person at a time in the hatch tower. She could only sit and wait anxiously while Pitt tried to contact the vessel, and for Giordino to tell them whether they were about to be saved or not.

"They haven't seen us," Giordino groaned between shouts across the water and wildly waving the flashlight. The beam barely cast a glow. The batteries were about gone. "They're passing us by."

"Hello, hello, please respond," Pitt implored.

His only reply was static.

Disappointment settled over the submersible like a soaking blanket, as Giordino watched the lights begin to fade into the darkness. No one on the passing vessel had seen them, and with a sinking heart he could only watch it continue on its course toward the northwest.

"So near, yet so far," he murmured dejectedly.

Suddenly a voice cracked over the submersible's speaker. "Who am I talking to?"

"Castaways!" Pitt snapped back. "You sailed right past us. Please reverse course."

"Hold tight. I'm coming around."

"He's turning!" Giordino shouted happily. "He's coming back."

"Where off my bow are you?" the voice shouted.

"Al!" Pitt yelled up the hatch. "He wants a position."

"Tell him to steer twenty degrees to his port."

"Steer twenty degrees to your port and you should see us," Pitt relayed the message.

After a minute, the voice said, "I have you now — a dim yellow glow about a hundred yards dead ahead."

The approaching boat's owner switched on an array of exterior lights. One was a large spotlight that swept the surface of the water before finally stopping on Giordino, still waving the flashlight like a madman in the hatch tower.

"Do not be alarmed," came the voice again. "I will pass over you and stop above your little tower when it is aligned with my stern. I've dropped a ladder for you to climb aboard."

Pitt missed the rescuer's meaning. "Pass over?" he repeated. "I do not read you."

There was no reply, only Giordino's baffled voice, shouting. "I think he means to run us down!"

Pitt's first thought was that they had been

found by someone out to kill them, maybe even the same group behind the man who had tried to murder Kelly Egan. He put his arms around Misty. "Hold on to me for the collision. Then hurry through the hatch before we go under. I'll you push through."

She started to say something, but then buried her face in his chest as his strong arms embraced her. "Call out when you're sure of a collision!" he ordered Giordino. "Then jump clear!"

Giordino prepared to launch himself out of the hatch tower as he stared aghast at the brightly lit vessel bearing down on him. It looked like no oceangoing yacht he'd ever seen. It was shaped like a great green-and-white manta or devil ray, with its cephalic forward fins encircling its huge plankton-gathering mouth. A wide sloping deck on the bow swept up and around a large arched picture window and then past a circular wheelhouse.

His state of mind quickly turned from dire apprehension to vast relief as the twin catamaran hulls slipped past the submersible with five feet of clearance to spare on either side. He gazed in awe as the underhull of the main superstructure moved overhead slowly until the submersible was directly below the stern between the twin hulls. Almost on reflex, he grabbed a chrome ladder built like a small staircase that abruptly appeared less than two feet away.

Only then did he think to bend down and report to Pitt and Misty. "Not to worry. It's a catamaran. We're directly under his stern." Then he disappeared.

Misty came out of the hatch like a champagne cork, astounded at her first view of the incredible vessel above. She stood on the luxurious rear deck with its table and couches without remembering scrambling up the stairway.

Pitt reset the beacon on the submersible, then closed and secured the hatch before climbing onto the catamaran. For a few moments, they stood there alone. No crew or passengers greeted them. The boat moved forward as the helmsman steered the vessel clear of the submersible. After traveling two hundred yards, the boat slowed and drifted. They watched as a figure stepped down from the wheelhouse.

He was a large man, the same height as Pitt but fifteen pounds heavier. He was also thirty years older. His gray hair and beard gave him the appearance of an old waterfront wharf rat. His blue-green eyes had a glint to them, and he readily smiled as he examined his catch.

"Three of you," he said in amazement. "I thought there was only one in that little life raft."

"Not a life raft," said Pitt. "A deep ocean submersible."

The old man started to say something, discarded his thoughts and simply said, "If you say so."

"We're investigating the wreck of a sunken cruise ship," explained Misty.

"Yes, the *Emerald Dolphin*. I'm aware of it. A terrible tragedy. A miracle so many people survived."

Pitt didn't elaborate on their role in the rescue, but simply offered their rescuer a brief summary of how they came to be lost at sea.

"Your ship was not there when you surfaced?" the old man inquired skeptically.

"It had vanished," Giordino assured him.

"It is imperative that we call our headquarters in Washington and advise the director of NUMA that we've been found and picked up."

The old man nodded. "Of course. Come on up to the wheelhouse. You can use the ship-to-shore radio or the satellite telephone. You can even send e-mail if you wish. The *Periwinkle* has the finest communications systems of any yacht on the water."

Pitt studied the old man. "We've met before."

"Yes, I suspect we have."

"My name is Dirk Pitt." He turned to the

others. "My shipmates, Misty Graham and Al Giordino."

The old man warmly shook hands with all. Then he turned and grinned at Pitt.

"I'm Clive Cussler."

17

Pitt looked at the old man curiously. "You get around."

"We were certainly lucky you happened past," said Misty, enormously happy to be off the cramped submersible.

"I'm on a round-the-world cruise," Cussler elaborated. "My last port was Hobart in Tasmania. I'm bound for Papeete, Tahiti, but I guess I'd better make a detour and set you folks on the nearest island with an airport."

"And where would that be?" asked Giordino.

"Rarotonga."

Pitt looked around the luxurious catamaran. "I see no crew."

"I'm sailing alone," answered Cussler.

"On a motor yacht this large?"

Cussler smiled. "The *Periwinkle* isn't your average yacht. Between her automated systems and computers, she can sail herself, and usually does."

"May I take you up on your offer to use the boat's satellite phone?" Pitt inquired.

"Most certainly."

Cussler led the way up a stairway to the wheelhouse. None of the NUMA people had ever seen anything like it. The tinted windows ran in a 360-degree circle, providing vision on every horizon. There was nothing traditional about the layout. There were no conventional instruments or gauges, no wheel for a helm or throttle levers. A large overstuffed executive chair sat in front of seven LCD, liquid crystal display, screens. The chair's right arm held a computer trackball while the left armrest was fitted with a joystick. The screens were all encased in burled walnut cabinets. The helm station was more elegant than the bridge of the *Starship Enterprise.*

Cussler motioned for Pitt to sit in the helm chair. "The Globalstar phone is mounted in the panel to your right. Just press the blue button and you can all speak and listen to your party on the other end."

Pitt thanked him and dialed up Sandecker's private line at NUMA headquarters. The admiral, as always, answered on the first ring. "Sandecker."

"Admiral, this is Dirk."

There was a pregnant pause. Then the

voice came slowly. "You're alive and well?"

"Hungry for solid food and a bit dehydrated, but otherwise healthy."

"And Al?"

"He and Misty Graham from the *Deep Encounter* are standing beside me."

Pitt could hear the admiral's sigh of pleasure through the earpiece. "I've got Rudi here in my office. I'll switch to the speaker."

"Dirk!" boomed Rudi Gunn's voice. "You don't know how happy I am to hear you're still with us. We've had every rescue unit from Australia and New Zealand out searching for you and the ship."

"We got lucky and were picked up by a passing yacht."

"You're not on *Deep Encounter*?" Sandecker asked sharply.

"After we spent several hours on the sea bottom investigating the wreck of the *Emerald Dolphin*, we ascended to the surface and found that the ship and everyone on it had vanished."

"Then you couldn't know?"

"Know what?"

"We can't be absolutely certain, but it's beginning to look like the *Deep Encounter* was hijacked."

"What gave you that idea?"

"It wasn't until this time yesterday that our security systems detected a difference in the speech pattern of Captain Burch's voice during his status reports to NUMA head-quarters. Until then the reports were accepted as genuine. We had no cause for suspicion."

"When we left the ship, all was normal."

"The last report by the genuine Captain Burch said the *Abyss Navigator* was about to be lowered in the water. We know now the hijackers boarded while you were on the bottom."

"Do you have any idea where the ship was taken?" asked Giordino.

"No," Gunn said candidly.

"It couldn't have evaporated," said Misty. "It wasn't swept into space by aliens."

"Our worst fear," Sandecker said ominously, "is that she was intentionally sunk." He pulled back from suggesting that the entire crew might be lying under the sea.

"But why?" questioned Giordino. "What earthly good is an oceanographic survey ship to pirates? There is no treasure on board. The ship can't be used for smuggling. It's too slow and too recognizable. Where's the motive?"

"Motive . . ." Pitt let the word slide off his tongue and hang in the air. "The same people who torched the cruise ship and then sank her wanted to prevent us from discovering evidence of arson."

"Were you able to survey the wreck?" asked Gunn.

He nodded. "There's no doubt about it, the bottom was blown out of the *Emerald Dolphin* in at least six places, sending her to the bottom of the Tonga Trench."

"From what I've heard," said Sandecker, "she came within a hair of taking the tugboat with her."

Giordino said slowly, "Twenty thousand feet deep in the ocean makes for a pretty effective hiding place."

Gunn said, "The murderous scum never figured on a NUMA survey ship working in the area, one with a pair of submersibles that could go down twenty thousand feet."

Misty's eyes suddenly looked stricken. "Which brings us to the horrible possibility that everyone on the *Deep Encounter* has been killed in the cover-up."

There was silence on the yacht and ten thousand miles away in Washington. They were all loath to consider the prospect. There was no doubt in their minds that anyone who lacked a conscience about burning alive or drowning everyone on board a cruise liner would have any hesitation about sending the survey ship and its crew to the bottom of the sea.

Pitt's perspective began to focus. He considered every avenue and gambled that the pirates had not yet set their murderous plan in gear. "Rudi?"

Gunn removed his glasses and began polishing the lenses. "Yes."

"The pirates could have just as easily sunk the *Deep Encounter* after they captured it. But you say they faked voice transmissions of Burch giving his scheduled reports. Why would they have bothered to stall off any suspicion if the ship was already sunk?"

"We don't know that it wasn't sunk," said Gunn.

"Perhaps, but we saw no sign of an oil slick or debris after we broke the surface. Nor did we hear the acoustic sounds of a ship breaking up under great pressure on its passage through the extreme pressures of the deep. My guess, my fervent hope, is that they took the ship and everyone on board and hid them as bargaining chips should their plans go wrong."

"And when it begins to look like they're in the clear and not hunted," Gunn continued, "will they dispose of the proof of their crimes?"

"We can't let that happen," said Misty, distressed. "If what Dirk suggests is accurate, we only have a little time to save our friends."

"The problem is where to look," said Sandecker.

"There is no trace of it anywhere?" asked Misty.

"None."

"Not even the hijacker's vessel?"

"No," Sandecker replied helplessly.

"I'll bet I know how to find both ships," said Pitt confidently.

In Washington, Sandecker and Gunn stared at each other. "In what waters are you fishing?" the admiral inquired cautiously.

"We expand our search grid," Pitt replied.

"I don't follow," said Gunn.

"Suppose the pirate ship and our survey vessel were out of the range of the satellite cameras that were focused on a narrow path."

"I can safely say that's a given," Sandecker conceded.

"I'm assuming you widened the path on the next orbit."

"We did," Gunn admitted.

"And found no sign of either ship."

"Not a trace."

"So we still don't know where the *Deep Encounter* is, but now we know where she's not."

Sandecker pulled at his neatly trimmed beard. "I know where you're going, but your theory won't fly."

"I must side with the admiral," said Gunn. "The top speed of *Deep Encounter* is no more than fifteen knots. There is no way she could have sailed out of the original satellite camera range."

"Chief Engineer House got twenty knots out of her during our dash toward the burning cruise ship," Pitt informed him. "I admit it's a stretch, but if the hijackers had a fast ship, they might have taken our vessel in tow and increased her speed by another four to six knots."

Sandecker's voice was skeptical. "Makes no difference. Once we increased the range and path of the satellite cameras, there was still no sign of *Deep Encounter*."

Pitt played his wild card. "True, but you were looking on the water."

"Where were we supposed to look?" asked Sandecker, becoming intrigued.

"Dirk has a point," said Gunn thoughtfully. "We didn't consider focusing the cameras on land."

"Forgive me for asking," Giordino spoke up, "but what land? The nearest landmass from where the cruise liner sank is the northern tip of New Zealand."

"No," said Pitt quietly, for effect, "there are the Kermadec Islands no more than two hundred nautical miles to the south, an easy eight-hour sail at a speed of twenty-five knots." He turned and looked at Cussler.

"Are you familiar with the Kermadec Islands?"

"I've cruised around them," answered Cussler. "Not much to look at. Three small islands and l'Esperance Rock. Raoul Island is the largest, but it's only a pile of rock thirteen miles square with lava rock cliffs that rise steeply up to Mount Mumukai."

"Any inhabitants or settlement?"

"There's a small meteorological and communications station, but it's automated. Scientists only visit it every six months to check and repair the equipment. The only permanent residents are goats and rats."

"Is there a harbor large enough to anchor a small ship?"

"More like a lagoon," replied Cussler, "but it's a safe anchorage for two, maybe three small ships."

"How about foliage for camouflage?"

"Raoul is lush and heavily wooded. They could cover a pair of small ships well enough for someone who wasn't looking real carefully."

Pitt said into the phone, "You heard?"

"I heard," said Sandecker. "I'll ask that the next satellite that passes over that part of the Pacific aim its cameras on the Kermadecs. How do I contact you?"

Pitt was about to ask Cussler for his communications code, but the old man had already written the numbers down and handed them to him on a slip of paper. Pitt informed Sandecker and punched off the connection.

"Is there any possibility you could make a detour by the Kermadecs?" Pitt asked.

The blue-green eyes glistened. "You have something devious in mind?"

"You wouldn't happen to have a bottle of tequila on board?"

Cussler nodded solemnly. "I do. A case of the best. A little touch of the blue agave now and then keeps me quick and nimble."

After the glasses were filled with Porfirio tequila — Misty preferred a margarita — Pitt told the old man what he had in mind, but only as much as he thought was advisable under the circumstances. After all, he thought as he looked around the elegant yacht, no one in his right mind would risk destroying such a beautiful vessel in a desperate scheme.

18

The malachite green sea merged with the peridot green water flowing through the channel of the large lagoon that nestled between the volcanic lava cliffs of Raoul Island. Once inside the narrow channel, the lagoon widened into a small but respectable anchorage. Beyond was the tributary mouth of a stream that ran down the rugged slopes of Mount Mumukai and into the waters of the lagoon. The sandy, horseshoe-shaped beach was interspersed with sea-worn black lava rock and framed by a marching army of coco palms.

From the sea, only a tiny section of the lagoon could be seen through the chasm whose cliffs rose on each side of the channel. It was like peering through a telescope into a distant narrow slit. High atop the west side of the entrance, more than three hundred feet above the surf crashing

266

against the shore, a small shack built of palm fronds perched dangerously close to the edge. The native look was a facade. Beneath the palm fronds were walls built of concrete blocks. The interior was air-conditioned, and the windows were tinted. A security guard sat inside a comfortable little house, studying the vast expanse of ocean with a large pair of binoculars mounted on a stand for any sign of a ship. He sat in a soft executive chair before a computer, radio and a VCR with a monitor. A chain smoker, he had heaped an ashtray with dead butts. Across from him, neatly stacked in a rack against one wall, were four missile launchers and two automatic rifles. With this arsenal, he could have held off a small navy trying to force its way into the lagoon.

Thirty years old, wiry and in good physical shape, he stared almost vacantly at the brilliant sea as he rubbed a hand over the stubble of new beard growth. He was blond and blue-eyed and a former Special Forces veteran, hired by the in-house security department of a vast corporate empire about which he knew little and cared even less. His assignments covered the world and occasionally included assassination, but he was paid and paid well. That's all that mattered.

He yawned and changed the discs in his

CD player. His taste was eclectic and ran from classical to soft rock. He had just pushed the play button when his eye caught a movement around the outcropping of rock that fell off just beyond his security shack. He swung the binoculars and focused on a bright blue-and-white object that was coming very fast over the water.

It was a yacht, the strangest-looking yacht he had ever seen; not a sailboat but a twin-hulled catamaran power cruiser, and it was cutting through the sun-danced water at what he guessed as close to forty knots. He rubbed his eyes and stared through the big, powerful binoculars again.

The boat was a good seventy feet, he estimated. He couldn't decide if he loved her design or hated it. The more he examined her lines, the more elegant and exotic she appeared. She reminded him of a pair of ice skates cut down and molded together with a circular wheelhouse on the top. On the upper open deck, two people, a man and woman, lounged in a Jacuzzi, drinking out of tall glasses and laughing. All the craft's windows were tinted, and he could not see any suggestion of other crew members or passengers.

He turned to the radio, switched on the transmitter and began speaking. "This is Pirate. I have a private yacht approaching from the northeast."

"The northeast, you say," replied a voice like sandpaper.

"Probably on a cruise from Tahiti to New Zealand."

"Any sign of weapons or armed personnel?"

"None."

"She doesn't look threatening?" asked the rough voice.

"Not unless you consider two naked people in a Jacuzzi threatening."

"Is she making toward the channel?"

The security guard examined the heading of the twin bows as the yacht sped closer. "She looks to be going past."

"Stay on the air and report any suspicious movement. If she turns into the channel, you know what you have to do."

The guard glanced at one of the missile launchers. "A pity to destroy such a handsome boat." He swung in his chair and gazed at the boat through the glasses again, somewhat pleased at seeing it continue on a course past the channel. He watched until it became a tiny speck in the distance. Then he called over the radio again. "This is Pirate. The yacht is gone. It appears as if she dropped anchor in the open lagoon on the south end of Macaulay Island."

"Then she's harmless," said a rough voice.

"It would seem so."

"Watch her lights after dark and make sure she stays put."

"I suspect she settled in for the night. Her passengers and crew are probably going to barbecue steaks on the beach. They just look like yachtsmen on a South Pacific cruise."

"I'll fly a reconnaissance in the helicopter and see if you're right."

Misty and Giordino were not naked in the hot tub. They were wearing swimsuits provided by Cussler. They were, however, sipping rum collinses as the boat cruised under the steep palisades of Raoul Island. Cussler and Pitt were not as lucky. The old man sat at the helm station with a chart in his lap, eyeing the depth sounder and examining the bottom coral reefs that could have sliced the *Periwinkle*'s twin hulls like razor blades through cardboard. Pitt had the worst job of all. He lay sweating under a pile of pillows and towels on the lower lounge deck, videotaping the guardhouse at the top of the cliffs overlooking the channel entrance.

Once the yacht was anchored, they all settled into the main salon and gazed at the monitor while Pitt played the tape on the VCR. The telephoto lens on the camera, combined with the video enhancement, revealed the guard through the windows of the guardhouse in slightly fuzzy detail but clear enough to distinguish him peering at them through a pair of huge binoculars. Added to the video was the soundtrack of the conversation between the guard and the coarse voice of his colleague somewhere in the Raoul Island lagoon, as traced and recorded by Cussler's high-tech communications systems.

"We fooled them," said Misty, unhesitating.

"Lucky we didn't attempt to run up the channel with all flags flying," Giordino said, pressing a bottle of cold beer against his forehead.

"They didn't give the impression they take kindly to strangers," Pitt agreed.

As if to affirm his statement, the thump of rotors and roar of engine exhaust sounded throughout the cabin as a helicopter flew over the yacht.

"The man said he was going to reconnoiter us," said Pitt. "What say we go out and wave to them?"

A red-and-yellow-painted helicopter, with its registration number and ownership lettering on its fuselage hidden under duct tape, hovered no more than a hundred feet in the air and slightly off the stern of the *Periwinkle*. Two men wearing flowered shirts peered down at the yacht.

Pitt lay sprawled on a couch on the lounge deck while Giordino stood partially under the deck overhang videotaping the aircraft with the camera hidden under his shirt and armpit. Misty and Cussler stood beside the Jacuzzi and waved to the men above. Pitt held up a glass and motioned for the pilots to join them. Seeing a woman and an older man with gray hair and beard must have dismissed their suspicions. The pilot of the helicopter waved back and banked the aircraft around the yacht and headed back to Raoul Island, satisfied that the tourists were no menace.

As soon as the craft was a speck in the blue sky, they all headed back into the saloon. Giordino pulled a videotape from the camera under his shirt and slid it into the VCR. The zoom focus clearly showed a sandy-haired man with a grizzled beard at the controls and a black man flying as copilot.

"Now we have faces to go with the plot," mused Giordino.

Cussler clicked off the remote. "What happens now?"

"As soon as it's dark, we build a small raft and attach lights on it so it looks like a boat lit up from a distance. Then we sail back under cover of the cliffs near the channel just out of sight of the guard above the cliffs. The boat won't be detected because the video shows no indication of radar equipment. Then Al and I will go in the water and take a swim up the channel to the lagoon, a little fishing expedition to have a look around. If we're right, and the *Deep Encounter* is hidden under camouflage netting, we sneak aboard, overpower the hijackers, free our friends and sail off into the blue."

"That's the plan?" asked Giordino, his eyes squinting as if seeing a mirage in the desert.

"That's the plan," Pitt echoed.

Misty looked dumbstruck. "You can't be serious? The two of you going up against fifty or more armed hijackers? That's the craziest scheme I've ever heard."

Pitt shrugged. "I admit I may have oversimplified things just a shade. But I really don't see any other way of handling the job."

"We could call up the Aussies and have them send a special force," suggested Cussler. "They can be here in twenty-four hours."

"We may not have the time," said Pitt. "If the hijackers haven't sunk the *Deep Encounter* and everybody on it by now, chances are they'll do it tonight after dark. Twenty-four hours from now may be too late."

"It's madness to throw your lives away," Misty persisted.

"We have no choice," Pitt said firmly. "Time is not on our side."

"What about weapons?" asked Giordino, as casually as if he were asking the price of an ice-cream cone.

"I have a pair of automatic rifles I carry for protection," offered Cussler. "But I can't say how well they and the ammo will perform after being dragged a mile under water."

Pitt shook his head. "Thank you, but it's better we swim in unencumbered. As far as firepower, we'll worry about it when the time comes."

"What about dive equipment? I have four filled air tanks and two regulators."

"The less equipment the better. Dive equipment would only hinder us once we came ashore. We'll snorkel into the lagoon. Nobody could spot us in the dark from twenty feet away."

"You'll have a long swim," said Cussler. "From where I'll moor the boat, the inside of the lagoon is over a mile."

"We'll be lucky to get in by midnight," muttered Giordino.

"I can cut your time by two hours."

Pitt looked at Cussler. "How?"

"I have a dive thruster that will pull you through the water. You can use it to propel you both in tandem."

"That will be a great help, thank you."

"Is there nothing I can say to talk you out of this senselessness?" Misty pleaded.

"No," said Pitt, his lips spread slightly in a comforting smile. "This thing has to be done. There wouldn't be a security facility at the entrance to the channel if there wasn't something inside someone wanted to hide. We have to find out if it's the *Deep Encounter*."

"And if you're wrong?"

The smile was gone suddenly, and Pitt's face became tense. "If we're wrong, then our friends on board the ship will die because we failed to save them."

Beginning just after sunset, it took the three men two hours to tie several palm tree trunks together into a raft and then construct a rough outline of the *Periwinkle* with framing scrounged from driftwood. For a finishing touch, a small battery was connected to a string of lights on the framework. Then the raft was anchored on the shore side of the yacht.

"Not a bad facsimile if I do say so," Cussler assented.

"It ain't pretty," said Giordino, "but it should fool the security guard sitting in his little hovel five miles away."

Pitt splashed seawater on his face to wash away the sweat brought on by the humidity. "We'll turn on the lights of the raft at the same moment we turn off the lights of the yacht."

Within minutes, Cussler engaged the *Periwinkle*'s big engines and eased the yacht forward as he pressed the switch to the winch that raised the anchor. Then he shifted the lights to the raft and threw the yacht into darkness. He ran the yacht out past the reef, keeping an eye on the depth sounder, gauging the depth of the coral that lurked below the surface like malicious killer teeth, waiting to send the yacht sinking into the depths beyond.

He steered toward Raoul Island by radar, watching carefully to see if the boat was stirring up any phosphorescence in her wake. He kept the speed down to ten knots, and was thankful that the star-carpeted sky held no moon. Pitt joined him at the helm station with Misty, who had resigned herself to the operation and had prepared snacks in the galley. She passed them around and sat next to Al, who was wearing headphones, trying to mimic the gravelly voice recorded during the security guard's conversation.

Cussler laid out the chart showing the water depths around the island and aimed the twin bows toward the tiny light high on the cliffs that came from the security guard's little house. "I'll bring us inside the outcropping of rocks just in front of the channel," he explained. "From there you'll have to rely on the thruster. Keep well clear of the surf pounding on the cliffs until you reach calm water."

For the first time, Cussler was showing something approaching trepidation. He rarely threw a glimpse out the window into the pitch-black night. He reserved his attention for an occasional glance at the compass. He steered the yacht almost exclusively by depth sounder and radar, seated extravagantly, his hands resting on the joystick and computer trackball. He slid open a window and heard the unmistakable sound of surf crashing against solid rock.

Pitt could hear it, too. They were behind the rock outcropping and out of the security guard's line of sight. The water beyond the surf line was incredibly calm. Cussler pressed a button on the joystick that was the throttle and decreased the speed to a slow crawl. Finally satisfied that he was as near to the rocks as he dared go, he set the engines in neutral and turned to Pitt, the expression in his eyes saying, "This is not a good idea," but voicing nothing.

Studying the craggy bottom only fifteen feet below the *Periwinkle*'s twin hulls on the depth sounder and staring thoughtfully at his drift readings, he let go of the anchor. As soon as the boat was safely moored with her bows dipping into the incoming tide, he nodded.

"This is as far as I go."

"How long can you stay?" asked Pitt.

"I'd like to say until you return, but the tide turns in another three hours and twenty minutes. Then I'll have to move farther off the shore or risk losing the boat and steer back around the island to stay out of the guard's view."

"How will we find you in the dark?"

"I have an underwater radio transmitter I use to study fish reactions to different sounds. In two hours, I'll begin playing a Meat Loaf recording."

Misty looked at him. "You listen to Meat Loaf?"

Cussler laughed. "Can't an old rooster like rock?"

"Does he attract sharks?" asked Giordino warily.

Cussler shook his head. "They prefer Tony Bennett."

Pitt and Giordino pulled on borrowed fins and masks. Cussler lowered the stern ladder and stood back. He patted both of them on the shoulder. "Remember, stay clear of the rocks at the entrance of the channel and then wait for the swells to carry you inside. No sense draining the thruster's batteries unnecessarily." Then he paused almost solemnly. "Good luck. I'll wait as long as I can."

They dropped into the warm, ink black water with only a slight splash and swam a short distance from the boat, Giordino following in Pitt's wake. Pitt guessed the water temperature at close to eighty degrees. There was a slight offshore breeze and a mild chop came with the incoming tide. After stroking for several minutes, they paused and looked back. Once past one hundred feet, the *Periwinkle* became invisible. Pitt held up his wrist and studied the luminescent needle and degree markings on the compass lent to him by the old man. He tapped Giordino on the head and motioned into the distance. Giordino wrapped his arms around Pitt's legs and hung on as the thruster was switched on; the motor hummed and the jets began pulling them through the water at nearly three knots.

Pitt could only navigate by the little compass and by the sound of the surf that beat against the rock cliffs with a low, sullen boom. The menacing rocks could have been a hundred yards away or two hundred. There was no way of telling in the darkness.

Then his ears distinguished two separate booms, suggesting that the waves were striking on opposites sides of the channel. He twisted the thruster and let it pull them toward the island until the surf was heard thundering on his right and left, but not ahead. Then, as instructed by Cussler, he switched off the thruster and allowed the waves to carry them through the channel entrance. It was sound advice.

There were no giant plunging breakers between the steep walls of the channel. Because of the deeper water in midchannel, and with no obstructions, the surf here merely rolled forward without building and curling under, sweeping them safely through the rocks as if they were corks.

Pitt floated facedown, legs outspread, as relaxed as a turtle sleeping on the surface. His breathing was slow and steady through the snorkel. Thanks to the thruster, they were nowhere near the point of exhaustion. Giordino had released his grasp momentarily and was drifting alongside Pitt.

Neither man rolled over and looked up to see if they had been spotted. They didn't have to bother. If they couldn't see a guard standing on the edge of the cliff, no guard could have seen them in the darkened waters far below. Belatedly, Pitt began to wonder if the hijackers had posted guards around the lagoon. He doubted they would be that security-conscious. It was next to impossible to scale the cliffs surrounding the island in the dark and then penetrate the thick jungle while hiking over jagged lava rock. He felt certain the only pair of eyes watching for intruders was that of the guard over the channel entrance.

From the brief glimpse he'd had of the lagoon through the channel hours earlier when the *Periwinkle* had passed the entrance, he estimated that it stretched in a straight line approximately a third of a mile from the sea. Feeling the impetus of the waves slacken until they were little more than two feet high, he alerted Giordino to hang on as he engaged the thruster again.

In less than fifteen minutes, the stars above opened and spread across the sky as they passed under the high cliffs into the open lagoon. Pitt angled the thruster off to the side of the beach and kept the power on until he could feel sand beneath his feet. Only then did he shut it down.

There was no indication of inhabited structures on the beach, but the lagoon was far from deserted. Two vessels lay moored side by side in the middle of the lagoon. Their shapes and outlines were indistinguishable in the dark. As Pitt suspected, they were made even more formless by camouflage netting that was draped over both ships. But for a few dim lights emitting from their ports, they were unrecognizable. Without a closer look, it was impossible to identify the *Deep Encounter* in the black night.

"Take off your face mask," Pitt whispered to Giordino. "The lights might reflect off our lenses."

Leaving the thruster on the beach, they swam toward the larger of the two ships.

She was anchored with her bow facing into the channel. The vessel had a graceful raked bow, the same as the research vessel, but they had to be positive. Without the slightest hesitation, Pitt pulled off his fins, handed them to Giordino and began climbing the anchor chain. It was damp but reasonably free of rust and slime. He pulled himself up until he was even with the hawse pipe and hung there for a full minute.

From the light from an open port, he could just barely make out the name on the welded letters on the bow.

They read, *Deep Encounter.*

19

The hawse pipe was a good ten feet below the top edge of the bow gunnels. Without a rope and a grappling hook, there was no way Pitt and Giordino could climb onto the foredeck. The rest of the hull held out little hope of boarding either. No protrusions beckoned as a means of climbing on board. Pitt cursed his lack of planning for such an elementary contingency.

He lowered himself back down the anchor chain. "She's *Deep Encounter*," he informed Giordino quietly.

Giordino gazed upward, and his expression in the dim light was one of puzzlement. "How do we get aboard without a gangplank or a ladder?"

"We don't."

"Naturally, you have an alternate plan," he said mechanically.

"Of course."

"Give me the bad news."

Pitt's slight grin was lost in the darkness. "The hijacker's ship is smaller. We can probably go over the stern, then work our way on board *Deep Encounter*."

Pitt felt comfortable, on an even keel again. He'd guessed right. The pirates' vessel was not a sailing ship bristling with muzzle-loading guns but a 135-foot utility work boat, whose stern was not only low enough for them to struggle aboard but showed them all the consideration in the world by providing a diver's boarding ladder and a small platform.

Giordino murmured, "I hope we find a length of good old-fashioned pipe to dent heads with. I feel naked with only my bare hands."

"I'm not concerned," Pitt said airily. "I've seen what you can do with those big hams. You forget. We have the element of surprise. They won't be expecting visitors, especially disreputable characters like us, skulking through the back door."

Pitt was in the act of climbing over the stern railing when Giordino's fingers dug into his arm. "What's wrong?" he muttered, rubbing his pulped forearm.

"Someone's standing in the shadows by the aft deckhouse, smoking a cigarette," Giordino spoke softly in Pitt's ear.

Pitt slowly raised his head until he could

peek across the work deck. Giordino's remarkable night vision was on target. A barely seen figure was outlined in the darkness only by the movement of his puffing on a cigarette while he leaned over the railing, enjoying the tropical air. He did not appear alert, but as though he was lost in his thoughts.

Quiet as a wraith, Giordino climbed over the stern railing, hoping the water dripping from his body couldn't be heard above a slight breeze rocking the fronds of the palm trees, padded silently across the deck and hooked those big hands around the man's neck, cutting off all air to the lungs. There was a brief struggle, and then the body went limp. With only a slight whisper of sound, he dragged the hijacker back to the stern and behind a large winch.

Pitt searched through the man's clothing, discovering a large folding knife and a snub-nosed revolver. "We're in business," he proclaimed.

"He's still breathing," said Giordino. "What do we do with him?"

"Lay him on the diver's boarding platform out of sight."

Giordino nodded and easily lifted the hijacker over the railing and dropped him in a heap on the boarding platform, where he came within inches of rolling into the sea and drowning. "Evil deed done."

"Let's hope he stays in slumberland for the next hour."

"Guaranteed." Giordino stared into the darkness, his eyes probing the open decks. "How many of them do you think there are?"

"NUMA has two similar work boats of about the same size. They accommodate a crew of fifteen, but they can carry more than a hundred passengers."

Pitt passed the knife to Giordino, who studied it morosely. "Why can't I have the gun?"

"You're the one who always watches old Errol Flynn movies."

"He used a sword, not a cheap switch-blade."

"Just pretend."

Without another word of complaint from Giordino, they crossed the expansive cargo and work deck at a steady, unhurried pace to a hatch on the aft bulkhead. The hatch door was closed to take full advantage of the work boat's air-conditioning. This might have been a time to fear the unknown, but that was unacceptable. There was only the ice-cold dread that they had arrived too late to save the men and women of the *Deep Encounter*. Pitt's mind registered the worst, but he disregarded it, just as he disregarded any concern about being killed.

They halted before coming to the gangplank between the two ships and sneaked a look inside one of the ports that had a light issuing through it. Pitt counted twenty-two of the hijackers sitting around in a large mess room playing cards, reading or watching satellite television. There were enough guns stacked around to start a revolution. None seemed the least bit wary of uninvited visitors, nor did they display any anxiety that their prisoners might escape. The mere sight made Pitt extremely uneasy. The hijackers appeared extremely lax, too lax to have fifty hostages on their hands.

"Remind me not to hire any of these guys to guard my worldly goods," mumbled Giordino.

"They're dressed more like professional mercenaries than backwater pirates," muttered Pitt.

He shrugged off any inclination to seek revenge on the hijackers aboard their own vessel. One six-shot revolver and a knife against more than twenty armed men hardly offered desirable odds of success. Their primary objective was to see if anyone was still alive on the research ship, then save them if at all possible. He and Giordino flattened themselves against the port superstructure for a few moments, listening and peering into the darkness. Hearing and seeing nothing menacing, they moved soundlessly across the deck before Pitt suddenly stopped.

Giordino froze alongside and whispered, "See something?"

Pitt pointed to the wide patch of painted cardboard that was crudely taped on the side of the superstructure. "Let's see what they're hiding."

Slowly, with infinite caution, he peeled off the duct tape that held the cardboard on the metal side. When he had removed most of it, he curled the end back and stared at the markings that were barely visible under the muted light falling through the ports.

He could just discern the stylized image of a three-headed dog with a serpent for its tail. Directly beneath was the word CERBERUS. It meant nothing to him, so he pushed the cardboard cover back in place and retaped it.

"See anything?" Giordino asked.

"Enough."

They continued to the narrow metal gangplank laid between the two ships and crossed warily, half expecting hijackers to step out of the shadows and blast away at them with automatic weapons.

They stepped over the water onto the deck of the survey ship without encountering trouble, and paused in the shadows. Now Pitt was on home ground. He knew every inch of the *Deep Encounter* and could easily make his way along her decks blindfolded.

Giordino cupped his hand and spoke softly into Pitt's ear. "Do you want to split up?"

"No," Pitt whispered. "Better we stick together. Let's start in the pilothouse and work down."

They could have gone up the outside stairways to the pilothouse, but elected to stay out of sight of any of the hijackers who might step outside the mess room and spot them. Instead, they slipped through a hatch and moved up a companionway four decks to the pilothouse. They found it dark and empty. Pitt went into the communications room and closed the door, while Giordino stood guard outside. He picked up the Globalstar phone and dialed Sandecker's cell phone number. While the connection went through, he checked his orange-faced Doxa dive watch. The dial read two minutes past ten. He mentally adjusted the eight-hour difference with Washington time. It would be six in the morning there. The admiral would be out running his daily routine of five miles.

Sandecker answered on his global phone. After running three miles he was still breathing normally. Time was too short for Pitt to say anything vague to throw off anyone homing in on the call. He gave a brief, concise report on finding the *Deep Encounter* and gave its exact location.

"My crew and scientific team?" asked the admiral, as if they were members of his immediate family.

"The issue is still in doubt," answered Pitt, repeating Major Deverieux's famous message just before the fall of Wake Island. "I will contact you when I have a positive answer." Then he closed the connection.

He stepped from the communications room. "See or hear anything?"

"Quiet as a grave."

"I wish," he said moodily, "you wouldn't use the word grave."

They left the pilothouse and dropped down to the next deck below. It was the same story. The staterooms and hospital were as silent as body trays in a morgue. Pitt entered his stateroom, fumbled in a drawer and was surprised to find his faithful old Colt automatic right where he'd left it. He shoved it under the waistband of his shorts and handed the revolver to Giordino, who took it without a word. Next, Pitt retrieved a small penlight, flicked it on and swung the beam around the room. Nothing had been touched. The only item not where he'd left it in the closet was Dr. Egan's leather case. It was sitting open on the bed.

Giordino found the same scene in his stateroom. None of his belongings had been searched or moved about.

"Nothing about these guys makes sense,"

said Giordino quietly. "I never heard of hijacking pirates who weren't interested in plunder."

Pitt aimed the light into the passageway. "Let's move on."

They continued down the companionway to the deck that contained eight more staterooms, the mess room, galley, conference room and lounge. Dishes with decaying food still sat on the mess table, magazines were strewn on tables and couches in the lounge as if recently cast off by their readers. Cigarettes that had burned to their filters lay in ashtrays in the conference room. Pots and pans still sat on the galley stove, their contents turning green. It was as though everyone on board the ship had vanished in a puff of smoke.

How long Pitt and Giordino searched the area desperately hoping to find a trace of life they couldn't be sure. Maybe five minutes, maybe as long as ten. Maybe they were waiting to hear a voice or a sound, any sound — or maybe they were just fearful of not finding answers. Pitt removed the .45 from his waistband and held it at his side, leery of firing a shot even if attacked that would alert the horde of hijackers relaxing on their ship.

As they dropped down to the engine and generating room, Pitt was beginning to believe his worst fears were realized by the total lack of security guards. They should have been standing watch over their prisoners, if indeed there was still anyone on board to imprison. And then there was the absence of lights. Guards would not sit around in darkness. His despondency deepened until they passed the engineering-deck staterooms and found lights on in the chief engineer's office.

"At last," muttered Giordino, "someone wants light to see by."

At the end of the passageway was the door to the engine and generating room. They took up positions opposite each other along the bulkheads and approached the door. From ten feet away they could hear the faint murmur of voices. Their eyes met for a brief instant. For a few moments, Pitt put his ear to the steel door and listened. The voices seemed to be taunting and heavy with scorn. Occasionally came the sound of laughter.

Pitt pushed the long metal door handle a fraction of an inch. It moved noiselessly. He made a mental note to thank Chief Engineer House for having the hatch door latches oiled periodically. He eased the handle downward with infinite slowness so it wouldn't be noticed on the other side. When the handle reached the end of its stop, he gently cracked open the door the way he'd have done it if he knew that inside were a dozen alien monsters who digested humans for nourishment.

They clearly heard the voices now. There were four of them. Two came from strangers, but the other two were as familiar as his own. Pitt's heart leaped within his chest. The voices were not indulging in idle conversation. The two unknowns seemed to be taunting the others.

"Won't be long now and the whole lot of you will see what it's like to drown."

"Yeah, it's nothing like falling asleep in the Arctic," said his partner nastily. "Your head feels like it's being filled with exploding firecrackers. Your eyes pop from your head. Your ears burst like they were punctured with icepicks. Your throat feels like it's being torn out and your lungs feel like they're being swabbed with nitric acid. You'll have a blast."

"You sick scum," spat Captain Burch.

"Talking like that in front of women, it only proves that you're nothing but a bunch of degenerate animals," came the voice of Chief Engineer House.

"Hey, Sam, did you know you were a degenerate?"

"Not since last week."

The last remark was followed by deep laughter.

"You kill us," said Burch angrily, "and every investigative force in the world will surely track you down and hang your butts higher than a kite."

"Not without evidence of the crime," the hijacker called Sam said with a sneer.

"You'll just be another one of the thousands of ships that sailed off and were lost with all hands."

"Please?" came the voice of one of the female scientists. "We all have loved ones at home. You can't do this terrible thing."

"Sorry, lady," said Sam coldly. "To the people who pay our wages, your lives aren't worth two cents."

Sam's partner said, "Our crew should be coming aboard in another half hour." Then he paused and looked beyond Pitt's vision. "Two hours after that, you NUMA people will get to study all them denizens of the deep first hand."

From his limited view through the crack in the hatch, Pitt could see that the hijackers were holding automatic weapons in the ready position. Pitt nodded at Giordino. Both men crouched forward and prepared for a fight, as they opened the door and walked in the engine room shoulder to shoulder.

The two hijackers sensed the movement behind them, but they didn't bother to turn, thinking it was their friends showing up early for the execution. Sam said, "You guys are early. What's the rush?"

"We've been ordered to set a course for Guam," said Giordino, in a reasonably good imitation of the hijacker with the gravelly voice.

"That's it," said Sam, laughing. "You people better start praying. It's almost time to meet your maker —"

That was as far as he got. Giordino picked him up off the deck by his head and smashed it against a bulkhead, as Pitt whipped his .45 in a sidearm swing against the other guard's jaw, sending him crumpling in a heap on the deck.

Then it was fiesta time. Saturday night all over again. All that was missing were the balloons and champagne.

They were all there. Sitting on the floor around the ship's generators with their legs chained together like galley slaves was the entire company of *Deep Encounter*. Their ankles were encased in steel bands attached to a long chain that was locked to the mounting of the main generator. Pitt made a quick count, while everyone sat there in shock at seeing the two men they'd thought were lost and gone forever. Burch, House, the crew and scientific team looked like they were in a dream. Then they began coming to their feet and were within a twinkling of launching into wild cheering when Pitt threw up his hands and hissed, "Quiet! For God's sake, remain silent or we'll have an army of armed guards rushing in here."

"Where in Hades did you come from?" asked Burch.

"From a very luxurious yacht," answered Giordino. "But that's another story." He looked at Chief Engineer House. "What have you got to cut the chain?"

House pointed to a side compartment. "In the toolroom. You'll find a pair of cable cutters hanging on the bulkhead."

"Release the crew first," Pitt said to Giordino. "We've got to get the ship under way before the hijackers come on board."

Giordino returned in thirty seconds and began feverishly cutting the chain. In the meantime, Pitt had rushed up to the outer deck and made sure the rescue had gone undiscovered. The decks of the pirate ship were still empty. As far as he could determine, they were all still in the mess room licking their chops like hungry hyenas, he thought, in happy anticipation of sending the *Deep Encounter* and its people to a watery grave.

When he returned, Chief House and his engine room crew were already manning the main control station in preparation for getting the survey ship under way. "This is where I leave you," he said to Burch.

The captain looked blank. Even Giordino turned and stared at Pitt queerly.

"There is a guard in a house on the cliffs

above the entrance to the channel. I'm guessing that besides keeping a lookout for intruders, he has enough firepower to stop any ship leaving the lagoon."

"What brought you to that conclusion?" asked Giordino.

"If one didn't know better, you'd think the hijackers were guarding a flower garden against marauding deer. Two men guarding fifty, the rest sitting around like they were on vacation? Not likely. They have to be confident that this ship could never get through to the open sea if the crew somehow managed to regain control. The channel is a good four hundred feet deep in its center. *Deep Encounter* could easily be sent to the bottom and never be found, while the pirate ship would still have plenty of water under her keel to sail out of the lagoon."

"It's a black night," said Burch. "We might be able to sneak out to sea without the guard spotting us."

"No good," said Pitt. "The minute you get under way, the hijackers on board their ship will know about it and give chase. They're bound to get wise when the anchor comes up and the engines begin pounding. The first thing they'd do is alert the channel entrance guard. I've got to get there first and remove the threat."

"I'll come with you," Giordino said firmly.

Pitt shook his head. "You're the best man to repel boarders before the ship slips away."

"Horatio at the bridge — that's me."

"You'll never get there in time," said House. "It's a good half mile uphill through the jungle."

Pitt held up his small penlight. "This will light my way. Besides, the hijackers have to have a well-beaten path between here and the guardhouse."

Giordino shook Pitt's hand. "Good luck, pal."

"Same to you."

And then Pitt was gone.

20

It was odd the way the crew hurried about their duties as calmly as if they were leaving the dock in San Francisco. There were no wasted words. It was equally odd that there was no discussion about the danger they were in. There was no apprehension, no foreboding. The scientists, bent on keeping out from underfoot, went to their staterooms and stayed there.

Captain Burch crouched low on the bridge wing, staring through the darkness at the hijackers' work boat. He held the ship's portable phone to his mouth and said softly, "Ready when you are, Chief."

"Then bring up the anchor," replied House. "Soon as it's off the bottom, call me and I'll give her every pound of torque these engines got in them."

"Stay tuned," said Burch. There was a time when anchors were brought up by crewmen operating switches and levers. All Burch had to do with the modern systems on board the *Deep Encounter* was punch a code into the computer. Then it was all automatic. But there was nothing he could do, there was nothing anybody could do, to muffle the rattle and clank as the chain scraped through the hawse hole into the chain locker.

His years of experience told Burch the instant that the anchor broke free of the bottom. "Okay, Chief. Full speed. Take us the hell out of here."

Down below in his kingdom, House's hands played over the control panel. He felt a measure of pleased satisfaction as he felt the propellers bite the water and drag down the stern as the ship lurched forward.

Giordino took the automatic rifles gathered from the two hijackers he and Pitt had overpowered and stationed himself behind the gunnel a few feet away from the gangplank leading to the pirate ship. He lay on the deck, one rifle held in the crook of his arm. The other rifle he laid on the deck beside him next to the revolver. He didn't fool himself into thinking he could win a heavy firefight. But his line of fire could easily keep boarders off the survey vessel once it got under way. He could have pushed the gangplank between the two ships into the water, but thought better of making any unnecessary sound. It would fall of its own accord after the *Deep Encounter* began to move away.

He felt the vibrations through the deck as Chief Engineer House switched on the big generators and set the diesel electric engines at full speed. Two of the survey ship's crewmen crawled along the deck under the steel gunnel shields and cast off the mooring lines to the work boat from the starboard bollards, before scrambling back inside the undercover of the superstructure.

Now comes the fun part, Giordino thought to himself, as he heard the clatter from the anchor chain. To the people on board *Deep Encounter*, the sound came like twenty hammers striking an anvil. True to expectations, three of the hijackers rushed out of the mess room to see what the noise was about.

Confused at seeing the anchor of the *Deep Encounter* being raised and unaware that their partners in crime had been subdued, one started yelling at the top of his voice. "Stop, stop! You can't leave ahead of schedule. Not without a crew!"

It was not in Giordino's nature to lie quiet. "Don't need no crew," he said, in a grating voice, still mimicking the frog-throated hijacker. "I'm gonna do the job myself."

There was growing confusion as more of the hijackers burst out onto the deck. Then a familiar rasping voice shouted out, "Who are you?"

"Sam!"

"You're not Sam. Where is he?"

Giordino could feel the beat of the engines increase as the ship began to make headway. Another few seconds and the gangplank would be pulled off the ship. "Sam sez you're a drooling imbecile who can't be trusted to raise a toilet seat."

Curses and shouts erupted as a crowd of hijackers made a run for the gangplank. Two of them made it and were halfway across when Giordino took careful aim and shot them in the knees. One hijacker fell backward on the work boat, the other sagged, clutching the railing on the gangplank, crying out in pain. At that moment, the end of the gangplank fell away as the survey ship got under way and began her dash through the channel.

The hijackers rallied in the blink of an eye. Before the *Deep Encounter* had covered a hundred yards, the anchor was hoisted on the work boat and her stern dug in the water as she leaped to the pursuit. A volley of shots rang out and echoed off the lava rock hills, answered by Giordino, who unleashed several shots through the bridge windshield of the work boat.

Rounding the bend into the channel, the survey ship was temporarily out of sight of the hijackers' guns. Giordino took the lull in the firing to run up the stairs to the pilothouse.

"They're not happy campers," he said to Burch, who was manning the helm.

"All they can do is bounce bullets off us," Burch said through teeth clenched on a pipe that was turned upside down. "They won't be boarding us as easily as they did the first time."

They were pounding through the channel now. House was running the big electric diesels as fast as they could turn. The channel looked like a black pit. Only the vague shapes of the cliffs soaring above them, silhouetted against the stars, offered any visual sense of direction, but Delgado was bent over the radar screen quietly giving course changes. Everyone else in the pilothouse was casting anxious glances through the rear ports as the lights of the work boat came into view as she entered the channel.

She was coming on at nearly twice the speed of the *Deep Encounter*. Black and sinister in the night, she loomed against the ragged outline of the palm trees on shore. Then all eyes turned and looked upward toward the steep cliffs and the tiny light that shone from the security guard's watch house. All in the pilothouse wondered if Pitt could get there before they reached the channel entrance. Only Giordino seemed confident, as he blasted the last of his ammunition at the rapidly approaching work boat.

The path, if you could call it that, was barely a foot wide and twisted tortuously up the rising cliffs from the lagoon. Pitt ran as fast as he was able to push his body. His feet ached from the pounding on the lava rock and had begun to bleed. He had worn only sweat socks under the dive fins he'd borrowed from the old man, and they were soon reduced to shreds. He ran hard, his heart pounding faster with every stride, never once reducing his pace to a trot. The sweat quickly burst from his pores and ran down his face and upper torso in streams.

He shaded the penlight with his hand to keep the beam from being seen by the guard in his watch house. It was during times like this that he wished he had indulged in more workout projects. Sandecker could have made the run without breathing hard, but Pitt's only exercise was his physically active life. He was gasping now and his feet felt as if they were treading on hot coals. He threw a quick glance back over his shoulder at hearing the sound of gunfire. He was confident that his friend of thirty years would never allow any attackers past the gangplank. The movement of the lights shining through the ports and flickering on the waters of the lagoon told him the *Deep Encounter* was under way. The shouting that echoed up the rock walls also told him the pirate ship was rapidly taking up the chase. Then came more gunfire as Giordino peppered the pursuing ship's bridge.

He was less than fifty yards from the guardhouse. He slowed to a walk and then froze in position as he saw a shadow pass in front of the light streaming from a window. The watch guard had come out of his house and was standing on the edge of the cliff, staring down at the survey ship surging through the channel. Pitt moved forward, making no attempt at concealment. He ran crouched from behind the guard, whose concentration was focused on the events unfolding below. The door of the guardhouse was open, and enough light filtered out to reveal that the guard was holding some kind of weapon in his hands. Either he was alerted by the shattering echo of the gunfire in the lagoon, or he was warned by radio that the NUMA crew had somehow managed to escape in their ship and were coming through in an attempt to reach the sea.

Moving closer, Pitt tensed as he recognized the weapon as a missile launcher. There was also a small wooden crate sitting on the ground next to the guard that held a supply of missiles. He watched as the guard raised the missile launcher to his shoulder.

All thought of stealth was forgotten. He doubted that he could close the distance and rush the guard without being detected, even coming out of the night. His rush was an act of desperation. If the guard fired a missile into the *Deep Encounter* before he could be stopped, fifty innocent people would die, including his closest friend. Recklessly, he hurled himself across the final ten yards.

Pitt materialized out of the night like an angel of death, running with all the determination he could gather. The agony that erupted from his cut and torn feet was willed away as he sprinted the final few feet. He neither flinched nor faltered. Too late, the guard became aware of Pitt's assault. He was in the act of activating the firing mechanism of the missile launcher when he sensed a figure hurtling toward him. Pitt leaped and launched himself through the air, striking the guard just as he fired the missile.

The blast from the launcher flashed over Pitt's head, singeing his hair as he smashed his head and shoulder into the guard's chest. They crashed to the ground as the missile, its aim altered by the impact of Pitt's body into the guard, flashed through the night and struck the side of a cliff fifty feet above and slightly behind the stern of the *Deep Encounter*. The explosion sent lava rock bursting across the channel, fragments raining down on the survey ship, but causing no casualties and little damage.

The guard, stunned and with two broken ribs, struggled to his feet and swung his clutched hands in a vicious judo chop, missing his assailant's neck but pounding into the top of his skull. Pitt came within a hair of blacking out but recovered in an instant, came to his knees and swung his right fist with every ounce of strength he had into the guard's stomach just above the groin. The guard doubled over, the air escaping out of his mouth in an audible grunt. Then Pitt grabbed the missile launcher and swung it like a club. It struck the guard in the hip, knocking him sideways. Despite his injuries, the man was tough, his body hard from years of dedicated physical training. He reeled around, straightened and lunged at Pitt like a wounded boar.

Using brain instead of muscle, Pitt deftly jumped to his feet and stepped aside. The guard reeled past, stumbled and fell over the edge of the cliff. His unexpected defeat came so quickly, he failed to cry out. The only sound came from a distant splash far below. With cold efficiency, Pitt quickly pulled a missile from the wooden crate, shoved it in the launcher and aimed it at the pirate ship plunging through the channel no more than a hundred yards behind the *Deep Encounter*. Pitt thanked the gods that it didn't require the complicated procedure of a Stinger. The firing sequence was elementary enough for any retarded terrorist to operate. He aimed the barrel through the simple sights at the pirate ship and pulled the trigger.

The missile screeched away into the night, striking the work boat square amidships of the hull, just above the waterline. For an instant the explosion came as an insignificant blast. But it had penetrated the plates of the hull before bursting inside the engine room. Then came a shrieking bedlam of roar and flame as the pirate ship tore herself apart. The entire channel was suddenly illuminated, as a brilliant orange-and-red ball painted the towering cliffs. The detonation had ruptured the fuel tanks, turning the work boat into a raging inferno. The entire superstructure seemed to lift from the hull like a toy disassembled by an unseen hand. And then the brilliant flash abruptly snuffed out and darkness fell on the channel again, except for small pieces of flaming debris that fell into the water around the dying work boat as it vanished into the black water of the channel. In one brief holocaust, the lives of the hijackers were snuffed out.

Pitt stood erect and stared entranced into the channel where only moments before a boat had been storming through the water. He felt few feelings of remorse. The men on board had been killers intent on murdering the entire fifty-one people of the survey vessel. The *Deep Encounter* and everyone on her were free from harm now. In Pitt's mind, that was all that mattered.

He hurled the missile launcher far over the cliff into the water below. The pain in his cut and bleeding feet came back to torment him, and he limped up to the guardhouse and entered. He rummaged around the cabinets until he found a first-aid kit. Minutes later, after a heavy swabbing with antiseptic, his throbbing feet were encased in bandages thick enough for him to walk on. He searched the small enclosure for any papers in the drawers of the cabinet beneath the communications equipment and found only a notebook. A fast scan told him the entries had been made by the watch guard. He shoved it in the pocket of his shorts. He emptied a can half filled with gasoline for the portable generator that provided energy for the lights and radio and lit it with a box of wooden matches sitting in an ashtray stacked with cigarettes smoked down to their filters.

Pitt stepped from the guardhouse, fired the matchbox and threw it through the doorway. As the interior erupted in flames, he hobbled back down the path leading to the lagoon. When he arrived, he found Giordino and Misty waiting for him on the beach. Resting with its bow in the sand was a launch with two crewmen from the survey ship.

Giordino walked up to him and embraced him. "For a while there, I thought you'd been sidetracked by a luscious native girl."

Pitt hugged his friend in return. "I guess I *did* cut it a mite close."

"The guard?"

"At the bottom of the channel with his buddies."

"You do nice work."

"Any damage or casualties on the ship?" asked Pitt.

"A few dents, a few scratches, nothing serious."

Misty ran up and threw her arms around him. "I can't believe you're still alive."

Pitt gave her a gentlemanly kiss and then looked around the lagoon. "You came in the ship's launch?"

Misty nodded. "The old man brought his yacht alongside *Deep Encounter* and transferred me on board."

"Where is he?"

Misty shrugged. "After talking briefly with Captain Burch, he sailed off to continue his round-the-world cruise."

"I never got a chance to thank him," said Pitt regretfully.

"He was a funny old guy," said Giordino. "He said we'd probably meet up again."

"Who knows," Pitt said wistfully. "Anything is possible."

Part Two

GUARD OF HADES

THE FORD AND THE FOKKER

21

Under orders from Admiral Sandecker, Captain Burch steered a course straight to the port city of Nuku'alofa, the capital town of the island nation of Tonga, the only remaining Polynesian monarchy. A car was waiting for Pitt and Giordino to rush them to the international airport at Fua'amotu, where they could immediately board a Royal Tongan airliner for Hawaii. From there, a NUMA jet would take them on to Washington.

Fond and tearful farewells were said with the men and women from the *Deep Encounter*. Despite their hair-raising ordeal, almost all of them had voted to return to station and continue their deep-ocean survey of the Tonga Trench. Misty cried, Giordino kept blowing his nose, Pitt's eyes were moist, even Burch and House looked as if they had lost their family dog. It was all

Pitt and Giordino could do to break away and jump in the waiting car.

After boarding a 747, they just had time to settle in their seats and fasten their seat belts before the big jet was thundering down the runway and rising in a lazy climb. The lush green landscape of Tonga quickly vanished behind them, and then they were climbing over an indigo sea above scattered clouds that looked thick enough to walk on. Thirty minutes into the flight, Giordino had drifted off to sleep in the aisle seat. Sitting by the window, Pitt retrieved Egan's leather case from the floor beneath the seat ahead of him and flicked open the clasps. He lifted the lid carefully, leery that it might be filled with oil again. A ridiculous idea, he thought with amusement. There was nothing magical about a prankster doing the deed.

The case was empty except for a towel and the cassettes containing the video taken of the *Emerald Dolphin* by the cameras of the *Abyss Navigator*. He gently unwrapped the towel until he held the strange-looking misshapen object with the greenish tint they had picked up from the chapel floor. He turned it over in his left hand, using the fingers of his right. This was the first opportunity he'd had to eye it up close.

There was a strange kind of greasy feel about it. Instead of being jagged and coarse, like most badly incinerated inorganic material, the object was rounded and smooth and twisted in a spiral. Pitt didn't have a clue as to its composition. He rewrapped the object in the towel and set it back in the case. He was certain the chemists in the NUMA lab would identify it. Once he delivered the material, his part of the mystery was finished.

Breakfast came, but he begged off, and had only tomato juice and coffee. Hunger eluded him. As he sipped the coffee, he again stared out the window. An island was drifting under the aircraft far below, an emerald speck set on a blue topaz sea. He studied it for a moment and recognized the shape as Tutuila, one of the American Samoan islands. He could make out the harbor of Pago Pago, where he'd visited the naval station many years ago with his father, then a United States congressman on a junket around the Pacific.

He recalled the trip well. He was a boy in his middle teens and he'd taken every opportunity to dive around the island while his father was inspecting the naval facilities, gliding among the coral and the brilliantly colored fish with a spear gun. He'd rarely released the old surgical rubber sling, sending the thin spear shaft at a fish. He'd preferred simply to study or photograph the wonders beneath the surface. After a day spent enjoying the water, he would relax on the sandy beach under a palm tree and contemplate his future.

And then, he remembered another beach, this one on the island of Oahu in Hawaii. He was still in the Air Force then. He saw himself as a young man with the woman whose memory had never left him. Summer Moran was the loveliest woman he'd ever known. He could recall in vivid detail the first time they'd met in the bar at the Ala Moana Hotel on Waikiki Beach. Her enchanting gray eyes, the long fiery red hair, the perfectly shaped body in a tight oriental silk green dress slit on the sides. Then came the vision of her death as it had a thousand times. He'd lost her during an earthquake in an underwater city built by her mad father, Frederick Moran. She'd swum down to save him and never returned.

He closed down that part of the memory as he had done so often in the past and stared at his reflection in the window. The eyes still radiated an intensity that had never dimmed, and yet there was a slight hint of age and weariness creeping into them. He wondered what it would be like to meet himself as he was twenty years ago. Suppose the young Dirk Pitt of two decades ago walked up and sat down next to him on a park bench. How would he receive the fresh young buck who had served with distinction as an Air Force pilot? Would he even recognize him? How would the youth see the old Dirk Pitt? Could he remotely foresee the wild adventures, agonizing heartbreaks and bloody encounters and injuries? The old Pitt doubted it. Would the young Pitt be repulsed at what he saw and shy away from what lay ahead, taking a totally different direction in their lives?

Pitt turned back from the window, closed his eyes and put the vision of his youth and what-might-have-been out of his mind. Would he do it all over again if given the chance for a restart? For the most part, the answer was yes. Oh sure, he would have made a few alterations and fine-tuned different episodes of his life. But on the whole, it had been extremely satisfying and filled with achievement. He felt thankful simply to be alive, and let it go at that.

His thoughts were interrupted by the bouncing of the plane as it hit turbulence. He complied when the FASTEN YOUR SEAT BELT light gonged on. He stayed awake and read magazines until the plane landed at the John Rodgers International Airport in Honolulu. He and Giordino were met by the pilot from NUMA who was to fly them to Washington. He escorted them to the carousels so they could pick up their luggage and then drove them to a turquoise-painted NUMA Gulfstream jet on the far side of the airport. When they took off, the sun was falling in the western sky and the blue was slowly turning black in the east.

For most of the trip, Giordino slept like a zombie, while Pitt fitfully dozed off and on. When he woke, his mind began to work. Was his end of the *Emerald Dolphin* tragedy finished? There was little doubt that Admiral Sandecker would put him to work on a new project. He made up his mind to argue against that possibility. He decided he had to see the mystery through to its conclusion. Those who had caused the terrible fire of the cruise liner must pay. They had to be tracked down, their motives dissected and then punished.

His mind slowly turned from the inhuman unpleasantness to the lure of sleeping in his own down-filled bed in his aircraft hangar apartment. He wondered if Congresswoman Loren Smith, his current lady love, would meet him after the plane landed, as she did so often. Loren, with her cinnamon hair and violet eyes. They had come so close to marriage on several occasions, but never quite got over the hump. Maybe now was the time. God only knows, thought Pitt, I can't be bounding all over the oceans and falling in a pit of devilment for many more years. Age, he knew, was creeping over his body like a layer of molasses, slowing it down infinitesimally, until one day he would wake up and say, My God, I'm eligible for Social Security and Medicare.

"No!" he said aloud.

Giordino awoke and looked at him. "Did you call?"

Pitt smiled. "Talking in my sleep."

Giordino shrugged, rolled to his side and reentered dreamland.

No, Pitt thought silently this time. I'm not going out to pasture, not for a long while yet. There would always be another undersea project, another maritime investigation. There was no way he would quit until they closed the lid on his casket.

When he woke up for the final time, the aircraft was touching down at Langley Air Force Base. The day was dark and rainy, the water streaking across the windows. The pilot taxied to the NUMA terminal and stopped just short of an open hangar. When Pitt stepped to the asphalt, he paused and looked toward the nearby parking lot. His hopes were in vain.

Loren Smith was not there to greet him.

Giordino went to his condo in Alexandria to clean up and call a bevy of his girlfriends to let them know he was back in circulation. Pitt postponed the comforts of home and took a NUMA jeep to the NUMA headquarters on the east hill overlooking the Potomac River. He parked the jeep in the underground parking lot and took the elevator up to the tenth floor, the domain of Hiram Yaeger, the agency's computer genius, who headed up a vast network. Yaeger's library contained every known scientific fact or historical event about the oceans since recorded history, and then some.

Yaeger came out of Silicon Valley and had been with NUMA almost fifteen years. He looked like an old hippie, with his graying hair tied in a ponytail. His standard uniform for the day was a pair of Levi's, a Levi jacket and cowboy boots. Nobody knew it to look at him, but he lived in an elegantly designed house in a fashionable residential section of Maryland. He drove a BMW 740 il, and his daughters were honor students and equestrian trophy-winners. He'd also created and designed a technically advanced computer named Max that was nearly human. He'd programmed photos of his wife into the holographic image that appeared when he talked to it.

Yaeger was studying the latest results sent from a NUMA expedition off Japan that was drilling into the sea floor in a search of life under the silt in the fractured rock, when Pitt walked into his sanctum sanctorum.

He looked up, then stood and smiled as he extended his hand. "Well, well, the scourge of the dismal deep is home again." He was taken aback at Pitt's appearance.

The NUMA special projects director looked like a lost soul off the street. His shorts and flowered shirt were ratty, and he was wearing slippers over heavily bandaged feet. Despite several hours of sleep on the airplanes, his eyes looked tired and washed out. His face had over a week's growth of scraggly beard. This was clearly a man who had seen hard times. "For the man of the hour, you look like second-class roadkill."

Pitt shook Yaeger's hand. "I came directly from the airport just to harass you."

"I don't doubt it for a moment." He looked into Pitt's eyes with pure admiration. "I read the report about the incredible rescue performed by you and the *Deep Encounter*'s crew, followed up by your fight with the pirates. How do you become involved in so much havoc?"

"It *finds* me," said Pitt, throwing up his hands in a modest gesture. "Seriously, the lion's share of the credit goes to the entire complement of the research ship, who worked like fiends in saving the passengers. And Giordino did most of the work in rescuing the crew of the survey ship."

Yaeger well knew Pitt's aversion to words of praise and compliments. The guy was too self-conscious for his own good, Yaeger thought. He skipped over any more talk of the recent events and motioned for Pitt to sit down.

"Have you seen the admiral yet? He has about fifty media interviews lined up for you."

"I'm not ready to face the world just yet. I'll see him in the morning."

"What brings you to my world of electronic manipulation?"

Pitt laid Egan's leather case on Yaeger's desk and opened it. He unwrapped the object taken from the cruise liner and handed it to him. "I'd like to have this analyzed and identified."

Yaeger examined the odd-shaped thing for a moment, then nodded. "I'll have the chemistry lab do a number on it. Unless it has a complicated molecular structure, I should have an answer for you in two days. Anything else?"

Pitt passed over the videocassettes from the *Abyss Navigator*. "Computer-enhance and digitize these into three-dimensional images."

"Can do."

"One final thing before I head home." He laid a drawing on the desk. "Have you ever seen a company logo like this?"

Yaeger examined Pitt's crude drawing of the three-headed dog with a snake for a tail and the word *Cerberus* beneath. He stared at Pitt queerly. "You don't know what outfit this is?"

"No."

"Where did you see it?"

"It was covered up on the side of the pirates' work boat."

"An oil rig work boat."

"Yes, the same type," Pitt replied. "You're familiar with it?"

"I am," replied Yaeger sagely. "You're opening a real can of worms if you connect the Cerberus Corporation with the hijacking of the *Deep Encounter*."

"The Cerberus Corporation," Pitt said, uttering each syllable slowly. "How stupid of me. I should have known. The conglomerate owns most of the U.S. domestic oil fields, copper and iron mines, and its chemical division makes a thousand different products. It was the three-headed dog that threw me. I failed to make the connection."

"All very relevant when you think about it."

"Why a three-headed dog as a corporate logo?"

"Each head stands for a division of the company," answered Yaeger. "One for oil, one for mining and the other for the chemistry division."

"And the serpent's tail?" asked Pitt half facetiously. "Does that represent something dark and sinister?"

Yaeger shrugged. "Who can say?"

"What's the source for the dog?"

"Cerberus . . . sounds Greek."

Yaeger sat at his computer and typed on the keyboard. In a chamber just opposite his console, the face and figure of an attractive woman appeared in three dimensions. She was dressed in a one-piece bathing suit.

"You called," she said.

"Hello, Max. You know Dirk Pitt." The hazy brown eyes flicked from Pitt's feet to his face. "Yes, I am familiar with him. How are you, Mr. Pitt?"

"Fair to middlin', as they say in Oklahoma. And you, Max, how are you?"

The face changed to an angry pout. "This stupid bathing suit Hiram put on me. It doesn't flatter me at all."

"Would you prefer something else?" asked Yaeger.

"An elegant Armani suit, Andra Gabrielle lingerie, and high-heel, ankle-strap sandals by Tods would be nice."

Yaeger smiled a cocky smile. "What color?"

"Red," Max replied without hesitation.

Yaeger's fingers flew in a blur over the computer keyboard. Then he sat back to admire his handiwork.

Max faded for a few moments and then reappeared in an elegant red suit with blouse, jacket and skirt. "Much better," she said happily. "I hate to look mundane when I'm on the job."

"Now that you're in a good mood, I

would like you to produce data on a subject."

Max ran her hands over her new outfit. "Just name it."

"What can you tell me about Cerberus the three-headed dog?"

"From Greek mythology," Max came back instantly. "Hercules — Latin for Herakles, as the Greeks called him — in a fit of temporary insanity murdered his own wife and children. The god Apollo ordered him to serve King Eurystheus of Mycenae for twelve years as punishment for his terrible act. As part of his sentence, Hercules had to perform twelve labors, feats so challenging they looked impossible. He had to overcome all sorts of hideous monsters, the most difficult being the submission of Cerberus, again Latin for the Greek Kerberos. This was the three-headed grotesque dog who guarded the gates of Hades and prevented the dead souls from escaping from the underworld. The three heads represented the past, present and future. What the serpent tail signified is not known to me."

"Did Hercules destroy the dog?" asked Pitt.

Max shook her head. "Near the gates of the Acheron River, one of five running into the underworld, he wrestled the monstrosity into submission after being bitten, not by the dog's jaws, but by the serpent on the tail. Hercules then took Cerberus to Mycenae and showed him off before returning him to Hades. That's about it in a nutshell, except that Cerberus's sister was Medusa, the hussy with snakes for hair."

"What can you tell me about the Cerberus Corporation?"

"Which one? There must be a dozen businesses around the world that go under the name Cerberus."

"A widely diversified corporation that does business in oil, mining and chemistry."

"Oh, that one," said Max, enlightened. "Have you got about ten hours?"

"You have that much data on Cerberus?" Pitt asked, constantly amazed at Max's enormous library of information.

"Not yet. But I will after I've entered their network and those of the companies who do business with them. Since their interests are international, various world governments must also have extensive files on them."

Pitt looked at Yaeger suspiciously. "Since when is hacking into corporate networks legal?"

Yaeger's expression took on that of a canny fox. "Once I give Max a command to search, far be it from me to interfere with her methods."

Pitt rose from his chair. "I'll leave it to

you and Max to come up with the answers."

"We'll get to work on it."

Pitt turned and gazed at Max. "So long for now, Max. You look stunning in that outfit."

"Thank you, Mr. Pitt. I like you. A pity our circuits can't integrate."

Pitt approached Max and extended his hand. It went through the image. "You never know, Max. Someday Hiram may be able to make you solid."

"I hope so, Mr. Pitt," said Max in a husky voice. "Oh, how I hope so."

The old aircraft hangar, built in the nineteen thirties for a long-since defunct airline, stood off in one corner of Ronald Reagan International Airport. The corrugated metal walls and roof were coated with orange/brown rust. Its few windows were boarded over, and the door to what once had been the office was weather-worn, with fading and peeling paint. The rounded roof structure sat at the end of an airport maintenance dirt road not far from a guard gate.

Pitt parked the NUMA jeep in the weeds outside the hangar and paused at the entrance door. He glanced at the security camera atop a wooden pole on the other side of the road to see that it had stopped its swivel and was aimed directly at him. Then he punched a sequence of numbers, waited for a series of clicks inside the hangar and turned the brass latch. The ancient door swung open noiselessly. The interior was dark except for a few skylights above an upstairs apartment. He switched on the lights.

The sudden effect was dazzling. Set off in their most elegant magnificence by the bright overhead lights, white walls and epoxy floor were three rows of beautifully restored classic automobiles. Sitting incongruously at the end of one row, but just as dazzling as the others, was a 1936 Ford hot rod. On one side of the hangar sat a World War II German jet fighter and a 1929 trimotor transport. Beyond was a turn-of-the-century railroad Pullman car, an odd-looking sailboat mounted on a rubber raft and a bathtub with an outboard motor attached on one end.

The collection of automotive mechanical masterpieces of art represented events in Pitt's life. They were relics of his personal history. They were cherished, maintained by him and seen by only his closest friends. No one driving the Mount Vernon Memorial Highway past Ronald Reagan Airport who glanced at the obsolete aircraft hangar across the end of the runways could have imagined the incredible array of breathtaking artifacts inside.

Pitt closed and locked the door. He took a brief tour, as he always did after returning home after an expedition. Several rainstorms in the past month had kept down the dust. Tomorrow, he told himself, he would run a soft cloth over the gleaming paint and remove the light coating of dust that had seeped inside the hangar while he was gone. Finishing his inspection, he climbed the antique iron circular staircase to his apartment that was perched above the main floor against the hangar's far wall.

The interior of his apartment was just as unique as the eclectic transportation collection below. Here there were all sorts of nautical antiques. No self-respecting interior decorator would have set foot in the place, certainly none who endorsed clutter. The 1,100 square feet of living space that included the living room, bathroom, kitchen and a bedroom were crowded with objects from old ships sunk or scrapped. There was a large wooden-spoked helm from an ancient clipper ship, a compass binnacle from an old Orient tramp steamer, ships' bells, brass and copper divers' helmets. The furniture was an assemblage of antique pieces that came from ships that had sailed the seas in the nineteenth century. Ship models in glass cases sat on low shelves, while marine paintings of ships crossing the seas by the respected artist Richard DeRosset hung on the walls.

After taking a shower and shaving, he

made reservations at a small French restaurant that was only a mile from the hangar. He could have called Loren, but decided he wished to dine alone. Relationships could come later, once he'd wound down. An enjoyable dinner alone and then a night in his large goosedown-mattress bed would serve to rejuvenate him to face the next day.

After dressing, he had twenty minutes to kill before leaving for the restaurant. He took the slip of paper with Kelly's phone number on it and called her. After five rings, he was about to hang up, wondering why her voice mail didn't come on, when she finally answered.

"Hello."

"Hello, Kelly Egan."

He could hear the intake of breath over the line. "Dirk! You're back."

"Just got in and thought I'd call."

"I'm so glad you did."

"I'm due for a few days' vacation. How busy are you?"

"Up to my ears in charity work," she answered. "I'm chairman for the local Handicapped Children's Organization. We're putting on our annual children's flying roundup, and I'm chairman of the event."

"I hate to sound stupid, but what is a flying roundup?"

Kelly laughed. "It's like an air show. People fly in old vintage airplanes and take the kids for rides in them."

"You have your work cut out for you."

"Tell me about it," she said, with a quaint laugh. "The man who owned a sixty-year-old Douglas DC-3 was scheduled to take the kids on flights over Manhattan, but he had a problem with the landing gear and can't make the show."

"Where is the roundup?"

"Just across the Hudson River in New Jersey, at a private field near a town called Englewood Cliffs. It's not far from Dad's farm and laboratory." The voice seemed to sadden.

Pitt walked out onto the balcony of his apartment with the portable phone and gazed at the classics below. His eyes fell on the big three-engine transport plane from 1929. "I think I can help you out on your aerial sightseeing project."

"You can?" Kelly asked, brightening up again. "You know where you can get an old transport plane?"

"When is the roundup?"

"Two days from now. But how can you arrange for one on such short notice?"

Pitt smiled to himself. "I know somebody who is an easy touch for beautiful women and handicapped kids."

22

Pitt was up early the next morning, shaved and put on a dark business suit. Sandecker insisted his top-level directors dress the part. He ate a light breakfast and drove across the river to the NUMA headquarters. The traffic was heavy as usual, but he was in no great hurry and used the delays to collect his thoughts and plan his schedule for the day. He took the elevator from the underground parking area straight up to the fourth floor, which held his office. When the doors opened, he stepped out onto an ornate mosaic tile floor with scenes of ships at sea that stretched down the corridor. The entire floor was empty. At seven o'clock, he was the first to arrive.

He stepped into his corner office, removed his coat and hung it on an old-fashioned coat rack. Pitt seldom spent more than six months out of the year at his desk.

He preferred working in the field. Paper-work was not his favorite area. He spent the next two hours sorting through his mail and studying the logistics of future NUMA scientific expeditions around the world. As special projects director, he oversaw those projects that dealt with the engineering side of oceanography.

At nine o'clock sharp, his secretary of many years, Zerri Pochinsky, entered the outer office. Seeing Pitt at his desk, she rushed in and gave him a kiss on the cheek. "Welcome back. I hear you're to be congratulated."

"Don't you start in," Pitt grumbled, happy to see Zerri.

Zerri was just twenty-five and single when she was hired as Pitt's secretary. Married to a Washington lobbyist now, she had no children of her own, but they had adopted five orphans. Extremely bright and intelligent, she worked just four days a week: an arrangement Pitt was happy to accommodate because of her mastery of the job, and the fact that she was always two steps ahead of him. She was the only secretary he knew who could still take shorthand.

Vivacious, with an endearing smile and hazel eyes, her fawn-colored hair fell to her shoulders, a style she had never changed in all the years Pitt had known her. In the early years, they had often flirted with each other, but Pitt had an unbroken rule about fooling around in his own office. They'd remained close friends without romantic attachments.

Zerri came around behind Pitt's desk chair, clasped her arms around his neck and shoulders and gave him a squeeze. "You'll never know how glad I am to see you in the flesh. I always anguish like a mother whenever I hear you're reported missing in action."

"Bad pennies always turn up."

She straightened up, smoothed her skirt and her tone became official. "Admiral Sandecker wants you in the conference room at eleven o'clock sharp."

"Giordino, too?"

"Giordino, too. Also, don't make plans for the afternoon. The admiral has set up interviews with the news media. They've gone crazy without any on-the-scene witnesses of the burning of the *Emerald Dolphin* to grill."

"I told all I knew in New Zealand," muttered Pitt.

"Not only are you in the United States, but in Washington. The news media considers you a local hero. You have to play along and answer their questions."

"The admiral should make Al endure the blitz. He loves the attention."

"Except that he works under you, which makes you the front man."

For the next few hours, Pitt worked on his detailed report of the crazy events of the past two weeks, beginning with his sighting of the burning cruise liner to the battle and escape of the *Deep Encounter* from the hijackers. He left out the part dealing with the possible Cerberus Corporation connection, because at this point he didn't have the slightest notion where the giant company entered into the picture. He left it to Hiram Yaeger to continue tracing the thread.

At eleven, Pitt entered the conference room and closed the door behind him. Sandecker and Rudi Gunn were already seated at the long conference table that had been constructed from planking salvaged from a schooner sunk in Lake Erie in 1882. The large room was paneled in teak, and enhanced by a turquoise carpet and a Victorian mantelpiece. Hanging on the walls were paintings of historical U.S. naval battles. Pitt's worst fears were realized when two other men rose from their chairs to greet him.

Sandecker remained seated as he made the introductions. "Dirk, I believe you know these gentlemen."

A tall blond man with a mustache and light blue eyes shook Pitt's hand. "Good to see you, Dirk. It's been, what, two years?"

Pitt pressed the hand of Wilbur Hill, a director of the CIA. "Closer to three."

Charles Davis, the special assistant to the director of the FBI, stepped forward. At six foot six, he was by far the tallest man in the room. He always reminded Pitt of a dog with sad, droopy eyes in search of his food dish. "We last met when we worked together on that Chinese immigration case."

"I remember it well," Pitt replied cordially.

While they chatted briefly about old times, Hiram Yaeger and Al Giordino walked into the room. "Well, it looks like we're all present," said Sandecker. "Shall we get to it?"

Yaeger began by passing around folders with copies of photos the cameras had taken of the sunken *Emerald Dolphin*. "While you gentlemen study these, I'll run the VCR."

A huge three-sided monitor dropped from a hidden recess in the ceiling. Yaeger pressed the buttons on a remote control and the images taken by the video cameras of the *Sea Sleuth* began to sweep in three dimensions across a stage in front of the screens. The wreck had a ghostly and pathetic look on the seabed. It was hard to believe that such a beautiful ship could have been reduced to such an incredible degree of devastation.

Pitt gave a narration as the submersible moved along the hull of the sunken cruise liner. "The wreck lies nineteen thousand seven hundred and sixty feet deep on a smooth slope of the Tonga Trench. She's broken into three pieces. The wreckage and debris field cover a square mile. The stern, and a fragment of the midships section, lies a quarter of a mile from the main forward section. This is where we concentrated our search. At first we believed she shattered upon impact with the bottom, but if you study the way the gaps in the hull are torn outward, it appears obvious that a series of explosions blew out the hull beneath the waterline while the fire-destroyed derelict was under tow by the Quest Marine tugboat. We can safely assume her internal structure, weakened by a series of synchronized detonations, broke up during her plunge to the bottom."

"Couldn't the hull have been blown apart when smoldering fire reached the ship's fuel tanks and caused them to explode while the ship was being towed?" asked Davis.

Wilbur Hill's eyes alternated between the photos and the images on the monitor. "I've had a fair amount of experience investigating terrorist bomb explosions, and I believe I'm on solid ground in saying Dirk is correct. The bottom of the *Emerald Dolphin* was not blown out by a concentrated explosion. As the photos and video show, the hull burst in several places, as demonstrated by the shattered hull plates extending outward.

It also looks as if the explosive devices were spaced equidistant from one another. A sure sign the destruction was well planned and executed."

"For what purpose?" asked Davis. "Why go to all that trouble to sink a burned-out hulk? Better yet, who could do it? No one alive was left aboard when it was taken in tow."

"Not so," said Gunn. "The tug's captain" — he paused to scan a large notepad — "his name was Jock McDermott, reported pulling one of the cruise ship's officers from the sea immediately after the ship went down."

Davis looked skeptical. "How could the man have survived the fire?"

"Good question," Gunn said, tapping a pen on his notepad. "McDermott was at a loss to explain the miracle. He stated that the man acted as if he was in shock until the tug reached Wellington. Then he slipped ashore before he could be questioned and disappeared."

"Did McDermott give a description?" Davis probed.

"Only that he was a black man."

Sandecker didn't ask for permission from the others seated in his presence to smoke. NUMA was his territory, and he lit up one of the legendary huge cigars that he highly treasured and almost never passed out, even to his closest friends. He exhaled a cloud of smoke toward the ceiling and spoke slowly. "The prime issue here is that the *Emerald Dolphin* was deliberately sunk to block any investigation by the insurance companies to find the cause of the fire. The sinking was a cover-up. At least that's how it looks to me."

Davis stared at Sandecker. "If your theory is on target, Admiral, that leads to the terrible possibility that the fire was an act of arson. I can't conceive of any motive, even by terrorists, to destroy a cruise ship and twenty-five hundred crew and passengers. Certainly not without a terrorist group claiming responsibility, and none has come forward."

"I agree the thought is incomprehensible," said Sandecker. "But if that's where the facts lead us, that's where we'll go."

"What facts?" Davis persisted. "It would be impossible to find evidence the fire was caused by man and not by an accident or a fault of the ship's systems."

"According to the accounts of the surviving ship's officers, every fire system on board ship failed to function," said Rudi Gunn. "They tell of their frustration at watching the fire rage out of control without any means of stopping it. We're talking twelve different main systems, including backups. What are the odds of their all failing?"

"About the same as a man on a bicycle winning the Indianapolis 500," answered Giordino cynically.

"I believe Dirk and Al have given us the evidence to prove the fire was deliberate," said Yaeger.

Everyone at the table looked at him expectantly, waiting for him to continue, but Pitt spoke first. "Our lab identified the material we brought back so soon?"

"They worked through the wee hours of the night and nailed it," Yaeger said triumphantly.

"What are we talking about?" asked Hill.

"A substance we found when we searched the wreck in a submersible," answered Giordino. "We spotted it in the chapel area, where reports claim the fire started, and brought back a sample."

"I won't bore you with a lengthy lecture on how the elements were broken down," Yaeger continued. "But our NUMA scientists identified it as a highly incendiary material known as Pyrotorch 610. Once it has been ignited, it's almost impossible to extinguish. The stuff is so unstable that even the military won't touch it."

Yaeger reveled in the mixture of expressions around the table. Pitt reached over and shook Giordino's hand. "Good work, partner."

Giordino grinned proudly. "It seems our

little trip in the *Abyss Navigator* paid off."

"Too bad Misty isn't here to hear the news."

"Misty?" inquired Davis.

"Misty Graham," said Pitt. "A marine biologist on board the *Deep Encounter*. She accompanied Al and me on the dive in the submersible."

Sandecker idly knocked the ashes of his cigar into a large brass ashtray. "It looks to me like what we'd thought was just a devastating tragedy has turned into a hideous crime —" He stopped as a blank look that turned to exasperation crossed his face.

Giordino had pulled out a cigar from his breast pocket that was the exact mate to the admiral's, and slowly lit it.

"You were saying," prompted Hill, not knowing the behind-the-scenes dance between Sandecker and Giordino and their cigars. The admiral was almost certain Al was stealing his cigars, but he could never prove it. None ever appeared to be missing. He never caught on that Giordino was secretly buying his cigars from the same source in Nicaragua.

"I was saying," Sandecker spoke slowly, giving the evil eye to Giordino, "that we have a grievous crime on our hands." He paused to look across the table at Hill and Davis. "I hope you gentlemen and your agencies will launch an immediate in-depth investigation into the atrocity and bring the guilty parties to justice."

"Now that we definitely know a crime was committed," said Davis, "I believe we can all work together to find the answers."

"You can begin with the hijacking of the *Deep Encounter*," said Pitt. "I don't harbor the slightest doubt there is a connection."

"I read a brief report on the incident," said Hill. "You and Al are very brave men for saving your vessel and defeating the pirates."

"They were not pirates in the strict sense of the word. Hired mercenary killers are closer to the truth."

Hill wasn't sold. "What possible grounds could they have had for stealing a NUMA ship?"

"It was hardly a simple theft," Pitt said acidly. "They meant to sink the ship and kill every man and woman on board, all fifty of them. You want a grounds for a motive? They were out to stop us from making a deep-water survey of the wreck. They were afraid of what we might discover."

Gunn's expression was thoughtful. "Who in God's name could be responsible for such evil?"

"You might start with the Cerberus Corporation," said Yaeger, glancing at Pitt.

"Nonsense," snorted Davis. "One of the nation's largest and most respected companies involved with murdering more than two thousand people on the other side of the world? Can you imagine General Motors, Exxon or Microsoft committing crimes of mass murder? I certainly can't."

"I couldn't agree with you more," said Sandecker. "But Cerberus hardly has lily-white hands. They've been involved with some pretty shady business deals."

"They've been investigated by congressional committees on several occasions," added Gunn.

"None of which amounted to more than political wool-gathering," retorted Davis.

Sandecker grinned. "It's pretty tough for Congress to reprimand an outfit that gives both political parties enough funding every election to launch ten third-world countries."

Davis shook his head. "I'd have to see hard proof before you sold me on investigating Cerberus."

Pitt caught the glitter in Yaeger's eyes, as the computer wizard spoke. "Would it help if I told you that the scientists at Cerberus's chemical division created Pyrotorch 610?"

"You can't be certain of that," said Davis, his tone filled with doubt.

"No other company in the world has come close to duplicating its Pyrotorch 610's properties."

Davis quickly came back. "The material

was probably stolen. Anybody could have gotten hold of it."

"At least the FBI has a place to start," said Sandecker to the FBI agent. He turned to Hill. "And what of the CIA?"

"I think the first thing is to mount a salvage expedition on the remains of the pirate ship and see what turns up."

"Can NUMA help you with that project?" asked Pitt.

"No, thank you," said Hill. "We have a private company we work with on underwater investigations."

"So be it," Sandecker said, between puffs of his cigar. "If you need our services, you have but to call. NUMA will cooperate fully."

"I would like your permission for my people to interrogate the crew of the *Deep Encounter*," said Davis.

"Granted," Sandecker agreed without hesitation. "If there is nothing else?"

"One other question," said Hill. "Who owned the *Emerald Dolphin*?"

"She sailed under British registry," replied Gunn, "but she was owned by the Blue Seas Cruise Lines, a British-based company owned primarily by American stockholders."

Hill smiled faintly at Davis. "A domestic as well as an international act of terror. Looks like our two agencies *will* have to work closely together."

Davis and Hill left together. After the door closed, Sandecker sat down again. His eyes narrowed until they had a fierce twinkle in them. "As long as both crimes took place at sea, there's no way they're leaving NUMA out of the investigation. We'll go our own separate way without rocking the CIA and the FBI's boat." He looked at Pitt and Giordino. "You two take three days off and rest up. Then come back and get to work."

Pitt looked candidly back at Sandecker, then around the table. "Where do we start?"

"I'll have a plan when you return. In the meantime, Rudi and Hiram will gather all the data possible."

"What are you going to do for relaxation?" Gunn asked Pitt and Giordino jointly.

"Before I left for the Pacific, I bought a thirty-six-foot sailboat that I keep at a marina near Annapolis. I thought I'd gather up a couple of ladies and cruise Chesapeake Bay."

Gunn turned to Pitt. "And you?"

"Me?" Pitt shrugged casually. "I'm going to an air show."

23

The day could not have been more perfect for the air show and the benefit for the disabled children. More than ten thousand people attended under a cobalt sky free of clouds. A slight breeze blew in off the Atlantic Ocean and cooled the warm summer temperatures.

Gene Taylor Field was a private airport in the middle of a housing community whose residents all owned airplanes. The streets were laid out so families could taxi their aircraft from their houses to the runway and back. Unlike most fields, the immediate area around the runway was landscaped with small bushes, hedges and flower beds. Acres of grass surrounded most of the paved area for car parking and picnicking. The crowds could congregate on the grassy lawns to watch the planes and their pilots performing acrobatics in the air, or they could walk among the vintage aircraft that were parked on display around one end of the runway.

The disabled children were brought in by families, schools and hospitals from four states. There was no shortage of volunteers to escort them around the aircraft on display. It was an emotional event, and everyone was proud to be a part of it.

Kelly was stressed to the limit. She knew her blood pressure was reaching the point of no return. Until now, everything had run smoothly, no glitches, no problems, the volunteers incredibly helpful. The owners and pilots of the ninety aircraft were happy to give their time and participate at their own expense. They were extremely gracious in allowing the children to sit in the cockpits while explaining the story behind their airplanes.

But the one aircraft Kelly was counting on, the transport that was scheduled to give rides to the children, flying them over the skyscrapers of Manhattan, had failed to show. She was on the verge of announcing the bad news to the children when her close friend and co-worker Mary Conrow approached her.

"I'm sorry," she said sympathetically. "I know you were counting on him."

"I can't believe Dirk didn't call me if he couldn't arrange for a plane," Kelly murmured dejectedly.

Mary was a very attractive woman, in her middle thirties, stylishly groomed and fashionably dressed. She wore her autumn-leaf blond hair in long ringlets that fanned out over her shoulders. Wide pale-green eyes stared at the world with a self-assurance that accented her high cheekbones and tapered chin. She was about to say something, when suddenly she shaded her eyes with one hand and pointed into the sky.

"What's that flying in from the south?"

Kelly stared in the direction where Mary gestured. "I can't make it out."

"Looks like an old transport plane!" said Mary excitedly. "I think he's coming!"

Vast relief flowed through Kelly's veins, and her heartbeat increased. "It has to be him!" she shouted. "Dirk didn't let me down."

They watched, the children watched, the whole crowd watched, as the strange-looking old aircraft lumbered across the sky only a few hundred feet above the tops of the trees surrounding the field. It came slowly, no more than seventy-five miles an hour. There was an awkward sort of grace in her flight through the sky, the reason she had been affectionately known as the Tin Goose, the most successful commercial airliner of her time.

The 5-AT Trimotor had been built by the Ford Motor Company in the early nineteen thirties; Pitt's was one of the few that still survived in museums or private collections. Most had color schemes painted with the identifying schemes and emblems of the old airlines they served. He had retained the pure silver look on the corrugated aluminum wings and fuselage, with only the registration number and Ford logo as markings.

Since it was the only plane in the air at that moment, the crowd and participating pilots all paused and gazed skyward at the legendary aircraft as it banked and lined up on the runway. The toothpick-fixed propellers on the engines flashed in the sun and whipped the air with a distinctive buzzing sound.

Two engines hung from the wings while the third protruded from the bow of the fuselage. The big, thick wings looked like they could lift a plane twice its size. The forward vee-windshield had a comical look to it, but the side windows were large, offering the pilots more than ample vision. The ageless machine seemed to hang motionlessly for a moment, like a true goose just before its feet touched water. Then, very slowly, she settled to the ground, her big tires biting the asphalt with a slight puff of white smoke and a barely audible squeal.

A volunteer raced across the runway in a World War II restored jeep and motioned the trimotor to follow toward its assigned parking place near the end of a row of vintage and antique aircraft. Pitt taxied between a World War I Fokker DR.1 triplane, painted a bright red like Baron Von Richthofen's famous aircraft, and a blue 1932 Sikorsky S-38 amphibian that could land on water as well as land.

Kelly and Mary drove up to the aircraft, chauffeured by a volunteer in his private 1918 Cadillac touring car. They hopped out and waited until the twin-bladed propellers spun to a stop. A minute later, the passengers' door opened and Pitt leaned out. He dropped a boarding stool to the ground before stepping down.

"You!" Kelly gasped. "You didn't say the aircraft belonged to you."

"I thought I'd surprise you," he said, with a devilish smile. "Forgive my tardiness. I encountered strong headwinds on the way from Washington." His eyes were drawn to Mary. "Hello."

"Oh, I'm sorry," said Kelly. "This is my very dear friend Mary Conrow. She's my assistant chairman for the event. And this is —"

"Yes, I know. The Dirk Pitt you never stop talking about." Mary sized Pitt up and was immediately swept into his green eyes. "A pleasure to meet you," she murmured.

"The pleasure is mine."

"The children are excited about flying in your plane," said Kelly. "That's all they've talked about since they saw you coming. We're already lining them up for the flights."

Pitt stared at the crowd of disabled children, many in wheelchairs, who were assembling for the rides. "How many of them want to go? The plane can only carry fifteen passengers at a time."

"We have about sixty," replied Mary. "So it will take four trips."

Pitt smiled. "I can handle it, but if I'm going to carry passengers, I'll need a copilot. My friend Al Giordino couldn't make it."

"No problem," said Kelly. "Mary is a pilot with Conquest Airlines."

"For very long?"

"Twelve years in seven thirty-sevens and seven sixty-sevens."

"How many hours in prop planes?"

"Well over a thousand."

Pitt nodded. "Okay, climb in and I'll give you a quick flight check."

Mary's face lit up like a child's on Christmas morning. "Flying a Ford trimotor will make all the male pilots I know green with envy."

Once they were belted into their bucket seats in the cockpit, Pitt lectured Mary on the controls and instruments. The forward instrument panel was a study in no-nonsense simplicity. Several mandatory switches and slightly more than a dozen fundamental instruments were spread strategically across a large pyramid-shaped black panel. But only the nose engine's instruments were set in the panel. Oddly, the tachometer, oil pressure and oil temperature gauges for the two outboard engines were mounted outside the cockpit on the mounting struts.

The engine's three throttles were mounted between the seats. The control columns sported steering wheels with wooden spokes that operated the ailerons and looked like they came out of old automobiles. Never one to waste a dime, Henry Ford had insisted his company could save money by using existing Model T Ford car steering wheels. Trim was altered by a small crank over the pilot's head. The big brake stick that swung left and right to steer the airplane when it was on the ground also rose between the pilot's and copilot's seats.

Pitt fired up the engines, watching them shudder and vibrate in their mountings to the accompaniment of a series of pops and coughs, before the combustion inside the cylinders smoothed out into a steady beat. After running them up, he taxied to the end of the runway. He explained the takeoff and landing procedure before turning the controls over to Mary, reminding her that she was flying a plane with a tail wheel instead of a jetliner with tricycle gear.

She had a light and graceful touch and quickly learned the quirks of flying a seventy-two-year-old aircraft. Pitt demonstrated how the aircraft would stall at sixty-four miles an hour, fly without effort on two engines, and still have enough power left to make a controlled landing on only one.

"It seems strange," she said loudly, over the roar of the triple exhaust, "to see engines sitting out in the open without any cowling."

"They were made to take the elements."

"What is her history?"

"She was built by the Stout Metal Airplane Company in nineteen twenty-nine," Pitt lectured, "which was a division of the Ford Motor Company. Ford built a hundred and ninety-six of them, the first all-metal airplanes in the United States. This was the one hundred and fifty-eighth off the assembly line. About eighteen still exist, and three are still flying. She began service with Transcontinental Air Transport, which later became TWA. She flew the New York-to-Chicago leg and carried many of the celebrities of the day — Charles Lindbergh, Amelia Earhart, Gloria Swanson, Douglas Fairbanks, Sr., and Mary Pickford. Franklin Roosevelt chartered her to fly to the Democratic convention in Chicago. Anybody who was somebody flew in her. There was no better air transport in her day for comfort and convenience. The Ford trimotor was the first to carry a rest room and service with a stewardess. You may not realize it, but you are sitting in the airplane that ushered in modern commercial aviation. The first queen of the skies."

"She has an interesting pedigree."

"When the Douglas DC-3 came out of production in 1934, Old Reliable, the nickname she picked up along her career, was retired. For the next several years, she flew passengers in Mexico. Unexpectedly, in 1942, she showed up on the island of Luzon in the Philippines and evacuated a score of our soldiers on island-hopping flights to Australia. She disappeared in the mists of time after that. She next turned up in Iceland, where she was owned by an aircraft mechanic who transported supplies to isolated farms and towns. I bought her in 1987 and flew her to Washington, where I gave her a painstaking restoration."

"What are her specs?"

"Three Pratt and Whitney four-hundred-and-fifty-horsepower engines," Pitt elaborated. "She carries enough fuel to fly five hundred fifty miles at a cruising speed of one hundred fifteen miles an hour. If pushed, she can do one hundred thirty-five.

She can climb at one thousand one hundred feet a minute and reach a ceiling of seventeen thousand three hundred feet. Her wingspan is seventy-seven feet and she is forty-nine feet in length. Did I miss anything?"

"That pretty well covers it," said Mary.

"She's all yours," said Pitt, as he lifted his hands from the controls. "She's strictly a hands-on plane. You have to fly her every second."

"I see what you mean," said Mary, having to use her muscles to twist the wheel and move the big ailerons. After a few minutes of banks and turns, she set up for a landing.

Pitt observed Mary land and touch down with just the slightest bump before settling the tail wheel on the asphalt. "Very nice," he complimented her. "Done like an old trimotor pro."

"Thank you, sir," she said, with a pleased laugh.

Once the trimotor was parked, the children began to come on board. Most had to be lifted through the doorway by volunteers into Pitt's arms, who then carried them to seats and buckled their seat belts. Seeing the severely disabled children showing such courage and humor despite their sad physical disabilities deeply touched Pitt's heart. Kelly came along to attend to the needs of the children, joking and laughing with them.

After takeoff, she pointed out the sights of Manhattan from the air as Pitt headed across the Hudson River toward the city.

The old aircraft was perfect for sightseeing. Its slow speed and the big square windows along her fuselage offered unobstructed panoramic viewing. The children sat in the old wicker chairs with their padded cushions and jabbered excitedly at seeing the buildings of the city reach upward toward them.

Pitt made three trips, and while the plane was being refueled, he walked over and admired the triwing World War I Fokker that was parked next to the trimotor. At one time during the war it had been the scourge of the Allied air services, flown by the German aces Manfred von Richthofen, Werner Voss and Hermann Göring. Von Richthofen had claimed it climbed like a monkey and maneuvered like the devil.

He was studying the guns mounted onto the engine cowling when a man in old flying togs walked up to him. "What do you think of her?" he asked.

Pitt turned his head and looked into the olive eyes of a dark-skinned man, who had the sharp features of an Egyptian. There was an almost imperious look about him. He stood tall and straight, with what looked to Pitt to be a military bearing. His eyes were strange, with a hard quality that seemed focused straight ahead without orbiting left or right.

Both men studied each other for a moment, noting that they were of equal height and weight. Finally, Pitt said, "I'm always surprised at how small the old fighters look in pictures, but become quite large when you stand next to them." He pointed at the twin guns mounted behind the propeller. "They look like the genuine articles."

The man nodded. "Original Spandau 7.92 millimeters."

"And the ammunition belts? They're loaded with rounds."

"Purely to impress the onlookers," said the dark-skinned man. "She was an excellent killing machine for her time. I like to retain the image." He removed a gauntlet-style flying glove and offered his hand. "I'm Conger Rand, the owner of the plane. You're the pilot of the trimotor?"

"Yes." Pitt had the strange feeling that the man knew him. "My name is Dirk Pitt."

"I know," said Rand. "You're with NUMA."

"Have we met?"

"No, but we have a mutual acquaintance."

Before Pitt could reply, Kelly called out. "We're ready to load for the last flight."

Pitt turned and was about to say "Well, I guess I have to go," but the pilot of the

Fokker had swiftly spun away and stepped out of view behind his aircraft.

The fuel tanks were capped, and as soon as the fuel truck had driven away, the trimotor was loaded with children for the final flight over the city. Pitt let Mary handle the controls while he went back and talked with the children, pointing out the Statue of Liberty and Ellis Island as they circled them at a thousand feet. He returned to the cockpit and took over, heading the plane over the East River and the Brooklyn Bridge.

With the outside temperature in the high eighties, Pitt slid open his side window and let the air rush into the cockpit. If he hadn't had children on board, he might have been tempted to fly under the venerable old bridge, but that would have cost him his license. Not a wise move, he decided rationally.

He was distracted by a shadow that appeared alongside and slightly above the trimotor.

"We have a visitor," said Mary, as he heard the children begin squealing in delight in the passenger's cabin.

Pitt looked up to see a bright splash of red against the dazzling blue sky. The pilot of the Red Fokker triplane waved from his cockpit no more than fifty yards away. He was wearing a leather flight helmet and goggles with a silk ribbon streaming from the top of his head. The old Fokker was so close Pitt saw the pilot's teeth flash in a wide grin, an almost evil grin. He was about to wave back when the antique plane suddenly veered away.

Pitt watched as the red triplane performed a loop and then abruptly swooped back toward the Ford trimotor, angling in from the forward port side.

"What is that crazy nut doing?" asked Mary. "He can't perform acrobatics over the city."

Her question was answered when twin bursts of laserlike light flashed from the muzzles of the twin Spandau machine guns. For a brief instant, Mary thought it was part of a staged aerial stunt. But then the glass in the windshield burst into fragments, quickly followed by a spray of oil and an eruption of smoke from the engine in front of the cockpit.

24

Pitt sensed the peril before the hail of bullets struck. He threw the trimotor into a steep 360-degree bank until he could see the Fokker moving below and to his left before it banked and returned for another attack. He shoved the throttles to their stops and followed, in the vain hope of staying on its tail. But it was a losing proposition. With three healthy engines, Pitt might have given the Fokker and its insane pilot a run for the money. The trimotor's top speed was more than thirty miles an hour faster than the ancient fighter plane. But now, with the loss of one engine, his advantage in speed was canceled by the Fokker's agile maneuverability.

Smoke poured out of the exhaust stacks of the center engine, and it was only a matter of seconds before it caught fire. He reached down between his legs and turned off the fuel selector switch and then the ignition on a panel below the throttles, watching the propeller on the center engine come to a stop in the horizontal position.

Mary's face was flushed in confusion. "He's shooting at us!" she gasped.

"Don't bother asking me why," Pitt fired back.

Kelly appeared in the doorway of the cockpit. "Why are you throwing us all over the sky?" she demanded furiously. "You're frightening the children." Then she caught sight of the smoking engine, the shattered windshield, and felt the rush of air. "What is happening?"

"We're under attack by a lunatic."

"He's shooting at us with real bullets," Mary said loudly, holding up a hand and shielding her face from the onrush of air.

"But we have children on board," argued Kelly.

"He knows it and doesn't seem to care. Go back and calm the kids. Make them think we're playing a game. Urge them to sing. Do whatever it takes to occupy their minds and play down the danger." He turned his head slightly toward Mary and gave her a nod of encouragement. "Get on the radio and give a Mayday. To anyone who answers, report the situation."

"Can anyone help?"

"Not in time."

"What are you going to do?"

Pitt watched as the red Fokker triwing swept around for another pass at the trimotor. "Keep everyone alive if I can." Kelly and Mary both marveled at Pitt's unruffled calm, the grim determination that shone in his eyes. Mary began shouting a Mayday into the radio microphone while Kelly ran back into the main cabin.

He scanned the sky, searching for clouds to enter and lose the Fokker, but the few that floated in the sky were several miles away and a good twenty thousand feet above the ground, three thousand feet above the ceiling of the trimotor. No clouds to hide in, no place to escape. The old transport plane was as defenseless as a lamb in a pasture stalked by a wolf. Why was the pilot he'd met earlier doing this? Pitt's brain churned with questions, but there were no simple answers.

Pitt might have attempted to set the plane down in the East River. If he could make a water landing that didn't damage the airplane or injure the children, and if it floated long enough for them to escape: the thought quickly came and was rejected. With the trimotor's rigid landing gear, the potential for a watery crash was too high, and he couldn't be sure the blood-crazed pilot of the Fokker would not strafe the helpless passengers if they weren't injured in the landing. If he intended to shoot them out of the air, Pitt thought, the guy would have no qualms about killing them in the water.

Pitt made his decision and circled the trimotor back toward the Brooklyn Bridge.

The red Fokker stood on its wingtips and followed the trimotor on a reverse course down the river. Pitt eased back on the throttles to his two remaining engines and allowed his attacker to close. Unlike modern jet fighters with missiles that could down an enemy plane from a mile away, the aces of World War I held their fire to less than a hundred yards away. Pitt was counting on the Fokker's pilot to wait until the last minute to fire at the trimotor.

Like the historic days on the Western Front, the warnings of Allied pilots held true. Pitt thought of the old adage: Watch for the Hun in the sun. It was just as relevant now as it had been then. The Fokker's pilot pulled his nose up in a steep climb, nearly hanging it on its propeller, before dipping downward in a shallow dive out of the sun. At a hundred yards, the pilot opened fire as he swooped on the trimotor, the bullets tearing into the corrugated aluminum sheets on the right wing behind the engine. But time was too short — the twin Spandaus were on target for less than two seconds before Pitt pushed the trimotor in a near-vertical dive.

The plane plunged down toward the

water, the Fokker pilot right on its tail but not firing until he could line up his sights again. Down Pitt went until it looked to the people walking along both shores, those crowded on the upper deck of an excursion boat and firemen on a passing fireboat, as if the plane would surely smash into the water. But at the last instant, Pitt pulled back on the control column and sent the trimotor on a course that would take him directly under the Brooklyn Bridge.

The famous bridge loomed like a giant spiderweb with its maze of support cables. Completed in 1883, the bridge carried more than 150,000 cars a day, 2,000 bikers and 300 pedestrians. Traffic was stopping and people were gawking from their cars at the sight of the two old aircraft speeding toward the span. Pedestrians and bikers on the wooden walkway that was elevated over the traffic came to a halt and rushed to the railings. No one could believe the World War I fighter was actually pumping bullets into the old three-engine plane.

"Oh lord!" muttered Mary. "You're not going under the bridge."

"Watch me," Pitt said doggedly.

Pitt hardly took notice of the towers rising 271 feet in the air. He swiftly estimated the distance between the roadway and the water at 150 feet when it was actually 135. With smoke trailing from the center engine, the trimotor flashed under the bridge and broke out into the open, dodging a tugboat pushing a pair of barges.

Thrilled at seeing the bridge pass above, the children thought it was part of the ride. Kelly instructed them to sing. Blissfully unaware of the deadly seriousness of their plight, they broke into song:

This old man, he played one.
He played knick knack on my thumb.
With a knick knack paddy whack, give
   the dog a bone.
This old man came rolling home.

The air controllers at La Guardia, Kennedy and the surrounding smaller airports all picked up the Mayday message sent frantically by Mary, and the police radios were alive with reports of the aerial battle. The controller at Kennedy Airport called over his chief.

"I've got a Mayday from a woman in an old Ford trimotor from that air show today. She claims she's under attack by a World War I fighter plane."

The chief controller laughed. "Sure, and Martians are landing at the Statue of Liberty."

"There must be something to it. I'm receiving police calls saying a red triplane chased an old three-motored aircraft under the Brooklyn Bridge and smoked one of its engines."

The humor quickly faded. "Do you know if the transport is carrying passengers?"

"The police say it has fifteen disabled children on board." He paused and his voice hesitated. "I . . . I can hear them singing."

"Singing?"

The controller nodded silently.

The chief controller's face took on a pained expression. He stepped over to the radar array and put his hand on the controller monitoring incoming flights. "What do you read over Manhattan?"

"I had two aircraft over the East River, but the larger one just went offscreen."

"It crashed?"

"Looks that way."

The chief controller's eyes went sick. "Those poor kids," he murmured sadly.

The pilot of the Fokker pulled up and soared over the arched cables of the bridge with only feet to spare. Then he dove ahead to pick up additional speed and made a 180-degree turn, flying head-on toward the trimotor.

Rather than wait to be shot at like a tin can on a rock, Pitt stood the trimotor on its port wingtip and sent the aircraft on the sharpest turn possible, heading directly over piers eleven and thirteen and crossing the FDR Drive and South Street at a ninety-degree angle. He flattened out as he soared less than two hundred feet above Wall Street and swooped over the statue of George Washington taking the oath of office, the roar from the exhaust of the Pratt-Whitney echoing off the buildings and vibrating their windows. The seventy-seven-foot, ten-inch wingspan barely cleared the fronts of the buildings as he struggled to climb out of the glass-and-concrete canyon.

Mary sat in shock, blood trickling down one cheek cut by a flying shard of glass. "This is madness."

"Sorry," Pitt said flatly. "I don't have a wide range of choices."

Pitt pulled back the control column as he saw what looked to be a wide street that turned out to be the lower reach of Broadway. With only a few feet to spare, he made a sharp bank and swept up the famous thoroughfare only a block from the New York Stock Exchange past Saint Paul's Chapel and across from City Hall Park. Police cars with sirens attempted to follow in the path of the airplane, but it was no contest. They could not make their way through traffic at half the same speed.

The pilot of the red Fokker temporarily lost Pitt in the jungle of buildings. He circled over the East River before climbing to a thousand feet and heading over lower Manhattan. He passed above the tall ships at the South Street Seaport and leaned from the cockpit, trying to locate the trimotor again. And then he caught a flash of silver that reflected in the sun. He raised his goggles and stared disbelieving at the trimotor flying below the tops of the buildings up Broadway.

Pitt knew he was endangering lives, knew that having the red Fokker send him down in flames along with the children was also jeopardizing the people below on the streets and sidewalks. His only hope was to elude his nemesis long enough to gain a substantial lead and wing out of the city, leaving the crazed Fokker pilot to deal with police helicopters. He became fixed in his dedication to save the children as he heard their voices singing:

This old man, he played four.
He played knick knack on my door.
With a knick knack paddy whack, give
  the dog a bone.
This old man came rolling home.

Suddenly he saw the pavement below the trimotor explode in a spray of asphalt as the red Fokker swung onto his tail and unleashed a burst of 7.62 shells. The shells carved their way through the hood of a yellow taxicab and into a mailbox on the corner without hitting anyone. At first, Pitt thought the trimotor had escaped unscathed, but then he felt a noticeable lack of response in the controls. A quick check revealed that the rudder was sluggish and the elevators refused to respond. Only the ailerons still functioned normally. Pitt realized that a bullet must have struck either the pulleys or their mountings to the control cables that traveled from the cockpit to the rudder and elevators on the exterior of the fuselage.

"What's wrong?" asked Mary.

"The last burst caught our elevators. I can't pull her into a climb."

The Fokker's approach had been near-perfect, but the sight of buildings rising above his wings unhinged him, and he overshot the trimotor before his guns could do any fatal damage. The pilot pulled up in a sharp vertical climb and performed an Immelmann maneuver by entering a roll and coming out flying in the opposite direction. It was immediately apparent to Pitt that his opponent was not going to waste time with a frontal assault. He was content to come up from the rear and attack from behind the trimotor's big tail section.

"Can you keep him in sight?" Pitt asked Mary.

"Not when he's directly behind," she said calmly. She loosened her seat belt so she could twist around in her seat. "I'll lean out as far as I can and watch our tail."

"Good girl."

Kelly appeared in the doorway. "The children are incredible. They're taking it in stride."

"Because they don't know we're on borrowed time." Pitt glanced down and guessed that they were flying through Greenwich Village. Then they flashed over Union Square Park. He could see Times Square approaching ahead. He knew the theater district was only a block off to his left. The lights from the huge signs flashed past as he flew over the statue of George M. Cohan. He tried to pull the plane higher to rise from the city, but the elevator controls refused to respond. For the moment, all Pitt could do was maintain a straight-and-level flight. He was all right as long as Broadway was angling slightly to the west, but when it took a slight dogleg at Forty-eighth Street near Paramount Plaza, he knew he was in trouble. There was no feel to the elevators, and he had to push the pedals with all his strength to get the slightest response from the rudder. The ailerons were all he had, but the slightest miscalculation, the tiniest twitch of the control wheel, would send the plane smashing into the side of a building. He was reduced to maintaining a straight course up Broadway by orchestrating the throttles.

Pitt was sweating freely and his lips were dry. The sheer walls of New York City's buildings seemed close enough for him to reach through the side window and touch. The street ahead looked endless and he felt as if it were closing in and becoming narrower. The crowds of people on the sidewalks and crossing the intersections stood dumbstruck at seeing the trimotor flying down the middle of Broadway only ten stories above the pavement. The roar of the two engines was deafening, and they could hear it coming blocks away. Office workers who looked down at the plane from their windows as it roared past were frozen in disbelief at the bizarre sight. All who watched the trimotor's progress thought it was about to crash.

Pitt tried desperately to bring the nose up, but it simply would not rise. He throttled back to reduce the speed to a bare seventy miles an hour, only six miles an hour above stalling. The pilot of the red Fokker was a good flyer and skilled as a fox stalking a chicken. Pitt was in a battle that took every ounce of pure courage or fearless defiance. This was a conflict between two men of equal skill and technique, of patience and tenacity. He was not merely fighting for his life but the lives of two women and fifteen disabled children, and God only knew how many would die if the trimotor fell and exploded on the crowded streets of the city.

Behind him, the children were beginning to feel the first tentacles of fear at seeing the buildings so close to their windows, and yet they still managed to sing, urged on by Kelly, who was too frightened to look outside at the blur of passing office buildings and see the faces of stunned workers behind the glass windows.

At a thousand feet, the pilot of the Fokker gazed down at the trimotor threading its way between the stores and buildings of Broadway. His was the patience of the devil waiting for the soul of an honorable man. He did not feel the need to dive and strafe the old transport again just yet. There was every likelihood it would crash on its own. He watched with fascination as a police helicopter appeared and took up the chase, flying at an altitude just above the rooftops between the Fokker and the Ford.

Cool and precise, he eased the control stick forward, nosing the Fokker into a dive directly toward the helicopter. A policeman on board who had kept an eye on the red Fokker could be seen frantically shouting and pointing upward to the pilot. The helicopter swung to meet what they assumed was the onslaught, but the hand weapons carried by the crew were no match for the rapid-fire machine guns whose bullets spat from the twin muzzles and smashed into the engine below the rotor. The attack was executed with single-minded viciousness and savagery. The burst of gunfire lasted no more than three seconds. But they were three seconds that transformed the helicopter from a sleek flying machine into a shredded, falling wreck that dropped onto the roof of an office building.

Several people on the sidewalks were lacerated by flying debris, but incredibly none was seriously injured, nor were any killed. The two policemen, pulled from the wreckage by building maintenance employees, suffered a few broken bones but nothing that was life threatening.

It was inhuman. Inhuman action that served no earthly purpose. The pilot of the Fokker could just as easily have broken off the chase when he felt assured the trimotor had only seconds to remain in the air. His sole reason for shooting down the police helicopter was not self-preservation. It was a cold-blooded act of pure enjoyment. He hardly glanced back at the destruction before taking up the pursuit of the trimotor again.

Pitt was not aware of the catastrophe in the wake of his aircraft. Mary, looking back through the cockpit side window, saw it, but she was frozen into silence. The street was making a slight curve and he compressed his concentration to jockey the plane into a turn.

Broadway angled left as it crossed Columbus Circle. He gave the right rudder a hard kick and slewed the plane around to the right as it broke free of the long chasm of tall buildings. His left wingtip missed the seventy-foot-high statue of Christopher Columbus by less than ten feet as he banked over Central Park West and Fifty-ninth Street. At the southwest entrance to Central Park, he dodged around the monument to the victims of the battleship *Maine* and headed out over the park. Riders on the bridle path struggled to stay in the saddle as their horses reared when the trimotor roared overhead.

Thousands of people who were enjoying the park on a warm summer afternoon stopped their activities and stared at the drama unfolding above them. Police cars from all over the city were converging on the park, sirens screeching. More police helicopters were sweeping into the park from Fifth Avenue, accompanied by a squadron of helicopters from the television channels.

"He's coming back!" Mary shouted. "He's eight hundred feet above and diving on our tail!"

Pitt could bank and barely turn, but he couldn't gain a foot of altitude without the elevators that were shredded with bullet holes and frozen in the neutral position. A plan formed in his mind, a plan that would only work if the red Fokker made a strafing run directly over the trimotor and then overshot. He reached over and flicked the ignition and fuel switches of the middle engine to the on position. The battered engine coughed several times, then caught and began turning over. Then he banked the trimotor sharply to the right, knowing his insane attacker was thundering in from above. The evasive action momentarily caught the pilot off his mark, and the twin streams of fire from the red Fokker went wide to the left.

The old transport was no match for the maneuverability of the triwing plane flown with great success by Imperial Germany's finest pilots eighty years ago. The Fokker's pilot quickly compensated, and Pitt felt the thumping of bullets tearing into the upper wing of the trimotor and ripping into the starboard engine. Flames erupted inside the nacelle behind the engine, but its cylinders still beat strongly. He twisted the old plane in the opposite direction, waiting with infinite patience for the right moment to go on the attack.

Suddenly a storm of bullets swept the cockpit, smashing into the instrument panel. The mad pilot was anticipating Pitt's every move. The man was cunning, but it was Pitt's turn as the red Fokker flashed over the shattered windshield and roared ahead.

Pitt shoved all three throttles to their stops. With two engines, his speed matched that of the Fokker, but with his center engine throwing out clouds of smoke and oil but running on all cylinders, the trimotor leaped forward like a thoroughbred out of the chute.

His face streaking blood from windshield glass that had been hurled into his cheeks and forehead, splattered with oil and barely able to see through the smoke, Pitt shouted out in glorious defiance.

"Curse you, Red Baron!"

Too late, the leather-helmeted head in the red cockpit spun around and saw the silver trimotor boring through the air within twenty feet. He hurled the Fokker into a violent bank, flipping it on its wingtips. It was the wrong move. Pitt had outguessed him. If he'd pulled up in a steep climb, the trimotor would have been helpless to follow, not with the damaged elevators. But on a ninety-degree angle with its three starboard wings rising toward the sky, the red Fokker was vulnerable. One of the trimotor's big landing wheels smashed through the wood and fabric, shattering and splintering the upper wing into shreds.

Pitt only had time for one brief glimpse of the pilot as the Fokker catapulted crazily in an out-of-control spin. In a show of unabashed audacity, he shook his fist at Pitt.

Then Pitt lost sight of the red plane as it spun and crashed into the trees around the Shakespearean Gardens. The wooden propeller splintered into a hundred pieces as it struck the trunk of a large elm. The fuselage and wings crumpled like a boy's model airplane made from balsa wood, tissue paper and glue. Within minutes, the wreckage was surrounded by police cars, their red-and-blue lights flashing like colored lightning strikes.

With fortitude he didn't believe possible, Kelly was still leading the children in song as the battered aircraft struggled to stay aloft:

> *This old man, he played ten.*
> *He played knick knack on my hen.*

Pitt shut down the center and the starboard engines before they turned the trimotor into a torch. Like a badly wounded warhorse that never faltered in charging forward, the old bird fought to claw the air. Streaming smoke and flame, her one good engine racing at full rpm, Pitt made a flat circle and aimed the plane toward the largest open space in sight, a large grassy area known as the Sheep Meadow.

Hordes of people, who were picnicking or lying in the sun tanning, suddenly began scattering like ants when they saw the bullet-riddled aircraft losing altitude and coming their way. They didn't need an illustration to realize the plane might crash and burn in their midst. Leaning out the side window to avoid the smoke flooding the cockpit, Pitt squinted at the green field and lined up for a landing. Under normal circumstances, he knew he could land her on a quarter and give a dime for change, but with almost no control, all bets were off. He eased back on the throttle and slowly dropped her toward the grass.

Two thousand people stood in shocked silence, many praying the badly damaged plane engulfed by smoke and flame could somehow land safely without exploding on impact. Breaths were held, fingers crossed. They gazed fascinated and listened to the howling roar of the one engine running at full rpm. They stared and stared, numb with anticipation, fear and disbelief, as it brushed through the tops of the trees on the edge of the meadow. Years later, none who witnessed the incredible sight could describe it accurately. Their memory became hazy trying to recall the sight of the ancient aircraft lumbering toward the grassy field.

In the main cabin, the children were singing the final chorus:

This old man came rolling home.

The plane wavered as Pitt sideslipped it. Then it seemed to hang for a moment before the big wheels met the grass, bounced twice and then the plane was down, the tail wheel dropping to the ground. To everybody's amazement, the trimotor rolled to a stop in less than fifty yards. None who watched believed it possible.

Seeing the crowd pour toward the airplane, Pitt cut the remaining engine, watching its propeller come to a stop, the blade stopping in a vertical position. He turned to Mary and started to say something, to compliment her on her intrepid assistance. But he remained silent when he saw her face, drained of all color. He reached out and put his fingers against her neck, feeling for a pulse. Then his hand dropped and clenched.

Kelly leaned breathlessly into the cockpit. "You did it!" she burst out happily.

"The children?" Pitt asked in a distant voice.

"All unharmed."

Then she saw the back of Mary's copilot seat, the almost perfectly spaced pattern of small holes, punched by the Spandaus of the Fokker. Kelly stood absolutely still in shock as Pitt solemnly shook his head. At first, she refused to believe Mary was gone, her friend of many years dead, but she looked down and saw the expanding pool of blood on the cockpit floor and realized the awful truth.

Deep sorrow brushed her face, matched by the confusion in her eyes. "Why?" she murmured vacantly. "Why did this have to happen? There was no reason for Mary to die."

People came from all over the nearby streets and park to look at the peppered old aircraft and marvel. Thousands were shouting and waving at the cockpit. But to Pitt it was as if they were not visible and they could not be heard. He felt surrounded, not by the people, but by the futility of it all. He looked at Kelly, and he said, "She wasn't the only one killed by the man who flew that plane. There were many others who needlessly lost their lives."

"It's all so stupid," murmured Kelly, through hands covering her face as she sobbed.

"Cerberus," Pitt said quietly, barely audible above the cheering outside. "Someone — I don't know who yet — is going to Hades to meet him."

25

After the children's bumps and bruises caused from being knocked around during the fight with the Red Fokker and its unknown pilot were tended to by paramedics, they were reunited with their parents. Pitt stood by a grief-stricken Kelly as the body of her friend Mary Conrow was carried from the plane to an ambulance. After the police cordoned off the airplane, Pitt and Kelly were escorted to police cars to be taken to the nearest precinct for questioning.

Before he was led off, Pitt walked around the old Ford trimotor, amazed and saddened at the amount of punishment she had endured. Yet, she had miraculously hung in the air until he set her down safely in the Sheep Meadow. He studied the bullet-ripped tail section, the neatly stitched holes in the upper wings, the shattered cylinder heads on the two Pratt & Whitney engines, still crackling from the heat and emitting light swirls of smoke.

He laid a hand on the fender over a landing wheel and murmured, "Thank you."

Then he asked the police officer in charge if they might stop by the wreckage of the Fokker before heading for the precinct. The officer nodded and motioned to the closest police car.

The red Fokker looked like a crumpled kite as it lay embedded in a huge elm tree twenty feet off the ground. Firemen, working from a ladder on a fire truck, were standing under the wreckage, staring up at the mangled plane. Pitt exited the police car and walked under the plane. He stopped and stared at the engine that had been torn from its mountings and was lying partially embedded in the grass. He was surprised to find it wasn't an updated, modern engine, but an original Oberursel 9 cylinder that put out 110 horsepower. Then he stared up into the open cockpit.

It was empty.

Pitt looked into the branches of the tree and then studied the ground beneath the plane. A leather flying jacket, along with a helmet and goggles, its lenses smeared with streaks of blood, was the only trace of the pilot.

Almost miraculously, he had vanished.

While Kelly was being interrogated by police officers, Pitt was allowed to call a local aircraft-maintenance company and arrange for the trimotor to be disassembled and trucked back to Washington, where he would have it repaired and reconstructed to her previous pristine condition by aircraft-restoration experts. Then he called Sandecker and reported on the situation.

His calls made, Pitt calmly sat at an empty desk in the precinct and worked on the *New York Times* crossword puzzle until he was called. He and Kelly embraced as she left the office where four detectives were waiting at a scarred oak desk that showed its age by the number of old cigarette burn marks on its surface.

"Mr. Pitt?" asked a small man with a thin mustache. The detective was coatless and wore narrow suspenders.

"That's my name."

"I'm Inspector Mark Hacken. My fellow detectives and I would like to ask you a few questions. Do you mind if we record the session?"

"Not at all."

Hacken made no offer to introduce the other three men in the room. None looked like the police as depicted on TV. They all appeared like ordinary neighbors who mowed their lawns every Saturday.

Hacken began by asking Pitt to talk about himself briefly, explain his job at NUMA and tell how he came to bring his old aircraft to the Disabled Children's Air Show benefit. The other detectives asked an occasional question but mostly took notes, as Pitt described the flight from the moment he'd taken off with the disabled children from Gene Taylor Field until he'd landed on the Sheep Meadow in Central Park.

One of the detectives looked at Pitt and said, "I'm a pilot myself, and I hope you realize you could go to jail for your antics, not to mention losing your pilot's license."

Pitt gazed at the detective with a faint trace of a confident grin. "If saving the lives of fifteen disabled children makes me a criminal, so be it."

"You still might have accomplished that by not turning off the river and into the city streets."

"If I had not turned onto Wall Street when I did, we would have surely been shot down and crashed in the river. Trust me when I say there would have been no survivors."

"But you must admit, you took a terrible chance."

Pitt shrugged indifferently. "Obviously, I wouldn't be sitting here if I hadn't taken the gamble."

"Do you have any idea why the other pilot

would risk a million-dollar aircraft, load it with antique operational weapons and attack an old plane full of disabled kids?" asked Hacken.

"I only wish I knew," said Pitt, sneaking past the question.

"So do I," said Hacken sarcastically.

"Do you have any idea who the pilot was?" Pitt asked in return.

"Not a clue. He melted into the crowd and escaped."

"The aircraft has to have a registration number that would lead to the owner."

"Our experts haven't had a chance to examine the plane yet."

"Surely the air show officials have his entry papers," said Pitt. "We all had to fill them out for insurance purposes. They should tell you something."

"We're working with New Jersey law enforcement from that end. All they can tell us until they are further into the investigation was that an aircraft collector called and said an identical plane was hangared at a small field near Pittsburgh. He claimed the owner was one Raul St. Justin."

"Sounds phony," offered Pitt.

"We agree," said Hacken. "Did you know St. Justin, or whatever his true name is?"

"No." Pitt stared steadily into Hacken's eyes. "We talked briefly before I took off."

"What did you talk about?"

"His triplane. I've always been fascinated by antique aircraft. Nothing more."

"Then you had never met him previously."

"No."

"Can you give a description and assist our crime artist in making a likeness of his face?"

"I'll be happy to cooperate."

"We're sorry to have put you and Miss Egan through this, but with the death of Mary Conrow, we're looking at a murder investigation as well as charges of endangering public lives. It was a miracle no one was killed when the red airplane strafed you in the city streets and our police helicopter was shot down near a busy intersection."

"We can all be thankful for that," said Pitt sincerely.

"I think that will be all for now," said Hacken. "You and Miss Egan will, of course, have to remain in the city until our investigation is concluded."

"I'm afraid that is impossible, Inspector."

Hacken's eyebrows rose. He wasn't used to having a witness in a prominent case tell him he was leaving town. "May I hear why?"

"Because I'm a part of the ongoing government investigation into the fire on board the cruise ship *Emerald Dolphin*, as well as the hijacking of a NUMA survey ship. My presence is required in Washington." Pitt paused for effect. "Naturally, you'll want to clear this with my superior, Admiral Sandecker of the National Underwater and Marine Agency." He pulled out his wallet and handed Hacken his NUMA card. "Here is his phone number."

Hacken silently passed the card to one of his detectives, who left the room.

"Are you through with me? I'd like to take Miss Egan home."

Hacken nodded and gestured toward the door. "Please wait outside until we confirm your connection with the government and the investigation."

Pitt found Kelly sitting curled up on a wooden bench. She looked like a pathetic little girl left on the steps of an orphanage. "Are you all right?"

"I can't get over Mary's death," she said sadly. "She was a close friend of my father's for many years."

Pitt's eyes strayed across the busy precinct office to see if anyone was listening to their conversation. Satisfied that no one was within earshot, he asked, "Just how close *was* Mary to your father?"

She looked at him angrily. "They were lovers over the years, if that's what you want to hear."

"That's not what I want to hear," Pitt said softly. "How knowledgeable was she about your father's projects?"

"She was no stranger to them. Because I had my own career and was away most of the time, she acted as his close confidante, secretary, maid and housekeeper when she wasn't flying with the airlines."

"Did he ever talk to you about his work?"

She shook her head. "Dad was a very secretive man. He always said that explaining his work to anyone other than a scientist or engineer would be impossible. The only time he lectured me on his work was on board the *Emerald Dolphin*. He was quite proud of his engineering concepts for the ship's engines, and he explained their magnetohydrodynamics principle to me over dinner one night.

"That's all he ever told you?"

"After a few martinis in the lounge, he did say that he had created the breakthrough of the ages." Kelly shrugged wistfully. "I thought it was the gin talking."

"Then Mary was the only person aware of his activities."

"No." She looked up as if seeing someone. "Josh Thomas."

"Who?"

"Dr. Josh Thomas was my father's friend and sometimes his assistant. They went to MIT together and received their doctorates, Dad in engineering and Josh in chemistry."

"Do you know where you can get in touch with him?"

"Yes," she answered.

"Where is your father's laboratory?" Pitt asked.

"At his home not far from Gene Taylor Field."

"Can you call Dr. Thomas? I would like to meet him."

"Any particular reason?"

"You might say I'm dying to find out what the breakthrough of the ages is all about."

26

Admiral Sandecker stood at a podium and fielded questions thrown at him by the news media. If there was one thing the admiral was not, it was a media narcissist. Though he always had good relations with press and TV reporters and often enjoyed their company on a one-to-one basis, he simply was not at home in the spotlight, nor was he comfortable evading or dancing around probing inquiries. There were times when Sandecker was simply too honest and outspoken for bureaucratic Washington.

After forty minutes of hard questions about NUMA's role in the investigation of the tragic loss of the *Emerald Dolphin*, Sandecker was thankful that the news conference was winding down.

"Can you tell us what your people found inside the wreck during their probe with the submersible?" asked a nationally recognized female TV reporter.

"We believe we have found evidence suggesting that the fire was deliberately caused," replied Sandecker.

"Can you describe the evidence?"

"What looks like an incendiary material was found in the area where the ship's crew reported the fire started."

"Have you identified this substance?" asked a reporter from the *Washington Post*.

"It's over at the FBI lab as we speak," Sandecker hedged. "They should have results shortly."

"What can you tell us about the terrorist hijacking of your survey vessel, the *Deep Encounter*?" This from a reporter with CNN.

"Not much that you already don't know from previous reports. I wish I could tell you why criminal elements hijacked a NUMA ship, but unfortunately none of the pirates responsible lived to tell the tale."

A woman in a blue suit from ABC News raised her hand. "How did your NUMA crew manage to destroy the pirate ship and everyone on board?"

The question had to come, and Sandecker had prepared himself for it. As much as he hated to, he lied to protect the NUMA scientists and ships' crew from being labeled killers. "As near as we can tell, one of the hijackers guarding the entrance to the lagoon fired a missile in the dark at the *Deep Encounter*. He missed and the missile struck the pirate ship."

"What happened to the guard?" the woman persisted. "Didn't he live to be arrested?"

"No, he accidentally died during a struggle with my special projects director, who was attempting to stop him from firing a second missile at our survey ship."

A reporter from the *Los Angeles Times* caught Sandecker's attention. "Do you know what possible connection there might be between the two incidents?"

Sandecker threw up his hands and shrugged. "It's a mystery to me. You'll probably have better luck finding answers from the FBI and CIA during their ongoing investigation."

The *L.A. Times* reporter motioned for one more question, and Sandecker nodded.

"Would that be the same NUMA special projects director who was in on the rescue of the twenty-five hundred people on the *Emerald Dolphin*, who saved your survey vessel from being destroyed, and who saved the lives of those disabled children in New York yesterday during the dogfight?"

"Yes," Sandecker said proudly. "His name, as you already know, is Dirk Pitt."

The woman in the back of the room shouted the next question. "Do you think there is a connection — ?"

"No, I do not." Sandecker cut her off. "And please don't ask me any more questions on that subject because I haven't talked to Mr. Pitt since the incident, and I only know what I read in your newspapers and see on your television news programs." He paused, stepped back from the podium and raised his hands. "Ladies and gentlemen, that's all I know. Thank you for your courtesy."

Hiram Yaeger was waiting in Sandecker's outer office when the admiral returned. Dr. Egan's old leather case was sitting on the floor beside his chair. He had a fondness for the old case and had begun using it to take his workload home because it was larger and more square than the common briefcase. He rose and followed Sandecker through the door.

"What have you got for me?" asked Sandecker, sitting at his desk.

"I thought you might like an update on the CIA's dive project on the hijackers' ship," he said, opening the case and removing a file folder.

Sandecker stared at Yaeger over a pair of reading glasses, his eyebrows arched. "Where did you get your information? The CIA has given out nothing yet. I know for a fact they've only been diving on the wreck" — he paused to glance at his watch — "for the past ten hours."

"The project manager insists on running a constant data program every hour. You might say that we'll know what they've discovered almost as soon as they will."

"If they find out Max is hacking secret CIA files, we'll catch twenty different kinds of hell."

Yaeger grinned deviously. "Believe me, Admiral, they'll never know. Max is gaining the data from the salvage ship's computer before it's cryptogrammed and sent on for analysis at their headquarters at Langley."

Now it was Sandecker's turn to grin deviously. "So tell me what Max found."

Yaeger opened the file folder and began reading. "The hijackers' boat was identified as a one-hundred-thirty-five-foot crew/utility work boat built by the Hogan and Lashere Boat Yard of San Diego, California. She was designed to service the offshore oil industry in Indonesia. She was considered to have great flexibility and speed."

"Did they establish who owned her?" asked Sandecker.

"She was last registered to Barak Oil Company, a subsidiary of Colexico."

"Colexico," Sandecker echoed. "I thought they ceased to exist after they were bought out and shut down."

"A situation that didn't go down well with the Indonesian government when their main source of oil income disappeared."

"Who acquired Colexico?"

Yaeger gazed at him and smiled. "Colexico was taken over and disbanded by the Cerberus Corporation."

Sandecker leaned back in his chair, a smug expression on his face. "I'd like to see Charlie Davis's face when he hears this."

"There won't be a direct tie-in," said Yaeger. "Ownership of the boat was never transferred. A check through our own library finds no trace of the boat from 1999 to the present. And it's extremely unlikely the hijackers kept any evidence leading to Cerberus on the boat."

"Have the CIA salvage people identified any of the hijackers yet?"

"There's not much left of the bodies to ID, and the guard at the lagoon entrance went out to sea with the tide. As Dirk suspected, dental records and fingerprints will probably find that those guys were former Special Forces warriors who took discharge and went to work as mercenaries."

"A common occurrence with the military these days."

"Unfortunately, there's more money to be made outside than inside."

"Has Max come up with any theories on what possible motives the directors of Cerberus could have for committing mass murder?"

"She can't create a scenario that makes sense."

"Perhaps Dr. Egan is the key," Sandecker said pensively.

"I'll put Max to work on researching the good doctor's life."

Yaeger returned to his vast computer department and sat down at his keyboard. He called up Max and sat there staring into nothingness while she appeared in holographic form and waited. Finally, he looked up at her over his console.

"Anything happen while I was with the admiral?"

"The salvage divers reported finding virtually nothing relating to the pirate crew. No personal effects, no notebooks, nothing except their clothes and weapons. Whoever was in charge of the hijacking operation was a master of the cover-up."

"I'd like to take you off that project and have you do an in-depth biography on Dr. Elmore Egan."

"The scientist?"

"The same."

"I'll see what I can find that goes beyond the normal bio."

"Thank you, Max."

Yaeger felt tired. He decided to leave and go home early. He had been neglecting his family since he became immersed in the

Dolphin Incident, as it was becoming known. He decided to take his wife and two daughters out for dinner and a movie. He set the leather case on an open space of the console and opened it to deposit some files and papers inside.

Yaeger was not a man who startled easily. He was known as being as calm and laid-back as a bloodhound. But what he saw stunned him down to his socks. Cautiously, as if he were reaching into a bear trap, he dipped his hand inside the case. He rubbed the substance he encountered between his thumb and forefinger.

"Oil," he muttered to himself, staring blankly at the liquid that half filled the leather case. It's not possible, he thought in confusion. The case had not been out of his hands since he'd left Sandecker's office.

27

Kelly drove up Highway 9 on the west bank of the Hudson River. The day was soggy, with wind gusts throwing sheets of rain against the car. She handled the Jaguar XK-R hardtop sports car easily over the wet pavement. With a 370-horsepower supercharged engine under the hood and computer-activated suspension and traction control under the chassis, she didn't hesitate to propel the car at speeds far above the posted limit.

Pitt relaxed in the soft leather passenger's seat and enjoyed the drive, his eyes occasionally shifting to the left and marking the needle on the speedometer. He wanted to trust Kelly's driving abilities, but he hadn't known her long enough to know how sharp they were in the rain. To Pitt's relief, the traffic was light on an early Sunday morning. He relaxed and returned to watching the countryside roll by. The rocky land above the palisades was green, and forested with tall trees so thick he could rarely see for more than a quarter of a mile except when they opened up into farm fields.

He must have counted two dozen antique shops before Kelly turned right on a narrow asphalt road not far above Stony Point, New York. They passed several picturesque houses with flower gardens and well-manicured lawns. The road curved like a snake and finally ended at a gate that cut across the middle. It was not what one would expect in such a rural atmosphere. The tall rock walls leading from the gate looked rustic enough, despite their ten-foot height. But the gate was a steel-barred affair that would have stopped a speeding semi–truck and trailer loaded with lead. Two television cameras sat atop high poles opposite the road twenty yards behind the gate. The only way to put them out of operation was with well-aimed rifle bullets.

Kelly leaned out her window and punched a code in a box embedded in a rock pillar beside the road. Then she took a remote from the glove compartment and punched in another code. Only then did the gates slowly swing open. Once the car was through, they closed quickly so another vehicle behind could not have followed the Jaguar inside.

"Your father was certainly security conscious. His system is much more elaborate than mine."

"We're not through his security just yet. You can't see them, but there are four guards."

The road meandered through fields of corn, alfalfa and grain. They were passing between a vineyard thick with grapevines when a large barricade suddenly popped up in front of the car. Kelly was aware of the obstacle and had begun to slow down. The minute she stopped, a man stepped out of a large tree trunk with an automatic rifle, leaned down and peered inside the car.

"Always good to see you, Miss Egan."

"Hello, Gus. How's the baby girl?"

"We threw her out with the bathwater."

"How very wise of you." She motioned ahead toward a house that was barely visible through a copse of trees. "Is Josh here?"

"Yes, ma'am," answered the guard. "Mr. Thomas hasn't left the premises since your father died. I'm real sorry. He was a fine man."

"Thank you, Gus."

"Have a nice day." Almost before the guard finished speaking, he had melted back into the tree trunk again.

Pitt looked at her questioningly. "What was all that about throwing the baby out with the bathwater?"

"A code," Kelly explained with a smile. "Had I asked about his baby boy instead of girl, he'd have known I was being held hostage and shot you dead before alerting the other three guards."

"Did you grow up in this environment?"

Kelly laughed. "Oh my heavens, no. There was no need for security when I was a little girl. My mother died when I was ten, and because of Dad's long hours and dedication to his work, he thought it best if I move to the city and live with my aunt. So I grew up on the sidewalks of New York."

Kelly stopped the Jaguar in a circular drive in front of a large two-story Colonial house with tall columns around the front porch. Leaving the car, Pitt followed her up the steps to a large double door carved with the images of Vikings.

"What's the significance?"

"Nothing enigmatic. Dad loved to study Viking history. It was only one of his many passions besides his work." She held up a key but punched the doorbell. "I could let myself in, but I'd rather alert Josh."

In half a minute, a bald-headed man in his early sixties opened the door. He was wearing a vest with a striped shirt and bow tie. The remaining hair was gray, and he had the limpid blue eyes of someone who was constantly lost in thought. He wore a neatly clipped gray mustache beneath a long, rounded nose, reddened by a constant supply of alcohol.

At seeing Kelly, he broke into a wide smile, stepped forward, and swept her in his arms. "Kelly, how wonderful to see you." Then he eased her back and his face clouded with sorrow. "I'm so sorry about Elmore. It must have been horrible seeing him die."

"Thank you, Josh," said Kelly quietly. "I know what a shock it must have been for you."

"I never expected him to go, not that way. My greatest fear was *they* would do him mortal harm."

Pitt made a mental note to ask Josh Thomas who *they* were. He reached out and shook the offered hand as Kelly introduced them. The grip was not as firm as Pitt would have liked. But Thomas seemed like an affable man.

"Happy to meet you. Kelly told me a great deal about you over the phone. Thank you for saving her life, not once but twice."

"I'm only sorry I couldn't have helped Dr. Egan, too."

Thomas's face reflected agonized grief, and he put his arm around Kelly's shoulders. "And Mary. What a wonderful lady. Why would anybody want to kill her?"

"She is a great loss for us both," Kelly said grievously.

"Kelly has told me you were very close to her father," said Pitt, trying to get off the subject of death.

Thomas motioned them inside. "Yes, yes, Elmore and I worked together off and on for more than forty years. He was the smartest man I've ever known. He'd have given Einstein and Tesla a run for their money. Mary was brilliant in her own right. If she hadn't loved flying so much, she might have been a first-rate scientist."

Thomas led them into the comfortable living room decorated with Victorian furniture and offered them a glass of wine. He returned in a few minutes with a tray, holding a bottle of Chardonnay and three glasses. "I feel odd, entertaining Kelly in her own house."

"It will be a while before the estate is settled," said Kelly. "In the meantime, consider it your home." She held up her glass. "Cheers."

Pitt stared at the wine inside the glass as he spoke. "Tell me, Mr. Thomas, what was Dr. Egan working on when he died?"

Thomas looked at Kelly, who nodded. "His big project was the design and development of a proficient and reliable magnetohydrodynamic engine." He paused and looked Pitt in the eye. "Kelly tells me you're a marine engineer with NUMA."

"Yes, that's right." Pitt had a vague

feeling that Thomas was shielding something.

"Then she's told you Dr. Egan was on the *Emerald Dolphin*'s maiden voyage because the engines he created and whose construction he supervised were mounted in the cruise ship."

"Kelly made me aware of it. But what I would like to know is what Dr. Egan's contribution was. Magnetohydrodynamic engines have been in the experimental state for twenty years. The Japanese built a ship using the same propulsion principles."

"True, but it was not efficient. The ship was slow and never became commercially efficient. Amazingly, Elmore created a successful source of power that would revolutionize the field of maritime propulsion. He designed the engines almost from scratch in a little over two years. An amazing achievement, considering that he worked alone. The research and development should have taken over a decade, but he built a working model in less than five months. Elmore's experimental units went far beyond any MHD technology. They were self-sustaining."

"I explained to Dirk how Dad's engines were able to use seawater as a source for fuel, which created the energy source to pump the water through thrusters," said Kelly.

"As revolutionary as the idea was,"

Thomas continued, "the first engines did not function properly and would burn out from the extremely high rate of friction buildup. I went to work with Elmore to solve the problem. Between us, we came up with a new formula for oil that would not break down under extreme heat and friction. This threw open the door for engines that could operate indefinitely without breaking down."

"So the two of you developed a super oil," said Pitt.

"Yes, you could call it that."

"What would its advantages be if used in internal combustion engines?"

"Theoretically, you could run an automobile engine two million miles or more before the internal workings required any repair," replied Thomas matter-of-factly. "Heavy-duty diesel engines could conceivably operate efficiently for ten million miles. Aircraft jet engines would especially benefit with longer life and less maintenance. The same for every industrial vehicle from forklifts to earthmovers."

"Not to mention boat and ship-propulsion units," added Pitt.

"Until new technology for energy is perfected that does not rely on moving parts," said Thomas, "our formula, which Elmore and I jokingly called Slick Sixty-six, will have enormous consequences for every mechanical power source that depends on oil for lubrication."

"How expensive is it to refine and produce?"

"Would you believe three cents a gallon more than normal motor oil?"

"I don't imagine the oil companies will be particularly happy about your discovery. They could very well lose billions of dollars, even trillions over twenty years. Unless, of course, they buy your formula and market it themselves."

Thomas shook his head slowly. "Never happen," he said decisively. "Elmore never intended to make a dime. He was going to give the formula to the world free of charge, no strings attached."

"From what you've said, the formula was half yours. Did you also agree to contribute it to the common good?"

Thomas uttered a quiet laugh. "I'm sixty-five years old, Mr. Pitt. I have diabetes, acute arthritis, an iron-overload disease called hemochromatosis, and cancer of both the pancreas and liver. I'll be lucky to walk the earth five years from now. What would I do with a billion dollars?"

"Oh, Josh," Kelly said despondently. "You never said . . ."

He reached over and patted her hand. "Even your father had no inkling. I kept it from everyone until now, when it no longer matters." Thomas paused and picked up the wine bottle. "More wine, Mr. Pitt?"

"Not quite yet, thank you."

"Kelly?"

"Yes, please. After what you've told me, I could use some courage."

"I see you have heavy security," said Pitt.

"Yes," acknowledged Thomas. "Elmore and I have had our lives threatened many times. I was wounded in the leg after a thief attempted to break into the laboratory."

"Someone tried to steal your formula?"

"Not just someone, but an entire industrial conglomerate."

"Do you know who?"

"The same corporation that threw Elmore and me out the door after twenty-five years of dedicated work."

"You were both fired?"

"At the time, Dad and Josh were still working to perfect the oil formula," replied Kelly. "The company's directors prematurely began making future plans to produce Super Slick and sell it with the goal of gaining enormous profits."

"Elmore and I wouldn't hear of it," said Thomas. "We agreed that it was too vital for the human good to sell it only to those who could afford it. Foolishly, the directors thought their other chemists and engineers had enough data to produce it on their own, and they gave us our walking papers, threatening to sue us into the gutter if we attempted to complete the experiment on our own. Bodily harm and death were also veiled threats. But we went ahead anyway."

"Do you believe it was your old company who tried to kill you and steal the formula?" asked Pitt.

"Who else was aware of our work?" Thomas said, as if Pitt knew the answer. "Who else had the motive and stood to benefit? When they failed to find the key to our formula, their program became a disaster. Then they came after us."

"Who are they?"

"The Cerberus Corporation."

Pitt felt as if he had been hit over the head with a mallet. " 'The Cerberus Corporation,' " he echoed.

"You're familiar with it?" asked Thomas.

"There is evidence that links them with the burning of the *Emerald Dolphin*."

Surprisingly, Thomas did not appear shocked. "I would not put it past them," he said evenly. "The man who owns and controls the company will stop at nothing to protect his interests, even if it meant burning a cruise ship along with every man, woman and child on board."

"He doesn't sound like somebody you'd want as an enemy. What about stockholders? Don't they have a clue about what's going on under the table?"

"Why should they care, when they're pocketing enormous returns on their investments? Besides, they had little to say about anything. Curtis Merlin Zale, the man at the top of the empire, owns eighty percent of the stock."

"A terrible thing for a giant American corporation to murder for company profit."

"More of it goes on than you might suspect, Mr. Pitt. I can give you the names of men who were connected with the Cerberus Corporation and who, for whatever reasons, have disappeared or been found dead in what were called accidental circumstances. Some supposedly committed suicide."

"How strange the government hasn't investigated their criminal operations."

"Cerberus has its claws into every agency in the state and federal government. They think nothing of paying a million dollars to a minor official to work undercover for them, relaying useful information of importance. Any politician who toes the line in behalf of Cerberus will find himself very wealthy, with a fortune in an offshore bank account, when he retires from politics." Thomas paused to pour himself another glass of wine. "And don't kid yourself into thinking someone might turn informer if they think they've been slighted or suddenly feel a desire to go honest. Cerberus has a program to prevent their dirty laundry from going public. The informer's family might be threatened by bodily harm, and that'd be backed up by a son or daughter suffering a broken arm or leg in what would look like an innocent accident. If that didn't keep the informer silent, he or she would simply become a suicide. Or maybe he'd succumb to a fatal disease injected into his body unknowingly in a crowded situation. You'd be surprised at how many news media investigations were called off by the heads of the newspapers or television networks after meetings with Cerberus directors. One who threw them out of his office came into the fold when one of his daughters was found badly beaten in a supposed mugging. Believe me, Mr. Pitt. These are not nice men."

"Whom do they hire to do their dirty work?"

"A covert organization called the Vipers. They only take their orders from Zale personally. I know this because Elmore was secretly told by an old friend in the Vipers who warned him that he and I were on the murder list."

"What happened to the old friend?"

"He disappeared," Thomas answered offhandedly, as if it was a foregone conclusion.

Something tugged in the back of Pitt's mind. "The tail of Cerberus, the guardian of Hades."

Thomas looked at Pitt, intrigued. "You

know about the three-headed dog."

"The corporation logo. The end of the dog's tail is the head of a snake."

"It's become a corporate icon," said Thomas.

"What is morale like among the employees?" Pitt asked.

"From the day they come on the job, they are indoctrinated like recruits in a cult. The company goes out of its way to provide a four-day workweek, large year-end bonuses, perks that go far and above what other corporations provide. It's almost as if they've been enslaved and don't know it."

"Cerberus has no problems with the unions?"

"Unions have never made a dent in Cerberus. If union officials make an appeal, word quickly goes out that anyone who wants to unionize will not be fired, but lose their bonus and fringe benefits, which as I've said are considerable. When an old employee dies or retires, his job usually goes to his children; it's that hard to break into the company infrastructure. The relationships from the top on down to the janitors are like parishioners in a church. Adoration of the company has become a religion. In the workers' eyes, Cerberus can do no wrong."

"How is it you and Dr. Egan survived for so long after leaving the company?"

"Because the man who directs corporate

operations left us alone, planning to steal the formula for the oil and the designs for Elmore's magnetohydrodynamic engine designs at his convenience."

"But why wait until Dr. Egan's engines were perfected and installed in the *Emerald Dolphin*?"

"So they could destroy the ship and blame the cause on the engines," replied Thomas. "If they ruined the engines' reputation for reliability, it'd discourage buyers and they could snatch up the patents for a song."

"But the fire did not start in the engine room."

"I was not aware of that," answered Thomas in bewilderment. "If what you say is correct, my only guess is that the operation to burn the ship somehow miscarried, didn't go as planned. But that's only a guess."

"Perhaps a good one," Pitt said in agreement. "We found incendiary devices in the ship's chapel where the crew said the fire started. A string of them was probably timed to go off in sequence, beginning in the engine room and traveling to the upper decks until the last one ignited in the ship's chapel. But as you suggest, something went wrong."

Pitt did not say it, but he realized that failing to condemn the MHD engines for the disaster was another reason for the ship to be sunk before an official investigation.

Thomas dropped his voice, speaking softly. Pitt could barely hear him. "I only hope and pray they don't attempt the same criminal act on the *Golden Marlin*."

"The new luxury submarine that's designed like an underwater cruise ship?"

"Yes, it begins its maiden voyage two days from now."

"Why should you be concerned?" inquired Kelly.

Thomas looked at her. "You don't know?"

"Know what?" Pitt came back.

"The *Golden Marlin* is owned by the Blue Seas Cruise Lines. The engines that Elmore and I developed were built and mounted in her, too."

28

Pitt immediately alerted Admiral Sandecker, who dispatched a NUMA jet to pick him up at the Gene Taylor airfield. Kelly drove even faster on the return trip down the river, arriving only minutes before the jet landed. She insisted that she could be useful, and no argument from Pitt held enough water to keep her from boarding the plane and accompanying him to Washington.

Giordino and Rudi Gunn were waiting on the tarmac when the plane taxied to a stop at Langley Field. They'd no sooner boarded the plane than it was airborne again, flying south to Fort Lauderdale, Florida, and the corporate headquarters of the Blue Seas Cruise Line. Gunn had arranged for a Lincoln Town Car as transportation, and within minutes of the jet landing, they were heading toward the harbor with Giordino at the wheel.

The Blue Seas building towered 900 feet above the waterfront on an island where the Blue Seas cruise ships docked. The exterior design was shaped like a gargantuan sailboat. The outside elevators were housed in one huge shaft that rose into the sky like a mast. The rest of the mostly glass-enclosed building was arched like a giant sail. The glass walls were blue, with a center wall of stretched white fabric that could withstand winds up to 150 miles an hour. The lower forty floors of the building housed the offices of the cruise line, while the upper fifty floors housed a hotel for the passengers to stay in before boarding the fleet of cruise ships.

Giordino turned into an underground tunnel that ran under the water to the island holding the huge building. A valet took the car, and they entered one of the outer elevators and rode three levels up to the main lobby, which was situated under an atrium that rose 700 feet in the middle of the office and hotel floors. The secretary to the CEO of the Blue Seas Cruise Lines was waiting for them and escorted them up a private executive elevator to the head office on the fortieth floor. Warren Lasch, the president of the cruise line, came from behind his desk to greet them.

Rudi Gunn made the introductions, and everyone took a chair.

"Now, then." Lasch, a tall man with graying hair and slightly on the heavy side, looked as if he might have played football in college. He peered through dark, coffee brown eyes that moved from Pitt to Kelly to Giordino to Gunn like a panoramic camera recording a scenic vista and then back again. "What is this all about? Admiral Sandecker seemed quite adamant over the phone that we postpone the sailing of the *Golden Marlin*."

"There is fear the ship may suffer the same fate as the *Emerald Dolphin*," Gunn replied.

"I have yet to see a report that says it was anything but an accident," Lasch said, his face expressing doubt. "I find it impossible that another disaster could happen."

Pitt leaned forward slightly in his chair. "I can assure you, sir, that NUMA has found irrefutable proof that the fire was intentionally ignited and evidence that clearly shows explosives were used to sink the ship while she was under tow."

"This is the first I've heard about it." The sudden anger in Lasch's voice was distinct. "The insurance companies that covered the ship have not reported to me or my corporate directors that the fire was deliberately set. All we've been told is that the fire emergency systems, for whatever reason, failed to operate properly. Blue Seas will, of course, file lawsuits against the companies who manufactured the systems."

"That may present a problem if it is proven conclusively that the fire systems were purposefully disabled."

"You'll never sell me on that fairy tale."

"Believe me," said Pitt, "it is no fairy tale."

"What possible motive could anyone have for destroying the *Emerald Dolphin* and murdering thousands of passengers?"

"We believe the motive was the destruction of Dr. Elmore Egan's new magnetohydrodynamic engines," explained Giordino.

"Why would anyone want to destroy the greatest propulsion technology of the new century?" asked Lasch, seemingly baffled.

"To eliminate competition."

"Frankly, gentlemen" — he nodded at Kelly and smiled — "and ladies, I cannot help but find your story anything but pure fabrication."

"I wish we could explain in more elaborate detail," said Gunn, "but at the moment our hands are tied until the FBI and CIA make their conclusions public."

Lasch was no fool. "Then this is not an official NUMA inquiry, nor is it authorized."

"In all honesty," Gunn answered, "no."

"I hope you're not going public with such outlandish speculation."

"Admiral Sandecker agreed that any official report should not be released until the investigation is concluded by all the agencies involved," said Pitt. "I might also add that he believed that it would harm the cruise ship industry if the news media began sensationalizing the incident with stories of terrorists destroying ships and killing passengers."

"I couldn't agree more heartily on that point," Lasch conceded. "But why prevent the *Golden Marlin* from sailing? Why not a hundred other cruise ships? If the sinking of the *Emerald Dolphin* was a terrorist act, why not alert other cruise lines around the world?" Lasch threw up his hands. "You cannot convince me to delay the sailing of the *Golden Marlin* on her maiden voyage. As the first underwater cruise ship, she will usher in a new age of luxury sailing. People made their reservations as long as two years ago. In good conscience, I cannot disappoint the four hundred passengers who have booked passage. Many have already arrived and are staying in the hotel. I'm sorry. The *Golden Marlin* will sail tomorrow as scheduled."

"Since we cannot persuade you otherwise," said Pitt, "can we make a case for increased security and a crew of marine inspectors to maintain a constant check of all equipment and systems on board the ship during the voyage?"

"Boat," Lasch interrupted, grinning. "Submarines are called boats."

"Isn't it a luxury liner?" asked Kelly.

"When sailing on the surface, but this vessel is built to cruise underwater."

"Will you agree to extra security and an inspection team?" persisted Gunn.

"Yes, most certainly," Lasch said affably.

Pitt was not finished with his requests. "I would also like to have a dive team inspect the hull below the waterline."

Lasch nodded curtly. "I can arrange for divers. We have them on staff for underwater repair and maintenance to both ships and building."

"Thank you for your cooperation," said Gunn.

"Though I believe the precautions are unnecessary, I don't want a repeat of the *Emerald Dolphin* tragedy. If not for Lloyds of London, Blue Seas would have surely filed for bankruptcy."

"Giordino and I would like to go along, if you have no objection," said Pitt.

"Include me," Kelly insisted. "I have a vested interest in my father's work."

Lasch rose from his chair. "I see no problem. Despite our differences of opinion, I'll be happy to arrange for staterooms. All the passenger accommodations are booked, but there may be a few no-shows. If not, I'm sure we can arrange something in the crew's quarters. The boat will arrive at the dock front of the hotel tomorrow morning at seven o'clock. You may board then."

Gunn shook Lasch's hand. "Thank you, Mr. Lasch. I hope we haven't unduly alarmed you, but Admiral Sandecker felt you should be aware of any potential danger."

"I quite agree. Please tell the admiral I'm grateful for his concern, but I foresee no serious problems. The *Golden Marlin* has undergone extensive sea trials, and Dr. Egan's engines *and* all the boat's emergency systems performed beautifully."

"Thank you, Mr. Lasch," said Pitt. "We'll keep you informed of any new developments."

As they left Lasch's office and were riding down in the elevator, Giordino sighed. "Well, we tried."

"I'm not surprised," said Gunn. "The *Emerald Dolphin* disaster has left the company hanging on the ropes. Postponing the sailing of the *Golden Marlin* would have closed the cruise line for certain. Lasch and his directors have no choice but to send the ship on her maiden voyage and hope for an uneventful cruise."

After Gunn returned to the airport for the flight back to Washington, Pitt, Giordino and Kelly arranged through Warren Lasch's private secretary to book rooms at the hotel for the night. As soon as he was settled in, Pitt called Sandecker.

"We failed to talk Lasch into postponing the sailing," Pitt explained.

"I thought you would." Sandecker sighed.

"Al and I, along with Kelly, are sailing on the boat."

"You cleared this with Lasch?"

"He agreed without argument."

Pitt could hear the admiral shuffling papers on his desk over the phone. Then Sandecker said, "I have a bit of news for you. The FBI think they have identified the man behind the fire on the *Emerald Dolphin* from descriptions given by the surviving passengers."

"Who is he?"

"A real sour apple, this one. His real name is Omo Kanai. Born in Los Angeles. He built a five-page rap sheet by the time he was eighteen and enlisted in the Army to escape an assault charge. Worked himself up through the ranks before becoming an officer and transferring into a highly secret military organization called CEASE."

"Never heard of it."

"Considering their function, very few in government have," said Sandecker. "CEASE stands for Covert Elite Action for Select Elimination."

"I've still never heard of it," said Pitt.

"It was originally formed to combat terrorism by assassinating terrorist leaders before their actions could threaten American citizens. But a decade ago, the president curtailed their projects and ordered them disbanded, which was not a good idea as it turns out. Highly trained in political and covert murder, Omo Kanai, now a captain, resigned along with twelve of his men and formed a commercial assassination company."

"A Murder Incorporated."

"Along the same lines. They hire out for killings. There is a whole list of unsolved deaths over the past two years, from politicians to corporate directors to certain celebrities. They've even hit Mafia leaders."

"Aren't they under investigation?" asked Pitt.

"The FBI has files, but these guys are good. They leave behind no evidence of their involvement. Investigative agents are frustrated because they have yet to lay a finger on Kanai and his murdering gang. There is growing fear that future economic wars will lead to death squads."

"Murder and mayhem are hardly what economic forecasters have in mind."

"Repulsive as it may sound," Sandecker said conversationally, "there are a few corporate CEOs here and there who will stop at nothing to achieve power and monopoly."

"Which brings us to Cerberus."

"Correct," Sandecker answered succinctly. "And it's becoming more evident that not only was Kanai behind the fire on board the *Emerald Dolphin* and the explosions that blew out the hull of the liner while under tow, but it was he, impersonating a ship's officer, who sabotaged the fire-control systems."

"One man could not have done all that alone," Pitt said dubiously.

"Kanai doesn't always work alone. That's why I'm warning you and Al to be alert every second you're on the *Golden Marlin*."

"We'll keep a sharp eye out for any suspicious behavior by the crew."

"Better you keep an eye out for Omo Kanai."

"You lost me," Pitt said, puzzled.

"His ego is too great. He won't leave a job like this to his subordinates. You can bet he'll run the show himself."

"Any idea what he looks like?"

"You should know. You met him."

"I met him? Where?"

"I've just received word from New York police investigators. Omo Kanai was the pilot of the old plane that tried to shoot you down."

29

The *Golden Marlin* looked like no other cruise liner ever built. There were no promenade decks, no stateroom balconies, no smoke or exhaust funnels. Her rounded superstructure was covered with rows of large, circular viewing ports. The only prominent features were a round, domelike structure above her bow that housed the bridge and control room, while on the stern a high fin enclosed an opulent lounge and casino that revolved around stationary viewing ports.

At 400 feet in length and 40 feet wide, she was in the same class as most of the smaller luxury cruise liners that sailed the seas. Until now, undersea tourist excursions were undertaken in small submarines that were limited in depth and distance. The *Golden Marlin* was about to change the history of cruising. With her self-sustaining engines designed by Dr. Egan, she could travel throughout the Caribbean Sea, in depths up to 1,000 feet for two weeks, before coming into port for food and supplies.

Given the public's insatiable lust for leisure-time activity and with an economy that put increased amounts of spendable income in their pockets, ocean cruising had become a mushrooming segment of the three-trillion-dollar international travel and tourism market. Now, with a submarine cruise liner, the horizon for undersea travel was about to spread immeasurably.

"She's beautiful," exclaimed Kelly, as she stood on the dock in the early morning, staring up at the unique vessel.

"The gold is a bit much," muttered Giordino, adjusting his sunglasses from the glare that glinted off the superstructure from the rising sun.

Pitt was silent as he studied the seamless shape of the titanium hull. Unlike on older ships, no plates or rivets were visible. The big tourist submarine was a marvel of marine technology. He was admiring the workmanship when a ship's officer approached from the foot of the gangway.

"I beg your pardon, but are you the people from NUMA?"

"We are," answered Giordino.

"I'm Paul Conrad, the boat's first officer. Mr. Lasch advised Captain Baldwin of your joining us for the maiden voyage. Do you have any luggage?"

"Only what we carry," said Kelly, looking forward to seeing the interior of the boat.

"You'll have a stateroom, Miss Egan," said Conrad politely. "Mr. Pitt and Mr. Giordino will have to share a cabin in the crew's quarters."

"Next to the showgirls who perform in the theater?" asked Giordino with a straight face.

"No such luck," Conrad laughed. "Please follow me."

"I'll be with you in one moment," said Pitt. He turned and walked along the dock to a ladder leading to the water. A man and a woman wearing wet suits were checking their dive gear before stepping down the ladder and entering the water. "Are you the team who is going to inspect the bottom of the hull?"

A slim, handsome man looked at him and smiled. "Yes, that's right."

"My name is Dirk Pitt. I was the one who requested your services."

"Frank Martin."

"And the lady?"

"My wife, Caroline. Honey, this is Dirk Pitt from NUMA. We can thank him for the job."

"Pleased to meet you," said a lovely blonde who nicely filled out her wet suit.

Pitt shook her hand, surprised at the

strong grip. "I'll bet you're an expert diver."

"Been doing it for fifteen years."

"She can dive as well as any man," Martin said proudly.

"Can you tell us exactly what it is we're looking for?" asked Caroline.

"No sense in dodging the issue," replied Pitt. "You'll be looking for any sort of object that's attached to the hull, specifically an explosive device."

Martin looked unfazed. "And if we find one?"

"If you find one, you'll find others. Don't touch them. We'll arrange for an underwater demolition team to remove them."

"Who do we notify?"

"The captain of the ship. It's his responsibility at that point."

"A pleasure meeting you, Mr. Pitt," said Martin.

"Likewise," Caroline spoke, with a charming smile.

"Good luck," Pitt said warmly. "You'll make my day if you don't find anything."

By the time he reached the gangway, the Martins were in the water and diving under the *Golden Marlin*'s hull.

The boat's first officer led Kelly through a luxurious solarium and up a glass elevator etched with tropical fish to a comfortable stateroom on the Manta Deck. Then he showed Pitt and Giordino to a small cabin below the passenger decks in the crew's quarters.

"I would like to meet with Captain Baldwin as soon as it's convenient," said Pitt.

"The captain is expecting you for breakfast in the officers' dining room in half an hour. The boat's officers and an inspection team from the boatbuilder that came aboard late last night will also be present."

"I'd like Miss Egan to attend," said Pitt in an official tone.

Conrad looked uneasy but quickly recovered. "I'll ask Captain Baldwin if he'll permit the lady to sit in on the meeting."

"Since this boat wouldn't exist if it hadn't been for the genius of her father," said Giordino curtly, "I think it only proper that she be present."

"I'm sure he'll agree," Conrad said hastily, as he exited the cabin and closed the door.

Looking around the sparse and closetlike cabin, Giordino said, "I get the impression we're not welcome here."

"Welcome or not," said Pitt, "we've got to ensure the safety of the boat and its passengers." He reached into his duffel bag and handed Giordino a portable radio. "You contact me if you find anything. I'll do likewise."

"Where do we start?"

"If you wanted to send this vessel to the bottom and everyone with it, how would you go about it?"

Giordino looked thoughtful for a few moments. "If I got away with a fire on the *Emerald Dolphin*, I might try the same game again. But if I wanted to send her to the bottom with no fuss or muss, I'd blow out either the hull or the ballast tanks."

"My thoughts exactly. You start with that scenario and search the ship for explosives."

"What are you going to look for?"

Pitt smiled, but there was no humor behind it. "I'm going to look for the man who will light the fuse."

If Pitt had hoped the captain of the *Golden Marlin* was going to be a model of harmonious cooperation, he was wrong. Captain Morris Baldwin was a man who walked a straight line and never deviated. He ran a tight ship and did not intend to have outsiders come on board and disrupt his set routine. His only home was the ship he served. If he had a wife, which he did not, or a home, which he found a waste of time, he would have been an oyster without a shell.

His face was a stern mask, red, ruddy and never cheerful. He gazed through beady dark walnut eyes under heavy lids that were set and grim. Only the magnificent silver mane gave him an air of sophisticated authority. His shoulders were as broad as Giordino's, but he was a good ten inches heavier in the waist. He drummed his fingers on the table in the officers' dining room and stared steadily at Pitt, who stared back without so much as a blink.

"You say this ship is in danger?"

"I do," said Pitt, "and so does Admiral Sandecker and a number of other high officials with the FBI and CIA."

"Nonsense," he said distinctly, his knuckles whitening on his chair's armrest. "Just because one of our liners suffered a disaster doesn't mean there will be a repeat performance. This boat is as safe as they come. I've gone over every inch of her myself. Hell, I even supervised her construction." He looked around the table in irritation at Pitt, Giordino and the four-man inspection team sent by the shipbuilders. "Do what you think you have to do. But I warn all of you not to interfere with the operation of this boat during the voyage, or I swear I will put you ashore in the next port, regardless of whatever reprimand I receive from management."

Rand O'Malley, a man every bit as gruff as Baldwin, smiled sardonically. "As head of the inspection team, I can assure you, Captain, we will not get in your way. But I expect you to cooperate if we should find a problem with any of the safety systems."

"Search all you want," muttered Baldwin. "I promise that you'll find nothing that will endanger this boat."

"I suggest you wait until you receive a report from the divers who are inspecting the lower hull," said Pitt.

"I see no reason to wait," Baldwin snapped.

"There is the possibility they may find foreign objects attached to the hull."

"This is real life, Mr. Pitt," Baldwin said indifferently, "not some fantasy tale on television."

For perhaps nearly half a minute, there was silence, total silence. Then Pitt was on his feet, arms outstretched, leaning on the table with both hands, his lips parted in a brisk wintry smile, his eyes boring into Baldwin's.

Giordino knew all the signs. Here it comes. Good old Dirk, Giordino thought blissfully. Give the arrogant jerk hell.

"It appears that you have no idea of the danger your boat is facing," Pitt said solemnly. "I'm the only one at this table who witnessed the terrible havoc the fire created on the *Emerald Dolphin*. I saw men, women and children die by the hundreds, some burning alive in agony, others drowning before we could get to them. The sea bottom is littered with ships whose captains thought they were invincible and immune to catastrophe. The *Titanic*, *Lusitania*, *Morro Castle*, their captains all ignored the omens and the danger signs and paid a heavy price. When it comes, Captain Baldwin, as it surely will, to this boat and everyone on board, it will come with lightning speed before you and your crew can react. The crisis will strike with overwhelming suddenness from a quarter you never suspected. And then it will be too late. The *Golden Marlin* and everybody on it will have died, and their deaths will be on your head."

Pitt paused to stand up straight. "The people who are determined to destroy your ship are doubtless already on board as we speak, posing as one of your officers, your crew or perhaps passengers. Do you get the picture, Captain Baldwin? Do you?"

Strangely, Baldwin did not show anger. His expression was remote, without any show of emotion. Then he said tightly, "Thank you for your opinion, Mr. Pitt. I shall take your words under consideration." Then he came to his feet and walked toward the door. "Thank you, gentlemen. We sail in exactly thirty-seven minutes."

As soon as the room cleared, except for Pitt, Giordino and O'Malley, Giordino leaned back in his chair and irreverently crossed his feet on the conference table. " 'We sail in exactly thirty-seven minutes,' "

434

he mimicked Baldwin. "Exacting old bird, isn't he?"

"Made out of dung and concrete, that one," observed O'Malley.

Pitt took an instant liking to the man, as did Giordino. "I hope you take us more seriously than Captain Baldwin."

O'Malley grinned with every tooth. "If you're right, and I'm not saying you ain't, I'm not about to die on this extravagant folly to man's greed."

"I take it you're not fond of her," said Pitt, amused.

"She's overbuilt," snorted O'Malley. "More expense and planning went into the palatial decor than into the true guts of the engineering systems. Successful sea trials or not, I wouldn't be surprised if she goes down and doesn't come up."

"Somehow I hate to hear those words from an expert on ship construction," muttered Giordino.

Pitt folded his arms across his chest. "My primary concern is that the disaster will be caused by human hands."

O'Malley looked at him. "Do you know how many places a madman could set an explosive that would cause this tub to sink?"

"If the boat is deep underwater, a rupture almost anyplace on the hull would do the trick."

"That and a puncture in the ballast tanks."

"I haven't had time to study the plans and specifications of the boat, except very briefly last night," said Pitt. "But there must be an underwater system for evacuation."

"There is," answered O'Malley, "and a good one. Instead of lifeboats, the passengers enter their assigned pods; they can hold fifty people. Then the entry door is closed and sealed. At the same time, the outer doors open, a stream of air is sent into the ejection system and the pods shoot free of the ship and float to the surface. Take my word for it, the system is efficient. I know, I consulted on the project."

"If you wanted to make the evacuation system inoperable, how would you go about it?"

"Not a pretty thought."

"We've got to cover all the bases."

O'Malley scratched his head. "Causing a failure in the air-ejection system would be the way I'd go."

"I'd be grateful if you and your team would check out any tampering with the system very carefully," said Pitt.

O'Malley looked at him with his eyes half closed. "I wouldn't do a sloppy job of inspection if my life depended on it."

Giordino studied the fingernails on one hand objectively. "Truer words, I hope, were never spoken."

The mooring hawsers were lifted off the bollards by the dock crew and reeled aboard the *Golden Marlin* seconds before the starboard thrusters were activated and the boat begin slipping sideways from the dock. Over a thousand people had come to the dock to watch the maiden voyage of the first underwater cruise boat. On a reviewing stand, the governor of Florida and other officials and celebrities made mundane speeches. The University of Florida band played a medley of sea tunes and were followed by a Caribbean marimba-and-steel-drum band. As the ship began to edge from the dock, both bands and the boat's orchestra combined to play the traditional sailing song, "Until We Meet Again." Streamers and confetti were thrown as the passengers and people onshore waved and shouted. The scene was very moving. Pitt was amazed at how many women wiped away tears. Even Kelly was swept up by the rousing *bon voyage*.

Pitt saw no sign of the divers. His calls to Captain Baldwin on the bridge were not answered or returned. He felt extremely restive, but there was no way he could stop the ship from sailing.

The boat was still in the channel, heading toward the open blue-green sea off Florida, when all passengers were asked to be seated in the theater, where First Officer Paul

Conrad lectured on the operation of the submarine cruise boat and explained the evacuation system. Kelly sat on one side of the theater in the front while Pitt sat on the other side near the rear. There were six black families on board, but none of the men remotely resembled Omo Kanai. As soon as the lecture was over, a series of gongs rang and the passengers were directed to their evacuation pod stations.

Giordino worked with the team of inspectors, searching for explosives or signs of damaged equipment, while Pitt and Kelly cooperated with the purser in matching up the passengers with their names and staterooms. The search went slowly. By lunchtime, they were less than halfway through the passenger list without getting to the crew members.

"I'm beginning to doubt he's on board," said Kelly wearily.

"Either that or he's stowed away," Pitt said, as he studied the pictures of the passengers that had been taken by the ship's photographer when they'd come on board. He held up a photo to the light and studied the features of the image. Then he passed it to Kelly. "Look familiar?"

She looked at the photo for several seconds, read the name and then she smiled. "There's a definite resemblance. The only problem is that this Mr. Jonathan Ford is white."

Pitt shrugged. "I know. Well, back to the drawing board."

At four o'clock in the afternoon, chimes sounded over the speakers throughout the boat playing the song "By the Sea, By the Beautiful Sea." It was the signal that the boat was about to submerge. The passengers all hurried to find chairs in front of the viewing ports. There was no noticeable vibration or decrease in speed as the boat slowly began to slip beneath the surface. The sea seemed to rise as the boat descended in a maelstrom of bubbles that quickly faded away as the bright sun and sky transformed into a deep blue liquid void.

The magnetohydrodynamic engines ran silently, without tremor. Except for the water passing outside the view ports, the passengers had no sensation of movement. The air regenerators scrubbed out the carbon dioxide and refreshed the breathable air inside the boat.

Though there was little to see at first, they remained absorbed in viewing a different world below the one to which they were accustomed. Soon, fish began to appear, taking little interest in the huge vessel as it trespassed into their kingdom. Brilliantly colored tropical fish in fluorescent purples, yellows and reds swam past the view ports. The saltwater inhabitants were far more dazzling than their cousins in freshwater lakes and river. They soon faded above the sub as it sank into deeper water.

A school of barracuda, their long sleek bodies radiating as if coated with silver glitter, swam lazily alongside the boat, their dead black eyes peering for a meal, their lower lips protruding. They swam effortlessly, keeping pace with the boat. Then, in the blink of an eye, they darted away and were gone.

The passengers on the port side of the boat were treated to the sight of a huge sunfish, often called a Mola Mola. There was a white-and-orange metallic luster to its huge oval body, which was ten feet long and nearly as high and probably weighed in the neighborhood of two tons. A strange-looking fish with high dorsal and anal fins, its body looked as if it had forgotten to grow in length. The great tail was attached just behind the head. A friendly giant of the depths, the sunfish soon fell behind the boat.

Marine biologists brought on board by the cruise line described the fish and explained their characteristics, behavior and migration patterns in the sea. The sunfish was followed by a pair of small hammerhead sharks no more than five feet in length. The passengers marveled that a fish could have developed with such a large foil across the front of the head with its eyeballs perched on the ends. The sharks were curious and swam alongside the view ports, peering with one eye aimed at the strange creatures on the other side. Like the other fish, they soon tired of the giant intruder, swayed their tails gracefully and propelled their sleek bodies into the gloom.

Digital meters that read out the submarine's depth were mounted beside every view port. First Officer Conrad announced over the speaker system that they were at six hundred feet and approaching the bottom. As one, the passengers leaned closer to the view ports and peered downward as the seabed slowly materialized and spread below the boat, a landscape that once had held coral before the oceans had risen and was now covered with ancient shells, silt and jumbled lava rock encrusted with sea life. Because vivid colors were lost at this depth, along with reds and yellows, the sea floor took on a greenish-brown tint. The barrenness was garnished by the myriad fish that inhabited the bottom. The passengers watched in wonder at seeing this alien world with a visibility of more than two hundred feet.

In the forward dome that served as the bridge and control room, Captain Baldwin was carefully guiding the *Golden Marlin* fifty feet above the ocean floor, keeping a steady eye out for any unexpected change in the terrain. Radar and side-scan sonar read the bottom half a mile ahead and to the sides, giving the operators ample time to change course and ascend in the event of a sudden rise of rock. The course for the next ten days had been laid out with extreme care. A privately hired oceanographic survey had studied the sea floor through the channel islands and marked the depths for the voyage. The boat now steered the set course with her onboard computers.

The seabed suddenly fell away as the boat soared out over a deep trench that dropped three thousand feet into the depths, two thousand feet deeper than the limits set by the boat's architects for the hull. Baldwin gave the helm to his third officer and turned as the communications officer approached and handed him a message. He read it, his face taking on a questioning expression.

"Find Mr. Pitt and send him to the bridge," he ordered a seaman, who stared entranced by the sight outside.

Pitt and Kelly had not taken the time to enjoy the underwater scenery. They were still holed up in the purser's office, studying the personnel records of the crew. When he was notified that the captain wished to see him, he left Kelly and walked to the bridge. He'd no sooner stepped through the door than Baldwin thrust the message at him.

"What do you make of this?" he demanded.

Pitt read the message aloud. "Please be advised that the bodies of the divers engaged to inspect the bottom of your ship have been found tied to the dock pilings beneath the surface of the channel. Initial investigation shows they were murdered by person or persons unknown who stabbed them both from the back, the knife blade penetrating their hearts. Await your reply."

It was signed Detective Lieutenant Del Carter, Fort Lauderdale Police Department.

Pitt was suddenly stricken with guilt, knowing it was he who had unwittingly sent Frank and Caroline Martin to their deaths.

"What's our depth?" he demanded sharply.

" 'Depth'?" echoed a startled Baldwin. "We've passed the Continental Shelf and are in deep water." He pointed at a depth gauge mounted above the windows. "See for yourself. The bottom is two thousand four hundred feet below our keel."

"Turn around immediately!" Pitt ordered curtly. "Get into shallow water before it's too late."

Baldwin's face hardened. "What are you talking about?"

"The divers were murdered because they found explosives attached to the hull of this boat. I'm not asking you, Captain. For the sake of the lives of everybody on board this boat, turn back and get into shallow water before it's too late."

"And if I don't?" Baldwin challenged him.

Pitt's green eyes turned cold as the Arctic Sea and pierced Baldwin as if they were ice picks. When he spoke, it was as if the devil himself were speaking. "Then, in the name of humanity, I swear I will kill you and take command of the ship."

Baldwin jerked backward as if he was stabbed with a spear. Slowly, very slowly, he recovered and his white-mouthed lips spread in a taut smile. He turned and looked at the helmsman, who was standing stunned, his eyes as wide as automobile wheel covers. "Reverse course and come to full speed." Then, "Does that satisfy you, Mr. Pitt?"

"I suggest you sound the warning signal and send the passengers to the stations at the evacuation pods."

Baldwin nodded. "Consider it done." Then he turned to First Officer Conrad and ordered, "Blow the ballast tanks. We can double our speed once we hit the surface."

"Pray we make it in time," Pitt said, the tenseness lessening slightly, "or we have a choice between drowning or suffocating while watching the fish swim by."

★ ★ ★

Kelly was sitting inside the purser's office, sifting through the crew's personnel records, when she became aware of a presence. She looked up and saw a man who had walked in the room without making a sound. He was dressed in a golf shirt and shorts. There was an ominous smile on his face. She immediately recognized him as the passenger she and Pitt had discussed briefly earlier. As he stood there without speaking, she studied his face and a feeling of horror began creeping over her. "Your name is Jonathan Ford."

"You know me?"

"No, not . . . really," she stammered.

"You should. We met briefly on the *Emerald Dolphin*."

Kelly was confused. There was a close resemblance to the black ship's officer who had tried to kill her and her father, but the man standing in front of her was white. "You can't be . . ."

"Ah, but I am." The smile widened. "I can see that you're mystified." He paused and took a handkerchief from the pocket of his pants. He dabbed a corner on his tongue and then rubbed it against the top of his left hand. The white makeup came off, revealing coffee brown skin underneath.

Kelly stumbled from her chair and tried to run out the door, but the man grabbed

445

her by the arms and pressed her against the wall. "My name is Ono Kanai. My orders are to take you with me."

"Take me where?" she rasped in terror, hoping against all hope that Pitt and Giordino would walk in the door.

"Why, home, of course."

The answer made no sense to her. She was only aware of the evil in his eyes as he pressed a cloth damp with a strange-smelling liquid against her face. Then a black pit opened beneath her feet and she fell into it.

30

It was a race against death now. That explosives had been placed on the hull was a certainty in Pitt's mind. The Martins had discovered them, but were murdered before they could alert Captain Baldwin. Pitt called Giordino over the portable radio. "You can knock off the search and call in the inspectors. The explosives are not inside the ship."

Giordino simply acknowledged the message and hurried to the bridge. "What do you know that I don't?" Giordino asked, as he rushed through the door, followed by Rand O'Malley.

"We just got word that the divers were killed," Pitt told them.

"That nails it," Giordino muttered angrily.

"The divers inspecting the bottom of the boat?" asked O'Malley.

Pitt nodded. "It's beginning to look as

though the explosives were set to detonate while we were over deep water."

"Which is where we are now," said Giordino quietly, as he stared uneasily at the depth meter.

Pitt turned to Baldwin, who was standing at the control console with the helmsman. "How soon before we pass into shallow water?" he asked.

"Twenty minutes will put us over the edge of the trench and onto the Continental Slope," Baldwin answered, his face beginning to show signs of stress now that he had come to believe his boat was truly in danger. "In ten more minutes, we'll reach the surface, which will enable us to increase our speed by half and reach shallow water."

Abruptly, the seaman standing at the ship's main console called out. "Captain, something is happening with the evacuation pods."

Baldwin and O'Malley stepped over and stared at the console in shock. All sixteen lights representing the evacuation pods were showing red except for one that still read green. "They've been activated," Baldwin gasped.

"And before anyone could board," added O'Malley grimly. "We'll never get the crew and passengers off the boat now."

The vision of an explosion on the hull, water flooding inside and dragging the boat unhindered into the abyss with seven hundred passengers and crew, was too horrible to contemplate but too real to dismiss.

Pitt knew that whoever had activated the evacuation pods had probably abandoned the boat in one of them, which meant that the explosives could detonate at almost any moment. He stepped over to the radar screen that sat side by side with the side-scan sonar display. The Continental Slope was rising, but too slowly. There were still almost a thousand feet of water below them. The *Golden Marlin*'s hull was built to withstand the water pressure at that depth, but any hope of rescue would be next to impossible. Every eye stared at the depth meter, every mind counted the seconds.

The seabed rose with agonizing slowness. Only another hundred feet remained before the boat broke the surface. A collective sigh of relief was heard in the control room as the *Golden Marlin* passed the edge of the Continental Slope, and the bottom came within six hundred feet of the hull. The water outside the view ports was becoming much lighter now and the restless surface could be seen sparkling under the sun.

"Depth under hull five hundred fifty and rising," called out Conrad.

The words had barely left his mouth when the boat shuddered with sickening violence. There was barely time to react, to contemplate the inevitable disaster. The boat twisted, completely out of control. Those great technically advanced engines wound down to a stop as the hungry sea poured into the two wounds caused by the underwater explosives.

The *Golden Marlin* lay motionless, drifting in the mild current, but sinking foot by inexorable foot toward the sea floor. Tons of water began flooding into the hull in locations yet unknown to the men in the control room. The surface looked so tantalizingly near it seemed as if it could be touched with a yardstick.

Baldwin was under no illusions. His boat was going down. "Call the engine room and ask the chief to ascertain the damage," he snapped to his second officer.

The reply came back almost immediately. "The chief engineer reports they're taking water in the engine room. The baggage compartment is also flooding, but the hull is still intact. He has the pumps flowing at maximum capacity. He also reports that the ballast tank pump system was damaged by the forward blast water and is pouring into the tanks through the exhaust tubes. The crew is struggling to shut down the flow, but the water is rising too fast and they may have to evacuate the engine room. I'm sorry, sir, the chief says he can no longer keep the boat from losing neutral buoyancy."

"Oh, God," murmured a young officer standing at the control console. "We're going to sink."

Baldwin quickly came on keel. "Tell the chief to close all the watertight doors below and keep the generators going as long as he can." Then he looked at Pitt, silent, expressionless, and said, "Well, Mr. Pitt, I guess now is the time for you to tell me 'I told you so.' "

Pitt's face was set, stonily thoughtful, the face of a man who was considering every possible contingency, every potential to save the ship and its passengers. Giordino had seen the look many times in the past. Pitt shook his head slowly. "I take no satisfaction in being right."

"Bottom coming up." First Officer Conrad's eyes had never left the radar and side-scan sonar displays. He had no sooner spoken the words than the *Golden Marlin* struck the sea floor with loud creaking and groaning sounds of protest, as her hull settled into the silt, throwing up a vast brown cloud that blotted out all vision beyond the view ports.

It didn't take a motion picture of the event for the passengers to know something very tragic was in the making. Yet as long as the passenger decks remained water-free and none of the crew looked frightened — since this was their first voyage in a submarine, none of them realized what real danger they were in — no one panicked. Captain Baldwin came on the speaker system and assured everyone that although the *Golden Marlin* had lost power, things would be back to normal shortly. The story, however, did not fly with the passengers and crew who'd noticed that almost all the pod chambers were empty. Some milled around in confusion. Some remained at the view ports and gazed at the fish who appeared after the silt settled. Some retired to the lounge and ordered drinks that were now on the house.

Captain Baldwin and his officers began studying emergency procedures that came out of corporate manuals written by those who had no concept of how to deal with a submarine cruise liner lying helpless on the bottom with seven hundred souls on board. While the hull was sounded to make certain it was still mostly watertight and the bulkhead doors closed, the engineering crew set the pumps in operation to keep up with the sea flowing into the engine room and baggage compartment. Fortunately, all the systems but propulsion appeared unaffected by damage from the explosions.

Baldwin sat in the communications room like a man in a daze. With great effort, he opened up communications with Lasch at the company headquarters, the Coast Guard and any ships that were within fifty miles, in that order. He issued a Mayday and gave the *Golden Marlin*'s position. That done, he sat back and laid his head in his hands. At first, he worried that his long career at sea would be ended. Then it came to him how unimportant his career was under the circumstances. His first duty was to his passengers and crew. "Damn the career," he muttered under his breath. He stood and walked from the bridge, first to the engine room for a full report and then he roamed the ship reassuring the passengers that they were in no immediate danger. He gave out the story that there was a problem with the ballast tanks, and repairs were in effect.

Together, Pitt, Giordino and O'Malley went down to the evacuation pod deck. O'Malley began opening inspection panels and checking the system. There was something oddly reassuring about the big Irishman. He knew his job and knew it well. No lost motion with him. Less than five minutes after he began his inspection, he stepped back from the open panels, sat down in a chair and sighed. "Whoever activated the evacuation pods knew his business. He overrode the circuits leading to the bridge and set the pods in motion by using the emergency manual controls. Luckily, it looks like one pod failed to release."

"Small consolation," muttered Giordino.

Pitt slowly shook his head in defeat.

"They've been two steps ahead of us from the beginning. I have to give than an A for planning."

"Who's they?" asked O'Malley.

"Men who will murder children as easily as you and I would kill flies."

"It makes no sense."

"Not to sane people."

"We still have one pod to put the children in," said Giordino.

"It's the captain's job to give the order," Pitt said, staring at the remaining pod. "The question is, how many can we put in it?"

An hour later, a Coast Guard cutter arrived on the scene, hauled aboard the orange marker buoy released from the *Golden Marlin* with a telephone line and opened communications to the boat. Only then did Baldwin give the command to gather the passengers into the theater and explain the situation. He concentrated on minimizing the danger and stated that it was in keeping with company regulations to send the youngest to the surface in case of an emergency. None of it sat well. Questions were raised. Tempers flared, and it was all the captain could do to defuse the anger and fear.

Before the pod was loaded, Pitt and O'Malley sat at a computer in the purser's office and estimated the number of bodies the pod could carry beyond the safe limits as stated by the manufacturer and still float free to the surface.

While they were absorbed in their work, Giordino left them to look for Kelly.

"How many children on board?" asked O'Malley.

Using the purser's list of passengers, Pitt totaled up the number. "Fifty-four who are under the age of eighteen."

"The pods are constructed to carry fifty people with an average weight of one hundred and sixty pounds, for a total weight limit of eight thousand pounds. Anything above that and they won't float to the surface."

"We can cut that figure in half. The kids should average around eighty pounds or less."

"Now that we're down to four thousand pounds, that leaves room for some of the mothers," said O'Malley, feeling odd to be discussing whose lives would be saved.

"Take an average weight of one-forty and we have room for nearly twenty-nine mothers."

O'Malley punched up the families and number of children. "There are twenty-seven mothers on board," he said with a hint of optimism. "Thank God we can evacuate all of them and their children."

"We have to ignore the new tradition of keeping families together," said Pitt. "The men make up too much weight."

"I agree," O'Malley said heavily.

"We still have room for one or two more bodies."

"We can't exactly ask the other six hundred and seventeen passengers and crew to draw straws."

"No," said Pitt. "We have to send someone, one of us, who can give a detailed report on the situation down here that can't be fully interpreted through underwater communications."

"I'm more important here," O'Malley said firmly.

Giordino returned at that moment. The expression on his face was not one of pleasure. "Kelly has disappeared," he said simply. "I put together a search party, but we can find no trace of her."

"Bloody hell," Pitt swore. He did not question Giordino, did not doubt for a moment that Kelly had indeed vanished. Gut instinct alone told him it was true. Suddenly, the photo of a passenger filled his mind. He programmed in the passenger list on the computer and typed the name Jonathan Ford.

The picture of Ford taken as he stepped off the gangway onto the deck filled the monitor. Next, Pitt hit the print key and waited until a colored image rolled from the printer. While O'Malley and Giordino stood silent, he studied the face, comparing it mentally with the pilot of the red Fokker he'd met at the air show before the dogfight. He took the image over to a desk, took a pencil and began shading in the man's face. When he was finished, he felt as if a fist had struck him in the stomach.

"He was here on board and I missed him."

Completely adrift, O'Malley asked, "Who are you talking about?"

"The man who nearly killed me along with a planeload of children in New York, and the one responsible for us lying helpless on the bottom and releasing empty evacuation pods. I'm afraid that he escaped in one of the pods and took Kelly with him."

Giordino placed a hand on Pitt's shoulder. He could appreciate how bad Pitt felt. He felt that he had failed as well, and it came back to haunt him.

Pitt made a mental note of Ford's stateroom number, and hurried out into the passageway, followed by Giordino and O'Malley. Pitt was not in any frame of mind to take the time to ask the stateroom stewardess for a key. He hauled off and kicked the door open. The stewardess had made up the room, but there was no sign of luggage. Pitt pulled open the drawers of the dressers. They were bare. Giordino opened the closet and saw a white object far up on the top shelf. He reached up and pulled down a thick roll of paper and spread it out on the bed.

"The blueprints of the boat," muttered O'Malley. "Where did he get them?"

A chill ran through Pitt's body, as he realized that seizing Kelly had been another one of Ford's assignments. "He's backed by a superb intelligence operation. He was able to familiarize himself with every system and piece of equipment, every deck, bulkhead and structure in exacting detail."

"Which explains how he knew where to place the explosives and manually activate the evacuation pods," said O'Malley.

"There's nothing more we can do here," said Giordino, "except notify the Coast Guard on the surface to look for a vessel that was hovering over the area to pick this character and Kelly out of the pod."

Accepting Ford's escape and Kelly's abduction as horrible reality, Pitt felt a deep sense of grotesque inadequacy and futility. He was totally powerless to help or rescue her. Pitt sagged dejectedly into a chair. He felt an even deadlier chill pass through him, and this one had nothing to do with Kelly's fate. All the pods were gone, and there was no way they could be retrieved and loaded again. He saw little hope of saving the other six hundred–plus souls on board the sunken cruise liner. He sat there listlessly for a few seconds, then looked into the silent and expectant face of O'Malley and said softly, "You know every corner of the boat." He said it as a statement of fact rather than a question.

O'Malley hesitated, not sure of Pitt's intent. "Yes, I know her as well as anyone."

"Is there another evacuation system besides the pods?"

"I'm not clear what you mean?"

"Did the boatbuilder install a backup airlock system for a chamber rescue?"

"You mean a specially configured hatch on the top of the hull?"

"Exactly."

"Yes, there is one, but there is no way all six hundred of us can be rescued before we run out of air."

"How so?" asked Giordino. "As we speak, rescue operations are under way."

"You don't know?"

"Only if you don't tell us," Pitt said harshly.

"The *Golden Marlin* was never designed to remain underwater more than four days before surfacing. After that, the air quickly becomes unbreathable."

"I thought the air regenerators refreshed the inside atmosphere indefinitely," said Giordino in surprise.

O'Malley shook his head. "They're very efficient. They do a first-rate job of refreshing the air, but after a while the combined carbon dioxide buildup from seven hundred humans in an enclosed atmosphere becomes too much for the scrubbers and filters. Then the air purification begins to break down." He shrugged darkly. "All this speculation goes out the window if the flooding gets to the generator and we lose power. Then the air regeneration equipment will shut down."

"Four days, if we're lucky," Pitt said slowly. "Three and a half, actually, since we've already been down almost twelve hours since we submerged."

"The U.S. Navy has a deep submergence rescue vehicle that can do the job," said Giordino.

"Yes, but mobilization, transporting it and the operating team to the site, and then setting up the rescue procedures could easily take four days." O'Malley spoke slowly, emphatically. "By the time they drop it down and lock up with the air escape chamber, it will be too late to save more than a handful of us."

Pitt turned to Giordino. "Al, you've got to go topside with the mothers and children."

For perhaps five incredulous seconds, Giordino stood there looking blank. When shocked realization did come, his voice became indignant. "Mrs. Giordino's boy is no coward. I won't jump ship hiding behind women's skirts."

"Believe me, old friend," Pitt entreated, "you can do far more to save everyone by working with me from the surface."

Giordino started to say Why don't you go? but thought better of it and accepted Pitt's reasoning as correct. "Okay, once I reach the surface, what then?"

"It's essential that we get an open line down here to purify the air."

"And just where am I supposed to scare up five hundred feet of hose, an air pump capable of pumping enough air to keep six hundred and seventeen people alive until rescue and a method of attaching it to the sunken boat?"

Pitt looked at his old pal of almost forty years and grinned. "If I know you, you'll think of something."

31

Four vessels arrived over the site of the sunken *Golden Marlin* within five hours after it sank. The Coast Guard cutter *Joseph Ryan*; the oil tanker *King Zeus*; the U.S. Navy oceangoing tug *Orion*; and the coastal cargo carrier *Compass Rose*. They were soon accompanied by a fleet of sailing yachts and powerboats out of Miami and Fort Lauderdale that had arrived on the scene more out of curiosity than a desire to help in the rescue. Admiral Sandecker had dispatched a NUMA salvage ship from Savannah, but it wasn't due to arrive for another twelve hours.

The Navy's deep submergence rescue vehicle, *Mercury*, its operations team and mother ship, *Alfred Aultman*, were pounding toward the disaster scene from Puerto Rico, where they were in the midst of conducting a practice mission. Messages were relayed back and forth from the Coast Guard vessel to the captain of the *Aultman* from Captain Baldwin on every aspect of the sunken cruise boat's condition.

Down below on the *Golden Marlin*, the passenger's children and their mothers were loaded on board the evacuation pod after O'Malley repaired the release mechanism. There were tearful farewells with fathers, and in many cases older relatives such as grandparents. A number of small children cried up a storm when entering the confined enclosure of the pod. Calming them was difficult, if not impossible.

Giordino tried to shut out the screaming infants and their mothers, and looked more forlorn than ever to be the only man escaping from the boat. "I feel like the guy who entered a *Titanic* lifeboat wearing a woman's dress."

Pitt put his arm around Giordino's shoulder. "You'll be more crucial to the rescue operation topside."

"I'll never be able to live this down," Giordino groaned. "You'd better come through this, you hear? If it all goes wrong and you don't make it —"

"I'll make it," Pitt assured him, "but only with you leading the rescue where it counts."

They shook hands one final time as Pitt nudged him into the only open seat in the evacuation pod. Pitt did his best to keep from grinning as a harried mother thrust one of her crying children into a cringing Giordino's arms. The tough little Italian looked as uncomfortable as though he were sitting on broken glass. Pitt could not recall seeing a more mournful look, as the pod door hissed closed and the launch sequence was activated. Sixty seconds later, there was a whoosh sound and the pod was on its way to the surface, floating upward very slowly because it was loaded almost to its buoyancy limit.

"I guess all we can do now is wait," said O'Malley, who was standing behind Pitt.

"No," said Pitt. "We prepare."

"Where do we start?"

"With the airlock escape chamber."

"What do you want to know?"

"Is the hatch compatible with the one on the Navy submersible rescue vehicle?"

O'Malley nodded. "I know for a fact that it was designed to the Navy's specifications to mate with their rescue vehicle or bell chambers for just such an emergency."

Pitt was already at the door. "Show me the way. I want to check it out for myself."

O'Malley led him up the elevator to the upper deck where the dining room was located, through the galley where the chefs were busily engaged in preparing dinner as if the voyage had never been interrupted. The scene seemed terribly unreal, considering the circumstances. Pitt followed the boat's engineer up a narrow stairway to a small chamber with bench seats along the bulkhead. In the center were steps leading to a platform. Above the platform was a ladder that disappeared into a tunnel that rose up to a hatch three feet in diameter. O'Malley climbed the ladder into the tunnel and studied the hatch. It seemed to Pitt the inspector spent an inordinate amount of time in the tunnel. Finally, he climbed down and sat wearily on the platform.

He looked up at Pitt and said, "Your friend was a very thorough character."

"What do you mean?"

"The frame is buckled and jammed solid around the hatch. It would take a ten-pound plastic charge to blow it free."

Pitt's eyes traveled up the tunnel, and he gazed at the bent and distorted escape hatch with an understanding bordering on horror. "Then there is no escape into the rescue vehicle."

"Not through here," O'Malley said, knowing all hope of saving six hundred and seventeen souls was gone. He stared at the deck and repeated, "Not through here. Not through anywhere."

Pitt and O'Malley carried the disastrous news to Captain Baldwin on the bridge. He took it stoically. "You're positive? The escape hatch cannot be forced open?"

"A cutting torch might split it open," said Pitt, "but then we'd have no way of sealing it against the incoming water. At this depth we're looking at roughly seventeen atmospheres. Figuring one atmosphere for every thirty-three feet, the water pressure against our hull is two hundred and fifty pounds per square inch. No way the passengers could fight through the cascade into the rescue vehicle."

Baldwin's face was not pleasant to see. A man of few emotions, he could not bring himself to believe that he and everyone left on board the *Golden Marlin* were going to die. "We have no hope of rescue?"

"There is always hope," Pitt said gamely, "but not by the usual methods."

Baldwin's shoulder sagged as he stared vacantly at the deck. "Then all we can do is survive as long as possible."

First Officer Conrad handed Pitt a phone. "Mr. Giordino is calling from the surface."

Pitt held the receiver to his ear. "Al?"

"I'm here on the Coast Guard cutter," the familiar voice crackled back.

"How was the ride to the surface?"

"I'm not used to an army of screaming infants. My eardrums are blasted out."

"Did it go well?" Pitt asked.

"All kids and mothers safe and sound. They were taken aboard a coastal cargo carrier that had better facilities than the cutter. They're on their way to the nearest port. I can tell you the women weren't happy about leaving their husbands behind. I got more dirty looks than a rattlesnake in an ice-cream parlor."

"Any word on when the Deep Submergence Rescue Vehicle will arrive?"

"The word here is thirty-six hours," replied Giordino. "How are things down where you are?"

"Not good. Our friend Kanai was on board and jammed the escape hatch shut before he left."

Giordino did not immediately reply. Then he asked, "How bad?"

"It's jammed solid. O'Malley says there is no way of forcing it open without flooding half the ship."

Giordino could not find it in his mind to believe all was lost for those souls still on the *Golden Marlin*. "You're quite certain?"

"Dead certain."

"We won't throw in the towel at this end," Giordino promised decisively. "I'll call Yaeger and have him put Max on the problem. There has to be a way to get you up here."

Pitt could sense the emotion building in Giordino. He thought it best to let it rest for the moment. "Keep in touch," he said facetiously, "but don't call collect."

The crew and passengers on board the dead submarine cruise liner had no knowledge of the hurricane that was brewing over their heads. After inundating newspaper and television networks with a weeklong barrage of stories on the *Emerald Dolphin* tragedy, they returned like a tidal wave to cover the sinking of the *Golden Marlin* and the race against time to save those trapped on board the submarine. Celebrities and politicians also put in appearances.

Boatloads of cameramen appeared as if by magic, along with a horde of reporters in light aircraft and helicopters. Less than two days after the submarine cruise liner had slipped onto the sea bottom, a fleet of ships and boats numbering close to a hundred drifted over the site. In time all but the ones holding accredited journalists were chased away by the Coast Guard.

The fire aboard the cruise liner had been in a remote area of the Pacific Ocean. Not so, this story. The sinking happened only ninety-seven miles off the coast of Florida. Every angle was hyped. Excitement built to a fever pitch as the hours passed and the end came closer for those deep below the surface. By the third day, the media circus went into high gear in readiness for the final chapter.

They tried every bit of ingenious scheming to make contact with anyone on the sunken boat. Some tried to tap into the phone line attached to the buoy, but the Coast Guard would have none of it. Shots were actually fired across the bows of the news media boats to keep them out of the way of those working frantically to save the 617 people left on board.

Wives and children who'd survived in the pod were interviewed relentlessly. Reporters tried to reach Giordino, but he'd gone on board the NUMA survey ship when it arrived and refused to have any contact with them. He immediately worked with the crew to send down an ROV named the *Sea Scout* that was a sister vehicle to the *Sea Sleuth*, to investigate and inspect the *Golden Marlin* from the exterior of the hull.

As he sat and guided the ROV with a remote control in his lap, the hopeless despair came home as he hovered over the escape hatch on the top of the hull. The images on the video monitor only confirmed what Pitt had told him. The hatch was irreparably jammed closed. Nothing short of explosives or a cutting torch could tear it off, and then only to allow the sea to pour through the opening before any survivors could pass through it. Making a seal with the rescue vehicle was impossible. There was no other way for those on the other side of the hull to escape.

The next morning the naval support ship carrying the Deep Submergence Rescue Vehicle arrived. Giordino moved his operation over to the *Alfred Aultman*, whose crew lost no time in readying the Rescue Vehicle for its descent to the sunken boat. The captain of the ship, Lieutenant Commander Mike Turner, greeted Giordino as he came aboard.

"Welcome to the *Aultman*," said Turner, shaking Giordino's hand. "The Navy is always happy to work with NUMA."

Most Navy ship commanders have a guarded look about them, as if they had bought and paid for their ship out of their own pocket and treated it as a haven for select guests. Turner wore a friendly expression, and his manner reflected deep intelligence. He gazed at the world through hazel eyes under a thinning head of blond hair with a widow's peak.

"I only wish it was under less tragic circumstances," replied Giordino.

"It is that," Turner admitted seriously. "I'll have one of my officers show you to your quarters. Would you like something to eat? We won't be launching the *Mercury* for another hour."

"I hope you'll give me permission to go along if I don't take up needed space."

Turner smiled. "We have room for twenty bodies. You won't be crowding us one bit."

" 'Us'?" queried Giordino, surprised the ship's captain would not send a subordinate on the dive. "You're going, too?"

Turner nodded, and his friendly smile vanished. "It won't be the first time I've taken the *Mercury* down to a sunken vessel filled with people whose only hope of survival was our vehicle."

Prior to launch, the *Mercury*, painted yellow with a diagonal red stripe across its hull, hung poised over the work deck of the Falcon like a modern artist's interpretation of a huge banana with all kinds of strange protrusions overhanging its skin. She measured thirty-eight feet in length by ten feet in height by nine feet wide, and displaced thirty tons. Her maximum operating depth was twelve hundred feet and her speed was two and a half knots.

Captain Turner boarded a ladder to the main hatch, followed by a ship's crewman. He introduced his copilot, Chief Warrant Officer Mack McKirdy, a gray-haired, grizzled sea dog with a beard like that of a sailor on an old clipper ship. He acknowledged Giordino's presence with a curt nod and a wink of one blue eye.

"I hear you're an old submersible man," said McKirdy to Giordino.

"I've spent a fair amount of time in them."

"Word's out that you probed the wreck of the *Emerald Dolphin* at twenty thousand feet."

"Yes, that's true," admitted Giordino. "Along with my good friend Dirk Pitt and NUMA marine biologist Misty Graham."

"Then this dive to only five hundred and fifty feet should be a piece of cake."

"Not unless we can hook up with the rescue hatch."

McKirdy read the gravity in Giordino's eyes. "We'll set you right on top of it." And then he said as if to reassure him, "Don't worry. If anyone can open a jammed hatch, it's me and the *Mercury*. We carry the necessary equipment to do the job."

"I hope so," Giordino murmured. "Oh, how I hope so."

The *Mercury*, with Chief McKirdy at the control console, reached the sunken boat in less than fifteen minutes. The chief steered the rescue vehicle along the hull. It looked like some immense dead animal. All three men felt an eerie sensation at gazing through the view ports and seeing faces inside the *Golden Marlin* gazing back. At one port in the boat, Giordino thought he saw Pitt waving at him, but the vehicle passed by too quickly to be sure.

They spent three hours making a thorough inspection of the boat lying in the bottom silt. Their cameras kept videotape rolling and still shots clicking at two-second intervals.

"Interesting," Turner said quietly. "We've been over every square foot of the hull and I saw very few bubbles."

"That *is* unusual," McKirdy agreed. "Thankfully, we've only had to perform rescue operations on two submarines. The German *Seigen* and the Russian sub *Tavda*. Both vessels went down after collisions with surface ships. In each case, air bubbles cascaded from the gashes in their hulls long after the collisions."

Giordino stared out the view port at the morbid scene. "The engine room and baggage compartments were the only two where water gushed in. They must be completely flooded, with no more air to release."

McKirdy steered the submersible closer to the damaged areas blown inward by the explosions. He pointed through the port. "Amazing how small the actual wounds are."

"Large enough to sink her."

"Were the ballast tanks ruptured?" asked Turner.

"No," answered Giordino. "They maintained their integrity. And even though Captain Baldwin blew them empty, the boat was still dragged down by the flow of water entering through the breaks in the hull. The pumps could not keep up with the flow and lost ground. What saved the boat was the closing of the watertight doors, keeping the flooding in the cargo compartment and engine room."

"A great tragedy," said Turner slowly, motioning out the port at the two breaks in the hull. "A foot or two smaller and she might have made it to the surface."

"Sir, I suggest we check out the escape hatch," said McKirdy, "before we have to head topside."

"Affirmative, Chief. Sit us down on top of it, and we'll see if we can't make a seal. If we're lucky, we can come back with a work crew and go to work freeing it."

McKirdy guided the rescue vehicle over the top of the *Golden Marlin* and eased to a stop just above and off to the side of the hatch. Both he and Turner studied the damage from the explosives.

"Doesn't look encouraging," said McKirdy.

Turner didn't look hopeful. "The sealing flange around the bottom of the hatch is ripped to shreds. There's no way we can use the air lock in the rescue chamber to make repairs, because the hull is too damaged to make an airtight seal, pump out the water and have a crew go to work with cutting torches."

"What about divers?" asked Giordino.

"It's not rare for them to work at these depths."

"They'd have to work in shifts around the clock while living in a decompression chamber. We'd need at least four days to get a chamber on site and complete the repairs. By then . . ." His voice trailed off.

They all looked at the shattered area around the escape hatch for a long time, or what seemed a long time. Giordino suddenly felt unequivocally tired. He wasn't sure if it was from the increasingly foul air or the overwhelming sense of frustration. He was enough of a qualified engineer to know that it was impossible to breach the hatch without sending in a flow of water that would surely doom everyone left on board. Any attempt would have been fruitless. McKirdy hovered the rescue vehicle above the escape hatch for another minute.

"We'll have to lower a pressure chamber down on the hull, form a seal and then cut a hole through the plates large enough to evacuate everyone on *Mercury*." Turner described the process in terms so simple that he sounded like a schoolteacher issuing homework.

"How long will that take?" asked Giordino.

"We should be able to do the job in forty-eight hours."

"Too late," Giordino said bluntly. "They

don't have more than thirty hours of air left in there. You'll be opening a passage into a huge coffin."

"You're quite right," Turner conceded. "But according to the boat's plans that we received by helicopter from the builder before we left port, there's an outside air connector for this type of emergency. A connector for an umbilical hose from the surface is mounted just forward of the fin on the stern. We have the hose and a pump that puts out more than a thousand pounds per square inch. We can have it in place and ready to supply air in" — he paused to glance at his watch — "three hours max."

"At the very least," said McKirdy, "we can keep the poor devils alive down there until we can make a dry entry and rescue them."

Ever the pessimist, Giordino said, "Yes, I'm aware of the exterior air emergency inlet. But you'd better check the exterior connector before you bet your hand."

McKirdy did not wait for Turner's command. He turned the submersible on a sharp angle and headed for the forward part of the fin that reached up toward the surface and housed the boat's lounge. He hung the vehicle above a small, rounded chamber attached to the hull at the base of the fin.

"Is that the housing for the air connector?" he asked.

"That should be it," said Turner, consulting the boat's plans.

"Looks like it's intact."

"Praise God," said McKirdy, suddenly buoyant. "Now we can attach the hose and pump enough air to those people to keep them alive till we can lift them off."

"You have manipulators," said Giordino, not wanting to pour champagne just yet. "To be on the safe side, why not lift the lid and make certain your hose fitting will match the connector?"

"I agree," said Turner. "Since we're already in the neighborhood, we might as well set it up for coupling and save time later." He turned from the control console, picked up a small remote with hand toggles and began operating one of the two manipulator arms. Very carefully, he unlatched the four locks, one on each side of the chamber. Then he lifted the side opposite the hinges.

The sight was not what they expected. The female fitting for the male fitting attached to the air hose was missing. It looked as if it had been mutilated and removed with a sledgehammer and chisel.

"Who in the world would have done that?" Turner asked desperately.

"A very shrewd fiend," Giordino muttered under his breath, with murder in his heart.

"It's impossible to receive a replacement

and make repairs before their air runs out," said McKirdy, closely studying the damaged connector.

"You telling me that over six hundred men and women are going to die while we stand around like clay statues and watch?" Giordino said, his dark face impassive.

Turner and McKirdy stared at each other like men wandering lost in a blizzard. There was nothing in their minds to say. They were overwhelmed with incredulity at being stymied every step of the way. There was no predicting the unexpected damage. The extent of treachery was beyond their comprehension.

Giordino had a feeling of unreality. Losing a best friend in a quick accident was abhorrent enough, but waiting for a perfectly healthy person to simply die because no one could help him, because he was beyond the reach of modern science and technology, was totally unacceptable. A grief-stricken man is driven to defy the gods. Giordino determined to do something, anything, if it meant diving 550 feet down to the wreck himself.

Then with grave misgiving, and without an order from Turner, McKirdy blew the water ballast, trimmed the craft and sent it toward the surface. Every man on board knew, even though he refused to visualize it, that the crew and passengers inside the

Golden Marlin were watching the rescue vehicle fade until it was lost in the murky void, not knowing their hopes and illusions went with it.

32

The mood inside the *Golden Marlin* was macabre. The passengers entered the dining room and ate as scheduled, gambled in the casino, drank cocktails in the lounge, read in the library and went to bed, as though the cruise had never ended. There was nothing else they could do. If any of them felt the slowly decreasing amount of oxygen, none showed it. They talked about their situation as if it were the weather. It was almost as if they were in denial.

The passengers who had been left aboard were mostly senior citizens, with a few younger but childless couples, two dozen single men and women, and the fathers who'd stayed behind after their wives and children left in the one remaining evacuation pod. The service crew went about their usual duties waiting on tables, cooking in the galley, cleaning the staterooms and putting on shows in the theater. Only the engine room crew worked endlessly, maintaining the pumps and the generators that still provided power. Luckily, these were housed in a separate compartment from the engine room and were sealed off immediately after the explosions.

Pitt's worst fears were realized after he watched the rescue vehicle return to the surface, and Giordino passed on the bad news over the phone. Hours later, he sat in the bridge control room at the chart table and studied the plans of the ship again and again, searching for some tiny clue to survival. Baldwin came over and sat on a stool opposite the chart table. He had regained a measure of composure, but the grim prospects weighed heavily on his mind. His breathing became noticeably labored.

"You haven't closed your eyes in three days," he said to Pitt. "Why don't you get some sleep?"

"If I go to sleep, if any of us goes to sleep, we won't wake up."

"I've carried on the lie that help is just around the corner," Baldwin said in obvious anguish, "but the truth is coming home to them now. The only thing that keeps us from a nasty confrontation is they're too weak to do much of anything."

Pitt rubbed his reddened eyes, took a swallow of cold coffee and studied the builder's plans for what seemed like the hundredth time. "There has to be a key," he said in a low voice. "There must be a way to attach a hose and pump purified air into the boat."

Baldwin took out a handkerchief and wiped his brow. "Not with the hatch and air connector destroyed. And any attempt to punch a hole in the hull would end up flooding the rest of the ship. We must face the sad but fundamental fact. By the time the Navy can repair the damage, make an airtight seal and penetrate the hull so we can all be evacuated, our air will be used up."

"We can stop the generators. That would give us a few more hours."

Baldwin wearily shook his head. "Better keep the power on and let these poor people live as normally as possible until the end. Besides, the pumps have to stay ahead of the overflow from the flooded compartments."

Dr. John Ringer stepped into the control room. The ship's doctor, Ringer was swamped by passengers coming to the hospital and complaining of headaches, lightheadedness and nausea. He did his best to provide them with whatever care was at his command without elaborating on the ultimate state of their tribulation.

Pitt stared at the doctor, who was obviously exhausted and on the verge of collapse. "Do I look as bad as you, Doc?"

Ringer forced a smile. "Worse, if you can believe it."

"I do."

Ringer dropped into a chair heavily. "What we're faced with is asphyxia. Insufficient breathing caused by an insufficient intake of oxygen and insufficient exhalation of carbon dioxide."

"What are the acceptable levels?" asked Pitt.

"Oxygen, twenty percent. Carbon dioxide, three tenths of one percent."

"How do we stand at the moment?"

"Eighteen percent oxygen," Ringer answered. "Slightly over four percent of carbon dioxide."

"And the danger limits?" Baldwin put to him stonily.

"Sixteen percent and five percent, respectively. After that the concentrations become extremely dangerous."

"Dangerous, like in deadly," said Pitt.

Baldwin asked Ringer the question none of them wanted to face. "How much longer do we have?"

"You can feel the lack of oxygen the same as I," said Ringer quietly. "Two hours, maybe two hours and thirty minutes, certainly no more."

"Thank you for your candid opinion,

Doctor," Baldwin said honestly. "Can you keep some of them alive a little longer with the fire crew's respirators?"

"There are about ten young people under the age of twenty. I'll provide them with oxygen until it runs out." Ringer came to his feet. "I'd better get back to the hospital. I suspect I have a line down there."

After the doctor had left, Pitt went back to scrutinizing the boat builder's plans. "For every complex problem, there is a simple solution," he said philosophically.

"When you find it," said Baldwin, with a show of humor, "let me know." He rose to his feet and started for the door. "Time for me to put in an appearance in the dining room. Good luck."

Pitt merely gave a brief nod and said nothing.

Slowly, a numbing fear seeped into his mind, not a fear for his life, but a fear that he might fail with so many people's lives hanging on his finding a solution. But for a few moments, it also sharpened his senses and flooded him with extraordinary clarity. This was followed by a revelation that struck with such force, it stunned him momentarily. The solution *was* simple. It came suddenly, with appalling ease. As with so many inspirations that struck men, he could only wonder why he hadn't seen it much earlier.

He jumped up so quickly he knocked over the stool in his rush to get to the phone attached to the line running up to the buoy. He shouted into the receiver. "Al! Are you there?"

"I'm here," Giordino's voice replied gravely.

"I think I have the answer! No, I'm positive I have the answer."

Giordino was stunned at Pitt's eagerness. "One moment, I'll put you on the bridge speaker so Captain Turner and the rest of his crew can listen." A moment's pause, and then, "Okay, go ahead."

"How long will it take you to set up the air hose and get it down here?"

"You know, of course, Mr. Pitt, that we can't make a connection," said Turner, his face gray like a rain cloud.

"Yes, yes, I know all that," Pitt said impatiently. "How soon before you can be pumping air?"

Turner looked across the bridge at McKirdy. The chief stared down at the deck as if he were contemplating what was beneath it. "We can have it ready to go in three hours."

"Make it two or you can forget it."

"What good will it do? We can't make a connection."

"Your pump, will it overcome the surrounding water pressure at this depth?"

485

"She puts out five hundred pounds per square inch," answered McKirdy. "Twice the pressure of the water at your depth."

"So far so good," rasped Pitt. He was beginning to feel light-headed. "Get the air hose down here fast. People are beginning to drop. Be prepared to use the vehicle's manipulators."

"Do you mind telling us what you have in mind?" asked Turner.

"I'll explain in detail when you're on site. Call me when you arrive for further instructions."

O'Malley had stumbled groggily into the control room in time to hear Pitt's conversation with the Alfred Aultman. "What have you got up your sleeve?"

"A grand idea," said Pitt, with growing optimism. "One of the best I ever had."

"How do you intend to get air in here?"

"I don't."

O'Malley looked at Pitt as if he had already expired. "Then what's so grand about your idea?"

"Simple," Pitt explained casually. "If Mohammed won't go to the mountain . . ."

"You're not making sense."

"Wait and see," said Pitt mysteriously. "It's the most elementary high school physics class experiment in the book."

The *Golden Marlin* was on the verge of becoming an underwater crypt. The air had deteriorated to a frightening extent, and the atmosphere had become so foul that passengers and crew were only minutes away from becoming unconscious, the first step before coma and then death. The carbon dioxide level was rapidly reaching limits that could no longer support life. Pitt and O'Malley, the only ones left on the bridge, were hanging on by the skin of their teeth.

Because their minds were numbed by the lack of oxygen, the passengers were becoming zombies, no longer capable of rational thought. No one panicked in the final moments, because no one fully realized their end was near. Baldwin talked to those still sitting in the dining room, encouraging them with words that he knew were meaningless. He was on his way back to the bridge when he sagged to his knees in a corridor and crumpled to the carpet. An elderly couple walked past, looked at the fallen captain through vacant eyes and stumbled on toward their stateroom.

In the control room, O'Malley was still murmuring coherently but not far from the edge of unconsciousness. Pitt was sucking deep breaths to take in what little oxygen was left in the room. "Where are you?" he gasped over the phone. "We're about done in."

"Coming." Giordino's voice sounded desperate. "Look through the port. We're approaching the control room dome."

Pitt staggered to the main port in front of the control console and saw the *Mercury* descending from above. "Do you have the hose?"

"Ready to pump when and wherever you say," answered Chief Warrant Officer McKirdy. Captain Turner had remained on board the *Aultman* to command the operation from the surface.

"Drop down until you're scraping the bottom and move toward the break in the hull opposite the engine room."

"On our way," Giordino acknowledged without questioning Pitt's intent.

Five minutes later, Turner reported, "We are level with the gash caused by the explosion."

Pitt found that fighting to breathe was ironic, considering that all the air he'd need in a lifetime was only a few feet away. He gasped out the words. "Use your manipulators and insert the end of the air hose as far back into the engine room as possible."

Inside the submersible, McKirdy exchanged glances and shrugged. Then Giordino went to work moving the hose inside the gash with the manipulators, careful not to slice it open on the jagged and torn hull. Working as fast as possible, it took him nearly ten minutes before he felt the hose reach the far bulkhead and jam itself between the engine mountings.

"She's in," announced Giordino.

Pitt spoke, inhaling one word, exhaling the next. "Okay . . . start pumping."

Again, the two men inside the rescue vehicle complied without challenging the request. McKirdy gave the order to Turner on the surface, and within two minutes a surge of air began bursting out of the hose into the engine room.

"What are we doing?" asked Giordino, mystified and grief stricken as he listened to what he thought were his friend's final words.

Pitt rasped out the answer in a voice barely above a whisper. "A ship sinks when water under pressure floods inside the hull's airspace. But at this depth, the air from your hose is blasting out at twice the pressure of the water, forcing it back out into the sea."

The explanation drained what little fortitude he had left and he slumped to the deck beside the body of O'Malley, who had already slipped into unconsciousness.

Giordino's hopes were suddenly renewed as he saw the water gush out of the engine room, driven back into the sea by the overwhelming pressure from the air pump 550 feet away on the surface. "It's working!" he shouted. "The air is forming a bubble inside."

"Yes, but none of the air is escaping inside the other parts of the boat," said McKirdy.

But Giordino saw the method to Pitt's madness. "He's not trying to purify the air inside. He's trying to raise the boat to the surface."

McKirdy looked down and saw the hull of the boat embedded in the silt, and had grave doubts that it could break the suction and rise. After a pause, McKirdy said quietly, "Your friend isn't answering."

"Dirk!" Giordino roared into the phone. "Talk to me."

But there was no answer.

On board the Navy support ship *Alfred Aultman*, Captain Turner paced the bridge as he listened to the drama being played out far below. He also saw the brilliance behind Pitt's stratagem. In his mind it was too incredibly simple to work. Murphy's law seldom took a backseat to Occam's razor.

There were eight men on the bridge of the support ship. Fear and defeat hung like a wet blanket. They each thought the end had arrived and the *Golden Marlin* was in the midst of becoming a titanium cemetery. They found it almost impossible to believe that 617 people were taking their final breaths less than a quarter of a mile below their feet. They gathered around the speaker, conversing as softly as if they were in a church, waiting for word from the *Mercury*.

"Will they recover the bodies?" mused one of Turner's officers.

Turner shrugged bleakly. "It would cost millions for a salvage job to go that deep to retrieve them. They'll probably be left where they lie."

A young ensign abruptly pounded his fist against a counter. "Why don't they report? Why doesn't McKirdy tell us what's happening down there?"

"Easy, son. They have enough to worry about without us hassling them."

"She's coming up. She's coming up." Six words from the side-scan sonar operator who had never taken his eyes off the recorder.

Turner leaned over the sonar operator's shoulder and stared openmouthed at the recorder. The image of the *Golden Marlin* had moved. "She's coming up, all right," he confirmed.

A great groaning sound came over the speaker, a sure indication that metal was being stressed and expanded as the boat rose from the bottom. Then McKirdy's voice roared out. "She's broken loose, by God! She's on her way to the surface. Pumping air into the engine room did the trick. She gained enough buoyancy to break suction and pop out of the silt —"

"We're trying to stay with her," Giordino cut in, "so we can keep the hose pumping air inside her or she'll sink again."

"We'll be ready!" snapped Turner.

He began issuing orders to his engineering crew to climb aboard the cruise boat the minute she hit the surface, and cut a hole in the top of her hull to pump air inside to revive the passengers and crew. Then he put out a call to every boat within twenty miles to come quickly with any piece of resuscitating equipment and oxygen respirator they had on board. He also requested every doctor to stand by to board the *Golden Marlin* as soon as his crew gained entry. Time was priceless. They had to get inside quickly if they were to revive those passengers and crew who had passed out from lack of oxygen.

The atmosphere among the fleet of ships over the *Golden Marlin* transformed from one of subdued gloom to wild jubilation within minutes of the word being passed that she was on her way up. A thousand eyes were straining at the open water circled by the ships and boats, when a cauldron of bubbles rose above the surface and burst in a display of rainbow colors under the morning sun. Then came the *Golden Marlin*. She erupted from the water on an even keel, like an immense cork, before settling back in a great splash that sent a surge toward the surrounding vessels, rocking the smaller yachts as if they were leaves swept from a tree in a fall windstorm.

"She's up!" shouted Turner ecstatically, almost afraid that he was seeing a mirage. "Rescue boats!" he shouted through a bullhorn from the bridge wing at the launches already in the water. "Get over there fast."

Cheers shattered the nearly windless air. People shouted themselves hoarse, many whistled, every horn and siren sounded. Like Turner, none could believe what they were seeing. The resurrection came so suddenly, so abruptly, many had not fully expected it. Media cameramen on the boats and in planes and helicopters quickly ignored the threats and orders from Turner and the captain of the Coast Guard cutter to stay out of the area, and swarmed in anyway, a few determined to get on board the cruise boat.

The *Golden Marlin* no sooner settled in the water like a hen on a roost than the armada of rescuers rushed toward her. Boats from the *Alfred Aultman* arrived first and tied alongside. Turner canceled the order for cutting equipment and ordered his rescue crew to simply gain entry through the boarding and cargo hatches, which could be broached from the outside now that there was no danger of water pouring inside.

The *Mercury* surfaced beside the big boat, McKirdy maneuvering the submersible to keep the hose securely lodged in the engine room, pumping in the air that expelled the flooded water. Giordino threw open the hatch, and before McKirdy could stop him, dove from the submersible into the water and swam toward a boat with the rescue crew who was unlatching the starboard boarding hatch. Fortunately, one of the navy rescue crew recognized Giordino or they would have ordered him off. Giordino was hauled into the boat, and he put his muscles to work helping pull open the hatch that was coated and nearly bonded shut with bottom silt.

They heaved it open half an inch. Then heaved again. This time it swung open on its hinges and was pushed back against the hull. For a moment they simply stood mute and peered inside as a stale smell flowed into their nostrils. It was air that they knew was unbreathable. Though the generators were still turning, it struck them as odd to see the interior of the boat brightly lit.

In the same moment, the crew on the other side of the hull pulled open the port hatch, allowing a cross-ventilation of air to blow in and suck out the bad air. Stepping inside, both crews found bodies lying on the deck and went to work attempting to resuscitate them. Giordino recognized one of them as Captain Baldwin.

Giordino had his own priority and did not pause. He rushed into the lobby, turned and dashed through the passageway toward the bow and up the stairs to the control room. He ran with a sinking heart, gasping the foul air that was slowly being reoxygenated. He charged into the control room with a growing dread in his chest, a dread that he was too late to save his dearest friend since childhood.

He stepped over the inert form of O'Malley and knelt beside Pitt, who was lying outstretched on the deck, eyes closed, seemingly not breathing. Giordino wasted no time feeling for a pulse but bent down to apply mouth-to-mouth resuscitation. But suddenly, to his astonishment, those mesmeric green eyes fluttered open and a voice whispered, "I hope this concludes the entertainment part of the program."

Never were so many people so close to dying at the same time. And never had so many cheated the old man with the scythe and that three-headed dog that guarded Hades. It was a near thing, little short of miraculous, that none of the passengers or crew of the *Golden Marlin* actually died. All were brought back from the brink of death. Only seventeen, mostly elderly men and women, were airlifted by Coast Guard helicopters to hospitals in Miami, and all but two recovered without any harmful effects. The remaining two were released a week later after suffering severe headaches and trauma.

Most revived as fresh air was recirculated throughout the boat. Only about fifty-two required resuscitation with oxygen equipment. Captain Baldwin was feted by the news media and the directors of the Blue Seas Cruise Lines as a hero who'd helped prevent what might have been a major tragedy, as was the boat's doctor, John Ringer, whose courageous efforts had helped immeasurably in keeping the death toll at zero. Captain Turner and his crew also received acclaim and honors from the Navy for their part in the rescue.

Only a very few knew of the role Pitt and Giordino had played in saving the ship and all its passengers and crew. By the time the news media learned that the man who'd helped save over two thousand people from the *Emerald Dolphin* was also instrumental in the raising of the *Golden Marlin*, he and Giordino were gone, having been picked by a NUMA helicopter from the pad on the stern of the *Alfred Aultman*.

Any attempts by reporters to track Pitt down for interviews failed. It was as though he had fallen in a hole and covered it up.

Part Three

THOUSAND-
YEAR TRAIL

RUNESTONE

33

Tohono Lake was off the beaten track as far as lakes went in New Jersey. There were no lakeside homes. It was on private land owned by the Cerberus Corporation for the use of its top management. Employees were provided with another resort lake thirty miles away for their pleasure. Because the lake was isolated, there were no fences around it. The only security was a locked gate five miles away on a road that wound through the low hills and heavily forested land before reaching a comfortable three-story lodge built of logs; the lodge faced the lake and came with a dock with a boathouse protecting canoes and rowboats. No motorized boats were allowed on the lake.

Fred Ames was not a director of Cerberus. He wasn't even a lower-level employee, but one of several local people who paid no attention to the No Trespassing signs and hiked into the lake to fish. He set up a small camp behind the trees surrounding the lakefront. The lake was stocked with largemouth bass and rarely fished, so it didn't take an old pro long to catch several five-to-ten-pound bass before noon. He was about to step into the water wearing his waders and begin casting when he noticed a large black limousine pull up and stop at the boat ramp. Two men got out with their fishing gear, while the chauffeur pulled one of the several boats sitting beside the ramp down to the water.

For big-time corporate executives, Ames thought it unusual for them not to use an outboard motor. Instead, one of them rowed the boat out to the middle of the lake, where he let it drift while both men tied on their bass plugs and began casting. Ames melted back into the forest and decided to warm a pot of coffee on his Coleman stove and read a paperback book until the corporate fishermen left.

The man who sat in the center of the boat and rowed was slightly under six feet and reasonably trim for a man of sixty. He had reddish-brown hair with no gray, topping a tanned face. Everything about him seemed exactingly sculptured in marble by an ancient Greek. His head, jaw, nose, ears, arms, legs, feet and hands seemed in perfect scale. The eyes were almost as blue-white as those on a husky, but not piercing. Their soft look was often misread as warm and friendly, when they were actually dissecting everyone in range. His movements — rowing, tying his bass plug and then casting — were precisely measured without wasted motion.

Curtis Merlin Zale was a perfectionist. There was nothing left of the boy who used to hike across cornfields to complete his chores. After his father died, he'd dropped out of school at twelve to run the family farm, and had educated himself. By the time he was twenty, he had accumulated the largest farm in the county and hired a manager to run it for his mother and three sisters.

Demonstrating a cunning mind and a shrewd tenacity, he'd forged school records to get himself admitted to New England's most prestigious business school. Despite his lack of education, Zale was blessed with a brilliant mind and photographic memory. He'd graduated with honors and gone on to receive a Ph.D. in economics.

From then on, his life followed a pattern: he'd launch companies, build them until they were extremely successful and then sell them. By the time he was thirty-eight, he was America's ninth-richest man, with a net worth in the billions. He then bought an oil company low in profits but high in leases around the country, including Alaska. Ten years later, he combined it with an old, solid chemical company. Eventually, he merged his holdings into one giant conglomerate called Cerberus.

No one really knew Curtis Merlin Zale. He made no friends, never attended parties or social functions, never married nor sired children. His love was power. He bought and sold politicians as if they were pedigreed dogs. He was ruthless, tough and as cold as the Ice Age. No opponents in his business transactions ever met with success. Most ended up defeated and broken, the victims of dirty, treacherous fights that went far beyond ethical business procedures.

Because he was extremely shrewd and cautious, there was never the slightest suspicion that Curtis Merlin Zale had risen to success through blackmail and murder. Strangely, not one of his business associates, the news media or his enemies, ever had cause to wonder about the deaths of the people who crossed swords with him. Many who stood in his way died from what seemed to be natural causes — heart attacks, cancer and other common diseases. A number died of accidents — cars, guns or drowning. A few simply disappeared. No trail ever led to Zale's door.

Curtis Merlin Zale was a cold-blooded sociopath without a shred of conscience. He could kill a child as easily as he would step on an ant.

He fixed his blue-white eyes on his chief security officer, who was clumsily trying to untangle the line on his reel. "I find it most peculiar that three vital projects planned with such meticulous forethought and computerized analysis should have failed."

Unlike the stereotyped Asian, James Wong had never acquired an inscrutable look. Big for his culture, he was a former major with the Special Forces, highly disciplined and as swift and deadly as a black mamba and puff adder entwined. He was the chief of Zale's dirty tricks and enforcement organization, the Vipers.

"Events happened beyond our control," he said, maddened at the snarl in his fishing reel. "The *Emerald Dolphin* came apart when those NUMA scientists unexpectedly appeared and then managed to dive down and survey her. Then, when we hijacked the survey crew, they managed to escape. And now, according to my intelligence sources, NUMA personnel were instrumental in saving the *Golden Marlin*. It's as if they appear like the plague."

"How do you explain it, Mr. Wong? They're an oceanographic agency — not a military, intelligence or investigative department of the government, but an agency devoted to sea research. How are they able to frustrate activities devised and carried out by the finest professional mercenaries money can buy?"

Wong laid down his rod and reel. "I could not have predicted NUMA's tenacity. It was just bad luck."

"I do not endure mistakes lightly," said Zale tonelessly. "Chance occurrences are due to poor planning, blunders to incompetence."

"No one regrets failure more than I," said Wong.

"I also find that foolish stunt by Ono Kanai in New York especially disturbing. I still can't understand why he cost us the loss of an expensive antique aircraft while attempting to shoot down a planeful of children. Who authorized the incident?"

"He did it entirely on his own after running into Pitt. As your own directives state, those who present obstacles to our plans must be eliminated. And then, of course, there was the fact that Kelly Egan was on board."

"Why kill her?"

"She could recognize Kanai."

"We are very lucky the police cannot trace Kanai to the Vipers and through you to Cerberus."

"Nor will they," Wong promised. "We threw out enough red herrings to muddy the trail forever — the same as we have on a hundred other operations to secure our power base."

"I would have handled it differently," Zale said, with an icy edge in his voice.

"The results are what count," Wong argued. "Egan's engines will never be seriously considered as a means of propulsion, at least until the *Emerald Dolphin* and *Golden Marlin* investigations are over, which could take a year or more. And with him dead, his formula for Slick 66 will soon belong to you."

"Providing you can lay it in my hands."

"It's as good as done," said Wong boldly. "I've given the assignment to Kanai. He won't dare fail this time."

"What about Josh Thomas? He'll never give it up."

Wong laughed. "That old drunk will give us the formula very, very soon. I promise."

"You seem confident."

Wong nodded. "Kanai has made up for his rash venture by abducting Kelly Egan from the *Golden Marlin* after he arranged its sinking. He is flying her to her father's house in New Jersey."

"Where I suppose he intends to torture her in front of Thomas to prod him into producing the oil formula."

"Not exactly an ingenious plan, but one that will produce a harvest of information."

"What about the guards around the farm?"

"We have found a way of penetrating their security without setting off alarms and alerting them."

"It's lucky for Kanai that you'd ordered him back here before his men and ship were blown up in the Kermadec Islands."

"I needed him back here for other reasons."

Zale sat silent for a moment, then he said, "I want this matter settled for good. Our projects must be concluded without interruption by outside influences. There can be no more failures. Perhaps I should get someone who can direct Viper operations without complications."

Before Wong could respond, Zale's rod suddenly bent into a U as a bass hit the plug. The fish broke water before splashing under again. He guessed the weight at close to seven pounds. Both men went silent as Zale slowly tired the fish and began reeling it toward the boat. When it was alongside, Wong scooped it up with a net, watching as it flopped between his feet.

"Nice catch," he complimented Zale.

The chief executive of Cerberus had a pleased look on his face as he removed the hooks on the red-and-white plug from the fish's mouth. "An old Bassarino, tried and true — they never fail." He did not cast again, but reached into his tackle box and made a show of fumbling for another bass plug. "The sun is getting higher. I think I'll try a Winnow."

A warning light flashed in the back of Wong's mind and he looked into Zale's eyes, attempting to read the thoughts behind them. "You were suggesting that I am no longer useful as the chief of Viper?"

"I think that others may be able to conduct future enterprises to more productive conclusions."

"I have served you with loyalty for twelve years," said Wong in quiet anger. "Does that count for nothing?"

"Believe me, I am grateful —" Suddenly, Zale pointed behind Wong at the water. "You have a bite."

Wong turned and looked, realizing too late that his line was still tangled and he had no bait in the water. In a lightning move, Zale snatched a syringe from his tackle box, plunged the needle in Wong's neck and pushed the plunger.

The poison acted almost instantly. Before he could resist, numbness set in followed quickly by death. He fell back in the boat, his eyes wide with shock as his body went limp.

Zale calmly felt for a pulse, and finding none, he tied a rope around Wong's ankles that was attached to the boat's anchor, a large tin can filled with hardened concrete. Then he dropped the anchor over the side and pushed Wong's body after it. He watched indifferently until the bubbles stopped rising to the surface.

The fish was still flopping in the bottom of the boat, but its struggles were rapidly diminishing. Zale tossed it over the side to join Wong.

"Sorry, my friend," he said, staring into the green water, "but failure begets failure. When your senses dull, it is time you be replaced."

Becoming impatient, Fred Ames walked cautiously toward the lake, staying hidden in the trees. When he reached the shoreline, he stared over the water at the lone fisherman rowing back toward the waiting limousine.

"That's odd," he muttered to himself. "I could have sworn there were two of them in that boat."

34

Members of the reorganized Viper team, now led by Ono Kanai, had timed the change of the security guards on the Egan farm, tracking when the new shift drove in the gate and the earlier shift left for home. Then by using aerial video photography they'd been able to follow the guards to their hidden locations. The next step was to gain entry by dressing as sheriff's deputies and driving an auto painted like a county patrol car. After killing the unsuspecting camouflaged road guard, they'd entered the house, seized Josh Thomas and then called in the rest of the guards for a meeting ostensibly to talk about new security programs.

Once the guards arrived at the house, they were unceremoniously shot and their bodies thrown in a storm cellar under the barn.

When Ono Kanai arrived at the nearby airport in a private unmarked plane belonging to Cerberus, he threw a sedated Kelly into the trunk of his car and drove to her father's farm, now secured by his mercenary team. He carried Kelly through the front door and dumped her on the floor in front of Josh Thomas, who was bound and gagged in a desk chair.

Thomas tried to struggle against his ropes and muttered incomprehensible curses through his gag, but only incurred the laughter of the five men in the room, who had cast aside the fake deputy's uniforms and changed into their standard black work outfits.

"All went well?" asked Kanai.

A mountain of a man, who towered six and a half feet tall and weighed nearly three hundred hard pounds, nodded. "Egan's guards were not very high caliber. They bought the phony sheriff's story hook, line and sinker."

"Where are they?"

"Disposed of."

Kanai looked into the crooked grin of his efficient colleague and at the scarred face complete with broken nose, missing front teeth and cauliflower ear, and nodded in satisfaction. "You do nice work, Darfur."

Dark evil eyes flashed from under a thick black mane. Kanai and Darfur had worked together for many years since they'd first met while eliminating a terrorist group working out of Iran. The big Arab gestured at Thomas.

"Please observe. Not a mark on him, yet I believe he has been sufficiently softened up to tell you what you wish to know."

Kanai studied Thomas and saw the twisted expression of pain that came from a beating to his body. He didn't doubt that Darfur had broken the scientist's ribs. He also noted anger in the scientist's eyes at seeing Kelly lying drugged and semi-conscious on the floor. Kanai smiled at Thomas, before stepping over and viciously kicking Kelly in her stomach. An expression of torment flashed on her face, along with a pathetic wail, as her eyes flicked open.

"Come awake, Miss Egan. It's time for you to persuade Mr. Thomas to reveal your father's oil formula."

Kelly rolled into a ball and clutched her stomach, gasping for breath. The pain was unlike any she'd ever suffered in her life. Kanai was an expert at inserting his boot toe in exactly the right place to induce the most agony. After a minute, she struggled to raise herself on one elbow and gaze at Thomas. "Don't tell this scum, Josh —"

She spoke no further. Her breath was cut off as Kanai shoved his boot against her neck and pressed her head against the carpet. "You are an obstinate young lady," he said coldly. "Do you enjoy pain? Because you will surely receive it."

One of Kanai's men entered the room, holding a portable radio. "A car is reported approaching the front gate. Should we refuse it entry?"

Kanai thought a moment. "Better to let them enter and see who it is than turn them away and arouse suspicion."

"Okay, mastermind," said Giordino, yawning, still tired after the hurried flight from Miami. "How do you plan to open the castle gate?"

"I punch in the code," answered Pitt, sitting behind the wheel of an old Ford pickup truck they'd rented from a farm appliance dealer.

"Do you know it?"

"No."

"You drag me up here less than an hour after I carry you off the *Golden Marlin* under the cockamamie notion that Kanai took Kelly to her father's laboratory, and you don't know the security code?"

"What better place to force information out of her and Josh Thomas? The formula has to be hidden in the lab somewhere."

"So what clever device do you use to gain entry?" asked Giordino, studying the massive gate and the high wall.

Pitt didn't answer but leaned out the car's window and punched a series of buttons.

"That will have to do. Actually, Kelly had a backup remote with a different code."

"And let's suppose Kanai and his flunkies *have* compromised the security system and overpowered the guards. What makes you think he's going to open the gate for us?"

"Because I punched in the name Cerberus for the code."

Giordino rolled his eyes. "If I had an ounce of common sense, this is where I'd get out."

Pitt's green eyes looked grim. "If I'm wrong, the gate won't open and we wasted the trip and lost Kelly for good."

"We'll find her," Giordino said gamely. "We won't stop searching until we do."

They were on the verge of leaving when the huge gate slowly began to swing open.

"I do believe we struck a chord," Pitt said, vindicated.

"You know, of course, they'll be waiting in ambush to shoot us to pieces."

Pitt slipped the car in drive and drove through the gate. "We're armed, too."

"Oh, sure. You've got your antique .45 Colt, and all I've got is a screwdriver I found in the glove compartment. The guys we're going up against are loaded down with assault weapons."

"Maybe we can pick up something along the way."

Pitt drove past the farmland and slowed

as he came to the vineyard, waiting for the barricade to rise up from the road. It came right on schedule and one of Kanai's men in a security guard uniform came to the car and leaned in the window, clutching an assault rifle across his chest. "Can I help you, gentlemen?"

"Where's Gus?" asked Pitt innocently.

"He called in sick," answered the guard. His eyes searched the car for weapons and, finding none, he relaxed.

"How's his baby girl?"

The guard's eyebrows raised fractionally. "Healthy, the last I heard —"

He was cut off as Pitt gripped the Colt by the barrel that was out of sight under his right thigh and swung it across the steering wheel and into the guard's forehead. The eyes crossed and the head and shoulders slipped below the car door's window frame and disappeared.

Almost before the bogus security guard hit the ground, Pitt and Giordino were pulling him through the grapevines into a large tree trunk and down eight steps to a security surveillance room underground. Twenty monitors were mounted against one wall, their cameras sweeping the farm fields and interior of the house. Pitt stood transfixed at the sight of Thomas trussed up and Kelly writhing on the floor, angry at seeing her abused but elated that she was alive and only a few hundred yards away. The five Vipers in the room seemed to have no indication they were being observed by cameras.

"We found her!" Giordino said, his spirits suddenly lifted.

"She's still alive," Pitt said, his rage mounting. "But it looks like those scum have given her a hard time."

"Let's not charge in like the Seventh Cavalry at the Little Big Horn," said Giordino. "With the security system, we can cover the entire farm and house from here and pinpoint where the rest of Kanai's men are located."

"We'll have to make it fast. They'll be expecting a report on us from the guy on the floor."

Giordino sat down at the console as Pitt found the hired assassin's black clothing that he had removed when he'd donned Egan's security guard's uniform. He looked down at the motionless body and saw they were roughly the same size. He quickly removed his street clothes and slipped into the black pants and sweater. The boots were a tight fit, but he squeezed his feet into them and pulled a ski mask over his face and head, which completed the outfit.

"These guys have no inhibitions when it comes to murder," said Giordino, as one of the monitors revealed the bodies of Egan's security guards stacked like grain sacks in a cellar under the barn. He switched from one camera to the next, searching for Kanai's men. "Besides the five in the house, I count two more. One guarding the back door overlooking the river and another by the barn."

"That makes eight, counting our friend on the floor."

"Now is as good a time as any to call for reinforcements."

Pitt nodded at one of three phones sitting on the counter. "Notify the sheriff's department, report the situation and ask them to send in a SWAT team."

"And you? What's your gig?"

"In this outfit they'll think I'm one of them," said Pitt. "It won't hurt to have a friend inside the house when all hell breaks loose."

"And me?" asked Giordino.

"Stay here, monitor the situation and direct the SWAT team."

"And when Kanai calls and asks where the occupants in the car went?"

"Fake it. Say they were a couple of fertilizer salesmen and you took care of them."

"How are you going to get from here to the house?"

"The vineyard runs within a short distance of the front of the house. I'll make my way through the grapevines, and move onto the front porch from behind the columns.

Getting across the strip of grass will be the touchy part."

"Don't you get us into another fine mess, Stanley," said Giordino, with the trace of a grin.

"I promise to be good, Ollie."

Giordino turned back to the monitors, as Pitt went up the stairs through the old tree trunk and crept through the vineyard.

Pitt's mind registered two emotions, a fear that he could not rescue Kelly before Kanai's goons worked her over again and a stark, simple urge for vengeance. He found it difficult to believe all the dead bodies left in the wake of the Cerberus Corporation and its gang of murderous Vipers, and for what? Profit? An obsession for power? No one lived long enough to enjoy such rotten rewards for very long. In Pitt's eyes, it was insane.

Crouching below the upper branches of the grapevines, he ran between the rows, his boots sinking in the soft soil. He had not taken the automatic rifle from the incapacitated Viper. He seldom shot a rifle and preferred to travel light, with only his old .45 Colt and two spare ammo clips. The summer day was warm and humid and he began to sweat inside the ski mask. He did not remove it because it was standard wear for the Vipers, and he didn't want to look conspicuous.

He ran more than a hundred yards before the rows of grapevines ended near the front of the house, separated by a narrow strip of well-mowed lawn. He was out of view of the Vipers guarding the barn and back of the house, but moving across fifty feet of open space without being detected by anyone in the house was more like a study in playing invisible man than in acting with stealth. He looked at the windows and detected movement on the other side, which suggested he would be totally visible once he left the shelter of the grapevines.

Fifty feet lay between him and the first column on the porch of the house, fifty feet of open grass under brilliant sunshine. He edged across the end of the grapevines until his movements were veiled by curtains. A sudden dash might catch the eye of someone inside, so he moved very slowly across the yard, watching for any sign of the guard behind the house. One step at a time, he moved like a cat stalking a bird pulling at a worm.

Five wooden steps led up to the columned porch, and Pitt trod slowly, quietly, fearful of a loud creak that thankfully never came. In less than a few seconds, he was pressing his back against the house around the corner and two feet from the big bay window of the living room. Now he laid himself out prone and inched his body below the window until he reached the other side and could stand and step toward the front door. He slowly turned the knob and cracked the door. No one was in the foyer and he slipped inside like a shadow.

There was no door to the living room. It was entered through an open archway. A clay pot sat on a pedestal beside the archway, with a small tropical plant sprouting from it. Pitt used it as cover to peer into the living room — not a quick glance, but a slow study to firmly fix everyone's position in his mind.

Josh Thomas, with blood trickling down his head from thin cuts on his forehead, ears and nose, sat slumped and bound in a chair in the center of the room. He recognized Ono Kanai as the pilot of the red Fokker. Kanai sat in the center of a large leather sofa, casually leaning against one armrest, calmly smoking a cigar. Two of the Vipers, dressed in black, stood on opposite sides of the fireplace, weapons at the ready. Another stood beside Thomas, a knife in one hand poised above one of Thomas's eyes. The fifth Viper was a giant monster who gripped a struggling Kelly by her long hair with one hand and held her in the air, her feet inches above the carpet. No screams came through her mouth, only agonized moans.

Pitt pulled back a moment around the archway, wondering if Giordino was watching him on a monitor. It was ridiculous to think he could simply walk into the room and say, "All right, you varmints, reach for the sky," and live to a ripe old age. The men inside would think nothing of shooting him a hundred times if he tried anything so foolish. They had spent years training to kill and would not waste a microsecond in decision. Killing came as naturally to men like these as brushing their teeth. Pitt, on the other hand, had to gear himself to shoot another human being. Though he had killed in self-defense, cold blood did not run in his veins. He had to stiffen himself for the ordeal and justify his resolve by the fact that he would be saving the lives of Josh Thomas and Kelly Egan. But only if he was successful — a dim prospect in any light.

Though surprise was on his side and he would not be immediately suspect if he entered the room in black Viper clothing, he decided they'd be safer with another two-second advantage if he shot through the tropical plant while he was still partially hidden. Not immediately knowing where the bullets were coming from would slow their reaction time. He could select his targets in order of priority.

He quickly rejected the idea. He might get two or three of them, but those who remained would surely pepper him with bullets before he could finish the job. Then there was the very likely possibility that a stray bullet could catch Kelly or Thomas. He decided the only hope was to stall for time until the SWAT team showed up. He laid his Colt on the table behind a flower vase and stepped unobtrusively into the room and stood quietly.

At first, Pitt wasn't noticed. Everyone in the room was focused on Kelly, who was struggling with Darfur. He could see the tears streaming from her eyes at the ungodly pain, and it was agonizing for him to stand rigid without attempting to stop the torture. He figured another five minutes would pass before the SWAT team arrived, but he could not stand by and see Kelly and Thomas suffer.

He said calmly to Kanai, "Tell fat boy to let her go."

Kanai looked at Pitt, his eyebrows rising in puzzlement. "What did you say?"

"I said, tell your fat flunky to take his slimy hands off the girl." And he pulled off the ski mask.

Every Viper in the room immediately recognized Pitt as an imposter, and guns were swiftly raised and aimed at his chest.

"*You!*" Kanai muttered in astonishment. "Wait!" he shouted. "Do not kill him. Not just yet."

Kelly momentarily dismissed her suffering

and stared in stunned surprise. "No, no, you shouldn't have come!" she gasped through clenched lips.

"You'll be next to die, Kanai," said Pitt coldly, "if he doesn't release her."

Kanai gave Pitt a bemused look. "Oh really? And who's going to kill me? You?"

"A SWAT team will be arriving any second. The road is the only way out. You're trapped."

"You'll forgive me, Mr. Pitt, if I don't believe you." Then he gave a brief tilt of his head toward the giant. "Set the lady on her feet, Darfur." He turned his attention back to Pitt. "Did you kill one of my men?"

"No," Pitt said. "I merely knocked your pal in the security center unconscious and borrowed his clothes."

"I have a score to settle with you, Mr. Pitt. Would you disagree?"

"Speaking for myself, I think I should be awarded a medal for fouling up your rotten plans. You and your friends belong back in Jurassic ooze."

"Your death will be slow and painful."

There it was. Kanai was not going to kill Pitt quickly. In the killer's mind, it was payback time. Pitt fully realized he was in a precarious position. What was Giordino thinking as he viewed the scene over the monitor? The law was coming. That much he was sure of, but when? He had to stall as long as he could.

"Did I interrupt something when I crashed the party?" he asked innocently.

Kanai gave him a calculated look. "I was having a friendly discussion with Miss Egan and Mr. Thomas regarding Dr. Egan's work."

"The old find-the-oil-formula routine," Pitt said dismissively. "How uncreative of you, Kanai. It seems everybody in the state knows the formula but you and your pals at Cerberus."

Kanai's eyes widened marginally. "You are well-informed."

Pitt shrugged. "It's all in how you interpret the drums."

Kelly had moved over to Thomas. She removed his gag and was wiping away the blood from his face with her sweater, revealing her bra. Thomas looked up through dull eyes at her, murmuring his thanks. The huge Darfur stood behind Pitt, looking like a coyote who had a rabbit trapped in a gulch.

"You may prove to be a blessing in disguise," Kanai said to him. He turned to Kelly. "Now then, Miss Egan, you will kindly give me the oil formula or I will shoot this man in the knees, then the elbows, then I'll blast off his ears."

Kelly looked at Pitt in anguish. It was the

final blow. With Kanai threatening both Pitt and Thomas, she knew she didn't have the fortitude to hold out, and abruptly crumbled. "The formula is hidden in my father's laboratory."

"Where?" Kanai demanded. "We've already made a thorough search of it."

She started to answer, but Pitt interrupted. "Don't tell him. Better we all die than give his murderous friends at Cerberus a bonanza they don't deserve."

"Enough," Kanai snapped. He removed an automatic from a shoulder holster and aimed the muzzle at Pitt's left knee. "It seems Miss Egan has to be persuaded."

Darfur walked over and stood in front of Pitt. "Sir, I would consider it an honor if you'd allow me to obtain work on this dog."

Kanai looked at the big man and smiled. "I stand remiss. I'd neglected your powers of persuasion, old friend. He's all yours."

As Darfur turned to lay his rifle against a chair, Pitt, who'd pretended a look of fear, suddenly uncoiled like a rattler and lashed out at Darfur with his knee, catching the monstrous man in the groin. It should have been a stunning blow, or at least an incapacitating one, but Pitt's aim was slightly off and the major force caught Darfur just to the side of the genitals where the thigh joins the torso.

Darfur was taken by complete surprise

and doubled over with a hoarse gasp of pain, but only for a moment. He recovered almost instantly and struck Pitt in the chest with both hands clutched together in a sledgehammer punch that forced an explosive gasp of breath and knocked him over a table, crashing to the carpet. Pitt had never been struck so hard. He came to his knees, heaving to put air in his lungs. Any more of this punishment and he'd be a candidate for the morgue. He knew he could never take the giant down with his feet and fists, and he'd have required muscles the size of drainage pipes even to attempt any display of resistance. He needed a weapon, any weapon. He picked up a coffee table, lifted it high and brought it down on Darfur's head, shattering the wooden surface. The monster must have had a skull of iron. His eyes seemed to go out of focus, and he swayed unsteadily. Pitt thought he might go down and readied himself to leap for the gun in Kanai's hand, but Darfur shook off the blow, rubbed his head, refocused his eyes and renewed his attack.

Pitt was in the fight of his life, and he was losing. There is a truism in the world of boxing that says a good little man can never beat a good big man. At least not in a fair fight. Pitt frantically looked around for something to throw. He snatched a heavy ceramic lamp off an end table and threw it with both hands. It merely bounced off of Darfur's right shoulder like a rock off a Patton tank. Pitt threw a telephone, followed by a vase, followed by a clock off the mantel. He might as well have been throwing a barrage of tennis balls. None had the slightest effect on Darfur's massive body.

Pitt could read the cold, dead eyes and saw that the giant was tired of playing the game. Darfur launched himself across the room like a defensive guard against a quarterback. But Pitt was still agile enough to step aside and let the express train thunder past and crash into a piano. Pitt ran over and picked up the piano stool, preparing to smash it into Darfur's face. The blow never fell.

With Kelly's arms clutched around his neck, Kanai brushed her away as if he she were a small rodent and brought the butt of his gun down on the back of Pitt's head. The blow did not knock him unconscious but unleashed a sea of pain that dropped Pitt to his knees, briefly causing him to black out. Consciousness slowly returned, and through a darkness that clouded his vision, he became aware of Kelly screaming. As his vision cleared, he saw Kanai holding her at bay, twisting her arm until it was a millimeter away from breaking. Kelly had attempted to wrest the gun away from him while his attention was focused on the one-sided fight between Pitt and Darfur.

Pitt was suddenly aware of being jerked to his feet by Darfur, who circled his arms around Pitt's chest, clutched his hands together and began to squeeze. The breath was slowly, irreversibly being compressed within his lungs as if he were being wrapped by a boa constrictor. His mouth was open, but he could not even utter a gasp. The blackness was returning, and he had no illusions of seeing daylight again. He felt his ribs on the verge of cracking, and he was within two seconds of giving in and letting death relieve his agony, when abruptly the pressure released and the arms around his chest loosened.

As if in a dream sequence, he saw Giordino walk into the room and kidney-punch Kanai from the rear, doubling him over in agony. Kanai dropped the gun and released his grip on Kelly's arm.

The other Vipers froze, their guns now aimed at Giordino, waiting for the word from Kanai to shoot.

Darfur gazed apprehensively at the intruder for a moment, but when he saw that Giordino was not carrying a firearm and was a good foot shorter than he, the look on his face reflected an air of disdain. "Leave him to me," he said fiendishly.

In the same instantaneous movement, he

released Pitt, who fell in a heap onto the carpet, took two steps and swept Giordino up off the floor in a great bear hug and held him with his feet in the air. Instead of Darfur towering above his opponent, they stared face-to-face, no more than inches apart. Darfur's lips were drawn back in an evil leer while Giordino's face was expressionless, with a complete absence of fear.

When Darfur had grasped him around the back above the waist and locked his arms like a vise, Giordino had lifted his arms so that they were free and stretched in the air above the giant's head. Darfur ignored Giordino's raised arms and used every ounce of his enormous strength to constrict the life out of the short Italian.

Pitt, still dazed and in extreme pain, crawled across the room, drawing in great breaths, gasping in agony from his bruised chest and head. Kelly leaped onto Darfur's back with her hands around his face again, covering his eyes and wrestling with him, twisting his head back and forth. Darfur easily broke her hold with one hand and tossed her away as if she were a show window mannequin, sending her sprawling onto the sofa before he resumed his constricting grip around Giordino.

But Giordino didn't need saving. He lowered his arms and tightened his fingers around Darfur's throat. The giant suddenly realized that he was the one who was staring death in the eye. The leer on his face turned to contorted fear as the air was cut off from his lungs and he tried to beat desperately at Giordino's chest with his fists one moment and pry the steel fingers from his throat the next. But Giordino was remorseless. He gave no sign of yielding. He hung on like a relentless bulldog as Darfur thrashed around the room like a madman.

There was a horrible gasping wail as Darfur suddenly went limp and crashed to the floor like a timbered oak tree, with Giordino on top of him. At that instant, a fleet of sheriff's patrol cars and SWAT vans slid to a stop on the gravel driveway. Uniformed men with heavy weapons began dispersing around the house. The sound of approaching helicopters also came through the windows.

"Out the back!" Kanai shouted to his men. He clutched Kelly around the waist and began dragging her from the room.

"You harm her," Pitt said, his voice like cold stone, "and I'll blow you to pieces bit by bit."

He saw Kanai quickly calculating the odds of escaping with a struggling prisoner.

"Not to worry," Kanai replied derisively, as he threw her across the room at Pitt. "She's yours for now. That is, until we meet again, and we will."

Pitt tried to follow, but he was in no condition for a footrace and he stumbled to a stop, leaning on a credenza, waiting for the cobwebs to clear and the pain to subside. After a minute, he returned to the living room and found Giordino cutting away the ropes that bound Thomas, while Kelly dabbed a cloth soaked with Jack Daniel's sour-mash whiskey at the wounds on the scientist's face.

Pitt glanced down at Darfur on the floor. "He dead?"

Giordino shook his head. "Not quite. I thought it best if he lives. Maybe he can be persuaded to tell the police and FBI what he knows."

"You cut it a bit thin, didn't you?" Pitt said, with a tight grin.

Giordino looked at him and shrugged. "I was on my way two seconds after I saw you get sandbagged, but I had to stop and take care of the guard outside the barn."

"I'm grateful," said Pitt genuinely. "If not for you, I wouldn't be standing."

"Yes, my intervention is getting monotonous."

There was no getting the last word with Giordino. Pitt went over and helped Thomas to his feet. "How are you doing, old-timer?"

Thomas smiled bravely. "I'll be good as new after a few stitches."

Kelly gazed at Pitt as he put his arm around her and said, "You're one tough little lady."

"Did he get away?"

"Kanai?"

"I'm afraid so, unless the sheriff's deputies can chase him down."

"Not him," she said uneasily. "They won't find him. He'll come back to kill with a vengeance. His bosses at Cerberus won't rest until they have Dad's formula."

Pitt stared out the window, as if searching for something in the distance beyond the horizon. When finally he spoke, it was in a quiet voice, as if he was dwelling on each syllable. "I have a strange feeling that the oil formula is not the only thing they're after."

35

It was late in the afternoon. Darfur and the two Vipers that Pitt and Giordino had subdued were handcuffed and driven away in patrol cars to the Sheriff's Department and booked for the murder of Egan's security guards. Kelly and Thomas gave their statements to the sheriff's homicide investigators, followed by Pitt and Giordino. Kelly was correct in saying the deputies would never catch Ono Kanai. Pitt traced the killer's tracks to the high cliffs above the Hudson River, where he found a rope leading down to the water.

"They must have escaped in a waiting boat," observed Giordino.

Pitt stood with his friend in a gazebo at the edge of the palisade and stared down at the water. He lifted his gaze across the river to the green hills and forests. Small villages strayed along the New York shore in the part of the Hudson Valley made famous by

Washington Irving. "Amazing how Kanai covers every bet, every contingency."

"Do you think the Vipers will talk under interrogation?"

"It really wouldn't make much difference if they did," said Pitt slowly. "The Viper organization probably works in cells, each ignorant of the other, under the command of Kanai. As far as they know, the chain of command stops with him. I'll bet none of them are aware their true bosses sit in the corporate offices of Cerberus."

"It stands to reason they're too smart to leave a trail leading to their doorstep."

Pitt nodded. "Government prosecutors will never find enough hard evidence to convict them. If they're ever punished for their hideous crimes, it won't be under the law."

Kelly walked across the lawn from the house to the gazebo. "You two hungry?"

"I'm always hungry," Giordino said, smiling.

"I fixed a light dinner while Josh mixed the drinks. He makes mean margaritas."

"Dear heart" — Pitt put his arm around her waist — "you just said the magic word."

To say that Dr. Elmore Egan's taste in decorating was eclectic would be an understatement. The living room was furnished in early Colonial, the kitchen had obviously been designed by a high-tech engineer whose passion ran more to exotic appliances than gourmet cooking and the dining room looked like it had come straight from a Viking farm, its chairs and tables crafted from heavy oak, with matching chairs carved and sculpted with intricate patterns and designs.

While Pitt, Giordino and Thomas savored margaritas that could have jumped from their glasses and walked away, Kelly dished up a tuna casserole with coleslaw. Despite the trauma of the day, everyone ate normally.

Afterward, they retired to the living room and replaced the uprooted pieces of furniture to their proper positions while Thomas poured everyone a glass of forty-year-old port.

Pitt looked at Kelly. "You told Kanai that your father's formula was hidden in the laboratory."

She glanced at Thomas as if seeking permission. He smiled slightly and nodded his approval. "Dad's formula is in a file folder that fits in a hidden panel in back of the door."

Giordino swirled the port slowly in his glass. "He'd have fooled me. I would never have looked for it inside a door."

"Your dad was a clever man."

"And Josh is a brave man," Giordino said respectfully. "Despite a nasty beating, he told Kanai nothing."

Thomas shook his head. "Believe me, if Dirk had not walked into the room when he did, I would have spilled the secret of the formula's hiding place to save Kelly further torture."

"Maybe," said Pitt. "But when they saw they couldn't beat it out of you, they switched their efforts to Kelly."

"They could come back, perhaps even tonight," said Kelly uneasily.

"No," Pitt assured her. "Kanai would need time to put another team together. He won't try again soon."

"We'll take every precaution," said Thomas seriously. "Kelly must leave the house and go into hiding."

"I agree," said Pitt. "Kanai will no doubt assume that you'll secrete the formula someplace other than the farm, which still leaves the two of you their only key to finding it."

"I could go to Washington with you and Al," said Kelly, with a mischievous gleam in her eye. "I'll be safe under *your* care."

"I'm not sure yet whether we're going back to Washington." Pitt set down his empty glass. "Could you please show us Dr. Egan's laboratory?"

"There's not much to see," said Thomas. He led them from the house to the barn. Inside were three counters upon which sat the usual apparatus seen in most chemistry laboratories. "It's not very exciting, but it's where we formulated and developed Slick 66."

Pitt walked around the room. "Not exactly what I was expecting."

Thomas looked at him queerly. "I'm not following you."

"This can't be where Dr. Egan conceived and designed his magnetohydrodynamic engines," Pitt said firmly.

"Why do you say that?" asked Thomas cautiously.

"This room is a chemistry lab, no more. Dr. Egan was a brilliant engineer. I see no drafting tables, no computers programmed for displaying three-dimensional components, no facilities or machinery to construct working models. I'm sorry, but this is not where an inventive mind would create a great advance in propulsion technology." Pitt paused and stared at both Kelly and Thomas, whose eyes were cast on the stained wooden floor. "What I can't figure out is why you're both stroking me."

"Kelly and I are hiding nothing from you, Mr. Pitt," said Thomas seriously. "The truth is, we do not know where Elmore conducted his research. He was a fine man and a good friend, but he had a secretive streak that was nothing short of fanatical. Elmore would disappear for days, sometimes weeks, in a secret research laboratory whose location was known only to him. Kelly and I tried to follow him on different occasions, but he somehow always knew and eluded us. It was as if he were a ghost who vanished whenever he desired."

"Do you think the secret lab is here on the farm?" asked Pitt.

"We don't know," replied Kelly. "When we were certain Dad had left the farm on business or research trips, Josh and I looked everywhere, but never found a clue to its location."

"What was Dr. Egan researching when he died?"

Thomas shrugged helplessly. "I have no idea. He refused to take me into his confidence. He only said it would revolutionize science and technology."

"You were his closest friend," said Giordino. "It's odd that he never confided in you."

"You'd have to have known Elmore. He was two people. One minute the absent-minded but lovable father and friend. The next, a paranoid master engineer who trusted no one, not even those closest to him."

"Did he ever take time for pleasure?" inquired Pitt.

Josh and Kelly looked at each other.

"He was incredibly passionate about researching the Vikings," said Thomas.

"He was also a dedicated fan of Jules

Verne," added Kelly. "He read his works over and over."

Pitt motioned around the laboratory. "I see no indication of any such passions."

Kelly laughed. "We haven't shown you his library."

"I'd like to see it."

"It's in a separate building beside the house overlooking the river. Dad built it almost twenty years ago. It was his home away from home, his sanctuary from the pressures of his work."

The building that housed Egan's study was made of stone and appeared to be designed after an eighteenth-century grain mill. Slate covered the roof, and ivy rose on the rock walls. The only admission to modern convenience were the skylights in the roof. Thomas used a large, old-fashioned key to unlock the thick oak door.

The interior of the library was what Pitt had imagined. The rows of mahogany bookshelves and the paneled walls oozed finesse and refinement. The big overstuffed chairs and couch were leather, and the desk, still littered with research papers, was a huge rosewood rolltop. The ambience smothered the visitors with comfort and solace. This library must have fit Egan like a snug, well-worn glove, Pitt thought. It was an ideal setting in which to conduct research.

He walked along the bookshelves that ran

from floor to ceiling. A ladder with wheels on its upper frames moved along a track, enabling Egan to reach the top shelves. Paintings of Viking ships hung on the only open wall. On a table below the paintings sat a model of a submarine nearly four feet in length. Pitt guessed the scale at a quarter of an inch to the foot. As a marine engineer himself, Pitt studied the model closely, noting the exacting craftsmanship. The boat was rounded on the ends, with portholes along the sides and a small tower that sat toward the bow. The propeller's blades were shaped more like paddles than the curved tips of modern designs.

Pitt had never seen a craft quite like it. The only comparison he could think of was a diagram of a submarine he'd studied once that had been built by the Confederates during the Civil War.

The brass plaque on the base beneath the model read, *Nautilus. Seventy meters in length with an 8-meter beam. Launched 1863.*

"A beautiful model," said Pitt. "Captain Nemo's submarine, isn't it? From *Twenty Thousand Leagues under the Sea*?"

"Dad designed it from an etching in the original book and found a master model builder by the name of Fred Torneau to construct it."

"Classic work," said Giordino admiringly.

Pitt continued his tour, examining the titles of the books on the shelves. They all covered the Viking era from 793 to 1450 A.D. One entire section was devoted to the runic alphabets used by the Germanic and Norse people from the third to the thirteenth centuries.

Kelly watched Pitt's interest in the books and came up, holding his arm. "Dad became expert at translating the characters found on rune stones throughout the country."

"He believed the Vikings came this far south?"

She nodded. "He was convinced. When I was little, he dragged mother and me around half the midwestern states in an old camper while he copied and studied every rune stone he could find."

"Couldn't have been a large number," said Giordino.

"He found and recorded over thirty-five stones with ancient runic alphabets." She paused and pointed to one entire shelf of binders and notebooks. "It's all right there."

"Did he ever intend to publish his findings?" asked Giordino.

"Not as far as I knew. About ten years ago, it was as if a light switch had been turned off. He suddenly lost all interest in his Viking research."

"From one fixation to another," said Thomas. "After the Vikings, Elmore immersed himself in Jules Verne." He swept a hand across one entire bookcase. "He collected every book, every story Verne ever wrote."

Pitt pulled one of the books from the shelf and opened it. The covers were leather bound. Gold lettering on the spine and front cover read *Mysterious Island*. Many of the pages were heavily underlined. He returned it to the shelf and stepped back. "I see no bound papers or notebooks concerning Verne. Apparently, Dr. Egan read the books, but wrote no commentaries."

Thomas looked exhausted from the traumatic events of the day. He slowly lowered himself into a leather chair. "Elmore's dedication to Verne and the Vikings is something of a mystery. He was not the kind of man who drove himself to become an expert on a subject purely for pleasure. I never knew him to gain specific knowledge without a purpose."

Pitt looked at Kelly. "Did he ever tell you why he was so absorbed in the Vikings?"

"It wasn't so much the lore and history of the culture as the runic inscriptions."

Giordino took one of Egan's Viking notebooks from the shelf and opened it. His eyes squinted as he thumbed through the pages, his face registering bafflement. He flipped through the pages of a second notebook, then a third. Then he looked up, utterly mystified, as he passed the notebooks to the others standing beside him. "It looks like Dr. Egan was more of an enigma than any of you knew."

They all studied the notebooks and then looked at each other in puzzled incomprehension.

All the pages in all the notebooks were blank.

"I don't understand," said Kelly, looking totally lost.

"Nor I," added Thomas.

Kelly opened two more notebooks and found them empty as well. "I vividly remember the family trips into the backwoods searching for rune stones. When he found one, he would highlight the rune fonts with talcum powder before photographing them. Then, while we camped nearby in the evening, he would translate the messages. I used to pester him, and he'd shoo me away as he scribbled in his notebooks. I saw him make notations with my own eyes."

"Not in these books," said Pitt. "None of the pages look as if they'd been removed and replaced with blank pages. Your father must have hidden the original notebooks elsewhere."

"No doubt gathering dust in the lost laboratory you talk about," said Giordino, whose respect for Elmore Egan had dropped a couple of notches.

Kelly's lovely face was flushed with bewilderment, and her sapphire blue eyes seemed to be trying to see something that was not there. "Why would Dad do such things? I always remember a man who was so straight and honest he didn't have a devious bone in his body."

"He must have had a good reason," Thomas said, in an attempt to comfort her.

Pitt looked down at her compassionately. "It's getting late. We're not going to solve anything tonight. I suggest we sleep on it and maybe we'll come up with some answers in the light of day."

No one gave him an argument. They were all dead tired. All, except Pitt. He was the last one to leave the library. He pretended to lock the door before he handed the key to Thomas. Later, when everyone was asleep, he quietly returned to the library and entered through the unlocked door. Then he turned on the lights and began searching through Egan's research material on the rune stones. A trail and a story began to emerge.

By four in the morning, he had found what he was looking for. Many answers still eluded him. But the mud in the water had cleared just enough for him to get a glimpse of the bottom. Happily satisfied, he fell asleep in one of the comfortable leather chairs, inhaling the quaint smell of the old books.

36

Giordino surprised everyone by making breakfast. Afterward, Pitt, tired and bleary-eyed from lack of sleep, dutifully called Sandecker and brought him up-to-date. The admiral had little to report on the investigation into Cerberus and mentioned in passing that Hiram Yaeger was mystified as to how Pitt had filled Egan's leather case with oil behind his back. Pitt was mystified, too, and couldn't fathom who was behind the trick.

Giordino joined Thomas, who had some work to do in the lab while Pitt and Kelly returned to the library. Kelly noticed the books and papers stacked on the rolltop desk. "Looks like a little fairy was burning the midnight oil."

Pitt looked at her. "Believe you me, it was no fairy."

"Now I see why you look like the morning after," she said, smiling. She came over and gave him a light kiss on the cheek. "I thought you might have visited me last night instead of Dad's library."

Pitt started to say "business before pleasure," but thought better of it. "I'm not good at romancing women when my mind is a million miles away."

"Back a thousand years in time," she added, studying the open Viking books on the desk. "What were you after?"

"You said your dad traveled around the country and translated thirty-five rune stones."

"Give or take a couple. I don't remember exactly."

"Do you recall the locations?"

She tilted her head back and forth trying to remember, her long maple-sugar brown hair curling down her shoulders. Finally, she held up her hands emptily. "About five or six come to mind, but they were so far off the beaten track I couldn't tell you how to get anywhere near them."

"You won't have to."

"What are you driving at?" she challenged.

"We're going to launch an expedition to retrace your dad's trail to the rune stones and have them translated."

"To what end?"

"Call it gut instinct," said Pitt. "But your father didn't chase around the country looking for Viking inscriptions and then hide or destroy his translations for laughs. He set out to accomplish something. He had a mission. I believe it ties in somehow with his experiments."

Her lips were set in doubt. "If so, you're seeing something I fail to see."

Pitt grinned at her. "Can't lose by trying."

"Dad destroyed all his notes revealing directions to the rune-stone sites. How are you going to find them?"

He leaned over the desk, picked up a book and handed it to her. The title was *Messages from the Ancient Vikings*, by Dr. Marlys Kaiser. "This lady has compiled a comprehensive record of more than eighty rune stones throughout North America and their translations. Her earlier works are here in your dad's library. I think it might pay to visit Dr. Kaiser."

"Eighty runes —" She stopped herself, a thought tugging at her mind. "But Dad only studied thirty-five. Why did he stop at that number and not study the other forty-five?"

"Because he was only concerned with the inscriptions that related to the particular project he was pursuing at the time."

There was a glint in her blue eyes as curiosity dug deeper into her mind. "Why didn't Dad leave a record of the inscriptions he translated?"

"I'm hoping Dr. Kaiser can provide us

with answers," he said, squeezing her hand.

"When do we leave?" she asked, excitement building within her.

"This afternoon, or as soon as your new security guards are positioned around the farm."

"Where does Dr. Kaiser live?"

"A little town called Monticello. It's about sixty miles northwest of Minneapolis."

"I've never been to Minnesota."

"Lots of bugs this time of year."

Kelly gazed at the books on Vikings lining the shelves of her father's library. "I wonder if Dr. Kaiser knew Dad?"

"It stands to reason he would have consulted her," said Pitt. "We'll know some answers by this time Sunday."

"That's four days away." She looked at him questioningly. "What gives?"

He led her from the library and closed the door. "First, I have to make five or six calls. Then we're flying to Washington. There are people there on whom I rely for their expertise. I want to gather all the data possible before we beat the bushes for old rune stones."

This time when Pitt's NUMA jet landed at Langley Field, Congresswoman Loren Smith was waiting to greet him. As he stepped onto the tarmac, she embraced him, snaking her fingers through his wavy black hair and pulling his head down so she could kiss him.

"Hi there, sailor," she said in a sultry tone after she released him. "My wandering one is home."

Kelly hesitated in the doorway of the aircraft, watching Pitt and Loren looking into each other's eyes. She could easily see this was no casual friendship, and she felt pangs of jealousy. Loren was a very beautiful woman. Her face and body reflected a healthy aura from having grown up on a ranch on the western slopes of Colorado. An accomplished horsewoman, she had run for Congress and won. She was now in her sixth term.

Loren was dressed casually for the humid Washington heat and looked stunning in tan shorts, gold sandals and a yellow blouse. With prominent cheekbones set below violet eyes and framed by cinnamon hair, she might have been a fashion model instead of a public servant. Over the course of ten years, her relationship with Pitt had gone from intimate to platonic and back again several times. Once, they had seriously considered getting married, but both were married to their jobs and found it hard to live together on common ground.

Kelly came over, and the two women immediately sized each other up. Pitt introduced them, and, being a male, did not see the instant underlying conflict of territory between them.

"Kelly Egan, may I present Congresswoman Loren Smith."

"An honor to meet you, Congresswoman," said Kelly, with a tight little smile.

"Please call me Loren," she replied sweetly. "The honor is mine. I knew your father. Please accept my condolences. He was a brilliant man."

Kelly's face brightened. "You knew Dad?"

"He appeared before my committee investigating price-fixing among the oil companies. We also met several times in private and discussed matters of national security."

"I knew Dad had gone to Washington occasionally, but he never talked about meeting with members of Congress. I always thought his trips had something to do with the Commerce and Transportation Departments."

Giordino stepped from the plane at that moment and hugged Loren; they exchanged kisses on their cheeks. "Still gorgeous, I see," he said, gazing from his five feet four inches up at her height of five feet eight.

"How's my favorite Roman?"

"Still fighting the barbarians. And you?"

"Still battling the Philistines in the nation's capital."

"We should change places sometime."

Loren laughed. "I do believe I'd be getting the better of the bargain."

She gave Pitt another hard kiss. "Just when I think you've gone to the great beyond, you turn up again."

"What car did you bring?" asked Pitt, knowing she always showed up in one of his collector cars.

She nodded toward an elegant dark green 1938 Packard with long sweeping fenders and two covered spare tires set deep into wells. The beautiful lines of the custom body design by Earle C. Anthony, a noted Packard dealer for five decades, symbolized the very essence of a classic car. This particular car was a model 1607 formal, all-weather town car with a wheelbase slightly over 139 inches and a magnificently quiet V-12 engine with 473 cubic inches that Pitt had tweaked to put out 200 horsepower.

There is an erotic love between a woman and a spectacular automobile. Kelly ran her fingers lightly over the chrome cormorant mascot on the radiator, her eyes glinting with reverence at touching a masterwork of engineering art. She knew her father would have appreciated such a wonderful car. "To simply say it's beautiful," she said, "doesn't do it justice."

"Would you like to drive it?" asked Loren, giving Pitt an imperious look. "I'm sure Dirk wouldn't mind."

Pitt could see he had little choice in the matter and resigned himself to helping Giordino throw their luggage in the trunk and climbing in the backseat with Loren. Giordino sat in the open front seat next to Kelly, who was in seventh heaven behind the big steering wheel.

The divider window between the front seat and the rear passenger compartment was rolled up. Loren looked at Pitt provocatively. "Is she staying with you?"

"What an evil mind you have," Pitt answered with a laugh. "Actually, I was hoping she could stay with you at your town house."

"This isn't the old Dirk Pitt I once knew."

"Sorry to disappoint you, but her life is in danger and she's safer at your place. The Cerberus Corporation is run by maniacs who won't hesitate to kill her in order to lay their hands on her father's formula for a super oil. I assume they've traced me to my hangar, which is why I think it wise that she not stay too close to me."

Loren took his hand in hers. "What would the women of the world do without you?"

"Do you mind baby-sitting Kelly for me?"

Loren smiled. "I could use some feminine company for a change." Then the smile faded. "Seriously, I had no idea you were mixed up with Cerberus."

"The investigation has been kept quiet by the FBI and CIA."

"I'll say it's been kept quiet. Nothing has hit the news media. What do you know that I don't?"

"NUMA proved conclusively that the fire and sinking of the *Emerald Dolphin* and the explosion that put the *Golden Marlin* on the bottom were deliberate. We're certain that Cerberus and their covert Viper operation are behind the disasters."

She looked at Pitt steadily. "You're certain of this?"

"Al and I have been involved up to our ears since the beginning."

She sat back in the luxurious leather seat and stared out the window for a few moments. Then she turned back. "I happen to head up the committee that's looking into unfair practices by the Cerberus Corporation. We believe they are trying to build a monopoly by purchasing most of the oil and gas-producing wells in North America."

"For what purpose?" asked Pitt. "Nearly ninety percent of our oil comes from foreign producers. It's no secret that American producers can't compete on the cost of a barrel of oil."

"True," acknowledged Loren. "We cannot afford to produce the oil we need internally. With foreign producers playing a dangerous game by dropping production to drive up prices, every country in the world could find itself faced with severe shortages. What makes the situation even worse is that U.S. oil stockpiles and inventories have virtually dried up. Domestic producers are only too happy to sell their leases and fields to Cerberus and stick to refining the crude oil that is shipped from overseas. There's a long supply chain from the ground to storage to supertankers to storage again and finally to the refineries. Once this supply line is drained because of decreased production, it will take three to five months to bring it up to full flow again."

"You're talking about an economic disaster of epic proportions."

Loren's lips tightened. "Fuel prices will soar out of sight. Airlines will have to raise fares through the roof. Prices at the gas pump will skyrocket. Inflation will quadruple. We could be talking about an oil-price swing as high as eighty dollars a barrel."

"I can't conceive of five dollars a gallon or more for gas," said Pitt.

"We're staring it in the face."

"Wouldn't that hurt the foreign producers as well?" asked Pitt.

"Not with them cutting costly production while profits nearly triple. OPEC, for one, is angry over the way the West has manipulated them through the years. They're going to play hardball in the future and turn their backs on pleas for increased production at lower prices. Ignore our threats, too."

Pitt gazed out the window at the small boats sailing on the Potomac River. "Which brings us back to Cerberus. What's their angle in all this? If they're playing for a domestic monopoly on crude oil, why not take over and control the refineries, too?"

Loren made a mystified gesture with her hands. "It's entirely possible they've been in secret negotiations with the refinery owners to buy them out. If I were in their position, I'd cover every base."

"They must have a motive, and a big one, or they wouldn't go around leaving a trail of dead bodies."

Following Giordino's directions, Kelly turned through the gate on the end corner of Ronald Reagan International Airport and drove the old Packard down the dirt road that stopped at Pitt's old aircraft hangar. Pitt rolled down the divider window and spoke to Giordino.

"Why don't you drop the ladies off at Loren's town house and go on to your place to clean up? Then pick us all up around seven o'clock. I'll make reservations for dinner."

"Sounds wonderful," said Kelly. She turned in her seat and smiled at Loren. "I hope I'm not causing you any trouble."

"Not at all," Loren said graciously. "I have a spare guest bedroom, and you're welcome to it."

Then Kelly gazed at Pitt, her eyes aglow. "I just love driving this car."

"Just don't become too attached," he said, grinning at her. "I want it back."

As the Packard town car moved silently down the road, Pitt punched the security code on his remote, entered the hangar, dropped off his luggage and checked his Doxa watch. The hands indicated two-thirty. He reached in the open window of a NUMA Jeep SUV and made a call on its cell phone.

A deep, musical voice with a distinguished cadence answered, "I'm here."

"St. Julien."

"Dirk!" roared St. Julien Perlmutter, raconteur, gourmand and renowned maritime historian. "I was hoping I'd hear from you. Good to hear your voice. I received a report that you were on the *Golden Marlin*."

"I was."

"Congratulations on a narrow escape."

"St. Julien, I wonder if you have time for a little research job?"

"I always have time for my favorite godson."

"May I come over?"

"Yes, indeed. I want to try out a new

sixty-year-old port that I ordered from Portugal. I hope you'll join me."

"I'll be there in fifteen minutes."

37

Pitt drove down a tree-lined street in Georgetown filled with fashionable old houses built at the turn of the twentieth century, and turned into a driveway. The driveway ran past a huge brick home with ivy-covered walls and ended at a spacious carriage house in front of a roofed-over courtyard in the rear. What had once housed the manor's horse-drawn buggies and, later, automobiles had been expanded into a large home with a two-story basement that housed the largest library on the sea ever amassed by one individual.

Pitt parked the Jeep, walked to the door and rapped the big bronze knocker that was cast in the shape of a sailing ship. The door was swept open almost before the knocker struck its bolt. A huge man who weighed 400 pounds, wearing burgundy paisley silk pajamas under a matching robe, filled the doorway. He was not what you'd call soft or flabby fat. His girth was solid and he moved with an unexpected grace. His flowing hair was gray, as was his long beard beneath a rosy red tulip nose and deep sky blue eyes.

"Dirk!" he cried out. He crushed Pitt in a tight hug and stepped back. "Come in, come in. It seems I don't see enough of you anymore."

"I have to admit I do miss your fantastic cooking."

Pitt followed St. Julien Perlmutter through rooms and hallways stacked floor to high ceilings with books on ships and the sea. It was an immense library eagerly sought by universities and museums, but Perlmutter meant to keep every volume until the day he died. And only then would his last will and testament reveal the recipient of his collection. He led Pitt into a spacious kitchen with enough jars, cooking utensils and dinnerware to fill ten restaurants. He motioned Pitt to a chair beside a round hatch table with a compass binnacle standing in the center of it.

"Sit down while I uncork my rare port. I've been saving it for a special occasion."

"My presence hardly ranks as a special occasion," Pitt said, smiling.

"Any occasion is special when I don't have to drink alone," Perlmutter chortled. He was a good-natured man who laughed easily and was rarely seen without a happy grin. He removed the cork and poured the deep red liquid into port glasses. He handed one to Pitt. "What do you think?"

Pitt savored the port and swished it gently around his tongue before swallowing and voicing his approval. "Nectar fit for the gods."

"One of life's finer joys." Perlmutter sipped his glass dry and poured another. "You said you had a research project for me."

"Have you heard of Dr. Elmore Egan?"

Perlmutter stared at Pitt intently for a moment. "I most certainly have. The man was a genius. His efficient and cost-practical magnetohydrodynamic engines are a marvel of the technical age. A pity he had to be one of the many victims of the *Emerald Dolphin* on the eve of his triumph. Why do you ask?"

Pitt relaxed in the chair, enjoyed a second glass of port and related the story as he knew it, beginning with the fire on board the *Emerald Dolphin* and ending with the fight in Egan's home above the Hudson River.

"So where do I fit in?" asked Perlmutter.

"Dr. Egan was a devotee of Jules Verne, especially his book *Twenty Thousand Leagues under the Sea.* I thought that if anybody knew about Captain Nemo's submarine, the *Nautilus,* it had to be you."

Perlmutter leaned back and stared at the ornate ceiling above his kitchen. "Because it's a work of fiction, I have not put it on the list of my research projects. It's been a few years since I reread the story. Verne was either way ahead of his time or he could see into the future, because the *Nautilus* was extremely technically advanced for 1866."

"Could someone or some country have built a submarine that might have been half as efficient as the *Nautilus*?" asked Pitt.

"The only one that I recall that was proven practical before the eighteen-nineties was the Confederate submarine *H. L. Hunley*."

"I remember," said Pitt. "She sank a Union sloop-of-war called the *Housatonic* outside of Charleston, South Carolina, in 1864, and became the first submarine in history to sink a warship."

Perlmutter nodded. "Yes, the feat didn't happen again until fifty years later, in August of 1914, when the U-21 sank the HMS *Pathfinder* in the North Sea. The *Hunley* sat on the bottom buried in silt for a hundred and thirty-six years before she was discovered, raised and placed in a conservation laboratory tank to preserve her for public display. When she was inspected at first hand and the silt and remains of her crew removed from inside, she was found to be far more modern in concept than was supposed. She was quite streamlined, and she had a rudimentary snorkel system with bellows to pump air, ballast tanks with pumps, diving planes and flush rivets to reduce water drag. That last thing, by the way, was a concept that nobody thought had been used before Howard Hughes flushed the rivets on an aircraft he designed in the mid-nineteen-thirties. The *Hunley* even experimented with electromagnetic engines, but that technology was not ready, so eight men sat inside the submarine and turned a crank that spun the propeller for propulsion. After that, submarine science lagged until John Holland and Simon Lake began experimenting with and building submarines that were accepted by several countries, including us and the Germans. Those early efforts would have looked crude beside Captain Nemo's *Nautilus*."

Perlmutter ran out of steam and was about to reach for the port bottle again when a look of revelation swept over his face. "I just thought of something," he said, raising his great bulk out of his chair with ease. He disappeared down the hall for several minutes before reappearing with a book in one hand. "A copy of the board of inquiry minutes concerning the sinking of the U.S. Navy frigate *Kearsarge*."

"The ship that sank the famous Confederate raider *Alabama*?"

"The same," Perlmutter answered Pitt.

"I'd forgotten the strange circumstances behind her grounding on Roncador Reef off Venezuela in 1894."

"Strange?" asked Pitt.

"Yes, according to her commander, Captain Leigh Hunt, he was attacked by a man-made underwater vessel that resembled a whale. The vessel was chased, then sank into the water before surfacing again and ramming the *Kearsarge*, putting a large hole in her hull. She barely made it to Roncador Reef before she grounded. The crew then made camp on the reef until they were rescued."

"Sounds like the good captain was heavily into the rum locker," Pitt said, jokingly.

"No, he was dead serious," replied Perlmutter, "and what's important is that his entire crew backed him up. Not one of them who witnessed the spectacle varied his story. Their testimony described a large steel monster that was impenetrable to a series of cannon shots the *Kearsarge* poured into it — they simply bounced off. They also mentioned some sort of pyramid-shaped tower on its back that appeared to have viewing ports. Captain Hunt swore that he saw a face staring back at him through one of the ports, a man with a beard."

"Did they comment on the monster's size?"

"The crew agreed that it was cigar shaped, cylindrical with conical ends. As would be expected, they estimated the size anywhere from one to three hundred feet, with a beam of twenty to forty feet."

"Probably somewhere in between," Pitt said thoughtfully. "Somewhere slightly more than two hundred feet in length with a twenty-five-foot beam. Not exactly an underwater craft to be taken lightly in 1894."

"Come to think of it, the *Kearsarge* was not the only vessel reported sunk by an undersea monster."

"The whaling ship *Essex*, out of Nantucket, was rammed and sunk by a whale," offered Pitt.

"That," said Perlmutter sternly, "was a real whale. I'm talking about another U.S. Navy ship, the *Abraham Lincoln*, which reported an encounter with an undersea craft that rammed and shattered her rudder."

"When did that occur?"

"1866."

"Twenty-eight years earlier."

Perlmutter contemplated his bottle of port, which was now two-thirds empty. "Over that time, many ships disappeared under mysterious circumstances. Most of them were British warships."

Pitt set his glass on the table but refused another when offered. "I can't believe a supernatural vessel decades ahead of its time was built by private individuals."

"The *Hunley* was built by private individuals who funded the project," lectured Perlmutter. "Actually, she was the third boat built by Horace Hunley and his engineers. Each more advanced than the previous."

"It seems a stretch to think that the mysterious monster wasn't designed and constructed by an industrial nation," said Pitt, still skeptical.

"Who's to say?" said Perlmutter, with an indifferent shrug. "Perhaps Jules Verne heard of such a vessel and created Captain Nemo and his *Nautilus* around it."

"It's odd that such a vessel, if it truly existed, could cruise the world for almost thirty years without its being seen more often, or one of its crew deserting ashore and telling the story. And if it sailed around ramming and sinking ships, how come there were not more survivors to report the incidents?"

"I can't say," said Perlmutter slowly. "I only know what I find in recorded sea history. Which isn't to say there are not more reports, untapped by researchers, in archives scattered around the world."

"What about Verne?" Pitt inquired. "There must be a museum, a home or relatives that collected all his papers, research records and letters."

"There are. Verne scholars exist everywhere. But Dr. Paul Hereoux, president of the Society of Jules Verne in Amiens, France, which was Verne's home from 1872 until he died in 1905, is considered the most knowledgeable man on the author's life."

"Can we contact him?"

"Better yet," said Perlmutter, "in a few days, I plan to travel to Paris to dig through an archive for information on John Paul Jones's ship, the *Bonhomme Richard*. I'll run up to Amiens and talk with Dr. Hereoux."

"I couldn't ask for more," said Pitt, rising from his chair. "I have to run along and clean up. I'm having dinner with Al, Loren and Dr. Egan's daughter, Kelly."

"Tell them all I wish them a good life."

Before Pitt stepped through the front door, Perlmutter was opening another bottle of old port.

38

After he returned to his apartment above the hangar floor, Pitt made a call to Admiral Sandecker. Then he took a shower, shaved and changed into casual slacks and a knit shirt. At the sound of the Packard's horn, he slipped on a light fabric sport coat and exited the hangar. He slid into the leather seat on the passenger's side and nodded a greeting at Giordino, who was wearing a similar outfit, except that his coat was slung over the seat due to the warm evening temperature and ninety-five percent Washington humidity.

"All set?" Giordino asked.

Pitt nodded. "The admiral has arranged a little party, should we have a problem."

"You armed?"

Pitt pulled aside his jacket to reveal his old Colt in a shoulder holster. "And you?"

Giordino twisted in the seat to expose a Ruger double-action P94, 40-caliber automatic slung under one arm. "Let's hope we're being overcautious."

Giordino said no more and depressed the clutch, shifted the long curved stick with its onyx knob into first gear and slowly released the clutch as he stepped on the accelerator pedal. The big Packard town car rolled smoothly onto the road toward the airport gate.

A few minutes later, Giordino eased the car to a stop in front of Loren's town house in Alexandria. Pitt stepped up to the front door and rang the chimes. Two minutes later, the women arrived at the entrance. Loren, stunning in a cotton mock turtleneck with side slits and a straight-falling skirt that stopped just above the ankles, looked cool and radiant. Kelly wore an embroidered jacket dress of soft rayon georgette with ruffle trim that gave her a feminine edge.

After they were all settled in the Packard, Kelly in the front with Giordino again, he turned to Pitt and asked, "Where to?"

"Take Telegraph Road to the little town of Rose Hill. There is a restaurant there called the Knox Inn. They serve country-style, home-cooked dishes that send your taste buds to gourmet heaven."

"After that buildup," said Loren, "it had better live up to its laurels."

"Country style sounds good to me," Kelly said happily. "I'm famished."

They chatted on the ride to the inn, mostly small talk. Nothing was mentioned of their past experiences, nor was Cerberus brought up. The women talked mostly of places they'd visited during their travels, while Pitt and Giordino sat in quiet contemplation as they carefully watched the passing cars and the road ahead, ready for any unforeseen complications.

The summer sun set late in the evening, and passengers in other cars stared at the old Packard cruising down the highway like a dignified dowager on her way to a plantation ball. She wasn't nearly as fast as modern automobiles, but Pitt knew that it would take nothing less than a large truck to force the three-ton car off the road. She was also built like a tank. Her huge chassis and body offered her passengers solid protection in case of a collision.

Giordino turned into the parking lot of the inn, and the women left the car under the watchful eye of the men. Pitt and Giordino gazed around the parking lot surrounding the inn, but saw no sign of suspicious activity. They stepped into the inn that had been a stagecoach stop as far back as 1772, and were immediately shown by the mâitre d' to a nice table in the courtyard beneath a large oak tree.

"For what we're about to order," said Pitt, "I recommend we skip cocktails or wine and order a premium ale they brew on the premises."

Pitt and Giordino finally began to relax and the time went swiftly, as Giordino ran through his repertoire of crazy jokes that soon had the women clutching their sides in laughter. Pitt merely grinned politely, having heard them all at least fifty times. He scanned the walls of the courtyard and examined the other diners like a TV security camera swinging from side to side, but saw nothing that aroused his interest.

They ordered an assortment of barbecued pork and chicken, grits with shrimp and crab, a southern coleslaw salad and corn on the cob. It was only after they'd finished dinner and were having key lime pie for dessert that Pitt tensed. A man with a tanned face and reddish-brown hair, flanked by two deadpan characters who might as well have worn signs that proclaimed them as *armed killers*, were approaching their table. The intruder was dressed in an expensive tailor-cut suit and his shoes were solidly made British, not light-crafted Italian. As he walked across the courtyard between the tables, his blue-white eyes locked on Pitt. He walked gracefully, but with an arrogance that suggested that he owned half the world.

An alarm went off in Pitt's brain. He tapped Giordino's leg with his foot and made a gesture that the stocky Italian immediately recognized.

The man came directly to their table and stopped. He looked from face to face as if filing them in his mind for future referral. His eyes lingered on Pitt. "We have never met, Mr. Pitt, but my name is Curtis Merlin Zale."

No one at the table recognized Zale, but they were all well familiar with the name. Their reactions at seeing the legendary monster in the flesh varied. Kelly sucked in her breath, and her eyes widened. Loren explored him with amused curiosity, while Giordino's interest was focused on the two bodyguards. Pitt gazed at Zale with studied indifference despite a cold feeling in his guts. If anything, he was sickened at the sight of the man who seemingly enjoyed barbaric cruelty. He made no effort to rise to his feet.

Zale gave a short, aristocratic bow as he addressed the ladies. "Miss Egan, Congresswoman Smith, it is a pleasure to finally meet you." Then he turned to Pitt and Giordino. "Gentlemen, you are uncommonly stubborn. Your meddling has caused my company a great deal of frustration."

"Your reputation as a greed-driven sociopath precedes you," said Pitt acidly.

The two bodyguards took a step forward, but Zale gestured them back. "I had hoped we might have a congenial conversation of benefit to us all," he said, without a sign of malice.

This guy is smooth, Pitt thought to himself, smooth and slippery as a snake-oil con man. "I fail to see what we have in common. You murder men, women and children. Al and I are just your common, law-abiding, taxpaying citizens who became swept up in your crackpot scheme to create a domestic oil monopoly."

"It will never happen," said Loren.

If Zale was dismayed that Pitt and Loren were aware of his grand design, he didn't show it. "You realize, of course, that my resources far exceed yours. That should be apparent even to you by now."

"You're delusional if you think you're bigger than the U.S. government," argued Loren. "Congress will stop you before any of your plans get off the ground. First thing in the morning, I'm calling for a full congressional investigation into your involvement with the *Emerald Dolphin* and *Golden Marlin* disasters."

Zale gave her a patronizing smile. "Are you sure that's wise? No politician is immune from scandal . . . or accidents."

Loren leaped to her feet so suddenly she knocked her chair over backwards. "Are you threatening me?" she hissed.

Zale did not step back or alter his smile.

"Why, no, Congresswoman Smith, simply pointing out the possibilities. If you are set on destroying Cerberus, then you should be prepared to suffer the consequences."

Loren became outraged. She could not believe that an elected government official was being menaced with false dishonor and possible death. She slowly sat down, after Pitt set her chair upright, and stared at Zale, hard. Pitt appeared relaxed and said nothing, almost as if enjoying the fight.

"You're mad!" Loren spat at Zale.

"Actually, I'm quite sane. I know exactly where I stand at all times. Believe me, Congresswoman, do not think you can depend on your fellow legislators for support. I have more friends in the Capitol than you."

"No doubt bribed and blackmailed into submission," injected Pitt.

Loren's eyes blazed. "Yes, and when it's revealed whom you paid off and how much, you and your cohorts will be indicted on more criminal charges than John Gotti."

Zale gave an imperious nod of his head. "I do not think so."

"I couldn't agree with Mr. Zale more," said Pitt casually. "He will never stand trial."

"You have more intelligence than I gave you credit for," said Zale.

"No," Pitt continued, with the barest trace of a sardonic smile. "You will never be convicted of your crimes because you will most certainly die first. No man deserves to die more than you, Zale, along with every murdering scum in your Viper gang."

There was a coldness in Pitt's opaline green eyes that caused a hairline crack in Zale's composure. "As to that I'd take care, Mr. Pitt. You seem too well-informed yourself ever to become a senior citizen." The voice had the frigid edge of an iceberg.

"You may think you're immune to legal prosecution, but you're wide open to those who work outside the law. A group every bit as deadly as your Vipers has been assembled to put you out of business, Zale. Now it's your turn to look over your shoulder."

Zale had not expected that. He wondered if Pitt and Giordino could be more than ocean engineers with NUMA. His first thought was that Pitt was bluffing. If so, his facial expression showed no fear, but rather cold wrath. He decided to fight fire with fire.

"Now that I know where I stand, I shall leave you to your dessert. But my friends here will remain."

"What does he mean?" asked Kelly fearfully.

"He means that as soon as he is on his way down the highway, safe in his limousine, his flunkies intend to shoot us."

"Here, in front of all these people?" queried Giordino. "And without masks? Your flair for drama is pretty tawdry."

Caution was edging around Zale's blue-white eyes. Pitt's own eyes were inscrutable. Giordino sat demurely with his hands in his lap, called over the waiter and ordered a Rémy Martin. Only the women appeared tense and nervous.

Zale had been thrown off keel. He was a man who never failed to command a situation, but these men were not reacting in the way he'd expected. These men were not afraid of death. His normally decisive mind was at a dead end, and it was not an experience he relished.

"Now that we've seen the face of the enemy," Pitt said, in a voice as eerie as a tomb, "I suggest you leave the inn while you can still walk and don't even think of harming Miss Egan, or anyone else at this table."

It was no blustery threat, merely a simple matter of fact.

Zale controlled his rising anger superbly. "Although I resent your interference, I respect you and Mr. Giordino as worthy adversaries. But now I can see that you are fools, far greater fools than I could have ever imagined."

"What's that supposed to mean?" Giordino muttered nastily, as he gazed at Zale over his brandy snifter.

There was a malignant look in Zale's eyes, like those of a reptile. He glanced around at the diners at the other tables, but none seemed interested in the conversation in the corner of the courtyard between the three standing men and the four people seated. Zale nodded at his two bodyguards and turned to leave.

"Good-bye, ladies and gentlemen. A pity your futures are so short."

"Before you run off," said Pitt, "it might be wise to take your pals with you or they'll follow in an ambulance."

Zale turned back and stared at Pitt, as his men stepped forward and reached inside their suit coats. As if rehearsed, Pitt and Giordino lifted their weapons from beneath the table where they had been resting in their laps under napkins.

"Good-bye, Mr. Zale," Giordino murmured, with a tight smile. "Next time . . ." And his voice trailed off.

The assassins glanced at each other uneasily. This was not the elementary kill they'd planned. It didn't take Mensa intelligence to know that they would be dead men before they could draw their own weapons.

"I apologize for calling you fools," said Zale, spreading his hands harmlessly. "It seems you came to dinner fully equipped."

"Al and I were Eagle Scouts," said Pitt. "We like to be prepared." He nonchalantly turned his back on Zale and dipped his fork into his key lime pie. "I hope that when we meet again you're strapped to a table receiving a lethal injection."

"You have been warned," said Zale, his facial expression under control but the skin flushed with rage. Then he turned and strode from the courtyard through the inside restaurant and into the parking lot, where he entered a black Mercedes limousine. His two hired guns walked past several cars before entering a Lincoln Navigator, where they sat and waited.

Loren reached over and touched Pitt's hand. "How can you be so calm? He made my skin crawl."

"That man is pure evil," whispered Kelly, fear in her eyes.

"Zale showed his hand when he didn't have to," said Pitt. "I can't help but wonder why."

Loren stared toward the courtyard entrance as if expecting to see Zale's men return. "Yes, why would a man in his corporate position stoop to meeting the peasant rabble-rousers?"

"Curiosity," suggested Giordino. "He had to see with his own eyes the faces of the people who were fouling up his plans."

"This key lime pie is excellent," Pitt proclaimed.

"I'm not hungry," murmured Kelly.

"Can't let a good dish go to waste," said Giordino, finishing Kelly's dessert.

After coffee and espresso, Pitt paid the check. Then Giordino stood on a chair and peered into the parking lot over the wall of the inn's courtyard, keeping the top of his head hidden in a clump of ivy. "Hekyll and Jekyll are sitting in a big SUV under a tree."

"We should call the police," said Loren.

Pitt grinned. "Plans have already been made." He pulled a cell phone from his coat pocket, punched a number, spoke no more than four words and turned it off. He smiled at Loren and Kelly. "You girls wait in the entrance while Al gets the car."

Loren snatched the keys of the Packard from Pitt's fingers. "Al might find himself in a touchy situation. Better I get the car. They won't shoot a helpless female."

"I wouldn't count on it, if I were you." Pitt was about to refuse, but knew deep down that she was right. Zale's men were killers, but they weren't village idiots. They wouldn't shoot a lone woman; they wanted all four in their sights. He nodded. "Okay, but keep low between the rows of cars. Our friends are on the opposite end of the lot from the Packard. If they start up their car and move before you turn the ignition key, Al and I will come running."

Loren and Pitt had often run together. She was fast. When they sprinted, he beat her by no more than two feet after 100 yards. She ducked and took off like a wraith in the night, reaching the Packard in less than a minute. No stranger to the car's controls, she had the key in the ignition in almost the same motion as she pushed the starter button. The big V-12 fired instantly. She shifted and hit the accelerator a bit hard, spinning the big tires in the gravel. Sliding to a stop in front of the restaurant, she glided over to the passenger side of the bench seat as Pitt, Giordino and Kelly piled inside.

Pitt floored the pedal and the big car surged quietly up the road, accelerating smoothly as Pitt revved the V-12 and shifted gears. She was no tire burner and would never have smoked a drag strip. She was built for elegance and silence and not for racing. It took Pitt nearly half a mile to push her up to eighty miles an hour.

The road was straight, and he took ample time for a long look in the rearview mirror at the big Navigator swinging out of the inn's parking lot, its black paint reflected under a streetlight. That was about all he could see as darkness closed over the country road. The Navigator was coming up fast with its headlights off.

"They're coming after us," he said, in the monotone of a bus driver telling his passengers to move back from the door.

The road was nearly deserted with only two cars passing in the opposite direction. The dense thicket and trees just off the shoulder looked black and uninviting. Nobody but a terror-crazed fool would stop and attempt to hide in there. Once or twice, he glanced at Loren. Her eyes were gleaming from the dashboard lights, and her lips were pulled back in a faint trace of a sensual smile. She was clearly enjoying the excitement and danger of the chase.

The Navigator was gaining rapidly on the old Packard. Five miles from the restaurant, the driver had crept up to within a hundred yards. The Navigator was nearly invisible, but showed up in the headlights of cars coming from the opposite direction who blinked to warn the driver he was driving with no lights.

"Everybody down on the floor," said Pitt. "They'll be coming alongside any minute."

The ladies did as they were told. Giordino only crouched and aimed his Ruger automatic out the rear window at the approaching Navigator. A curve was coming up, and Pitt pushed the old car for every bit of horsepower her stout old V-12 engine could give. The Navigator was coming up on the outside, the driver steering recklessly into the lane of oncoming traffic. Another thirty seconds and Pitt swung the Packard around the turn, her big tires protesting as they skidded sideways across the pavement.

The instant Pitt had the car on an even track heading up a straight section of the road, he peered into the mirror in time to see two big Chevy Avalanches charge out of the woods like ghosts directly in front of the speeding Navigator. The appearance of the Avalanches, with machine guns mounted and manned in their cargo box, was as totally unexpected as it was abrupt.

The driver of the Navigator was caught completely off guard and whipped the wheel to one side, sending the big SUV into an uncontrollable skid across the road and onto the grassy shoulder, where it lost traction and rolled over three times, disappearing into the thick underbrush in a cloud of dust and a spray of leaves and branches. Armed men in combat camouflage night gear burst from the Avalanches and quickly surrounded the upside-down Navigator.

Pitt eased off on the accelerator, slowing the Packard down to fifty miles an hour. "The chase is over," he said. "Everybody can relax and breathe normally again."

"What happened?" asked Loren, staring out the rear window at the headlights angled across the road and the settling cloud of dust.

"Admiral Sandecker called a few friends and arranged a little entertainment for Zale's hired guns."

"Not a moment too soon," said Giordino.

"We had to make it to a place where two country roads crossed so our rescuers could let us through before moving forward and blocking off our pursuers."

"I have to admit you had me scared for a minute," said Loren, sliding across the seat and clutching Pitt's arm in a proprietary fashion.

"It was closer than I would have liked."

"You dirty dogs," she said to Pitt and Giordino. "You didn't tell us that the Marines were waiting to rescue us."

"The night has suddenly become glorious," Kelly said, inhaling the air blowing over the windshield and through the open divider window between the front and back seats. "I should have known you had the war under control."

"I'll take everyone home," said Pitt, steering toward the lights of the city. "Tomorrow, we take our act on the road again."

"Where are you going?" asked Loren.

"While you're forming your committee to investigate Cerberus's criminal destruction of the cruise ships, Al, Kelly and I are heading for Minnesota to look at old rune stones."

"What do you hope to find?"

"The answer to an enigma," Pitt said slowly. "A key that may well open more than one door."

39

Marlys Kaiser stepped from her kitchen onto the porch as she heard the thumping sound of a helicopter approaching her farm outside Monticello, Minnesota. Her house was typical of most midwestern farm structures: a wooden frame and siding, a chimney that rose from the living room through the upstairs bedroom and a peaked roof with two gables. Across a broad grassy lawn stood a red barn in pristine condition. The property had once been a working dairy farm, but now the barn was her office and the three hundred acres of wheat, corn and sunflowers were sharecropped and sold on the market. Behind the farm, the land dropped down a sloping bank to the shoreline of Bertram Lake. The blue-green waters were surrounded by trees, and the shallow water around the edges was filled with lily pads. Bertram was popular with fishermen, who drove up from Minneapolis because it was stocked regularly with bluegill, sunfish, pike and bass. It also had a large school of bullhead that began biting after sunset.

Marlys shielded her eyes from the early-morning sun in the east as a turquoise helicopter with the black letters NUMA painted on the sides dipped over the roof of the barn and hovered for a few moments above the yard, before settling its landing wheels into the grass. The whine of the twin turbines died away, and the rotor blades slowly drifted to a stop. A door opened and a ladder was dropped whose lower rung ended just above the ground.

Marlys stepped forward as a young woman with light brown hair that glimmered under the sun stepped from inside, followed by a short, stocky man with curly black hair who looked distinctly Italian. Then came a tall man with dark wavy hair and a craggy face etched with a broad smile. He walked across the yard in a direct manner that reminded her of her departed husband. As he came nearer, she found herself looking into the greenest eyes she had ever seen.

"Mrs. Kaiser?" he said softly. "My name is Dirk Pitt. I talked to you last night about flying from Washington and meeting with you."

"I didn't expect you so soon."

"We flew by jet to a NUMA research station on Lake Superior in Duluth late last night. Then we borrowed their helicopter and flew on toward Monticello."

"I see you had no problem finding the place."

"Your directions were right on the money." Pitt turned and introduced Al and Kelly.

Marlys gave Kelly a motherly hug. "Elmore Egan's daughter. This is a thrill. I'm so happy to meet you. Your father and I were great friends."

"I know," said Kelly, smiling. "He often talked about you."

She looked from one face to the other. "Have you had breakfast?"

"We haven't eaten since leaving Washington," Pitt answered truthfully.

"I'll have eggs, bacon and pancakes ready in twenty minutes," Marlys said warmly. "Why don't you folks take a stroll and check out the fields and lake?"

"Do you work the farm alone?" asked Kelly.

"Oh, my dear, no. I sharecrop with a neighbor. He pays me a percentage after the crops are sold at current market prices, which is all too low nowadays."

"Judging from the gate to the pasture across the road, the access door into the lower level of the barn and the hayloft above, you used to run a dairy herd."

"You're very observant, Mr. Pitt. My husband was a dairy farmer most of his life. You must have had a little experience yourself."

"I spent a summer on my uncle's farm in Iowa. I got so I could squeeze my fingers in sequence to squirt the milk in a pail, but I never got the hang of actually pulling it out."

Marlys laughed. "I'll give a shout when the coffee's on."

Pitt, Giordino and Kelly walked along the fields and then down to a boat dock, where they borrowed one of the boats Marlys rented to fishermen, and with Pitt manning the oars they rowed out on the lake. They were just returning when Marlys shouted from the porch.

As they gathered around the table in the quaint country kitchen, Kelly said, "This is very kind of you, Mrs. Kaiser."

"Marlys. Please think of me as an old family friend."

They engaged in small talk during the meal, discussing everything from the weather to lake fishing to the tough economy facing farmers across the country. Only after the dishes were cleared, with Giordino's able assistance in loading the dishwasher, did the talk turn to rune stones.

"Father never explained his interest in

rune stone inscriptions," said Kelly. "Mother and I went along on his excursions to find them, but we were more interested in the fun of camping and hiking than searching for old rocks with writing on them."

"Dr. Egan's library was filled with books on Vikings but didn't have any of his notes and reports," added Pitt.

"Norsemen, Mr. Pitt," Marlys corrected him. "*Viking* is a term for sea-roving raiders, who were fearless and fierce in battle. Centuries later, they probably would have been called pirates or buccaneers. The Viking age was launched when they raided the Lindisfarne monastery in England in 793. They came out of the north like ghosts, raping and pillaging Scotland and England until William the Conqueror, a Norman whose ancestors were Norse, won the battle of Hastings and became King of England. From 800 on, Viking fleets roamed throughout Europe and the Mediterranean. Their reign was short, and their power faded by the thirteenth century. Their final episode was written when the last of them left Greenland in 1450."

"Any idea why so many Norse rune stones have been found around the Midwest?" inquired Giordino.

"Norse sagas, especially those from Iceland, tell of the seafaring people and inhabitants of Iceland and Greenland who tried to colonize the northeast coast of the United States between 1000 and 1015 A.D. We must assume they launched expeditions of exploration into our heartland."

"But the only hard evidence that they came to North America is their settlement at L'Anse aux Meadows in Newfoundland," said Pitt.

"If they sailed and set up colonies in France, Russia, England, Ireland and the far reaches of the Mediterranean," Marlys argued, "it stands to reason they could easily have entered middle America down the St. Lawrence River or around Florida, into the Gulf and up the Mississippi. They could have used the inland river water systems to explore vast regions of the country."

"As indicated by the stones with runic inscriptions they left behind," offered Giordino.

"Not just by Norsemen," said Marlys. "Numerous people from the Old World visited the Americans before Leif Eriksson and Christopher Columbus. Ancient seafarers of many cultures sailed across the Atlantic and explored our shores. We've found stones with inscriptions in Egyptian hieroglyphs, Cypriot script, Nubian letters and numerals, Carthaginian Punic script, and Iberian Ogam. Well over two hundred stones inscribed with the Ogam alphabet, which was used mostly by the Celts of Scotland, Ireland and Iberia, have been found and translated. The landscape is littered with stones carved with scripts that have yet to be identified. Early peoples may have traveled on our home grounds as far back as four thousand years ago." She paused for effect. "And the alphabetic inscriptions are only the half of it."

Kelly stared in disbelief. "There's more?"

"The petroglyphs," Pitt guessed.

"The petroglyphs," Marlys echoed, with a nod of her head. "There are hundreds of recorded examples of carved images in stone of ships, animals, gods and goddesses. There are faces with beards that look identical to those from ancient Greece; heads of people that are nearly identical to those carved around the Mediterranean in classic times. Birds in flight are big favorites, as are horses and boats. There are even petroglyphs of animals that are foreign to the Americas, such as rhinos, elephants and lions. A great number of the images are astronomical, showing stars and constellations, whose positions in the stone correlate with positions in the sky thousands of years ago."

"As I told you over the phone," said Pitt, "we are investigating Kelly's father's fascination with a series of rune stones he discovered and studied fifteen years ago."

Marlys looked up at the ceiling for a moment, recalling. "Dr. Egan's studies concerned a series of thirty-five rune-stone inscriptions that told of a group of Norsemen who explored the Midwest in 1035 A.D. I recall he was obsessed with the inscriptions in the hope they would lead him to a cave. Where? I have no idea."

"Do you have any records of them?"

Marlys clapped her hands. "This is your lucky day. Come out to my office in the barn where I have them filed away."

What was once a barn built for a dairy herd had been converted into a giant office. The hayloft was gone and the high ceiling was open. Rows of library-style bookshelves took up half the space. A huge square table sat in the center of the room, with a cutaway entry to the middle where Marlys worked behind a pair of computers. The table was piled with photographs, folders, books and bound reports. There was an expansive monitor beyond the desk. Beneath it were shelves containing videotapes and discs. The old wooden plank floor was worn smooth and still showed nicks and dents from the hooves of the cows when they entered and exited during milking. Through a doorway a laboratory could be seen, the walls and floors of which looked to be coated with white dust.

One side of the spacious room was filled with artifacts, ceramic bowls shaped into pots, human heads and figures, and animals. Several were creative interpretations of almost comical humans in strange and sometimes contorted positions. At least a hundred smaller unidentifiable artifacts were preserved in a great glass case. Pitt was particularly taken by several stone masks, very similar to those he'd seen in museums in Athens, Greece. None could have been carved by American Indians depicting members of their own tribe. All the bas-reliefs were images of men with curly beards, an interesting phenomenon since the native inhabitants of North, Central and South America were lucky in never having to shave.

"These were all found in the United States?" asked Pitt.

"Discovered in every state from Colorado to Oklahoma to Georgia."

"And the artifacts?"

"Mostly tools, with a few ancient coins and weapons for good measure."

"You have an amazing collection."

"Everything you see goes to a university archive and museum when I pass on."

"Remarkable that so many ancient people came this way," said Kelly in awe.

"Our ancestors were just as curious as we are about what's over the horizon." Marlys swept her arm at chairs and a sofa as she searched the bookcases. "Make yourselves comfortable while I look for the records of the inscriptions that interested your father." After less than a minute, she found what she was looking for and pulled out two thick reports in metal binders and carried them over to the desk. One held over a hundred photographs, and the other was bulky with papers.

She laid down a photograph of a large inscribed rock, with Marlys standing next to it for perspective. "This is the Bertram Stone, found on the other side of the lake by a hunter in 1933." Then she went to a tall cabinet and removed what looked like a white plaster cast. "I usually shoot photos after highlighting the inscriptions with talcum powder or chalk. But if possible, I paint on several layers of liquid latex. After it dries, I transport it to my lab and make a mold with wet plaster. When that dries, I reproduce it on a blueprint machine and highlight the indented images or script. Letters and symbols then show up in the eroded stone that were not visible to the naked eye."

Pitt stared at the twiglike markings. "A few of the letters are the same as our current alphabet."

"The script is a combination of the old Germanic Futhark alphabet and the later

Scandinavian Futhork. The first used twenty-four runes or letters, the second, sixteen. The origin of runic script is lost in time. There is a slight similarity to ancient Greek and Latin, but scholars think the basic runic alphabet originated in the first century with Germanic cultures who linked it with the Teutonic language of the time. By the third century, it had migrated into the Nordic countries."

"How do you know the writing on the stone isn't fake?" The question came from Giordino, a worldly skeptic.

"A number of reasons," Marlys answered sweetly. "One, police forgery experts have examined several of the stones and unanimously agreed that the carved inscriptions were made by the same hand. All characteristics are identical. Two, who would travel two thousand miles around the country carving runic inscriptions about a Norse exploration expedition if it never happened? For what purpose? Also, if they were fake, they were made by someone who was a master of the language and alphabet, as attested to by modern experts on runology who found no incorrect variations in the letters. Three, the Bertram Rune Stone was first discovered, according to local historians, by a tribe of the Ojibways, who told early settlers about it in 1820. It was next recorded by French fur trappers. It seems extremely unlikely that someone else carved the stones long before the area was settled. And finally, four, although carbon-dating analysis only works with organic materials and not with stone, the only method to judge aging is to study the amount of erosion on the rock over the years. The weathering of the inscriptions and the hardness of the stone as exposed to the elements can give an approximate time of antiquity when the letters were carved. Judging from the wear and tear on the rock from wind, rain and snow, they were dated between 1000 and 1150 A.D., which seems reasonable."

"Have any artifacts been found in or around the stones?" Giordino pursued.

"Nothing that has survived the years of exposure."

"Not unusual," said Pitt. "Few if any artifacts ever turned up along Coronado's trail centuries after his trek from Mexico as far as Kansas."

"Here's the million-dollar question," Giordino asked Marlys. "What does the stone say?"

Marlys took a CD disc and inserted it in her terminal. In a moment the letters, highlighted on the mold cast from the liquid latex, were revealed in great detail on the monitor. There were four lines of almost 140 letters.

"We may never have a totally accurate

translation," she said, "but six runologists from here and Scandinavia agree that the inscription reads . . .

"Magnus Sigvatson passed this way in year 1035 and claimed the lands this side of the river for his brother, Bjarne Sigvatson, leader of our tribe. Helgan Siggtrygg murdered by Skraelings.

"*Skraelings* translates to barbarians or lazy heathen, or in the old vernacular, wretches. We must assume that Siggtrygg was killed during a clash with local native Indians, the early ancestors of the Sioux and Ojibway."

"Magnus Sigvatson." Pitt spoke the name softly, accenting each syllable. "Brother of Bjarne."

Marlys sighed thoughtfully. "There is a saga that mentions Bjarne Sigvatson along with several boatloads of colonists setting off from Greenland toward the west. Later sagas claim Sigvatson and his people were swallowed up by the sea and never seen again."

"The other thirty-four stones," said Pitt. "What do they reveal?"

"Most of them seem to be boundary markers. Magnus was quite ambitious. He claimed a quarter of what became the United States for his brother, Bjarne, and his tribe." She paused to scan another highlighted inscription mold on the monitor. "This one reads . . .

"Magnus Sigvatson came ashore here."

"Where was this stone found?" inquired Giordino.

"Bark Point, which sticks out into Siskiwit Bay."

Pitt and Giordino exchanged amused glances. "We're not familiar with the names," said Pitt.

Marlys laughed. "I'm sorry. Siskiwit Bay is on Lake Superior in Wisconsin."

"And where were the other rune stones found?" asked Kelly.

"These Norsemen were quite wordy when you consider that probably fewer than a quarter of the rune stones they carved have been located and translated. The first and last was discovered at Crown Point on the southern end of Lake Champlain." She paused and looked at Pitt with a sly grin. "That's in upstate New York."

Pitt smiled back courteously. "I know."

"From there," Maryls continued, "three stones are found at different sites in the Great Lakes, suggesting that they sailed the waterway north to the St. Lawrence River. They then came through the lakes until coming ashore at Siskiwit Bay. Once there, I believe they portaged their boats from one body of water to another until they reached the Mississippi River, where they began their journey south."

"But Bertram Lake is not on the river," stated Kelly.

"No, but we're only two miles away. My guess is the Norsemen would come ashore and conduct short treks into the countryside before continuing downstream."

"How far did they reach?" asked Giordino.

"Stone inscriptions were found on a meandering course through Iowa, Missouri, Arkansas and Kansas. The farthest stone was found by a Boy Scout troop near Sterling, Colorado. Then we estimate they trekked back to the Mississippi where they had left their boats. A stone was uncovered on the west bank of the river across from Memphis, which read,

"Boats stay here guarded by Olafson and Tyggvason."

She continued, "From that point they must have sailed up the Ohio River and into the Allegheny River, where they made their way to Lake Erie before retracing their path back the way they had come to Lake Champlain."

Kelly looked puzzled. "I'm unclear as to what you mean by the first and last stone."

"As close as we can tell, the Lake Champlain rune stone was the first inscribed at the beginning of the expedition. There must be others, but none have been found. When they returned nearly a year later, they made a second inscription on the stone below the first."

"May we see them?" Pitt asked.

Marlys typed on her keyboard, and a large stone appeared on the monitor. Judging from the man sitting on top of it, the height looked to be ten feet. The stone sat in a deep ravine.

Above ten rows of inscriptions was carved the petroglyph of a Viking ship, complete with sails, oars and shields on the sides. "This is a tough one," said Marlys. "None of the epigraphists who studied the stone have agreed one hundred percent on the message. But the translations are fairly similar in text." She then began to translate the lengthy inscription.

"After six days travel up the fjord from our families at the settlement, Magnus Sigvatson and his 100 comrades rest here and claim all the land within sight of the water for my kinsman and leader of our tribe, Bjarne Sigvatson, and our children.

The land is far larger than we knew. Larger even than our beloved homeland. We are well provisioned and our five small ships are stout and in good repair. We will not come back this way many months. May Odin protect us from the Skraelings."

She went on, "I must warn you that the translations are very vague and probably do not convey the original meaning. The second inscription carved on the return reads . . .

"Fourteen months after leaving our families, we are but a few days' sail down the fjord to the cave below the high cliffs to our homes. Of the 100, we are now 95. Bless Odin for protecting us. The land I claimed in my brother's name is larger than we have known. We have discovered paradise. Magnus Sigvatson."

"Then there is a date of 1036."

"Six days' sail down the fjord," Pitt repeated pensively. "That would suggest the Norsemen had a settlement in the United States."

"Has a site ever been discovered?" asked Giordino.

Marlys shook her head. "Archaeologists have yet to find one below Newfoundland."

"You have to wonder why it disappeared so completely."

"There are ancient Indian legends that tell of a great battle with strange wild men from the west with long chin hair and shiny heads."

Kelly looked confused. "Shiny heads?"

"Helmets," Pitt said, smiling. "They must be referring to the helmets the Vikings wore in combat."

"Strange that no archaeological evidence of a site has ever been discovered," said Kelly.

Pitt looked at her. "Your father knew where it was."

"What makes you say that?"

"Why else would he become so fanatical in his search for the rune stones? My guess is that your father was searching for the cave mentioned in the final inscription. The reason he suddenly dropped his research is because he must have found it."

"Without his files and papers," said Giordino, "we have no direction. Without a ballpark in which to launch a search, we're floundering in the dark."

Pitt turned to Marlys. "You have nothing from Dr. Egan that might give us a clue to what data he was accumulating?"

"He was not a man into correspondence or e-mail. I don't have so much as a scrap of paper with his signature. All our sharing of information was done over the phone."

"I'm not surprised," Kelly murmured resignedly.

"And rightly so," Giordino said. "Considering his problems with Cerberus."

Pitt's eyes stared into the vague distance

without seeing anything. Then they focused on Kelly. "You and Josh said you searched the farm for your father's hidden laboratory and turned up nothing."

Kelly nodded. "True. We searched every square inch of our property and those of the neighboring farms on both sides. We found nothing."

"How about the palisades facing the river?"

"One of the first places we looked. We even had rock-climbing clubs come in and check the rocky bluffs. They found no sign of caves or a path or a stairway leading across the face of the cliffs."

"If the only inscription about a cave was on the first rune stone, why run around the country beating the bushes searching for more inscriptions that revealed nothing?"

"He didn't know that when he launched his search," Pitt surmised. "He must have hoped that other stones might give him more clues. But his quest turned up dry, and the trail always came home to the first rune stone."

"What inspired him to search in the first place?" Giordino asked Kelly.

She shook her head. "I have no idea. He never told my mother and me what it was he was looking for."

"The cave in the high cliffs," Pitt said slowly.

"You think that's what he was looking for?"

"I do," Pitt came back positively.

"Do you think he found it?"

"I do," Pitt repeated.

"But there is no cave," Kelly protested.

"It's a question of looking in the right place. And if we find it, too, it will open the door to a closetful of mysteries, including your father's secret project."

"You might take a new direction in your search," said Marlys.

"What are you suggesting?" asked Pitt.

"I believe it would be helpful if you consulted with Dr. Jerry Wednesday."

"And he is . . . ?"

"A leading expert on the ancient Hudson River Valley Indian tribes. He might be able to throw some light on contact with the Norsemen."

"Where can we reach him?"

"Marymount College in Tarrytown, New York. Dr. Wednesday is a professor of cultural history."

"I know Marymount," said Kelly. "A Catholic women's college just across the river from Dad's farm."

Pitt looked at Giordino. "What do you think?"

"When searching for a historical treasure, you can never do enough research."

"That's what I always say."

"I thought I heard it somewhere."

Pitt turned and shook Marlys's hand. "Marlys, thank you. Thank you for your hospitality and for being so helpful."

"Not at all. You've given me gossip for the neighbors."

She stood and watched, hand shielding her eyes from the sun, as the NUMA helicopter rose into a cloudless sky and set a course northeast to Duluth. Her thoughts traveled back to Elmore Egan. He'd been a true eccentric, an oddball but lovable, she recalled. She fervently hoped that she had given them a direction for their search, and that Dr. Wednesday might provide the final clue to the adventure.

40

Inconspicuous-looking, dusty four-wheel-drive Jeeps, Durangos and a Chevy Suburban cruised down the private road to the Cerberus-owned lodge beside Tohono Lake. None of the SUVs were new, and none were younger than eight years. They were chosen by design to blend in with the vehicles driven by the local residents of the county. As they passed through nearby towns on their way to the lake, no one paid the least bit of attention to their passengers, who were dressed as fishermen.

They arrived ten to fifteen minutes apart and entered the lodge, carrying fishing tackle boxes, rods and reels. Oddly, none gave the slightest glance at the dock or the boats that had been tied to the mooring cleats. Once they disappeared into the lodge, they stayed inside and made no attempt at baiting a hook or casting a plug.

Their mission went far beyond the solitude and joy of fishing.

Nor did they did gather socially in the main hall with the huge moss-rock fireplace and high log ceiling. There would be no relaxing in the chairs and sofas draped with Navajo rugs amid the Western decor enhanced by Russell and Remington paintings and bronze sculptures. Rather, they assembled in a large basement room beneath the lodge, a room separated by a massive steel door from an escape tunnel that traveled more than two hundred yards into the safety of the forest. From there a path led half a mile to an open field, where helicopters could be called in at a moment's notice. Security systems with alarms watched over the road and grounds around the lodge for intruders. The setting was planned to look unobtrusive and ordinary, but every precaution had been taken against surveillance by government agents or state and local law enforcement.

Down in the lavishly furnished basement room, six men and two women sat opposite one another around a circular pine conference table. The ninth person, Curtis Merlin Zale, was seated at one end. He passed out several leather-bound folders and leaned back in his chair, waiting for the others to study the contents.

"Commit what you read to memory," he

directed. "When we leave tomorrow evening, all paperwork and notes will be destroyed."

It was vital to the interests of the Cerberus empire that the strategy planning session be held in the strictest secrecy. The men and women seated at the table were CEOs of the largest oil companies in the Northern Hemisphere and had congregated to map strategy for the coming months. To the economists, the officials at the Commerce Department and reporters of the *Wall Street Journal*, these giants of the oil industry directed only the day-to-day operations of the autonomous corporations under their independent control. Only those present knew that they were linked behind the scenes to Curtis Merlin Zale and the long arms of Cerberus. A monopoly had been created unlike any attempted in the past. The parameters were rigid.

The oil tycoons had all made billions with their clandestine alliance with Cerberus, and none were about to go to jail for criminal business dealings. Though an extensive Justice Department investigation was sure to uncover the most enormous cartel formed to corner an oil market since Rockefeller and Standard Oil, precautions were taken to halt any such investigation before it got off the ground. The only very real threat was that one of them might sell out and inform the Justice Department of the criminal actions of the cartel. But potential deserters knew well that they and members of their families would quickly disappear or die in unfortunate accidents once word of their defection was out. Once in, there was no escape.

If the risk seemed heavy, the expected returns were stratospheric. It took no stretch of the imagination for these people to know that the ultimate yield of their nefarious enterprise would ultimately go beyond billions into trillions of dollars. Beyond money, the power that went with total success could only be measured in the eventual degree of control they'd achieve over the United States government, its legislators and the executive branch.

"You all know the predictions," said Zale, as he began the meeting. "I hasten to add they are not intentionally doctored figures. Between 1975 and 2000, the world's population grew fifty percent. The demand for crude oil followed suit. By 2010, the world's total oil production will peak. That's less than seven years from now. From then until 2050, production will drop to a small fraction of what it is today."

The forty-six-year-old head of Zenna Oil, Rick Sherman, who had the appearance of a grade-school math teacher but led the nation's third-largest oil producer peered at

Zale through thick rimless glasses. "Statistics are already coming up short. A permanent oil shortage has already begun ten years ahead of the predictions. Demand has exceeded global production, which will skid steeply from now on."

"If production looks gloomy, the resulting drop in the world economy looks absolutely pitch-dark," said Jesus Morales, the CEO of the CalTex Oil Company. "The shock will be paralyzing and permanent. Prices will skyrocket, accompanied by hyperinflation and even rationing. I shudder to think what level transportation costs will hit."

"I agree." Sally Morse polished the lenses of her reading glasses and studied Zale's report. The chief of Yukon Oil, Canada's largest oil producer, she'd been the last to reluctantly join the secret cabal five years earlier, but was beginning to have second thoughts. "There will be no major finds in the future. Since 1980, despite geologists' forecasts, few new fields have been found that produce over ten million barrels. The one thousand three hundred eleven known major oil-producing fields contain ninety-four percent of the world's known oil. As these fields diminish, oil and gas prices will rise on a steep, unending curve."

"The bad news," said Zale, "is that exploration finds only one new barrel of oil for every ten barrels we consume."

"A situation that will only get worse," added Morales.

Zale nodded. "The very reason we formed our alliance. With China and India's industrial capacity requiring more and more oil, competition between them, Europe and the United States will quickly become a hard-fought battle over prices."

"All to the gain of OPEC," said Sherman. "With worldwide demand increasing rapidly, the OPEC oil producers will squeeze every cent they can get out of a barrel of oil."

"It's as though the entire situation were falling into our hands," said Zale confidently. "By pooling our resources, our fields and refineries in North America, we can dictate our own terms and prices. We can also double production by drilling where the government has not allowed us to go before. Our newly built pipeline systems will carry the oil overland without the expensive use of tankers. If our strategy works according to plan, the only oil and gas sold north of Mexico will be American and Canadian. Or, to put it in simple terms, ninety-six percent of the income will go to enhance the profit of our respective organizations."

"The OPEC nations won't roll over and play dead." Old oilman Gunnar Machowsky had started as a rigger and had busted five times with dry wells before he'd struck a huge reservoir in the middle of Nevada. He was a big man with a round stomach and white hair circling a bald head. The sole owner of Gunnar Oil, he ran a notoriously tight company that never failed to show a healthy profit. "You can bet they'll undercut us at every turn on the price of a barrel of oil."

Zale grinned. "I don't doubt it for a moment. We'd all go bankrupt trying to match their price, but the plan is to make foreign oil so unpopular with American citizens that our elected officials will have to listen to the uproar and place an embargo on foreign oil."

"How many legislators do we have in our pockets?" asked Guy Kruse, the laid-back, bespectacled, soft-spoken director of Eureka Offshore Oil Ventures.

Zale turned to Sandra Delage, the cartel's chief administrator. Her attractive, demure looks were deceiving. An ash blonde with velvet blue eyes, Delage's lightning mind and razor-sharp organizational skills were admired and respected by everyone at the table. She studied a large notebook for a moment before looking up. "As of yesterday, we can safely count on thirty-nine senators and one hundred ten representatives who will vote as you direct."

Kruse smiled. "It looks as if our sugar money went further than we hoped."

"I think it's safe to say the White House will also accommodate your counsel," Delage added.

"That leaves the environmentalist lobbies and those members of both the Senate and Congress who want to save the beavers," said Machowsky gruffly.

Zale leaned across the table and waved a pencil in his hand. "Their protests will be swept aside by the public's outcry when the oil shortage and high prices become acute and hit home. We already have enough votes to open new oil fields from Alaska to Florida over the protests of the environmentalists. The American and Canadian governments have no choice but to allow our exploration operations expanded access on federal lands for drilling in areas where geologists have found rich reserves."

"Lest we forget, the government dug its own grave after it began opening up the Strategic Petroleum Reserve. They've dipped into it five more times, until there isn't enough left to supply the country's fuel needs for more than three weeks."

A scowl spread across Machowsky's face. "The whole thing was a politically activated joke. Our refineries were already running at full capacity. It accomplished nothing but selling the gullible public into thinking their government was doing them a favor."

Sally Morse nodded. "It seems they unknowingly played right into our hands."

Sam Riley, the chairman of Pioneer Oil, a company that owns vast reserves throughout the Midwest, spoke for the first time. "We couldn't have planned it better if we'd had a channel to the future."

"Yes," said Zale, "a combination of luck and our forecasts being on the mark." He turned to Dan Goodman of Diversified Oil Resources. "What's the latest report on our shale oil operation in western Colorado?"

A former Army general who'd headed the Fuel Supply Command, Goodman was a good ten years older than anyone at the table. Overweight at 250 pounds, he still possessed a physical toughness along with a dour sense of humor. "Because of a technological breakthrough in shale, our startup operation will be launched in one week. All shale recovery systems and equipment have been tested thoroughly and are on line. I can comfortably state that we now have an enormous potential source of oil, hydrocarbon gas and a solid fuel that can exceed coal. Our estimated yield of forty gallons of oil per ton of rock appears reasonable."

"How large do you figure the deposit?" asked Kruse.

"Two trillion barrels."

Zale looked at Goodman. "Say again."

"Two trillion barrels of oil from shale, and that's a conservative estimate."

"Good lord," muttered Sherman. "That's far below the estimates on government energy reports."

"Those were doctored," Goodman said, with a sly twinkle in his eye.

Riley laughed. "If you can get your cost below fifty dollars a barrel, you'll put the rest of us out of business."

"Not yet. At the moment we figure our cost will run around sixty dollars a barrel."

Morales leaned his chair back on two legs and placed his hands on the back of his head. "Now all that is left before we can begin our operation is the final completion of the oil pipeline system."

Zale did not immediately reply. He nodded at Sandra Delage, who pressed a button on a remote control that lowered a large screen. Almost instantly, a large map of Alaska, Canada and the lower forty-eight states filled the screen. A series of black lines traveled across national and state borders from oil fields to refineries to major cities. "Ladies and gentlemen, our oil transportation system. Thirty-seven thousand miles of underground pipeline. The final line from Sam Riley's Pioneer Oil fields in Nebraska, Wyoming, Kansas and the Dakotas will be in place and ready to send oil by the end of the month."

"Circumventing the environmentalists by

laying pipe underground was a brilliant stroke," said Riley.

"The excavation pipe-laying machinery developed by Cerberus engineers enabled our construction crews working around the clock to lay ten miles of pipe every twenty-four hours."

"An ingenious concept," said Jesus Morales, "leasing the right-of-way from the railroads and laying pipe along the track."

"I must admit it saved untold billions in litigation and hassles with private and public land owners," acknowledged Zale. "It also allows us to pump oil directly into every major city in both countries without restrictions or having to worry about strict governmental regulations."

"It's a miracle we've come this far without interference from the Justice Department," said Sally Morse.

"We've covered our trail well," said Zale. "Our moles in the Justice Department ensure that any mention or questions by their agents or from the FBI are quietly misplaced or filed away for future review."

Guy Kruse looked at Zale. "I understand a congressional committee led by Congresswoman Loren Smith is launching an investigation into your affairs at Cerberus."

"Smith's probe will go nowhere," Zale asserted firmly.

"How can you be so sure?" asked Morse.

"Loren Smith is one member of Congress who definitely is not on our side."

Zale looked at her, his eyes cold. "The matter will be handled."

"Like the *Emerald Dolphin* and the *Golden Marlin*?" Machowsky murmured sarcastically.

"The end justified the means," retorted Zale. "The ultimate goal was accomplished by blaming the disasters on malfunctions by Elmore Egan's engines. All contracts by shipbuilders to install his magnetohydrodynamic engines have been canceled. And with Egan dead, it's only a matter of days before we have the formula for his super oil. Once we go into production, we will control and share in the profits of the manufacture and sales of his engines. As you can see, we're covering every side of the fuel oil market."

"Can you assure us that there will be no more interference from NUMA?" asked Sherman.

"A temporary situation. They have no jurisdiction in our commercial affairs."

"Pirating their survey vessel and crew was not wise," said Riley.

"A circumstance that unexpectedly turned against us. But that is history. No trails lead to Cerberus."

Dan Goodman raised his hand. "I, for one, applaud your successful campaign to enrage the general public against foreign oil coming into the United States. For decades, no one cared where their fuel supplies were coming from. But with the supertanker disasters your Viper group caused in Fort Lauderdale, Newport Beach, Boston and Vancouver, where millions of gallons of oil spills invaded highly populated and affluent areas of the country, public outcry to become self-sufficient in oil has soared."

"All those arranged accidents within the space of nine months made the *Exxon Valdez* spill in Alaska look like a minor melodrama," agreed Morales.

Zale shrugged his shoulders indifferently. "A tragic necessity. The longer the cleanup goes on, the stronger the demand for domestic oil."

"But haven't we sold our souls to the devil to establish our market position and monopoly?" asked Sally Morse.

"*Monopoly* is a distasteful word, my dear lady," said Zale. "I prefer to call it a *market trust.*"

Morse held her head in her hands. "When I think of all the people, the birds, animals and fish that have died for us to achieve our goal, it makes me ill."

"Now is not the time for conscience," Zale admonished her. "We are in an economic war. There may be no need for generals or admirals, tanks, submarines or nuclear bombers, but to win we have to supply the public's insatiable appetite for fuel. Soon, very soon, we will be in a position to tell every person living north of Mexico what fuel to buy, when to buy it, and how much to pay for it. We will be accountable to no one. In time, our efforts will replace a governmental state with a corporate state. We cannot weaken now, Sally."

"A world without politicians," Guy Kruse murmured thoughtfully. "It seems too good to be true."

"The country is on the verge of mass demonstrations over foreign oil," said Sherman. "We need only one more incident to push them over the edge."

A foxlike grin cut Zale's features. "I'm one jump ahead of you, Rick. Such an incident will take place three days from now."

"Another tanker spill?"

"Far worse."

"What could be worse?" Morales asked innocently.

"A spill magnified by an explosion," Zale answered.

"Off a coastline?"

Zale shook his head. "Inside one of the world's busiest harbors."

There were a few moments of silence while the conspirators grasped the awesome consequences. Then Sandra Delage looked at Zale and spoke up quietly, "May I?"

He nodded without speaking.

"On Saturday, at approximately four-thirty in the early evening, an Ultra Large Crude Carrier, the *Pacific Chimera*, with a length of one thousand six hundred eight feet and a width of two hundred thirty-two feet — making her the largest oil tanker in the world — will enter San Francisco Bay. She will make for the Point San Pedro Mooring, where she would normally tie her bow and discharge her cargo. Only, she will not stop. She will continue toward the central section of the city at full speed, driving ashore at the Ferry Building's World Trade Center. Estimates are that she will plow nearly two blocks into the city before coming to rest. Then charges will be detonated and the *Pacific Chimera* and her deadweight cargo of six hundred twenty thousand tons of oil will go up in an explosion that will devastate the entire San Francisco waterfront area."

"Oh my God," muttered Sally Morse, her face suddenly pale. "How many people will die?"

"Could be in the thousands, since it'll take place during rush hour," answered Kruse callously.

"What does it matter?" asked Zale coldly, as if he were a coroner shoving a body into a morgue refrigerator. "Far more have died in wars that accomplished nothing. Our purpose will be served and we will all benefit in the end." Then he rose from his chair. "I think that will be enough discussion for today. We'll take up where we left off tomorrow morning, deliberate on our respective dealings with our governments and finalize our plans for the coming year."

Then the most powerful oil moguls of two nations stood and followed Zale to the elevators and up to the lodge's dining room, where cocktails were waiting.

Only Sally Morse of Yukon Oil remained, visualizing the horrible suffering that was about to fall on thousands of innocent men, women and children in San Francisco. As she sat alone, she came to a decision that could very well end her life. But she set her mind and left the room determined to carry it through.

When the driver of her Jeep stopped in front of her company Lockheed Jetstar after the conference ended, the pilot was waiting at the boarding steps. "Ready for the flight to Anchorage, Ms. Morse?"

"There's been a change in plans. I have to be in Washington for another conference."

"I'll draw up a new flight plan," said the pilot. "Shouldn't take but a few minutes before we take off."

As Sally sagged into a leather executive chair behind a desk with a computer and an array of phones and a fax, she knew she had entered a maze with no way out. She had never made a decision that was life threatening. A resourceful woman, she had directed the operations of Yukon Oil after her husband died, but this — she had no experience with this. She started to pick up a phone to make a call, but realized there was a very real danger her conversation might be listened into by Zale's agents.

She asked her flight attendant for a martini to beef up her resolve, threw off her shoes and began making plans to undermine Curtis Merlin Zale and his vicious operations.

The pilot of Zale's big Executive Boeing 727 sat in the cockpit and read a magazine as he waited for his employer to appear. He looked through the windshield and idly watched the Yukon Oil jet roll down the runway and lift off into a sky scattered with thick white clouds. He was still watching as the jet banked and headed toward the south.

Odd, he thought. He would have expected the pilot to turn northwest toward Alaska. He left the cockpit and stepped back into the main cabin, stopping before a man with his legs crossed, reading the *Wall Street Journal*. "Excuse me, sir, but I thought you should know that the Yukon Oil jet took off on a heading south toward Washington instead of north for Alaska."

Omo Kanai laid the paper aside and smiled. "Thank you for being so observant. That *is* an interesting piece of news."

41

Tarrytown, nestled in New York's Westchester County, is one of the more picturesque towns in the historic Hudson Valley. Its tree-lined streets are complemented by Colonial antique shops, homey little restaurants and stores selling locally produced craft items. The residential areas host gothic mansions and secluded estates in the grand style. Its most famous landmark is Sleepy Hollow, made famous by Washington Irving's classic story "The Legend of Sleepy Hollow."

Pitt lounged and dozed in the backseat of a rental car as Giordino drove, and Kelly admired the scenery from the passenger side. Giordino steered the car around the curves of a narrow road to Marymount's twenty-five-acre campus high on a hill overlooking the Hudson River and the Tappan Zee Bridge.

Founded in 1907 by a Catholic teaching order named the Religious of the Sacred Heart of Mary, Marymount College was the first of a vast network of Marymount schools around the world. The founder, Mother Joseph Butler, made it her life's mission to create places of learning where women could receive an education that would prepare them for occupations of authority and importance throughout every nation of the globe. An independent liberal-arts college in the Catholic tradition, Marymount was one of the fastest-growing women's institutes of learning in the United States.

The college buildings were austere and mostly constructed of tan-colored brick. Giordino could not help staring at the attractive girls hustling to and from class as he turned onto the main street of the campus. He drove past Butler Hall, a large building with a dome beneath a cross, and pulled to a stop in a parking lot beside Gerard Hall, where the faculty offices were located on the first two floors.

They walked up the steps of Gerard Hall, through the doors and to an information desk. A young blond student in her early twenties looked up at Pitt as he looked down at her and smiled.

"How may I direct you?" she asked cordially.

"Anthropology Department. Dr. Jerry Wednesday's office."

"Go up the stairs to your left. Then take a right. The Anthropology Department is through the door at the end of the hallway."

"Thank you."

"Seeing all these gorgeous young creatures makes me want to go to school again," said Giordino, as they passed a bevy of girls on the stairs.

"You're out of luck," said Pitt. "It's an all-girls school. No men allowed."

"Maybe I could teach."

"You'd be tossed out the door within a week for lecherous behavior."

Another young student working in the Anthropology Department ushered them into Dr. Wednesday's office. The man who turned from pulling a book from a tightly packed shelf smiled as the three strangers filtered into his cluttered office that smelled of musty academia. Dr. Jerry Wednesday wasn't any taller than Giordino, but much thinner. No tweed jacket with leather elbows or pipe-smoking for this man. He was dressed in a sweatshirt, Levi's and hiking boots. His narrow face was clean-shaven, and the thinning hair on his forehead suggested someone who was in his late forties. The eyes were a dark gray, and he smiled with straight, even, white teeth an orthodontist could be proud of.

"One of you gentlemen must be the man who called," he said jovially.

"I called," said Pitt. "This is Kelly Egan and Al Giordino, and I'm Dirk Pitt."

"Won't you please sit down? You caught me at a good time. I don't have a class for another two hours." Then he looked at Kelly. "Was your father Dr. Elmore Egan, by any chance?"

"He was my father," Kelly answered.

"I was very sorry to hear about his death," Wednesday said sincerely. "I met and corresponded with him, you know. He was researching a Viking expedition he thought had passed through New York in . . . 1035, I believe it was."

"Yes, Dad was very interested in the rune stones they left behind."

"We've just come from Marlys Kaiser in Minnesota," said Pitt. "It was she who suggested we meet with you."

"A grand lady." Wednesday sat down behind his cluttered desk. "I suppose Marlys mentioned that Dr. Egan thought the Vikings who settled in this area were massacred by the Indians in the valley."

Kelly nodded. "She touched on the subject."

Wednesday rummaged around an open desk drawer and retrieved a sheaf of wrinkled papers. "Very little is known about the early American Indians who lived along the

Hudson River. The first record and description of the local natives came from Giovanni da Verrazano in 1524. During his epic voyage up and down the East Coast, he entered New York Harbor, where he anchored and explored for two weeks, before continuing north to Newfoundland and sailing back to France."

Wednesday paused as he studied his notes. "Verrazano went on to describe the American natives as having sharp faces, long black hair and black eyes. They dressed in fox and deer skin and adorned themselves with copper ornaments. He noted that they carved canoes from individual logs and lived in either round or long houses constructed from split logs and thatched with long grass and tree branches. Except for Verrazano's earliest account, the ancient Indians left little for archaeologists to discover, study and record. Much of the early inhabitants' life can be only conjectured."

"So the history of the American Indians begins in 1524," said Giordino.

"Recorded history, yes. The next great navigator to leave an account was Henry Hudson in 1609. He sailed into the harbor and up the river that was given his name. Amazingly, he made it as far as Cohoes, about ten miles above Albany, where he was stopped by the falls. He described the Indians who lived on the lower part of the river as strong and warlike, while those farther up were friendly and polite."

"What did they use as weapons?"

"Bows and arrows, with points made of sharp stones and attached to the shafts with hard resin. They had also carved clubs and made hatchets fashioned with large flints."

"What was their food supply?" asked Kelly.

"Game and every kind of fish was plentiful, especially sturgeon, salmon and oysters. They farmed large fields of maize, or corn as we call it, which they cooked by baking, along with squash, sunflowers, and beans. They also produced tobacco, which they smoked in copper pipes. Copper was in abundance throughout the north around the Great Lakes and was the only metal Indians knew how to craft. They were aware of iron, but did not know how to process it."

"Then they had a comfortable lifestyle."

"Hudson found no sign of starvation or malnutrition among the Indians," Wednesday answered. Then he smiled slightly. "Interestingly, none of the early explorers ever reported seeing any indication of scalps, prisoners or slaves. We must assume such repugnant practices were introduced by foreigners from across the sea."

Pitt clasped his hands thoughtfully. "Did any of the early explorers mention any sign of previous contact with Europeans?"

"A few things were noted by Hudson and others. One was that there was no astonishment among the Indians, as you might expect at seeing strange vessels and white-skinned men with blond or red hair for the first time. One crewman of Verrazano's told of Indians wearing iron adornments that looked like old rusty knife blades. Another claimed he saw an iron axe hanging on the wall of an Indian house. There was also a rumor of a crewman finding a concave iron vessel used as a bowl."

"A Viking helmet," Giordino mused.

Wednesday smiled patiently and continued. "It wasn't until the Dutch began to settle the valley by building a fort near present-day Albany in 1613, and they began to learn the tribal languages, that the legends of the past began to emerge."

"What did the legends reveal?"

"It's difficult to separate myth from fact," replied Wednesday. "The tales passed down through the centuries by spoken word were very vague, of course, with no evidence to support them. One that surfaced told of wild, bearded men with white skin and hard heads that gleamed in the sun, who arrived and built a settlement in the valley. When some went away for a long time —"

"Magnus Sigvatson and his hundred men who set off to explore the west," Kelly interrupted.

"Yes, I'm familiar with the rune stones your father discovered and their translations," said Wednesday, unruffled. "The story goes on to say that when the Indians, who saw no crime in theft, began stealing and slaughtering livestock that had been carried across the sea in the newcomers' boats, there was retaliation. The wild men with hair on the face, as they were called, retrieved the livestock and cut off the hands of the thieves. Unfortunately, one of the thieves was a local chief's son. The angered chief gathered other tribes in the valley. One tribe was the Munsee Lenape, or Delaware, who were culturally related to the Algonkian. The combined forces attacked the foreigners' settlement and destroyed it, slaughtering them all. One version suggests that a few of the women and children were carried off as slaves, but that practice did not come in until much later."

"It must have been a shock for Magnus and his men to return and find their friends and families dead."

Wednesday nodded. "We can only speculate. But now it was their turn. The legend describes a great battle with the wild men with shiny heads, who killed more than a thousand Indians before dying to the last man."

"Not a pretty story," murmured Kelly.

Wednesday held up his hands in an absent gesture. "Who can say whether it's true or not?"

"Seems odd that no trace of the settlement has been discovered," observed Pitt.

"The legend goes on to say the Indians, understandably in a crazed wrath, destroyed and burned every last vestige of the newcomers' settlement, leaving nothing standing aboveground for later archaeologists to study."

"Was there ever a reference to a cave?"

"The only mention I'm aware of is on one of the rune stones Dr. Egan found."

Pitt looked at Wednesday, saying nothing and waiting in expectation.

Wednesday took the clue. "There *were,* however, a few unexplained circumstances. For example, a significant transition occurred in the Hudson Valley beginning about 1000 A.D. The inhabitants suddenly discovered agriculture and began to grow their own vegetables. Farming became a source of sustenance, along with hunting, fishing and gathering. About this same time, they began to fortify their villages with rock and vertical logs reinforced with earth embankments. They also constructed oval longhouses with sleeping platforms set in the walls, something they had never done in earlier times."

"So what you are suggesting is that the Vikings showed them how to farm crops and build sturdy houses. And, after the great battle, the Indians began throwing up stockades for defense in case of another mass attack by foreigners."

"I'm a realist, Mr. Pitt," said Wednesday. "I'm not suggesting anything. What I've told you is ancient hearsay and supposition. Until absolute proof is found that goes beyond the inscriptions on the rune stones, whose authenticity is in doubt by most archaeologists, we can only accept the stories as legends and myths, nothing more."

"I believe my father found evidence of a Viking settlement," said Kelly quietly. "But he died before revealing his research, and we cannot find his notes or journals."

"I sincerely hope you're successful," said Wednesday honestly. "I would like nothing better than to believe the Hudson Valley was visited and settled six hundred years earlier than the Spanish and Dutch. It might be fun to rewrite the history books."

Pitt rose, leaned across the desk and shook Dr. Wednesday's hand. "Thank you, Doctor. We're grateful for your time."

"Not at all, I enjoyed it." He smiled at Kelly. "Please let me know if you turn up anything."

"There *is* one more question."

"Yes?"

"Did any other Viking artifacts ever turn

up besides those mentioned by the early explorers?"

Wednesday thought a moment. "Come to think of it, a farmer reported finding old rusty chain mail back in the nineteen twenties, but I don't know what became of it or whether a scientist ever examined it."

"Thank you again."

They offered their farewells, left Wednesday's office and headed for the parking lot. Dark clouds were massing and it looked as if rain was only minutes away. They reached the car and climbed in just as the first drops began to fall. The mood was somber as Giordino inserted the keys in the ignition and started the engine.

"Dad found the settlement," Kelly said intently. "I know it."

"My problem," said Giordino, "is that I can't make a connection between a settlement and a cave. It looks to me as if no cave, no settlement."

"Though any trace of the settlement was destroyed, I'm betting there was a cave and that it still exists," said Pitt.

"I wish I knew where," Kelly said wistfully. "Josh and I never found it."

"The Indians could have sealed off the entrance," advised Giordino.

Kelly stared out the window dreamily at the trees surrounding the parking lot. "Then we'll never find it."

"I suggest that we make a search from the river below the palisades," said Pitt confidently. "Finding a cavity in the rock under the surface is very possible with the use of side-scan sonar. We can round up a NUMA boat and sensor and be ready to go the day after tomorrow."

Giordino was shifting into gear and pulling out of the college parking area when his cell phone buzzed. "Giordino." A pause and then, "One moment, Admiral. He's right here." He passed the phone to Pitt in the rear seat. "It's Sandecker."

"Yes, Admiral," said Pitt. Then, for the next three minutes, he went mute and listened without replying. Then finally, "Yes, sir. We're on our way." He handed the phone back to Giordino. "He wants us back in Washington as quickly as we can get there."

"A problem?"

"More like an emergency."

"Did he say what it was?" asked Kelly.

"It seems Curtis Merlin Zale and his pals at Cerberus are about to cause a catastrophe even worse than the *Emerald Dolphin*."

Part Four

DECEPTION

MONGOL INVADER
Liquefied Natural Gas Tanker

CORAL WANDERER
Luxury Submarine

42

Congresswoman Loren Smith felt as though she'd been tied to a wild horse and dragged across the desert. Though the directors of Cerberus had been subpoenaed to appear before her Congressional Investigative Committee into Illegal Marketing Practices, they had failed to show. Instead, they were represented by an army of their corporate attorneys who laid an impenetrable smoke screen over the entire proceedings.

"Spin-and-stall tactics," she muttered under her breath, as she gaveled the hearings to a close until the following morning. "They don't come any slimier than we've seen here this morning."

She was sitting there in utter anger and frustration when Congressman Leonard Sturgis, a Democrat from North Dakota, walked up and put a hand on her shoulder.

"Don't be discouraged, Loren."

"I can't say that you were much help today," she said, with a hard edge to her voice. "You agreed with everything they threw at us when you knew perfectly well it was nothing but distortions and lies."

"You can't deny everything they testified about was perfectly legal."

"I want to see Curtis Merlin Zale in front of the committee, along with his board of directors. Not a bunch of shysters throwing mud in the water."

"I'm sure Mr. Zale will appear at the proper time," said Sturgis. "I think you will find him a quite reasonable man."

Loren gave Sturgis a withering look. "Zale crudely interrupted my dinner the other night, and I found him to be utter vermin."

Sturgis frowned, which was atypical for him. His face was rarely without a smile. In Congress he was known as the great pacifier. He had the weathered look of a man who'd spent most of his life on a farm. His brothers still farmed the family homestead in Buffalo, North Dakota, and he was continually reelected because of his unending fight to preserve the farming way of life. His only liability, as Loren saw it, was his coziness with Curtis Merlin Zale.

"You met Zale?" he asked in genuine surprise.

"Your reasonable man threatened my life

if I didn't drop the investigation."

"I find that hard to accept."

"Believe it!" Loren said nastily. "Take my advice, Leo. Distance yourself from Cerberus. They're going down, and going down big time, and Zale will be lucky if he doesn't end up on death row."

Sturgis watched her turn and stride away, immaculate in a beige tweed wool suit cinched at the waist with a suede belt. She carried a briefcase whose dyed leather matched the color of her suit. It was her trademark.

Loren did not go back to her office. It was late in the evening, and she went directly to her car in the congressional underground parking level of her office building. Her mind wandered over the day's events as she made her way through the tail end of the rush-hour traffic. Forty-five minutes later, she reached her town house in Alexandria. As she stopped and clicked the remote to her garage door, a woman stepped from the shadows and approached her from the driver's side. Unafraid, Loren turned and rolled down her window.

"Congresswoman Smith. Forgive the intrusion, but it's most urgent that we talk."

"Who are you?"

"My name is Sally Morse. I am the chairman of the Yukon Oil Company."

Loren studied the woman, who was

dressed only in denim slacks with a light blue cotton sweater. There was a sincerity in the eyes that appealed to Loren. "Step into the garage."

Loren parked the car and closed the garage door. "Please come inside." She led the way into a living room. The decor was ultra-modern, each piece of furniture individually designed by artisans. "Please sit down. Would you like a cup of coffee?"

"I'd prefer something a little stronger, thank you."

"Name your poison," Loren said, as she opened a liquor cabinet whose glass doors were etched with exotic floral designs.

"Scotch on the rocks?"

"Spoken like a man."

Loren poured a shot of Cutty Sark scotch over ice and handed the glass to Sally. Then she opened a Coors beer and sat across a coffee table from her. "Now, Ms. Morse, why come to me?"

"Because you're heading the congressional investigation into the Cerberus empire and its impact on the oil market."

Loren's heart began to increase its beat and she forced herself to act composed. "Am I to assume you have information you'd like to share with me?"

Sally took a large swallow of the scotch, made a sour face and took a deep breath. "I hope you'll understand something. From this moment on, my life is in extreme danger, my property will likely be destroyed and my reputation and my position that I worked so long and hard to achieve will be scourged."

Loren did not push Sally, but sat patiently. "You're a very brave woman."

Sally shook her head sadly. "Not really. I'm only fortunate that I have no family for Curtis Merlin Zale to threaten or murder, as his henchmen have done with so many others."

Loren's adrenaline was beginning to pump. The mere mention of Zale's name came like a lightning strike on the roof.

"You're privy to his criminal activities," she ventured.

"From the time he recruited me and formed the cartel with other major oil companies' corporate executive officers."

"I wasn't aware of a cartel." Loren was beginning to feel she had struck the mother lode.

"Oh yes, indeed," said Sally. "Zale's plan was to form a secret merger of our companies in order to create a nation that is no longer dependent on foreign oil. At first, it seemed like a noble cause. But then it became apparent that his plans went far beyond simply cutting off OPEC supplies."

"What is his ultimate goal?"

"To become more powerful than the

United States government. To dictate his schemes to a country so dependent on fair-priced oil and abundant supplies that it'll applaud his efforts, never knowing that someday he'll pull the rug out from under it once he has a total monopoly and foreign oil is banned from our shores."

"I don't see how that is possible," said Loren, unable to grasp the full extent of what Sally was saying. "How can he achieve a monopoly without bringing in huge new oil fields in North America?"

"By having all American and Canadian restrictions on drilling and on exploiting government-owned lands lifted. By casting aside all environmental concerns. And by buying off and controlling Washington. Worst of all, convincing the American public to protest and riot against foreign oil shipments into the country."

"Impossible!" Loren snapped. "No one man can achieve that much power on top of the backs of so many."

"The protests have already started," Sally said somberly. "Rioting is just around the corner. You'll understand when I tell you his latest planned catastrophe. At the moment, little stands between him and a total oil monopoly."

"It's unthinkable."

Sally smiled grimly. "It's a cliché to say nothing can stand in his way or that he will not hesitate to use any means to achieve his goals, even mass murder, but it's all too true."

"The *Emerald Dolphin* and the *Golden Marlin.*"

Sally stared at Loren, confused. "You know about his involvement with those tragedies?"

"Since you're telling me what you know, I feel safe in telling you that the FBI, working closely with NUMA, has proven the disasters were not accidents, but caused by agents of Cerberus called the Vipers. From what we gathered, the burning of the cruise ship and the sinking of the underwater cruise boat were meant to be blamed on Dr. Elmore Egan's magnetohydrodynamic engines. Zale wanted to halt their production because of a revolutionary oil Egan had formulated that virtually eliminates friction. If sold on the market, it would put a huge dent in oil sales and make the difference between profit and loss for the refinery corporations."

"I had no idea government investigators were aware of Zale's secret circle of mercenary killers," said Sally in astonishment.

"So long as Zale doesn't know."

Sally spread her hands dejectedly. "He knows."

Loren looked skeptical. "How? The investigation is being conducted in the strictest secrecy."

"Curtis Merlin Zale has paid out more than five billion dollars to buy everyone in Washington that he can profit from. Over a hundred senators and representatives are in his pocket, along with officials in every department of government, including the Justice Department."

"Can you name names?" asked Loren intently.

Sally's expression turned almost fiendish. She pulled a computer disc from her purse. "It's all here. Two hundred and eleven names. I can't tell you how much they've been paid or when. But I came across a sealed file sent to me by mistake that was meant for Sandra Delage, the cartel's inside administrator. After making copies, I resealed the file and sent it to Sandra. Luckily, she did not suspect that I was having second thoughts about my involvement with Cerberus and Zale's mad scheme and she did not act the least suspicious."

"Can you tell me a few of the names?"

"Let's just say leaders of both houses and three top White House officials."

"Congressman Leonard Sturgis?"

"He's on the list."

"I was afraid of that," said Loren angrily. "And the president?"

Sally shook her head. "To my knowledge, he wants nothing to do with Zale. The president is not perfect, but he sees enough in the oil tycoon to know he's as rotten as a ninety-day-old truckload of fruit."

Loren and Sally talked until nearly three o'clock in the morning. Loren was horrified when Sally reported Zale's scheme to blow up a supertanker in San Francisco harbor. The disc was inserted in Loren's home computer and the contents printed out until there was a stack of papers the size of a small book manuscript. The women then hid the disk and the printed copies in a safe Loren had built in her garage floor beneath a storage cabinet.

"You can stay here for the night, but we've got to find you a safe hideout while the investigation is under way. Once Zale discovers you're going to blow the whistle on his insidious operation, he'll make every effort to silence you."

"*Silence*, a nice word for murder."

"They've already tried to torture Kelly Egan, Dr. Egan's daughter, for the oil formula."

"Did they succeed?"

"No, she was rescued before Zale's Viper pals could find out anything."

"I'd like to meet her."

"You can. She was staying with me, but after Zale found us together over dinner the other night, I had to hide her elsewhere, too."

"I came away with only an overnight bag. I have just a few cosmetics, jewelry and a couple of changes of clean underwear."

Loren gauged Sally's shape and nodded. "We're about the same size. You can borrow whatever of my wardrobe that suits you."

"I'll be a happy woman when this dirty business is over."

"You realize that by doing this you're going to be ordered to testify before Justice officials and my congressional investigating committee."

"I accept the consequences," Sally said solemnly.

Loren put her arm around her. "I'll say it again. You're a very brave woman."

"It's one of the few times in my life I've put good intentions in front of my ambition."

"I admire you," Loren said sincerely.

"Where do you want me to hide after tonight?"

"Because Zale has too many moles in the Justice Department, I don't think it wise to put you in a government safe house." Loren smiled craftily. "I have this friend who can put you up in an old aircraft hangar that has more security systems than Fort Knox. His name is Dirk Pitt."

"Can he be trusted?"

Loren laughed. "Honey, if the old Greek

philosopher Diogenes were still wandering around with a lantern looking for an honest man, he could have ended his journey at Dirk's door."

43

After Kelly left the aircraft in Washington, she was escorted to an unmarked van that transported her to a safe house in Arlington. Pitt and Giordino saw her off and entered a NUMA Lincoln Navigator and relaxed as the driver steered the car toward Landover, Maryland. Twenty minutes later, they turned onto Arena Drive and drove into the vast parking lot of FedEx Field, the stadium that is home to the Washington Redskins football team. Built in 1997, it can accommodate 80,116 fans in wide, comfortable seats. Restaurants on the end zones serve a wide variety of ethnic foods. Two huge video screens for replays and four scoreboards make it enjoyable for fans to follow the finer points of the game.

The Navigator rolled into the underground VIP parking area and stopped by a doorway guarded by two security men in combat gear, holding automatic rifles. They stopped Pitt and Giordino and studied their faces with photographs provided to them by NUMA's security department, before allowing them to pass into a long corridor that stretched beneath the seats of the stadium.

"Fourth door on the left, gentlemen," instructed one of the guards.

"Doesn't this strike you as overkill?" Giordino asked Pitt.

"Knowing the admiral, he must have a good reason."

They reached the door and found another armed guard outside. He merely studied them for a quick moment, then swung open the door and stepped aside.

"I thought the Cold War was over years ago," Giordino muttered quietly.

They were mildly surprised to find themselves in the locker room for the visiting football teams. Several people were already seated in the team management office. Loren was there, with Sally Morse. Admiral Sandecker, Rudi Gunn and Hiram Yaeger represented NUMA. Pitt recognized Admiral Amos Dover of the Coast Guard, Captain Warren Garnet of the Marines and Commander Miles Jacobs, who was a veteran of Navy SEAL operations. He and Giordino had worked with all of them in the past.

The only one who was not familiar was a tall man with the distinguished good looks you'd expect from a cruise ship captain. Adding to his image of a mariner was a black patch over the left eye. Pitt guessed him to be in his late fifties.

Pitt momentarily shuffled the stranger to one side of his mind as he greeted his NUMA associates and shook hands with the military men he'd known from past adventures. Dover, a great bear of a man, had worked with Pitt on the Deep Six project. Garnet and Jacobs had been engaged in a losing firefight in the Antarctic until Pitt and Giordino had made a timely appearance in Admiral Byrd's colossal Snow Cruiser. Only after a few pleasantries were exchanged did Pitt focus his attention on the man with the eye patch.

"Dirk," said Sandecker, "may I introduce Wes Rader. Wes is an old naval friend. We served in the Baltic Sea together, keeping an eye on Russian submarines heading out into the Atlantic. Wes is a senior deputy director at the Justice Department and will coordinate all activities from the legal end."

Questions rose in the back of Pitt's mind, but he waited until the proper moment to present them. Alone, he would have hugged Loren and kissed her boldly on the lips. But this was business and she was a member of Congress, so he merely made a slight bow and shook her offered hand. "Nice to see you again, Congresswoman."

"Likewise," Loren said, with a sly glint in her eye. She turned to Sally. "This is the man I was telling you about. Sally Morse, meet Dirk Pitt."

Sally looked deep into Pitt's opaline green eyes and saw what most women who met him saw, a man they could depend on. "I've heard a great deal about you."

Pitt gave a side glance at Loren and smiled. "I hope your source didn't lay it on too thick."

"If everyone will please find a chair and get comfortable," said Sandecker, "we'll start the proceedings." He sat down, pulled out one of his immense cigars, but in deference to the ladies present did not light it. He probably could have without protest. The women would probably have preferred it to the smells of sweat that still hung in the air of the locker room from the last football game.

"Gentlemen, as some of you are already aware, Ms. Morse is the CEO of the Yukon Oil Company. She will describe a grave threat to our national security and the citizens of our country that concerns us all." He turned to Sally. "The stage is yours."

"Pardon me for interrupting, Admiral," said Rader, "but I'm at a loss as to why we're playing all these security games.

Meeting in the locker room of a football stadium seems a bit overdone."

"You'll have your question answered as soon as Ms. Morse makes her report." He nodded at Sally.

"Please begin."

For the next two hours, Sally gave a detailed narrative of Curtis Merlin Zale's grand scheme to create an oil monopoly and gain enormous wealth while dictating terms to the United States government.

When she finished, there was a heavy cloud of incredulity in the room. Finally, Wes Rader spoke. "Are you certain what you've told us is true?"

"Every word," Sally said resolutely.

Rader turned to Sandecker. "This threat goes far beyond the people in this room. We've got to notify others immediately. The president, the leaders of Congress, the Joint Chiefs of Staff, my boss at the Justice Department — that's just for starters."

"We can't," Sandecker said, and passed out copies containing the names of members of Congress, agency officials, people in the Justice Department and close aides to the president in the West Wing. "And this is why. This is the reason for the secrecy," he said to Rader. "The names of the people you see in your hand have all been bought and paid for by Cerberus and Curtis Merlin Zale."

"Impossible," said Rader, scanning the names in utter disbelief. "There would have to be a vast paper trail."

"The money was paid through overseas companies owned by other companies owned by Cerberus," answered Sally. "All funds and payoff monies are in offshore accounts that would take Justice Department investigators years to track down."

"How is it possible one man corrupted the entire system?"

Loren answered for Sally. "The members of Congress who could not resist Zale's bribes are those who are not rich men. They may not have given up their ideals and ethics for a million dollars, but ten or twenty million was too much for them to pass on. Those who fell into Zale's trap do not know the full extent of his web. Until now, with thanks to Sally, we are the only ones outside of the Cerberus circle who know of the rampant influence Zale has achieved within the government."

"Do not forget the respected members of the news media," added Sally. "Those under Zale's thumb can bias the news in his favor. If they balk, he can threaten to expose them, and with their credibility gone, they'd be out of the newsroom and on the street within hours."

Rader shook his head. "I still can't believe

651

one man is responsible, no matter how wealthy he is."

"He didn't act alone. Zale had the backing of the most powerful oil barons in the United States and Canada. Not all the money came out of Cerberus."

"Yukon Oil, too?"

"Yukon Oil, too," Sally replied solemnly. "I'm as guilty as the others of falling under Zale's spell."

"You've more than atoned by coming to us," said Loren, squeezing Sally's hand.

"Why me?" asked Rader. "I'm only the number-three man at the Justice Department."

"As you've seen, your name is not on the list, and your direct superiors' are," answered Sandecker. "I've also known you and your wife for years. I know you to be an honorable man who can't be bought."

"You must have been approached," said Loren.

Rader looked up at the ceiling, trying to recall. Then he nodded. "Two years ago. I was walking my cocker spaniel near my house when a strange woman, yes, it was a woman, walked along beside me and struck up a conversation."

Sally smiled. "Ash blond hair, blue eyes, about five foot nine, one hundred thirty pounds. An attractive woman with a direct approach?"

"A faithful description."

"Her name is Sandra Delage. She's Zale's chief administrator."

"Did she make an outright offer of money?" Sandecker inquired.

"Nothing so crude," Rader replied. "As I remember, she talked in vague terms. What would I do if I won the lottery? Was I happy with my job, and was I appreciated for my efforts? If I could live anyplace but Washington, where would it be? Apparently, I failed the examination. She left me at an intersection and climbed into a passing car that stopped for her. I never heard another word after that."

"It is up to you to get the ball rolling. Zale and his cronies in the Cerberus cartel must be stopped in their tracks and brought to justice," said Sandecker. "We're looking at a national scandal of immense proportions."

"Where do we begin?" asked Rader. "If Ms. Morse's list of bribed officials is correct, I can't simply walk into the attorney general's office and announce that I'm arresting him for taking bribes."

"You do that," said Loren, "and Zale's team of Viper assassins would make sure your body was found in the Potomac River."

Sandecker nodded at Hiram Yaeger, who opened two large cardboard boxes and began passing around a bound set of documents several inches thick. "Utilizing Ms. Morse's account and our own investigations into Zale's criminal empire through our NUMA computer facilities, we put together a complete indictment with more than enough solid, established evidence to convince honest officials of what must be done." He looked Rader in the eye. "Wes, you have to put together a team at Justice whose loyalty you can absolutely depend on to build an airtight case. People who are not afraid of threats, like the Untouchables who put away Al Capone. There can be no leaks. If Zale gets the slightest hint of your actions, he'll send out his hit squad."

"I can't believe this could happen in America."

"Many nefarious things go on behind the scenes of business and government that the public doesn't know about," said Loren.

Rader stared apprehensively at the thick report on the table in front of him. "I hope I'm not biting off more than I can chew."

"I'll give you every assistance from the congressional end," Loren promised him.

"Our first priority," said Sandecker, pressing a series of buttons on a remote and lowering a monitor with a display of San Francisco Bay, "is to stop that oil tanker from wiping out half of San Francisco." He turned and looked at Dover, Garnet and Jacobs, who had remained quiet during the discussion. "This is where you gentlemen come into the picture."

"The Coast Guard will stop the *Pacific Chimera* from entering the bay," Dover stated flatly.

Sandecker nodded. "Sounds simple, Amos. You've stopped thousands of ships carrying everything from drugs to illegal immigrants to smuggled weapons. But stopping one of the world's largest super oil tankers will take more than firing a shot across its bow and a command through a bullhorn."

Dover smiled at Garnet and Jacobs. "Is this why we have the Navy SEALs and Marine Recon at the table?"

"You will, of course, be in command of the operation," said Sandecker. "But if the captain of the tanker ignores your commands to heave to and continues on his course into the bay, we don't have a whole lot of avenues open to us. The ship must be stopped outside the Golden Gate, but to fire on her and risk causing a monstrous oil spill is out of the question. As a last resort, a combat team will have to be air-dropped by helicopter onto the vessel itself and neutralize the crew."

"Where is the *Pacific Chimera* now?" asked Dover.

Sandecker pressed another button on the remote and the map enlarged to show the ocean to the west of the Golden Gate. The chart showed a small image of a ship heading toward the coast of California. "Approximately nine hundred miles out."

"That gives us less than forty-eight hours."

"We only received the devastating news from Ms. Morse and Congresswoman Smith in the early hours of the morning."

"I'll have Coast Guard cutters waiting to intercept fifty miles out," said Dover solidly.

"And I'll have a boarding team in the air as backup," Jacobs assured him.

"My SEAL team will stand ready to board from the sea," Garnet added.

Dover looked at Garnet dubiously. "Your men can board a supertanker from the water while it's under way?"

"An exercise we've rehearsed many times," said Garnet, with an almost imperceptible grin.

"*That* I'll have to see," said Dover.

"Well, ladies and gentlemen," Sandecker said quietly, "this is as far as NUMA can go in this project. We'll help in any way we're asked, and will supply the evidence we've accumulated pertaining to the fire and cover-up sinking of the *Emerald Dolphin* and the near-tragedy of the *Golden Marlin*, but we are a scientific oceanographic agency and not authorized to act as an investigative agency. I leave it to Wes and Loren to as-

656

semble a trusted team of patriots to launch the first phase of an undercover investigation."

"We have our work cut out for us," Loren said to Rader.

"Yes," replied Rader quietly. "Some of the people on this list are my friends. I'll be a lonely man when this is over."

"You won't be the only outcast," said Loren, with a dry smile. "I have friends on the list, too."

Dover pushed back his chair and stood and looked down at Sandecker. "I'll keep you informed every hour on the status of the operation."

"I appreciate that, Amos. Thank you."

One by one, they filed out of the locker room. Pitt and Giordino, along with Rudi Gunn, were asked by Sandecker to remain. As he left, Yaeger put his hand on Pitt's shoulder and asked him to drop by NUMA headquarters after he left there and come to the computer floor.

Sandecker relaxed in his chair and lit his big cigar. He stared at Giordino with an annoyed look, waiting for him to light up one of his special cigars, too, but Al merely stared back with a patronizing smile. "It looks as if you boys are sidelined for the rest of the game."

"I'm sure you and Rudi won't let us sit on the bench for very long," said Pitt, as he stared from Sandecker to Gunn.

Gunn adjusted his glasses. "We're sending an expedition to French Frigate Shoals northwest of the Hawaiian Islands to survey and examine the widespread death of the coral. We'd like Al to head up the investigation."

"And me?" asked Pitt.

"I hope you saved your cold-weather gear from the Atlantis Project," said Sandecker wryly. "You'll be returning to Antarctica in an attempt to penetrate the ice down to the vast lake scientists believe is under the ice cap."

A shadow of dissent crossed Pitt's face. "I will, of course, follow your directives, Admiral, without argument. But I respectfully request five days for Al and me to clear up a mystery concerning Dr. Elmore Egan."

"The search for his secret laboratory?"

"You know?"

"I have my sources."

Kelly, Pitt thought. The old devil had played sympathetic uncle while protecting her from harm by Zale's henchmen. She must have told him about their search for the Norsemen and the puzzle behind the legend of the lost cave.

"I strongly believe it is a matter of national security to find out what Dr. Egan was working on when he died, before Zale gets there first."

Sandecker looked over at Gunn. "What

do you think, Rudi? Should we give these two scoundrels five days to search for an illusion?"

Gunn peered over the tops of his glasses at Pitt and Giordino like a fox eyeing a pair of coyotes. "I think we can be magnanimous, Admiral. It will take at least five days to finish equipping and supplying the survey ships I've scheduled for the projects, anyway."

Sandecker exhaled a cloud of blue aromatic smoke. "That's it, then. Rudi will inform you where and when to report on board your survey ships." Then he dropped his gruff edge and said, "I wish you luck on your quest. I'm also curious as to what Egan was conjuring up."

Yaeger was slouching in his chair, feet stretched out, in front of his keyboard conversing with Max, when Pitt arrived from the football stadium. "You wanted to see me, Hiram?"

"I'll say." Yaeger straightened and pulled Egan's leather case from a nearby cabinet. "You're just in time for the next act."

"Act?"

"Three more minutes."

"I don't follow."

"Every forty-eight hours, at precisely one-fifteen in the afternoon, this case turns to magic."

"It fills with oil," Pitt said hesitantly.

"Exactly." Yaeger opened the case, and waved his hand over the empty contents like a magician. Then he closed it and snapped the latches. He studied the sweep hand on his wristwatch, counting the seconds. Then he said, "To reverse the old cliché: Now, you don't see it — and now you do." He carefully unlatched and lifted the lid. The interior of the case was filled with oil less than an inch from the upper edge.

"I know you're not performing black magic," said Pitt, "since the same thing happened to Al and me after Kelly Egan gave me the case on the *Deep Encounter*."

"It has to be some sort of trick or illusion," said Yaeger, befuddled.

"It's not an illusion," said Pitt. "It's real enough." He dipped his finger in the oil and rubbed it between his thumb. "Feels frictionless. My guess is that it's Dr. Egan's super oil."

"The million-dollar question is: Where's it coming from?"

"Does Max have a read on it?" Pitt asked, staring at the holograph figure on the other side of Yaeger's desk.

"Sorry, Dirk. I'm as mystified as you," said Max. "I have a few ideas I'd like to pursue if Hiram doesn't shut me down when he leaves for home tonight."

"Only if you promise not to enter confidential or private sites."

"I will try to be a good girl." The words were there, but the delivery had a conniving tone to it.

Yaeger did not think it was funny. Max had gotten him in trouble before, going where she was forbidden to go. But Pitt could not help laughing.

"Have you ever regretted not making Max a male?"

Yaeger looked like a man who'd fallen into a sewer wearing a tuxedo. "Consider yourself lucky," he said wearily. "You're single. Not only do I have to contend with Max, but I have a wife and two teenage daughters at home."

"You don't know it, Hiram, but you're a man to be envied."

"That's easy for you to say. You never let a woman into your life."

"No," said Pitt wistfully. "That, I never did."

44

Unknown to Pitt, his days of lonely bachelor-hood would be temporarily interrupted. He returned to his hangar and observed that wily old Sandecker had sent a security team to patrol the area around him at the deserted end of the airport. He didn't question the admiral's concern for his safety. He didn't feel it was necessary, despite Zale's threats, but he was grateful all the same. The real reason did not become apparent until he entered the hangar and climbed to his apartment above the main floor.

The music coming out of his stereo system was on an easy-listening station instead of his preferred modern jazz. Then he smelled the aroma of coffee. He also detected the wisp of a fragrant feminine scent. He peered into the kitchen and found Sally Morse stirring the contents of an array of pots on the stove. She was in bare feet, wearing a sundress and little else.

Who invited you? Who said you could invade my personal domain as if you owned it? Who let you in through the security systems? All these questions ripened in his mind, but, mild-mannered marine engineer that he was, Pitt simply said, "Hello, what's for dinner?"

"Beef stroganoff," answered Sally, turning and smiling sweetly. "Do you like it?"

"One of my favorites."

She could tell by the adrift expression on his face that he hadn't expected her. "Congresswoman Smith thought I'd be safer staying here. Especially since Admiral Sandecker has placed a security ring around your hangar."

Questions answered, Pitt opened the cabinet above his bar to pour a drink.

"Loren told me you drink tequila, so I took the liberty of making margaritas. I hope you don't mind?"

Though Pitt preferred his expensive tequila straight over ice with a touch of lime and light salt rimming the glass, he enjoyed a well-mixed margarita. They were better made with cheaper tequila, though. To his way of thinking, it was a crime to dilute the top-quality brands with sweet mix. He looked forlornly at his half-empty bottle of good Juan Julio silver, 100 percent blue agave tequila. Just to be polite, he complimented Sally on the taste and went to his bedroom to take a shower and change into comfortable shorts and T-shirt.

His bedroom looked as if a bomb had gone off in it. Shoes and various items of female apparel littered the polished wooden plank floor. Bottles of nail polish and other cosmetics were stacked on the dresser and the bed's end tables. Why do women always drop their clothes on the floor? he wondered. Men at least throw them over a chair. He couldn't believe only one female could have created such chaos until he heard a voice humming in his bathroom.

The door was ajar, so he very slowly eased it half open with his toe. Kelly was standing in front of a half-steamed mirror wearing a towel around her body and a smaller one wrapped around her head. She was putting on eye makeup. She saw Pitt's blank stare in the mirror and smiled engagingly.

"Welcome home. I hope Sally and I haven't upset your routine."

"It was suggested you stay here, too?" he asked.

"Loren thought it safer than her place. And the government safe houses could not be trusted because of Zale's infiltration into the Justice Department."

"Sorry I have only one bedroom in the apartment. I hope you and Ms. Morse don't mind sharing the bed."

"It's king-size," Kelly said, returning to her makeup as if she and Pitt had lived together for years. "We won't mind." Then as an afterthought: "I'm sorry, would you like to use the bathroom?"

"Don't mind me," Pitt said wryly. "I'll pack some clothes and shower downstairs in the guest quarters."

Sally had stepped from the kitchen. "I fear we have inconvenienced you."

"I'll survive," Pitt said, as he began throwing some things in an overnight bag. "You ladies make yourselves at home."

From his dry tone, Sally and Kelly could tell that Pitt wasn't overjoyed at their intrusion. "We'll stay out of your way," promised Kelly.

"Don't get me wrong," Pitt said, sensing her uneasiness. "You're not the first ones who have stayed here and slept in my bed. I adore women and am actually quite fond of their curious mannerisms. I come from the old school that elevates them on a pedestal, so don't think I'm a nasty old grunt." He paused and grinned. "Actually, it will be enjoyable having a pair of gorgeous creatures like yourselves, cooking and cleaning house for me."

Then he walked from the bedroom and down the circular stairway to the main floor below.

Sally and Kelly watched in silence as he disappeared from view. Then they turned, looked at each other and broke out laughing.

"My God," burst Sally. "Is he for real?"

"Take my word for it," said Kelly. "He's bigger than life."

Pitt set up house in the *Manhattan Limited* Pullman railroad car that sat on rails along one wall of the hangar. A relic from a Hudson River search operation several years ago, he used it as guest quarters when visitors and friends stayed with him. Giordino often borrowed it for the night when he wanted to impress one of his string of lady friends. Women found the luxurious antique railroad car a very exotic setting for a romantic evening.

He had stepped from the shower and was shaving when the extension phone in the Pullman car rang. He picked up the receiver and simply said, "Hello."

"Dirk!" St. Julien Perlmutter's voice boomed in Pitt's ear. "How are you, my boy?"

"Fine, St. Julien. Where are you?"

"Amiens, France. I spent the day talking to Jules Verne scholars. Tomorrow, I have an appointment with Dr. Paul Hereoux, president of the Jules Verne Society. He has graciously given me permission to conduct research in the society's archives, which are inside the house where Verne lived and wrote until his death in 1905. Verne was an amazing man, you know — I had no idea. A true visionary. He established the genre of science fiction, of course, but he also anticipated flights to the moon, submarines that could circle the globe underwater, solar heating, moving escalators and walkways, three-dimensional holographic images — you name it, he was there first. He also foresaw asteroids and comets striking the Earth and causing wide devastation."

"Discover any new revelations about Captain Nemo and the *Nautilus*?"

"Nothing beyond what Verne wrote in *Twenty Thousand Leagues under the Sea* and *The Mysterious Island.*"

"That was the sequel, right? The one that told what happened to Nemo after the *Nautilus* was lost in a maelstrom off the Norwegian coast."

"Yes, *Twenty Thousand Leagues* came out in 1869 as a magazine serial. *The Mysterious Island* in 1875 revealed the history and biography of Nemo."

"From what I gathered from Dr. Egan's research on Verne, he seemed fascinated by how the author created Nemo and his submarine. Egan must have believed that Verne had more than a brilliant imagination working for him. I think Egan thought

Verne built the story around a real person."

"I'll know more in a couple of days," said Perlmutter. "But don't get your hopes up. Jules Verne's tales, however ingeniously clever, were fiction. Captain Nemo may have been one of the greatest protagonists in literature, but really, he was nothing more than the precursor of the mad scientist out to exact revenge for past wrongs. The noble genius gone wrong."

"Still," Pitt persisted, "for Verne to have created a technical marvel like the *Nautilus* from the keel up in his own mind seems incredible. Unless Jules Verne was the Leonardo da Vinci of his time, he must have had technical advice above and beyond what was generally thought available in 1869."

"From the real Captain Nemo?" asked Perlmutter cynically.

"Or some other engineering genius," Pitt answered seriously.

"You don't appreciate true genius," said Perlmutter. "I may glean new details from the archives, but I'm not betting my life's savings on the outcome."

"It's been many years since I read the books," said Pitt, "but Nemo was a man of mystery in *Twenty Thousand Leagues*. If I recall, it wasn't until near the end of *The Mysterious Island* that Verne offered an insight into Nemo."

"Chapter Sixteen," Perlmutter recited. "Nemo was born the son of a rajah in India. Prince Dakkar, as he was named, was an exceptionally gifted and intelligent child. Verne described him as growing up handsome, extremely wealthy and full of hatred for the British who had conquered his country. His lust for revenge affected his thinking as he grew older, especially after he led and fought in the Sepoy Rebellion in 1857. In revenge, British agents seized and murdered his father, mother, wife and two children.

"During the years he brooded over the loss of his family and country, he threw himself into the science of marine engineering. On a remote, uninhabited island in the Pacific, he used his wealth to build a shipyard, where he created the *Nautilus*. Verne wrote that Nemo harnessed electricity long before Tesla and Edison built their generators. The engines in the submarine powered the boat indefinitely without the need of refueling or regeneration."

"Makes me wonder if Verne didn't envision Dr. Egan's magnetohydrodynamic engines."

"After completing his undersea vessel," continued Perlmutter, "he brought on a loyal crew and vanished under the sea. Then in 1867 he took on three castaways who had fallen off an American Navy frigate that he had attacked. They recorded his secret existence and voyaged around the world with him underwater. The castaways — a professor, his servant and a Canadian fisherman — escaped when the *Nautilus* sailed into the maelstrom and Nemo disappeared. By the time he was sixty years old, his crew had died and he was interred in a coral cemetery beneath the sea. Alone with his beloved submarine, Nemo spent his final years in a cavern beneath a volcano on Lincoln Island. After aiding castaways on the island against pirates and helping them to leave and sail home, he died of natural causes. The volcano then erupted and Lincoln Island sank beneath the sea, burying Captain Nemo and his extraordinary *Nautilus* in the depths, where they are now enshrined in fictional history."

"But *was* it fiction?" Pitt mused. "Or based on nonfiction?"

"You'll never sell me that Nemo was anything more than a figment of Verne's imagination," said Perlmutter, in a quiet, authoritative voice.

Pitt said nothing for a few moments. He did not fool himself. He was chasing shadows. "If only I knew what Dr. Egan discovered about the Vikings and Captain Nemo," he said at last.

Perlmutter sighed patiently. "I fail to see a connection between two such totally different topics."

"Egan was a fanatic on both. I can't help but feel they somehow tied in with each other."

"I doubt that he uncovered any previously undiscovered facts on either. Certainly nothing that hasn't already been recorded."

"St. Julien, you're an old cynic."

"I'm a historian, and I do not chronicle or publish anything I can't document."

"Enjoy yourself in those dusty old archives," said Pitt humorously.

"Nothing stirs my blood more than finding a new angle on history in a forgotten log or letter. Except of course the taste of fine wine. Or a gourmet meal prepared by a great chef."

"Of course," Pitt said, smiling to himself as he pictured Perlmutter's great girth, which was a direct result of excessive indulgence in food and drink.

"I will call should I turn up anything of interest."

"Thank you." Pitt hung up the phone as Sally Morse called from the balcony above that dinner was ready. He shouted an acknowledgment but did not immediately leave the Pullman car and walk up the staircase.

Now that he was removed from any role in the operation to stop Curtis Merlin Zale, the murderous Viper organization and the Cerberus cartel, Pitt felt lost, without direction. It was not his nature to sit powerless on the outside looking in. He had run out of road — and he wished to high heaven that he had turned off earlier and turned down one he'd overlooked.

45

The Cerberus offices in Washington were housed in a large mansion that had been built for a wealthy senator from California in 1910. Set on ten acres on the fringe of Bethesda and surrounded by a high vine-covered brick wall, the mansion-turned-office-building did not contain spartan offices for the conglomerate's engineers, scientists or geologists. The four floors of lavish suites were filled with corporate attorneys, political analysts, high-level lobbyists and influential former senators and congressmen, all working to increase Zale's grip on the United States government.

At one o'clock in the morning, a van advertising an electrical contractor pulled up to the gate and was passed through. Security was tight. Two guards manned the house at the front gate while two more patrolled the grounds with attack dogs. The van eased to a stop in a parking slot near the front door. A large black man walked toward the entrance with a long box containing fluorescent light tubes. He signed in at the guard-reception desk and took an elevator to the fourth floor, where he stepped across a teak floor covered with expensive handwoven Persian rugs. There was no secretary in the foyer of the large office at the end of the hallway. She had left for home an hour earlier. He passed her empty desk and entered a spacious office whose door was open.

Curtis Merlin Zale was seated in a huge leather executive chair studying a geologist's seismic reports on a previously undiscovered oil and gas field in Idaho. He did not look up as the electrician entered. Instead of installing the light tubes, the electrician boldly sat down in a chair in front of the desk. Only then did Zale look up into the dark sinister eyes of Omo Kanai.

"Was your distrust validated?" asked Kanai.

Zale smiled smugly. "The unsuspecting fish took the bait."

"May I ask who?"

"Sally Morse of Yukon Oil. I began to doubt her dedication to the cause when she raised questions over our plan to ram the supertanker into the heart of San Francisco."

"Do you think she talked to authorities?"

"I'm certain of it. Her plane did not return to Alaska but flew to Washington."

"A loose cannon in the capital could be dangerous."

Zale shook his head. "She has no documentation. Only her word. Nothing can be proved. Little does she suspect that she did us a great service by turning renegade and defecting."

"If she testifies before Congress . . . ," said Kanai, without finishing his thought.

"If you handle your end, she'll have an accident before she can be interrogated."

"Has the government put her in a safe house?"

"Our sources inside the Justice Department say they have no knowledge of her whereabouts."

"Any idea where she can be found?"

Zale shrugged. "None at the moment. She must be hiding with private parties."

"Then she won't be easy to find," said Kanai.

"I'll locate her for you," said Zale confidently. "I have more than a hundred of our people looking for her. It's only a question of hours."

"When is she due to testify before the committee?"

"Not for another three days."

Kanai appeared satisfied.

"I assume all is in readiness," Zale said. "There can be no oversight, no unforeseen problems."

"I expect none. Your scheme is brilliant. The operation is planned down to the tiniest detail. I see no room for failure."

"Your Viper team is on board?"

"All except me. A helicopter is waiting to carry me to the tanker when it is a hundred miles out." Kanai glanced at his watch. "If I am to direct the final preparations, I must be leaving."

"The military cannot stop the tanker?" Zale asked hopefully.

"Those who try will be in for a rude awakening."

They stood and shook hands. "Good luck, Omo. Next time we meet, the U.S. government will have its strings pulled by new hands."

"And where will you be during the holocaust tomorrow?"

A sharp grin curled Zale's lips. "I will be testifying before Congresswoman Smith."

"Do you think she knows about your designs on domestic oil?"

"Sally Morse has no doubt revealed our agenda to her." Zale turned and stared out the window at the twinkling lights and the floodlit monuments of the capital. "But by this time tomorrow, it won't matter. Public outcry over foreign oil and gas will have surged like a tidal wave across the nation and all resistance against Cerberus will have been swept aside."

When Loren walked from her office in the Congressional Office Building into the hearing room, she was stunned as she stared at the table reserved for those subpoenaed to appear before her committee. There was no army of Cerberus corporate attorneys, no platoon of company directors or officials.

Curtis Merlin Zale sat alone behind the table.

No papers or notes were laid out on the surface before him. No briefcase on the floor. He simply relaxed casually in his chair, immaculately suited, and smiled at the members of Congress as they entered and sat down at the raised desks above the main floor of the hearing room. His eyes strayed to Loren as she sat down and laid a sheaf of papers on her desktop. She caught him staring at her, and she suddenly felt unclean. Despite his attractive looks and impeccable attire, she found him repulsive, like a venomous snake sunning itself on a rock.

She looked over to see if the other members of the committee were settled in their chairs and ready to begin the proceedings. She exchanged looks with Congressman Leonard Sturgis, who nodded politely, but his face appeared strained, as if he was leery of having to go through the motions of asking tough questions of Zale.

Loren said a few preliminary words to open the investigation and then thanked Zale for appearing. "You realize, of course, that you have the privilege of appearing with counsel," she advised him.

"Yes," he said in a calm voice, "but in the spirit of full cooperation and disclosure, I sit here before you ready to answer fully any and all questions."

Loren glanced up at the big clock on the far wall of the hearing chamber. It read 9:10 A.M. "The proceedings may run most of the day," she informed Zale.

"I am at your disposal for as long as it takes," said Zale in a quiet voice.

Loren turned to Congresswoman Lorraine Hope of Texas. "Congresswoman Hope, would you do the honor of beginning the investigation?"

Lorraine Hope, a heavy black woman from the Galveston shore of Texas, nodded and launched the proceedings. Loren knew that Hope's name was not on the list of those bought off by Cerberus, but she couldn't be positive of Hope's views on the company. Up to this point her probes had been moderate and seemingly independent. But that was soon to change now that she was confronted by Zale himself.

"Mr. Zale, is it your position that the United States would be far better off if we became self-sufficient in domestic oil and did not require the importing of foreign crude from the Middle East and Latin America?"

Oh God, thought Loren, she's playing right into his hands.

"Our reliance on foreign oil," began Zale, "is draining the economy. For the past fifty years, we have been at the mercy of OPEC, who has played with market prices like a yo-yo. Their insidious ploy was to raise the price of a barrel of oil by two dollars, then drop it one. Raise it two and drop it one, keeping the price edging slowly up and up until we are now looking at nearly sixty dollars a barrel for every barrel of imported oil. Prices at the gas pump are outrageous. Trucking companies and drivers who own their trucks are going under. Prices for airline tickets have skyrocketed because of higher aviation jet fuel prices. The only way to stop this madness that will eventually break the country is to develop our own fields and not have to rely on outside oil."

"Are there enough reserves underground to support American needs, and if so, for how long?" asked Lorraine Hope.

"Indeed," Zale said boldly. "There is more than enough oil in the continental United States and Canada, plus offshore oil reserves, to make North America completely self-sufficient for the next fifty years. I can also announce at this time that the enormous shale oil deposits throughout Colorado, Wyoming and Montana will be ready to process into crude oil within the next year. This alone will keep us from ever again becoming reliant on foreign oil. Then perhaps, by the middle of the century, technology will perfect alternative sources of power."

"Are you saying that there should be no environmental considerations in opening new fields?" asked Loren.

"The environmental protests are vastly overstated," retorted Zale. "Few if any animals have died because of oil-drilling rigs or pipelines. Migratory trails can be altered by wildlife-management experts. There is no contamination on the ground or in the sky due to drilling. And most important, by keeping foreign oil off our shores, we can eliminate the kind of tragedies that we've seen with the *Exxon Valdez* and the other oil spills the nation has suffered in the last few years. Without the need for tankers to bring oil into the United States, that threat is eliminated."

"You make a strong case," said Congressman Sturgis. "I, for one, lean toward your scenario. I have always been against blackmail by the foreign oil cartels. If American oil companies can supply the country's needs without leaving our shores, I'm in favor of it."

"What about the companies bringing up oil from around the world and shipping it into our ports and refineries?" demanded Loren. "If their flow to the United States is cut off, they'll most likely go broke."

Zale didn't look the least bit disconcerted. "They'll simply have to sell their output to other countries."

The questions were given out and the answers returned. Zale, Loren could see, was not about to be daunted. He well knew that he controlled three of the five members on the Unfair Practices Committee, and he felt in total control. Except for occasionally sneaking a look at his wristwatch, he was completely unfazed.

Loren lifted her eyes to the clock on the far wall just as often. She found it almost impossible to keep her mind from wandering to the disaster approaching San Francisco, and wondered if the Coast Guard and Special Forces were going to stop it in time. It was especially discouraging knowing she could not confront Zale with her knowledge and accuse him in advance of attempted mass murder.

46

The sea's surface rolled and marched in endless formation. There were no whitecaps, and the troughs curled like furrows in a plowed field. There was a strange silence about the sea. A light mist floated over the waves, muting any sound of moving water, barely hiding the stars dipping over the western horizon. San Francisco's lights glowed in a creamy cloud against the dark sky to the east.

It was an hour before dawn when the Coast Guard cutter *Huron*, running at full speed, intercepted the gargantuan super-tanker *Pacific Trojan* twenty miles west of the Golden Gate. Two Coast Guard helicopters circled the big ship, accompanied by the latest addition to Marine Air, a Goshawk copter that carried Captain Garnet and his thirty-man Marine Recon Team. A fast, armored Army patrol boat followed at the stern of the tanker. Onboard were Commander Miles Jacobs and his Navy SEAL team, prepared to shoot grappling hooks attached to ladders onto the vast deck of the tanker.

Admiral Amos Dover, who was in charge of the boarding operation, stood with binoculars pressed against his eyes. "She's a big one. As long as five football fields end to end, and then some."

"An Ultra, Ultra Large Crude Carrier," observed the cutter's commander, Captain Buck Compton. Twenty-three years in the Coast Guard, Compton had served around the world, commanding cutters in daring rescues in stormy seas, and stopping ships whose cargoes were illegal immigrants or drugs. "You'd never know that eighty percent of her mass is below her waterline. According to her specs, she can carry over six hundred thousand tons of oil."

"I wouldn't want to be within ten miles if her cargo of oil explodes."

"Better here than in San Francisco Bay."

"Her captain is making no attempt at skulking into the bay," Dover said quietly. "He's got every light from bow to stern turned on. It's almost as if he wants to announce his presence." He lowered his glasses. "Strange that he would advertise his presence so conspicuously."

Still studying the tanker, Compton could clearly see the ship's cook empty a pail of garbage into the sea, as gulls swooped down into the water rushing past the gigantic hull. "I don't like the looks of it," he said flatly.

Dover turned to his radioman, who was standing nearby with a portable radio plugged into the bridge speaker. "Contact our helicopters and ask if they see any signs of hostile activity."

The radioman complied and waited until a voice replied over the speaker. "Admiral Dover, Lieutenant Hooker in Chase One. Except for a crewman who appears to be checking pipe fittings and the ship's cook, the decks appear empty."

"The wheelhouse?" Dover inquired.

The message was relayed and the answer came back quickly. "The bridge wing is vacant. All I can make out through the bridge windshield is two officers on watch."

"Pass on your observations to Captain Garnet and Commander Jacobs and tell them to stand by while I hail the tanker."

"She carries a crew of fifteen officers and thirty crewmen," said Compton, studying the computer data on the tanker. "British registry. That means all hell will break loose if we board a ship flying a foreign flag without proper permission."

"That's Washington's problem. We're operating under strict orders to board her."

"Just so long as you and I are off the hook."

"You do the honors, Buck."

Compton took the transmitter from the radioman. "To the Captain of *Pacific Trojan*. This is the captain of Coast Guard Cutter *Huron*. Where are you bound?"

The supertanker's captain, who was in the wheelhouse as his ship neared the United States coast, answered almost immediately. "This is Captain Don Walsh. We are bound for the offshore oil-pumping facilities at Point San Pedro."

"The answer I would expect," muttered Dover. "Tell him to heave to."

Compton nodded. "Captain Walsh, this is Captain Compton. Please heave to for a boarding inspection."

"Is this necessary?" asked Walsh. "It will cost the company time and money to stop and it'll throw us off our schedule."

"Please comply," answered Compton, in an authoritative tone.

"She's riding low in the water," commented Dover. "Her tanks must be filled to the brim."

There was no answer of compliance from Captain Walsh, but after a minute Dover and Compton could see that the wake caused by the tanker's churning screws was falling off. She still held the bone of foam on her bow, but both men knew it would take nearly a mile to bring her huge mass to a complete stop.

"Order Commander Jacobs and Captain Garnet to board the ship with their assault teams."

Compton looked at Dover. "You don't wish to send over a boarding crew from the *Huron*?"

"They're better equipped to deal with resistance than our boys," answered Dover.

Compton gave the order and they watched as the pilot dipped the Marine helicopter around the stern of the supertanker, its blades beating above the superstructure until it was clear of the radar mast and funnel. Then it hovered for a minute while Garnet studied the deck for any indication of hostility. Satisfied that the huge upper deck was clear, he motioned for the pilot to descend to an open deck area forward of the superstructure.

Below in the water, Jacob's patrol boat closed along the hull just aft of the stern. Grappling hooks were shot out of a pneumatic gun and gripped their hooks onto the bulwarks. The SEALs quickly scaled the rope ladders and spread across the deck, moving toward the main superstructure, arms at the ready. Except for one startled crewman, there was no indication of other life.

Several men under Jacobs's command found bicycles used by the crew and mounted them to patrol the enormous deck and oil tank tunnels in search of explosives. Garnet split his men, sending one team down to the engine room and leading the other through the stern superstructure, rounding up the crew and making their way to the wheelhouse. As he stepped onto the bridge, Captain Walsh stormed up to him, indignation written across his face.

"What is the meaning of this?" he demanded. "You people aren't Coast Guard."

Garnet ignored him and spoke over his portable radio. "Admiral Dover. This is Team One. The crew quarters and wheelhouse are secure."

"Commander Jacobs?" inquired Dover. "Report on Team Two."

"We still have a lot of space to cover," replied Jacobs. "But no sign of explosives in the tank areas we've already covered."

Dover turned to Compton. "I'm going over."

A boat was lowered and carried Admiral Dover over to the tanker where Garnet's men had dropped the pilot's boarding ladder. He climbed to the deck and ascended five sets of stairs to the bridge, where he found an angry Walsh.

The captain of the *Pacific Trojan* seemed surprised at finding a Coast Guard admiral boarding his ship. "I demand to know what in Hades is going on," Walsh snapped at Dover.

"This ship has been reported to be carrying explosives," said Dover. "We are making a routine inspection to verify."

"Explosives!" burst Walsh. "Are you crazy? This is an oil tanker. No one in his right mind would bring explosives on board."

"That's what we intend to find out," Dover replied calmly.

"Your report is ridiculous. Where did it come from?"

"From a high-level official at Cerberus Oil."

"What has Cerberus Oil got to do with anything? *Pacific Trojan* belongs to the Berwick Shipping Company of Great Britain. We transport oil and chemical products around the world for any number of foreign clients."

"Whose oil are you carrying?" asked Dover.

"This voyage, it belongs to Zandak Oil of Indonesia."

"How long has Berwick been transporting oil for Zandak?"

"More than twenty years."

"Team One reporting," came Garnet's voice over Dover's radio.

"This is Admiral Dover. I'm listening."

"We can find no sign of explosive devices in the engine room or stern superstructure."

"Okay," said Dover. "Give Commander

Jacobs a hand. He has far more territory to cover."

An hour passed, while Captain Walsh fumed and paced the bridge like a man in the depths of frustration, knowing that each passing minute the ship was delayed cost his company many thousands of dollars.

Captain Compton came over from the *Huron* and ascended to the tanker's bridge. "I'm afflicted with impatience," he said, smiling. "I hope you don't mind my dropping in to see how it's going."

"Not well," said Dover in exasperation. "So far there is no sign of explosives or detonation devices. The captain and crew are not acting like men on a suicide mission. I'm beginning to fear we've been conned."

Twenty minutes later, Jacobs reported in. "She's clean, Admiral. We found no trace of explosive material."

"There!" roared Walsh. "I told you so. You people are crazy."

Dover made no attempt to soothe the irate captain of the tanker. He was beginning to harbor large doubts about Sally Morse's truthfulness. But he was also vastly relieved to find that the ship had no intention of blowing up half of San Francisco.

"Sorry for the intrusion and the delay," he told Walsh. "We'll be on our way."

"You can bet there will be a protest launched by my government against yours," said Walsh angrily. "You had no legal cause to stop and board my vessel."

"My apologies for any inconvenience," Dover said, with honest regret. He turned to Compton as they exited the bridge, and spoke in a low tone. "I'd hate to see the looks on everyone's faces in Washington when I notify them that they've been hoaxed."

47

Pitt was seated at his desk, clearing it of NUMA business before flying to Elmore Egan's farm in New York, when Admiral Sandecker abruptly walked past his secretary, Zerri Pochinsky, and entered his office. Pitt looked up in surprise. When the admiral wanted to discuss NUMA concerns, he nearly always insisted that his special projects director come up and meet in *his* office. It was obvious that Sandecker was deeply disturbed. His lips were taut beneath the red Vandyke beard and the authoritative blue eyes reflected uneasiness.

Before Pitt could say a word, Sandecker snarled, "Zale threw us a red herring."

"I'm sorry?" replied Pitt, confused.

"The *Pacific Trojan* came up empty. Admiral Dover just reported in. There were no explosives on board. The ship was clean, the captain and crew are completely innocent of any plot to destroy the San Francisco water-front. Either we were duped or Sally Morse was hallucinating."

"I trust Sally. I prefer to think we were duped."

"For what reason?"

Pitt looked thoughtful before answering. "Zale has the wits of a jackal. The chances are he fed Sally a fake story, knowing she was about to defect and would alert the government. He used the old magician's method of waving one hand to distract the audience while using the other to perform the trick." He looked directly at Sandecker. "I think he has another disaster up his sleeve."

"All right," said Sandecker. "I'll go along with your thinking, but where does it lead?"

"I'm counting on Hiram Yaeger and Max to come up with the answer," Pitt said, as he came to his feet, hurried around the desk and headed out the door.

Yaeger was studying pages of overseas bank accounts, whose computerized records Max had penetrated while tracking down Cerberus's illegal payoffs and bribes to almost a thousand members of the United States government. The total sum was nothing less than astronomical.

"You're sure about these totals, Max?" asked Yaeger, stunned by the amount.

"They seem a trifle bizarre."

Max's holographic figure shrugged. "I did the best I could. There are probably at least fifty or more I haven't tracked down as yet. Why do you ask? Do the amounts surprise you?"

"Maybe twenty-one billion, two hundred million dollars doesn't seem like big money to you, but to a poverty-stricken computer tech it's big bucks."

"I'd hardly call you poverty-stricken."

Pitt, with Sandecker two steps behind, rushed into Yaeger's office like someone being chased by a water buffalo. "Hiram, the admiral and I need you and Max to launch a new probe as quickly as possible."

Yaeger looked up and saw the look of gravity in both Pitt and Sandecker's faces. "Max and I are at your disposal. What do you wish me to search for?"

"Check all maritime ship arrivals at major U.S. ports, beginning now and for the next ten hours, with emphasis on super oil tankers."

Yaeger nodded and turned to Max. "You hear that?"

Max smiled bewitchingly. "I'll be back to you in sixty seconds."

"That fast?" asked Sandecker, always in awe of Max's potential.

"She hasn't failed me yet," Yaeger said, with a knowing grin.

As Max slowly vaporized and vanished, Yaeger handed Sandecker the results of her latest probe. "There it is. Not quite complete yet. But with over ninety-five percent of the findings in, here are names, offshore bank accounts and the amounts of deposit of those who were paid off by Curtis Merlin Zale and his Cerberus cronies."

Sandecker studied the figures and looked up in astonishment. "No wonder Zale has so many high officials in his pocket. The sums he paid out would cover NUMA's entire budget for a hundred years."

"Did the Coast Guard and Special Forces teams stop the oil tanker from entering San Francisco Bay?" Yaeger asked, uninformed of the events.

"Zale made fools out of us," said Sandecker curtly. "The ship was transporting a full load of oil all right, but it was empty of explosives. None could be found on board, and the ship continued on its voyage to its scheduled mooring terminal south of the Bay Area."

Yaeger looked at Pitt. "You think it was a decoy?"

"I believe that was Zale's plan. What bothered me from the beginning was the extraordinary draft of a fully loaded tanker the size of the *Pacific Trojan*. The bottom of the bay surrounding the city of San Francisco is too shallow for a ship that size to cross. It would have grounded long before it could have come ashore."

"So you're considering the prospect that Zale is sending another tanker into a different port city," Yaeger suggested.

They went silent as Max's feminine form materialized on her little stage. "I believe I have what you gentlemen were after."

"Did you check all supertankers entering our domestic ports?" asked Sandecker anxiously.

"There are several Very Large Crude Carriers arriving at several ports, but of the Ultra, Ultra Large Crude Carriers, there is one bound for Louisiana from Saudi Arabia, but her mooring terminal is a hundred miles from a major city. Another is headed for the offshore pumping station off New Jersey, but she isn't due until tomorrow, and finally, a UULCC bound for Long Beach, California, is still two days out to sea. That's the lot. It looks like your friend Mr. Zale has lost any opportunity of sneaking in another tanker."

"So the whole exercise was a waste," murmured Sandecker. "Zale never intended to devastate San Francisco or any other densely inhabited port city."

"Looks that way," said Pitt, dejectedly. "But if that's the case, why the subterfuge? What did he have to gain?"

"Maybe he was just testing us?"

"That's not his modus operandi."

"There are no mistakes?" Yaeger asked Max.

"I got inside the records of every port authority in the lower forty-eight states."

Sandecker made as if to leave the office and shook his head wearily. "I guess that ends that."

"Did you gentlemen ever consider a different type of vessel?" asked Max.

Pitt looked at her with interest. "What do you have in mind?"

"I was thinking on my own. An LNG ship could do far more damage than a UULCC."

The revelation struck Pitt like a hammer blow. "A Liquefied Natural Gas tanker!"

"One blew up in Japan back in the forties with nearly the explosive power of the Hiroshima atomic bomb," Max enlightened them. "The death toll ran more than a thousand."

"Did you check to see if any are bound for stateside ports?" asked Yaeger.

Max acted as if she were pouting. "You don't seem to have a high regard for my intuitive talents. Of course, I checked all incoming LNG ships."

"*Well?*" Yaeger prompted.

"The *Mongol Invader*, bound from Kuwait, is scheduled to dock in New York at ten-thirty."

"A.M. or P.M.?" asked Sandecker.

"A.M."

The admiral checked his watch. "We can eliminate her. She would have docked twenty minutes ago."

"Not so," said Max. "She was delayed by problems with her generators and had to heave to until repairs were made. She's running five hours late."

Pitt and Sandecker exchanged stricken expressions.

"That has to be Zale's plan," said Pitt. "Feint with the *Pacific Trojan* on the West Coast and strike New York from the east with the *Mongol Invader*."

Sandecker pounded his fist against a table. "He caught us napping like diapered infants."

"There's not much time to stop her before she reaches the lower bay and heads into the Narrows," Max remarked.

"What does the *Mongol Invader* look like?" Yaeger asked Max.

She revealed an image of the ship on the screen of a large monitor. The vessel looked like something out of a science-fiction comic book. The hull had the same lines as an oil tanker, with its engines and superstructure mounted at the stern, but there the resemblance ended. Instead of an expansive flat main deck, there were eight identical mammoth, freestanding, spherical tanks rising out of the hull.

Max began to tick off the ship's specifications. "The largest LNG tanker yet built. Overall length is one thousand eight hundred sixty feet with a three-hundred-sixty-foot beam. She carries a crew of only eight officers and fifteen crewmen. The low number is due to the fact that she is almost entirely automated. Her cross-compound, double-reduction gear turbine engines put out sixty thousand shaft horsepower to each of her twin screws. Her country of registry is Argentina."

Yaeger asked, "Who owns her?"

"I traced her pedigree through a facade of paper companies that led to the doorstep of the Cerberus empire."

Yaeger grinned. "Now, why did I think that's who you'd find?"

"LNG tankers have a much shallower draft than oil tankers due to the difference in weight between gas and oil," said Sandecker. "She could very well make it up the Hudson River before turning and running toward lower Manhattan, then slip between the docks without grounding until she struck the shore."

"Sally Morse said the *Pacific Trojan* was going to ram the city at the World Trade Terminal," said Yaeger. "Can we assume that Zale made a slip and meant the World Trade Center in New York?"

"Exactly where I would strike Manhattan's shore if I wanted to do the most damage," Sandecker said in agreement.

"What gas volume is she carrying?" Pitt asked Max.

"Seven million five hundred seventy thousand three hundred thirty-three cubic feet."

"Very bad," Yaeger muttered.

"And the gas cargo?"

"Propane."

"Even worse," Yaeger moaned.

"The fireball could be horrendous," explained Max. "A railroad tank car exploded in Kingman, Arizona, in the seventies. It held eight thousand gallons of propane, and the fireball extended almost an eighth of a mile. One gallon of propane will produce two hundred seventy of gas. Or, figuring one hundred sixty-two cubic feet of propane vapor per cubic foot of liquid, then multiply it by seven and a half million, you could conceivably produce a fireball almost two miles wide."

"What about structural damage?" Sandecker queried Max.

"Heavy," answered Max. "Major buildings such as the World Trade Center skyscrapers would still stand, but their interiors would be gutted. Most of the other buildings close to the center of the blast would be destroyed. I don't even want to speculate on the loss of life."

"All because that crazy Zale and the Cerberus cartel want to inflame the American public against foreign oil," Pitt muttered angrily.

"We've got to stop that ship!" said Sandecker in a cold tone. "There can be no mistakes this time."

Pitt said slowly, "This ship's crew won't allow it to be boarded like the *Pacific Trojan*. I'll bet a month's pay Omo Kanai has his Viper group operating the ship. Zale would never trust such an undertaking to amateurs."

Sandecker checked his watch again. "We have four and a half hours before she enters the Hudson River off Manhattan. I'll report what we've discovered to Admiral Dover and have him alert his Coast Guard units in the New York area to launch an intercept."

"You should also call the New York State Antiterrorist Division," suggested Max. "They train and run practice drills for just such a possibility."

"Thank you, Max," said Sandecker, warming to Yaeger's computer creation. Previously, he'd always thought Max was a strain on NUMA's budget, but he had come to realize that she was worth every nickel, and much more. "I'll see to it."

"I'll round up Al. Using NUMA's new tilt-wing *Aquarius* jet, we should be on the NUMA dock in New York inside an hour."

"What do you plan to do after you get

there?" inquired a curious Max.

Pitt looked at her as if she were asking Dan Marino if he knew how to throw a football. "Stop the *Mongol Invader* from destroying half of Manhattan. What else?"

48

Anyone gazing at a Liquefied Natural Gas tanker would have done so with grave skepticism, finding it hard to believe such a grotesque-looking ship could ever cross the oceans. The *Mongol Invader*, with her eight bulbous tanks rising from the upper half of her hull, was the largest of the LNG tankers ever built and did not look as if she belonged on the water, as she burrowed through choppy seas on a course dead set for the entrance to New York Harbor. Strictly utilitarian and painted an adobe brown, she had to be one of the ugliest ships afloat.

Her architects had designed her to envelop, support and protect her eight immense, insulated-aluminum spherical cargo tanks that right now were full of liquid propane that should have been refrigerated to a temperature of about minus 265 degrees Fahrenheit. But on this trip from Kuwait the temperature had been gradually raised until it was only twenty degrees below the danger level.

A floating bomb with the potential to devastate the lower half of Manhattan Island, the *Mongol Invader* was driven through the unruly waves at 25 knots by her great twin bronze screws, her forward underwater prow shrugging aside the water with deceptive ease. Flights of gulls came and circled but, sensing an ominous aura about her, they remained strangely silent and soon winged away.

Unlike on the *Pacific Trojan*, no crew could be seen exploring the *Mongol Invader*'s tanks or walking the long runway across their domed roofs. They remained unseen at their action stations. There were only fifteen of them scattered throughout the ship. Four operated the controls in the wheelhouse. Five ran the engine room while the remaining six were armed with portable missiles that could sink the largest Coast Guard cutter or bring down any aircraft that might attack. The Vipers were fully aware of the cost of indifferent vigilance. They were secure in the knowledge that they could easily repel any attempt to board by professional Special Forces, to whose military elements most of them had once belonged. They were supremely confident they could prevent any attempt to stop them before the ship entered the outer reaches of the city — and once they passed under the Verrazano Narrows Bridge it was even money whether the commander-in-charge of the intercept operation would risk igniting a massive fireball.

Leaning over the railing of the starboard bridge wing, Omo Kanai stared at the menacing dark clouds that drifted in an overcast sky. He was certain that any force arrayed against him would find it unlikely that fifteen men who were not fanatical terrorists, but simply well-paid mercenaries, would even think of committing suicide for their employer. This was not a James Bond movie. He smiled to himself. Only those on board the ship knew about the submarine attached to the hull one hundred feet forward of the rudder and twin screws. Once the ship was turned toward the Manhattan shoreline, Kanai and his Viper crew would board the hidden submarine and escape into deep water to avoid the ensuing fireball.

He walked back onto the bridge, crossed his arms and ran his eye along the course he'd laid out on the chart, following the red line that traveled past Rockaway Point, then Norton Point at Seagate, before moving under the Verrazano Bridge that spanned Brooklyn and Staten Island. From there the line ran up the center of the Upper Bay and beyond the Statue of Liberty and Ellis Island. Once past Battery Park, the red line made a sharp right turn into the shore and ended at the base of the twin World Trade Center towers.

He flexed his muscular shoulders, his body attuned to the speeding mass of the ship below his feet. The *Mongol Invader* would not be stopped, could not be stopped before reaching her destiny. He would be remembered a thousand years from now for achieving the worst man-made disaster ever attempted against the United States.

Kanai looked up through the bridge windshield and observed the cars moving over the bridge above the water turned a gray-green by the dark clouds. The colors on the cars' bodies flickered like insects as they crossed. He noted on the instrument console that brisk twenty-knot winds were blowing from the southeast. All the better to expand the killing distance of the fireball, he thought.

The thought of thousands of incinerated victims never entered his mind. Kanai was incapable of emotion. He was immune to death and had no hesitancy about facing it when his turn came.

His second in command, Harmon Kerry, a tough-looking customer with tattoos running up and down his arms, stepped onto the bridge from below. He picked up a pair of binoculars and peered at a cargo ship passing on their port side and heading out to sea. "It won't be long now," he said, with more than a hint of pleasure. "The Americans are in for a nasty surprise."

"No surprise," Kanai muttered, "not if they realize by now that the *Pacific Trojan* was a decoy."

"Do you think they're wise to the operation?"

"Zale has yet to come up with a flawless plan," Kanai said flatly. "Unexpected and unforeseen circumstances kept them from total success. What we have achieved this far, we have done well. But someone, perhaps many, in the United States government has put two and two together. The five hours we were delayed by generator problems cost us dearly. Instead of arriving unexpectedly at the same time as the *Pacific Trojan* was boarded, and under cover of darkness just before dawn, we may have to face everything they can throw at us. And you can bet they'll be better prepared this time."

"I look forward to seeing a smoldering and melted Statue of Liberty," said Kerry, with a diabolical grin.

The helmsman who stood at the control console reported, "Forty minutes until we reach the bridge."

Kanai stood and stared at the slowly approaching span. "If they don't try and stop us very soon, they'll never have another chance."

Admiral Dover had flown in aboard a Navy fighter jet from the Alameda Naval Air Station on the West Coast within fifteen minutes of Sandecker's dire alert. His pilot had requested an emergency landing between commercial jetliners at JFK International Airport. From there, an NYPD helicopter flew him over to the Sandy Hook Coast Guard Station, where two fast 110-foot patrol cutters were waiting for his arrival to intercept the *Mongol Invader*.

He stepped into the conference room of the station, his hands clenching and unclenching into fists from anxiety and desperation. He forced himself to think calmly. He could not allow himself to be overwhelmed by Zale's trick, or blame his powers of deduction for missing something that in hindsight seemed so obvious. Sandecker might still be wrong. There was nothing solid on which to hang another intercept operation, only conjecture, yet he was determined to see it through. If the *Mongol Invader* turned out to be another false alarm, so be it. They would keep searching until they got the right ship.

Dover nodded silent greetings to the ten men and two women clustered in the room as he walked to the head of the conference table. He wasted no time on niceties. "Have the police aerial patrols flown over the ship?"

A police captain who stood along one wall nodded. "We have a copter on station as we speak. He reports that the tanker is running at full speed toward the harbor."

Dover sighed with relief, but only slightly. If this was indeed the ship that was to devastate Lower Manhattan, it had to be stopped. "Gentlemen, you've all been briefed over the phone and fax by Admiral Sandecker in Washington and know what to expect. If we can't turn it away, it must be sunk."

A Coast Guard commander spoke off to Dover's side. "Sir, if we fire into the tanks, we could very well turn her into one immense explosion. Conceivably, the entire flotilla of intercepting boats, as well as the pilots flying the police patrol helicopters, could be caught in the fireball."

"Better a thousand than a million," Dover replied curtly. "But under no circumstances are you to fire forward of the stern superstructure. If the crew refuses orders to heave to, then I will have no choice but to call in U.S. Navy fighters to destroy the ship with air-to-surface missiles. In that event, everyone will be warned in ample time to put as much distance as possible between their vessels and the *Mongol Invader* before combustion occurs."

"What are our chances of boarding her, overpowering the crew and cutting off any detonation devices?" asked one of the police.

"Not good if she won't stop, and continues at full speed inside the harbor. Unfortunately, the military force we had in San Francisco was ordered to stand down and return to their respective stations when we found we had the wrong ship. We haven't had time to reassemble them again or fly in new teams in time. I realize New York's Antiterrorist Response Teams are trained for just such emergencies, but I don't want to commit them until we're certain the crew will put up no resistance." He paused to sweep the faces of the men and women in the conference room. "If you don't already know, the maximum flame temperature in the air of propane is three thousand six hundred degrees Fahrenheit."

One of two New York Harbor fireboat captains present raised his hand. "Admiral, I might add that should the tanker cargo be exposed to fire, the resulting vapor explosion of seven million cubic feet of propane could produce a fireball nearly two miles in diameter."

"All the more reason for us to stop that tanker before she comes anywhere close to the city," Dover answered tersely. "Any more questions?" There was no response.

"Then I suggest we launch the operation. Time is running out."

Dover left the briefing and went directly to the dock and walked up the gangway to the Coast Guard cutter *William Shea*. A deep sense of foreboding fell over him. If the *Mongol Invader* refused to be boarded and the Navy fighters failed to send her to the bottom short of her goal, time was far too short to evacuate Manhattan. Unfortunately, at this time of day the streets and buildings would be filled with office workers. The damage and loss of life would be horrendous if the LNG tanker were allowed to blow up.

The only other thought that briefly crossed his mind was Sandecker's quick mention that Dirk Pitt and Al Giordino would be involved with the intercept after all. But Dover had seen no sign of them. He wondered what had delayed them from attending the briefing, not that they might have made a difference. Dover doubted that they would have proved critical to the operation.

The sun was trying to probe through the clouds as the *William Shea* and her sister cutter, *Timothy Firme*, cast off and sailed toward their confrontation with the *Mongol Invader* and her deadly cargo of propane gas.

49

"It doesn't look like any submarine I've ever seen," Giordino remarked, staring at a sleek vessel that looked more like a luxury yacht than an undersea boat.

Pitt stood on the dock at Sheepshead Bay south of Brooklyn, admiring the eighty-five-foot craft whose exterior styling was that of an elegant powerboat. Giordino was right; above the waterline she looked like most any other expensive yacht. The only noticeable differences were what could be seen underwater. The large, rounded viewing ports in the forward sides of her hull were similar but smaller to those mounted in the hull of the *Golden Marlin*.

Able to sleep eleven passengers and crew in lavish comfort, the *Coral Wanderer* was the largest model the Meridian Shipyard of Massachusetts built of the Ocean Diver series. Displacing 400 tons, it was designed to operate at a depth of 1,200 feet with a range of 200 nautical miles.

Captain Jimmy Flett walked down the stairs from the deck to the dock and approached Pitt with an outstretched hand. He was short and burly, with a face turned ruddy from long years of a love affair with scotch whiskey, but his blue eyes had somehow managed to remain clear and bright. The skin on his arms and hands was not deeply tanned as one might expect on a man who had sailed on many voyages across warm, sun-splashed seas. Flett had spent most of his life on ships in the North Sea and had the tough, hardy look of a fisherman who returned home with a catch regardless of stormy seas. He had seen more than his share of hard blows and survived them all.

He squeezed Pitt's hand to a pulp. "Dirk, how long has it been since we trod a deck and drank a scotch together?"

"On the *Arvor III* back in 'eighty-eight."

"The search for the *Bonhomme Richard*," said Flett, in a voice surprisingly soft. "As I recall, we didn't find it."

"No, but we *did* stumble onto a Russian spy trawler that had gone down in a storm."

"I remember. The British Navy ordered us to forget we'd ever found her. I always thought they were diving on her hours after we gave them the position."

Pitt turned to Giordino. "Al, may I present Jimmy Flett. A good friend from times past."

"Glad to meet you," said Giordino. "Dirk has often spoken of you."

"Nothing good, I hope." Jimmy laughed, as he crushed Giordino's hand and got crushed in return.

"So you've gone soft and become a skipper of luxury boats," said Pitt warmly, nodding at the underwater yacht.

"I'm a seaman who prefers the surface. Nothing under the water has any interest for me."

"Then why do it?"

"The pay is good and the job easy. I'm getting old and can't fight the elements the way I used to."

"Did you clear it with your bosses for us to use it?" asked Pitt.

"They're not keen on the idea. She's still undergoing trials and is not certified yet. As soon as she passes all the regulations, I'm scheduled to sail her across the sea to Monte Carlo, where her new owners intend to put her out for charter to wealthy Europeans."

"This is an extremely critical situation."

Flett stared into Pitt's green eyes. "What do you want with her? All you said over the phone was that it was a NUMA charter."

"We intend to use her as a torpedo boat."

Flett stared at Pitt as though his gray matter were oozing from one ear. "I see," he murmured softly, "a torpedo boat. And what ship do you plan on sending to the bottom?"

"A Liquid Natural Gas tanker."

Now Flett could imagine gray matter flowing from Pitt's other ear as well. "And if I refuse your request?"

"Then you will carry the blame for more than five hundred thousand lost lives."

Flett instantly read the situation. "This tanker — are terrorists planning to blow her up?"

"Not terrorists in the strict sense of the word. But a team of criminals who intend to run the ship aground near the World Trade Center towers before igniting the combustible gas."

There was no hesitation, no more questions, no protests. Flett said simply, "Since the *Wanderer* doesn't carry torpedo tubes, what have you got in mind?"

"Did you ever hear of the Confederate submarine *Hunley*?"

"I have."

"We're taking a page from her history," Pitt said with a self-assured smile, as Giordino began unloading a van parked on the dock.

Twenty minutes later, the three men had

mounted a long pipe that acted as a spar and protruded thirty feet in front of the boat's bow. Two more pipes were secured along the deck beneath the raised cabin. Without wasting another minute, they boarded, while Flett fired up the big supercharged diesel turbine engines. Busily occupied on the bow, Giordino attached magnetic explosive canisters to the ends of the two extra spars. The one that was already mounted had a hundred-pound plastic underwater charge bound on the end to a detonator.

Flett took the helm as Pitt and Giordino cast off the bow and stern lines. The old captain stood at a console. Several levers protruding from its face controlled the surface and dive wings and directional thrusters, along with the throttle speed.

Under three-quarter throttles, the *Coral Wanderer* soon shot across Sheepshead Bay into the open water and toward the Verrazano Bridge. The Coast Guard cutters and a fleet of smaller patrol boats had already spread out across the water ahead of the *Wanderer*'s bow. Overhead they observed two Coast Guard and two New York Police helicopters circling like vultures above a huge repulsive-looking ship painted a dirty buff color.

Flett shoved the twin throttle levers to their stops, lifting the bow clear of the water. He hugged the north shoreline in the dash across the bay, rounding Norton Point at Seagate, and cut a course that would send the *Wanderer* on an angle toward the LNG's midships.

"What's her top speed?" Pitt asked Flett.

"Forty-five knots on the surface. Twenty-five beneath."

"We'll need every knot you can coax out of her once we submerge. The top speed of the *Mongol Invader* is twenty-five knots, too."

"Is that her name?" asked Flett, as he gazed at the tight colossal tanks bulging on the big ship. "*Mongol Invader?*"

"Somehow it fits her," Pitt replied caustically.

"We should come alongside before she passes under the bridge."

"Once she gets into the Narrows, it'll be too difficult to blast her from the air without taking out half of Brooklyn and Staten Island."

"Your *Hunley* plan better work if the Coast Guard and New York's finest fail."

Pitt pointed at the armada through the windshield. "The posse is closing in."

On board the *William Shea*, Admiral Dover opened contact with the LNG tanker *Mongol Invader*. "This is the United States Coast Guard. Please heave to immediately and prepare for boarding."

The tension on the bridge of the cutter was deepened by the absence of conversation. Dover hailed again, and a third time, but there was no reply. The *Invader* remained headed into New York Harbor without any indication of decreasing speed. The crew and captain on the bridge were all watching the admiral now, waiting for his orders to attack.

Then abruptly a calm steady voice settled over the quiet bridge. "Coast Guard, this is the master of the *Mongol Invader*. I have no intention of bringing this ship to a stop. You will be advised that any attempt to damage my vessel will bring dire consequences."

The uncertainty and suspense were suddenly swept away. There was no doubt now. The horror was real. Dover could have engaged the LNG's master in talk, but time was not on his side. There was a grave disadvantage to any stalling tactics. He gave the order for the helicopters to land their antiterrorist teams on the open deck forward of the tanks. At the same time, he directed the cutters to come alongside with their guns manned.

He gazed through binoculars at the bridge of the ungodly-looking ship surging toward the Narrows bridge, wondering what her crazy commander was thinking. He had to be crazy. No sane man would attempt to devastate a city and a million people purely for monetary profit. These were no terrorists fanatical to a cause or religion.

Dover could not believe any human could be so cold-bloodedly rotten. Thank God for a calm sea, he thought, as the helicopter hovered over the tanker in preparation for landing, and the cutters surged smoothly on a hundred-and-eighty-degree arc to approach and close on the great ship.

The two red-orange Coast Guard–modified Dolphin helicopters took up station behind the stern of the LNG tanker as the first blue-black Jayhawk police copter came in low over the bow. The pilot increased the throttle and the collective pitch of the blades, matching the speed of the massive vessel as he drifted over the bow railing and hovered a few moments, studying the deck for hatches, ventilators or anchor chains that might foul a safe landing. A tall radar-and-watch mast stood between the upper tip of the bow and the first gas tank. The pilot, satisfied that he had enough room for an unobstructed landing, flared out the helicopter only twenty feet above the bow.

That was as far as he got.

Dover stood shocked, staring through his binoculars, as a small missile launched from atop the first tank tore into the helicopter, bursting it open like a firecracker in a tuna can. Flames from the shattered fuel tanks enveloped the craft as it hung blazing for a moment before dropping into the water, taking the police antiterrorist team with it. In seconds, after it had sunk from sight, there were only a few bits and pieces floating on the water, along with a spiral of smoke that stretched into the brightening sky.

50

Kanai watched with detached indifference as the *Mongol Invader* bullied its way through the pitiful floating remains of the wreckage of the police helicopter. He felt no guilt about erasing twelve men from the earth in less than ten seconds. In his mind, the helicopter's attack was merely an annoyance.

Nor did the flotilla of Coast Guard cutters and the fireboats that surrounded his ship dispirit Kanai. He felt secure, knowing they would never dare assault him with guns blazing — not unless the commander of the fleet was either mad or incredibly stupid. If a stray shot penetrated one of the tanks and caused combustion, every ship and aircraft within a mile would be obliterated, including the cars and their passengers crossing the bridge far above.

He stared upward at the roadway of the great bridge, one of the longest spans in the world. The ship was almost close enough to where he could hear the rumble of traffic above. With growing satisfaction, he observed the other helicopters pulling away, their pilots realizing that they were exposed and defenseless against rocket fire. Kanai turned his attention to the two Coast Guard cutters, with their white superstructures and hulls and the wide-angled orange stripes and CG insignias set off from narrow blue bands behind them. The two cutters were approaching the LNG tanker on opposite sides of her great hull. Their intention was clear, but their guns looked woefully inadequate to cause major damage to the *Invader*.

Now it was his turn, he thought with amusement. But before he could give the order to his Viper teams to launch missiles against the cutters, they both opened fire simultaneously with twenty-five-millimeter Bushmaster guns mounted on their bows. The twin-barreled guns seemed insignificant to the task, too minuscule to cause damage to such a monster ship.

The starboard cutter concentrated its armor-piercing rounds on the three-eighth-inch steel bulkhead of the bridge and wheelhouse, while the cutter on the port side blasted away at the lower hull of the stern in an attempt to penetrate the thicker steel plates that shielded the engine room. The men manning both guns were careful not to aim anywhere close to the giant tanks filled with the deadly propane.

Kanai threw himself to the deck as the twenty-five-millimeter rounds slashed through the bridge, taking out the windows and ripping into the control console. The *Viper* at the helm was killed instantly. Another fell mortally wounded from the unanticipated assault. Scorning the storm of shells, Kanai reached up and snatched the radio from the bridge counter and shouted, "Launch surface-to-surface missiles now!"

He lay on the deck and looked up through the shattered windows. The *Invader* was less than a mile from passing under the bridge. He also noticed that the bow was swinging slightly to starboard. Shot to pieces, the navigation console was a mass of jagged holes, the computerized controls unable to send a course command to the rudder.

He called down to the engine room. "Report damage."

The Viper, who was a former chief engineer on naval ships used for secret operations, answered in a slow and deliberate voice. "Gunfire has disabled the port generator, but the engines are untouched. I have one man dead and one badly wounded. Shells are penetrating the bulkhead like wind-driven hail, but they're pretty well spent by the time they strike the machinery, which keeps damage to a minimum."

Kanai saw that the tanker was beginning to veer out of the channel toward a buoy. "The bridge controls are shot away. Helm the ship from down there. Bring her back on course three-five-five to port or we'll collide with a bridge span. Hold steady until I order you otherwise."

He crawled out on the bridge wing and peered down and saw a Viper lean over the starboard railing and fire missiles point-blank onto the bow of the *Timothy Firme*. The first passed through the thin deck and through the hull, exploding in the water. The other exploded against a bulwark and sent shredded steel cascading across the deck and cutting down the men manning the twenty-five-millimeter Bushmaster. Pieces of the gun flew in the sky like burning leaves.

Then the air on the opposite side of the *Mongol Invader* was torn apart, as another missile bored into the funnel of the *William Shea*. It struck like a giant hammer, heeling the ship ten degrees and sending out a huge spray of debris and a cloud of dense black smoke. But the lone twenty-five-millimeter Bushmaster on her bow still peppered away at the hull surrounding the *Mongol Invader*'s engine room.

A second missile slammed into the *Timothy Firme*. Her hull trembled and flames burst out of her stern. An instant later, another plowed into her superstructure below the bridge. The explosion scattered steel splinters throughout the forward part of the ship. Coast Guard cutters were not heavily armored, as most naval vessels were, and the damage was severe. Half the officers were down on the bridge. She lost headway and began to fall away from the LNG tanker, afire in two places, smoke pouring out of her, badly crippled and drifting helplessly. More savage crashes and explosions rocked both Coast Guard cutters, smoke and flame twisting into the sky.

Kanai had achieved the tactical advantage.

He was gratified at the way the battle was going in his favor. He threw a glance astern and saw both of the larger Coast Guard cutters battered and nearly reduced to burntout derelicts, drifting helplessly. There would be no further worry from surface ships.

With the police helicopters held at bay, he knew he wasn't home free, not yet. The *Mongol Invader* may have been closing in on the Verrazano Bridge, but Kanai was certain that whoever was in command of the intercept operation would call in military jet fighters before the ship reached relative safety under and beyond the bridge.

Dover checked his body for wounds. He

was bleeding from shrapnel cuts on his left shoulder and the side of his head. He felt for his ear and found it dangling by a shred of flesh. Out of frustration more than pain, he pulled it away and stuffed it in his pocket, certain that a surgeon could sew it back on later. He picked his way across the shattered wheelhouse. Dead and wounded men spread across the deck. They were young men who shouldn't be treated like this, he thought absently. This was not a war with a foreign enemy of the United States. This was a battle over internal economics. None of the slaughter made sense to him.

The cutters had been sitting ducks against the concentrated fire from at least four portable shoulder-fired guided-missile systems. He could feel the speed falling off and the ship slowing down. The damage below her waterline was severe, and she was beginning to sink.

Unable to assess the harm to the *Timothy Firme* on the other side of the *Mongol Invader*, but assuming the worst, Admiral Dover ordered the only officer of the *Firme* still standing to turn the cutter toward the nearest shore and ground her. The Coast Guard's struggle against the nightmare ship was finished.

The last throw of the dice, Dover thought grimly. Clutching the radio, he ordered in the three Air National Guard F-16C fighters that had assembled and were circling a few miles out to sea. He instinctively ducked as a missile from the LNG tanker flashed in front of the bridge and burst harmlessly in the water a hundred yards beyond. Then he crouched and peered over the railing, his eyes turned skyward.

He changed the frequency on his radio and said slowly, distinctly, "Blue Flight, Blue Flight, this is Red Fleet. If you hear and understand me, attack the LNG tanker. Repeat, attack the ship. But for God's sake, don't strike the tanks containing the propane."

"Understood, Red Fleet," replied the flight leader. "We will concentrate our fire on the stern superstructure."

"Try for the engine room under the funnel," ordered Dover. "Do whatever it takes to stop her and stop her quickly without setting off the gas."

"I copy, Red Fleet. Launching attack *now*."

The Blue Flight leader sent his two wingmen in, one five hundred yards behind the other, while he circled to observe the results of the strike and follow up should his lead planes miss the target. He feared that by being too cautious his pilots would fire too far aft on the stern and as far as possible from the tanks, missing the ship completely.

As it turned out, his fears were set in the wrong direction.

The first pilot banked and rolled as he dropped in an almost vertical dive. Aiming his fighter arrow-straight for the machinery room deep beneath the big funnel of the *Invader*, he locked in his missile guidance systems on his target, which was becoming hidden by smoke from the burning Coast Guard cutters. But a split second before he could press his fire switch, a surface-to-air missile fired from the LNG tanker blasted his F-16 into a giant fiery pyre that burst like a fireworks rocket. It seemed to hang for a moment, no longer a sleek fighter jet but a shattered and flaming pile of scrap falling crazily in a thousand pieces and splashing into the sea.

"Break off!" shouted the flight leader to the second aircraft.

"Too late!" broke in the pilot. "I'm locked on —"

He spoke no more. There was no time to take evasive action, no pulling out of his approach dive. No time to react. Another missile belched from its launcher and his plane exploded into a second fireball, which also seemed to hang suspended before plunging into the waiting arms of an apathetic sea, not more than a hundred yards from the watery burial shroud of the first F-16.

The flight leader froze, unable to believe

what he had witnessed. Two of his closest friends, National Guard pilots who had responded to the emergency, both businessmen with families, suddenly incinerated within seconds of each other and now lying within the wreckage of their aircraft on the bottom of lower New York Harbor. Numb with revulsion, he was too paralyzed with shock to launch another attack. Instead, he turned his aircraft away from the death and destruction and flew back to the National Guard field on Long Island.

Dover watched the destruction of the two aircraft in stunned horror. He understood instantly what it meant. Everybody on board the cutters, rescue boats and helicopters knew. The loss of the pilots was appalling, but their failed mission to stop the LNG tanker before she passed into the upper harbor spelled disaster now.

He suddenly straightened in awe as one of the small thirty-five-foot Coast Guard rescue boats abruptly shot across the water at full speed in the direction of the stern of the *Mongol Invader*. The crew, clutching the tops of their life vests, spilled over the sides as the boat's skipper gripped the helm and kept his bow on a straight, undeviating course toward the huge ship.

"Suicide," Dover thought wonderingly. "Pure suicide, but God bless him."

Small-arms fire erupted from the *Invader*.

Bullets clouded the rescue boat like swarms of hornets and whined around the young man at the helm. Splashes seemed to cover every inch of the water around the thin fiberglass hull. The man at the helm could be seen shaking the spray from his eyes with one hand while he gripped the wheel with the other. The little red, white and blue ensign flew stiff in the morning breeze.

After seeing the fighter jets crash, people had stopped their cars on the bridge and were standing in crowds along the railing, watching the drama unfold beneath them. The eyes of the men in the remaining helicopters were on the rescue boat, too, every man and woman silently urging the boat's commander to jump overboard before the collision.

"A glorious act of defiance," Dover muttered to no one but himself. "Close enough!" he yelled, knowing he could not be heard. "Abandon the boat!"

But it was not to be. Just when it looked like the skipper was about to leap clear of the cockpit, a spray of bullets stitched him across the chest and he fell backward onto the work deck. A thousand people gazed entranced as the boat, its engines racing in a crescendo, props churning the water into a froth, struck the big port rudder of the LNG tanker.

There was no fiery explosion, no burst of

smoke and flame. The little boat simply disintegrated when it struck the massive steel rudder. The only visible evidence of the collision was a small cloud of dust and debris that sprayed the water. The great menacing ship continued on like an elephant attacked by a mosquito without feeling the bite.

Dover dragged himself erect, not noticing the blood flooding out of his shoe from another shrapnel wound in his right ankle. He watched the massive LNG tanker sail on unmolested. Her bow was almost to a point where it was directly under the bridge.

"Dear God, don't let us lose her now," he muttered in abject fear and anger. "God help everyone if she gets under the bridge."

The words had hardly escaped his mouth when there was an explosion in the water under the stern of the *Mongol Invader*. He stared disbelieving as the bows of the giant ship slowly, inexorably began to make a sweeping turn to port away from the bridge. Ever so gradually at first, then faster and faster.

51

"That big Liquid Natural Gas carrier looks like a line of eight pregnant women lying on their backs in a spa," said Jimmy Flett, as he stood at the console helm and closed on the *Mongol Invader*.

"A helicopter, two cutters and two F-16s blasted to scrap within twenty minutes," Giordino muttered, eyeing the wreckage floating everywhere, scattered among the waves by the smaller boats that sped through it. "She's even deadlier than she is ugly."

"They'll never stop her now," Pitt said, gazing through a pair of thirty-by-fifty binoculars at the big ship doggedly heading for Manhattan and her rendezvous with nightmarish devastation.

"She's about a thousand yards from the bridge," judged Flett. "Just time enough for us to cut in, submerge and go for her screws and rudders."

From Giordino's point of view, it would be a near thing. "We'll only get one pass. Miss and we'll never be able to circle and come at her again. Her speed is too great. We couldn't surface, race ahead of her and submerge for another try until she was long past the bridge."

Pitt looked at him and grinned. "Then we'll just have to get it right the first time, won't we?"

The *Coral Wanderer* skipped over the waves like a smooth, flat stone thrown by a major-league pitcher. Pitt swung his glasses onto the burning Coast Guard cutters. The *William Shea* was crawling toward the Brooklyn shore, the *Timothy Firme* listing and down by the stern. The smaller Coast Guard rescue craft had gathered around to put on extra men for damage control. The New York fireboats also pulled alongside, their pipes and nozzles throwing a shower of water on the sections of the ships that were on fire. This was one time when the hounds were outclassed by a grizzly bear, he thought. He deeply regretted that they couldn't have arrived sooner and diverted the devastation.

He had acted cocksure in his words of optimism to Giordino, but deep down he felt the chilling fear of failure. He was determined to hinder the *Mongol Invader* and prevent her from entering the upper harbor, even if it meant putting his life and those of Giordino and Flett on the line.

It was too late to turn back; the point of no return had been passed. All trepidation and uncertainty were left far astern. He knew with calculated certainty that Omo Kanai was on board. There was a score to settle, and he felt a growing wave of rage.

He studied the shattered and shell-torn wheelhouse of the *Invader*, but saw no human figures moving inside. The hull below the funnel had more holes than a colander, but they were small and the damage looked slight.

It seemed to take half a lifetime for the *Coral Wanderer* to narrow the gap. Two hundred yards off the starboard bow of the LNG tanker, Flett eased back the throttles and switched on the ballast tank pumps. Faster than Pitt might have thought, the luxury submarine slipped beneath the surface of the water as smoothly as if guided by a giant hand. Once submerged, Flett picked up the speed again, pushing the *Coral Wanderer* faster than her designers had specified. From now on there could be no room for error.

Giordino stayed on the bridge with Flett, while Pitt dropped down to the main cabin and made his way forward to the bow and its big viewing port. Seated comfortably on a suede couch, he picked up a phone set in one armrest.

"Are we connected?" he asked.

"We have you on the speaker," answered Giordino.

Flett read off the numbers. "One hundred fifty yards and closing."

"Visibility is less than forty feet," Pitt reported. "Keep a sharp eye on the radar."

"We have a computer image of the ship as she sails," said Giordino. "I'll let you know what section of the hull we come in contact with."

Three agonizing minutes dragged by as Flett read off the closing distance. "One hundred yards out," he notified Pitt. "Her shadow is beginning to show above on the surface."

Pitt could hear the throb of the *Mongol Invader*'s engines and sense the rush of water under her keel. He peered into the green gloom and barely discerned the white foam that was sliding along her hull. And then her plates materialized out of the murk thirty feet ahead and ten feet above.

"We've got her!" Pitt said sharply.

Flett instantly threw the twin screws into reverse, stopping the *Wanderer* before she rammed the *Invader*.

"Take us down another ten feet, Jimmy."

"Ten feet, it is," acknowledged Flett, sending the *Coral Wanderer* on a course directly under the starboard side of the *Mongol Invader*'s hull.

To Pitt, seated inside the bow observation cabin, it was an eerie sight to watch the great hull sweep over the submarine like a Chinook wind out of the north, a vast mechanical monster with no mind of its own. The beat of the propellers came as a distant pulse but soon increased to the sound of a farm threshing machine. Something caught his eye, a large object that bulged from the bottom of the hull near the keel. But then it flashed from view.

Pitt was an extension of Flett's eyes. Only he could make the split-second judgment call when the great bronze screws came into sight. The movement of the huge ship through the water was blurring his visibility. He moved forward and lay down on the carpet deck with his face less than an inch from the viewing port, eyes straining to penetrate the froth and green pall to see the magnetic explosive charge on the end of the spar protruding from the bow of the *Wanderer*, but it was obscured by the restless water.

"Ready, Jimmy?"

"Say the word," Flett replied, his voice solid as a stone.

"You should see the starboard prop only three seconds after it comes into my view on the bow."

Nothing more was said as the suspense deepened. His mind and body as taut as banjo strings, Pitt's knuckles turned ivory as he clenched the phone only an inch from his lips. Then the green curtain parted in a white explosion of bubbles. "Now!" Pitt yelled.

Flett reacted with the speed of a lightning bolt, shoving the throttles forward until he felt a jar from the front of the boat and then whipping them into reverse, praying that his timing was on a thin dime.

Pitt could only watch, helpless and exposed, as the magnetic charge impacted against the steel plates of the hull and clung an instant before Flett went full speed into reverse. The massive propeller came like an out-of-control windmill, beating the water of the bay into sparkling foam.

From the control bridge, Giordino and Flett stared in rapt wariness, seeing the mighty blades pound toward them. For a brief instant, they were certain they would not pull clear in time, that the blades would beat the luxury boat into splinters and their bodies along with it. But in the final seconds, the *Coral Wanderer*'s diesels roared and her own propellers chewed the water in a violent frenzy. She leaped astern as the LNG tanker's fifty-foot-diameter propellers flailed past no more than two feet from the bow view port, rocking the submarine yacht like a tree whipped in a tornado.

As he lay on the deck, arm raised and

clutching the hand railing of a circular stairway for support, all Pitt could see out the view port was a maelstrom of enraged water, embellished by the ear-pounding drumming of the spinning blades. A brief thirty seconds later, the yacht came back on a smoother keel, the water calmed into the *Mongol Invader*'s wake and the throb of the propellers began to fade.

"Now is as good a time as any, Al," said Pitt, coming to his feet.

"You think we're far enough away."

"If this boat is built to withstand the water pressure at a thousand feet, she can take the stress of a detonation a hundred yards away."

Giordino held a small black remote control in both hands and pressed a tiny lever. A loud thud sounded, amplified by the acoustics through the water. This was followed by a pressure wave that struck the *Coral Wanderer* with the force of a twenty-foot swell before sweeping over and around. And then it was gone and the water calmed again.

Pitt popped his head above the deck at the head of the stairway. "Bring her up, Jimmy, and let's see if we did any good." He looked at Giordino. "Soon as we break the surface, let's mount another charge."

Unable to comprehend the source behind

the muted underwater explosion, Admiral Dover was overcome with fleeting relief at seeing the *Mongol Invader* swinging away from the channel and making a wide, sweeping turn back the way she had come. He could not have known that Pitt and Giordino on board a submarine yacht were responsible. Everyone who wasn't wounded on the *William Shea* had been too busy to notice the unusual craft before it slipped underwater and rammed a magnetic charge of explosives just ahead of the *Mongol Invader*'s starboard propeller. The explosion had blown an eight-foot hole in the hull below the base of the propeller shaft, shearing it apart, while the rudder mounting, already damaged by the heroic suicide run by the Coast Guardsman, became jammed in a forty-five-degree position to port.

The propeller dipped downward on a slanted angle, barely held by the outer stub of its severed shaft, while the big turbine-driven engine inside the machinery compartment abruptly tripled its rpm and raced out of control before the chief engineer could shut it down.

With the port propeller still turning at full speed and the starboard critically damaged, the bow of the ship pulled slowly, deliberately, toward Staten Island, around on a reverse course that would eventually return her to sea or keep her running in circles.

The worst of the disaster has been averted, thought Dover. But would the crazy man in command of the LNG tanker carry out his plans and blow her up, knowing that he could still cause great loss of life and billions in damage?

Dover had prepared for certain catastrophe after losing the fight, but now that a sudden miracle had occurred, he prayed that a holocaust might still be avoided.

If Admiral Dover was surprised at seeing the great ship suddenly reverse its course, Omo Kanai was stunned into absolute confusion. Though he had felt and heard the explosion deep beneath the *Mongol Invader*'s stern, he had felt no concern, since no vessel or aircraft within twenty miles would dare to attack him. Then, as the ship began its unscheduled turn, he shouted down to the engine room.

"Get back on course! Can't you see we've come around!"

"We've lost our starboard screw from some kind of explosion," replied the chief engineer, anxiety obvious in his tone. "Before I could shut down the port engine, its screw pulled the ship around."

"Compensate with the rudders!" Kanai ordered.

"Impossible. Something struck the port

rudder earlier, wreckage maybe, and jammed it, adding to the uncontrolled turn."

"What are you telling me?" demanded Kanai, beginning for the first time to lose his composure.

The words came back steadily and lifelessly. "Either we continue to go around in circles or we come to *all stop* and drift. The truth is, we ain't going nowhere."

It was the end of the trail, yet Kanai refused to accept defeat. "We're too close to give up. Once under the bridge, no one can stop us."

"And I'm telling you, with the starboard rudder jammed forty-five degrees to port and my starboard screw useless with a broken shaft, the sooner we get off this gas can, the better."

Kanai saw it was fruitless to argue further with his chief engineer. He stared up at the great bridge. He could almost look straight up at the suspended roadway as it began to fall away astern. Less than a few hundred feet had separated success and utter failure before the *Mongol Invader* had been diverted by the mysterious explosion. He had come so close and defied the odds — it seemed impossible that triumph had been snatched from him at the beginning of the end.

His eyes swept the water. It was at that moment that he saw what looked like a private yacht cruising in the wake of the *In-*

vader. There is a strange look to it, he thought. Kanai was about to turn away, but then stared with sudden understanding and anger as the yacht suddenly slipped beneath the waves.

"Okay, Jimmy," Pitt said to the submarine yacht's skipper. "We turned her. Now let's put those big balls of gas on the bottom."

"I only hope those devils don't set off the charges," Flett said, as he worked the controls to level the *Coral Wanderer* at thirty feet and make another run at the LNG tanker. If there was the slightest thought of hesitation, none showed in the old seaman's ruddy face. If anything, he looked as though he was enjoying himself for the first time in ages.

The *Wanderer* was running under the water as if she were a fish. Flett felt more at ease now that it looked as though they might not damage his precious boat. He set his eyes on the radar screen and the GPS to keep his course straight toward the *Invader*.

"Where do you want to hit her?" he asked Pitt.

"Below the engine room, port side of the stern, careful not to set off an explosion in the hull under one of those tanks. We put a charge too far forward and the whole ship could go up and everybody within two miles along with it."

"And our third and last charge?"

"Same area but on the starboard side. If we can put a pair of big holes in her stern, she should slip under the water quickly since she doesn't have a deep draft."

Giordino spoke with a curious look of satisfaction on his face. "With no screws to contend with, this run should be a piece of cake compared to the last one."

"Never count your chickens before the check clears the bank," Pitt retorted, as he had on other occasions. "We're not ready for bed yet."

52

"John Milton Hay wrote, 'Luckiest is he who knows just when to rise and go home,' " quoted Jimmy Flett, as a missile launched from the *Mongol Invader* flashed narrowly past the submerging control cabin, exploding on impact with the water less than a hundred feet astern. "Maybe we should have taken his advice."

"They're onto us, all right," said Pitt.

"They must really be mad now that they've discovered we're the ones who broke their boat," Giordino cracked.

"She looks like she's dead in the water."

"If her crew of rats is abandoning the ship," said Giordino, as the water rose past the windshield, "I don't see them lowering the boats."

The instant the water closed over the cabin roof and the *Coral Wanderer* was out of sight to those on the LNG tanker, Flett dove at full speed and hung a sharp turn to starboard. And not a moment too soon. An audible thump rocked the luxury submarine as another missile struck the water and exploded almost where they would have been if not for Flett's quick maneuver.

He straightened out and set the bow on a dead-set course for the port hull of the disabled LNG tanker. Another missile burst, but farther away. The Vipers had lost their chance to destroy their nemesis. The *Wanderer* was now shrouded by the water and invisible to those on the ship. What little wake her propellers left behind was mostly dissipated by the time it reached the surface.

Pitt returned to the observation view port in the bow and took up his vigil again. With the big ship heaved to, this run would not be nearly as intricate or hazardous as the first assault. The Viper crew must be preparing to escape, he thought. But where? They weren't lowering the boats. They couldn't just swim away. Then something he'd seen earlier flashed through his mind.

Now was not the time to ponder variables. He had to concentrate every brain cell, focus his eyes and be ready to warn Flett again . . . and then the mammoth hull burst across the view port. It was easier this time. Flett did not close the gap at full speed as before; they were approaching a stationary ship without having to dodge its propellers.

A minute, then two, then Pitt saw the hull fill up the viewport. "We're on her, Jimmy."

Flett expertly reversed the engines to slow speed and turned parallel to the hull. In a display of masterful seamanship, he brought the sub alongside no more than six feet away. Then he increased speed as they moved toward the section of the stern that contained the engine-room machinery.

In the control cabin, Giordino studied the screen of the computerized underwater radar system intently. Slowly, he raised a hand, then waved it. "Coming up in thirty feet."

Flett dutifully made a turn, using the reverse thrusters until the bow and the charge on the end of the spar were pointing directly against the *Invader*'s hull plates opposite the vulnerable engine room.

The magnetic charge clunked against the hull, and the luxury sub quickly backed away. When they reached a safe zone, Giordino grinned. "Once more with feeling." Then he pushed the detonator switch. Another dull boom raced through the water as the *Wanderer* shook off the pressure wave.

"There's a mortal blow," said Flett. "With that highly advanced explosive material you brought, she must have a hole bigger than any naval torpedo could have opened."

Pitt entered the control cabin from below. "Jimmy, I assume you have a safety escape chamber."

Flett nodded. "Of course. All commercial undersea craft are required by international maritime law to have them."

"Do you have dive gear on board?"

"I do," acknowledged Flett. "There are four sets of suits and gear for passengers who want to dive from the boat after she's put into charter."

Pitt looked at Giordino. "Al, what say you and I get wet?"

"I was about to suggest the same thing," Giordino said, as though he looked forward to it. "Better we reload the spar underwater than risk a missile down our throats."

They didn't waste a moment putting on wet suits. They decided that every minute counted and they could suffer the cold water wearing only their shorts in the time it would take them to place the third charge on the end of the spar. Going through the airlock, which was large enough for two people, they attached the explosive charge and were back aboard in less than seven minutes, their bodies numb from the sixty-five-degree water.

As soon as they returned inside the airlock, Flett sent the *Coral Wanderer* on her final attack. Before Pitt and Giordino had come up into the control cabin, he had rammed the charge against the hull and was running astern.

Pitt placed a hand on Flett's shoulder. "Nice work, Jimmy."

Flett smiled. "I'm not one to dillydally."

Giordino toweled his wet body and sat in a chair in his shorts. He picked up the explosive remote before putting on his clothes. At Flett's command, he flicked the little lever, detonating the charge and blowing another huge hole in the stern of the *Mongol Invader*.

"Dare we risk surfacing to see our handiwork?" Flett asked Pitt.

"Not yet. There's something I'd like to explore first."

The deck in the wheelhouse gave a lurch as the second charge blew a second gaping void in the tanker's hull. The blast seemed to come right beneath Kanai's feet. The stern superstructure shuddered from the blast. To those gazing at the tanker from shore, on the boats and the bridge, her bow was noticeably beginning to lift from the water.

Kanai thought they might survive the first blast and somehow get the ship headed back into the Narrows. It was purely wishful thinking. The next explosion sealed the ship's fate. The *Mongol Invader* was going to the bottom of the lower bay in two hundred feet of water. He sat in the captain's bridge chair and mopped the blood that was seeping from his forehead into his eyes where a piece of glass from the windshield had gashed the skin to the bone.

The engine's beat had ceased minutes before. He could only wonder if the chief engineer and his men had escaped from the engine room before the two blasts sent tons of water rushing inside. He glanced around the bridge, which looked as if it had been ransacked by a frenzied mob. Holding a towel to his forehead, he walked over to a cabinet, opened the door and stared at a panel of switches. He set the timer for twenty minutes, his mind foggy, without considering the possibility that the ship might sink before the charges laid beneath the gargantuan tanks of propane went off. Then he engaged the detonation switch to the *on* position.

Harmon Kerry stepped off of the ship's outside stairway. Blood oozed from half a dozen wounds, but he seemed not to notice. His eyes were glassy, and he was gasping for air as if from great exertion. He hung on to a navigation counter to catch his breath.

"Didn't you take the elevator?" asked Kanai, curious as if detached from the disorder around him.

"It was damaged and out of order," Kerry rasped. "I had to climb ten flights. A cable was shot off a pully, but I repaired it. I think it will get us to the bottom deck if we take it slow."

"You should have gone directly to the escape sub."

"I won't desert the ship without you."

"I'm grateful for your loyalty."

"Have you set the charges?"

"They're timed for twenty minutes."

"We'll be lucky to be a safe distance away," said Kerry, seeing the anguish of defeat on Kanai's profile. He looked like a man who had been cheated in a poker game. "We'd better get a move on."

The ship took a sudden lurch and the deck tilted backwards. "Are the men clear?" Kanai asked.

"As far as I know, they've all left their posts for the sub."

"There is nothing more to be accomplished here."

Kanai took one last look around at the bodies. There was one wounded man still breathing, but Kanai figured he was as good as dead and stepped over him to the elevator. As he turned inside, he took one last look at the panel with the explosive charge timer. The red numbers on the digital clock were ticking down toward detonation. At least the mission wasn't a total failure.

Some death and damage were better than none at all, he thought perversely.

Kerry pushed the button for the bottom deck after the doors closed and hoped for the best. The elevator trembled and jerked, but descended slowly until it reached its bottom stop at the bilge deck just above the keel.

By the time they reached the open hatch of the escape sub, which protruded up through a watertight seal in the hull, they were wading in a rush of water up to their knees and had to lean forward to compensate for the sharpening angle of the sinking stern.

The chief engineer was waiting for them, covered with sweat and oil. "Make it quick or the sub will be swamped. The ship's going down and going down fast."

Kanai was the last man to drop through the hatch into the main passenger cabin. Six men, three of them wounded, sat in seats opposite one another — all that remained of the entire Viper team.

After dogging the hatch, Kanai stepped into the control cockpit along with the chief engineer, who took the seat next to him and threw on the battery switches.

Above them they could hear the *Mongol Invader* groaning and howling in protest from the stress as her bow lifted into the air. She was only minutes away from sliding onto the bottom stern first.

He was about to engage the propulsion motors when he glanced through the bubble-shaped windshield and saw a strange craft approaching out of the murky water ahead. At first he thought it might be a private yacht that had been caught up in the battle and was sinking, but then he realized it was the vessel he'd seen earlier slipping beneath the waves. As it drew closer, he could see a long metal spar sticking out from the bow slanted up toward the hull above. Too late he discovered the mysterious boat's purpose.

It surged forward until its metal spar rammed into the mechanism holding the escape sub to the bottom of the LNG tanker's hull, effectively jamming the release pins. Kanai's face turned as rigid as a plaster death mask. Frantically, he worked the handle of the release mechanism. It failed to respond. The pins refused to pull out of their slots and drop the escape sub away from its cradle attached to the bottom of the hull.

"Why aren't we falling free!" shouted the chief engineer, on the verge of terror. "Good God, man, hurry before the ship sinks on top of us!"

While feverishly yanking on the release mechanism handle with every ounce of his strength, Kanai stared out into the green void at the sub hanging in the water just beyond the curving edge of the hull. To his growing horror, he recognized the man sitting inside the large viewing port on the boat's bow. Because of the magnification of the water through the port, he could discern the green eyes and black hair, and the satanic grin on the face.

"Pitt!" he gasped.

Pitt stared back at Kanai with morbid curiosity. There was a great rumble from the sinking LNG tanker as her stern struck the bottom on a sharp angle that produced a huge cloud of silt. Slowly, the rest of her hull began to settle, until the escape sub was only feet away from being buried in the silt by the colossal weight from above.

The expression of horror on Kanai's face abruptly switched to one of black fury. He shook his fist at Pitt as the great hull above began to press the escape sub into the bottom silt. Pitt had to get it in before it was too late. He spread his lips into a wide smile that showed every tooth and waved bye-bye, as Jimmy Flett moved the *Coral Wanderer* astern so they wouldn't be buried under the great ship, too.

Then the escape sub with the entire remaining Viper team vanished in a swirl of muddy water, interred for eternity under the wreck of the *Mongol Invader*.

Kanai died, crushed in the terror of total blackness, never knowing that the explosive charges had failed to erupt under the monstrous propane tanks. He died not knowing that a shell fired from the twenty-five-millimeter bow guns of the Coast Guard cutter *Timothy Firme* into the tanker's wheelhouse had sliced through the main wire leading to the detonators.

The heroic fight by the Coast Guardsmen had not been in vain.

Part Five

FULL CIRCLE

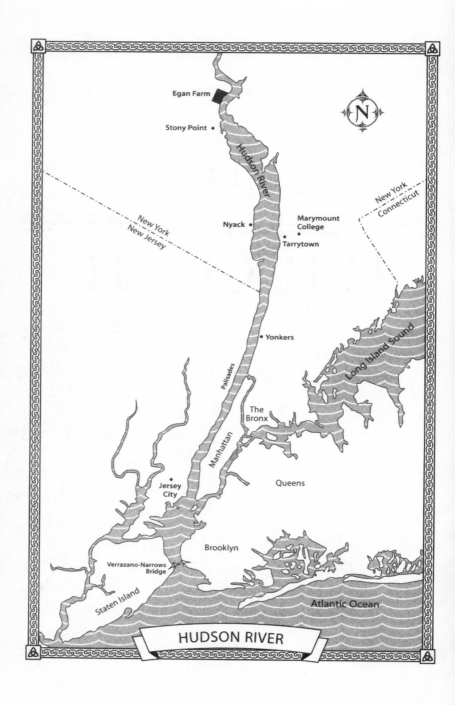

Egan Farm

Stony Point •

Hudson River

New York
Connecticut

Nyack •

Marymount
College

New York
New Jersey

• Tarrytown

• Yonkers

Long Island Sound

Palisades

The
Bronx

Manhattan

Queens

Jersey
City •

Brooklyn

Verrazano-Narrows
Bridge

Atlantic Ocean

Staten Island

HUDSON RIVER

53

The silver-and-green Rolls-Royce rolled silently, regally through the French city of Amiens. Situated in the Somme Valley north of Paris, the original village existed long before the Romans settled in the area. Battles were fought in and around the city for centuries between the Celts and Roman legions, during the Napoleonic Wars and then World Wars I and II, when it was occupied by the Germans.

The Rolls-Royce passed the splendid Amiens cathedral that was begun in 1220 and finished in 1270. Romanesque as well as Gothic, its walls included a rose-windowed facade running around ornate galleries enhanced by three portals and twin towers. The car continued on past the waterway where truck farmers sold their fruit and vegetables from small boats on the Somme River.

St. Julien Perlmutter did not travel with the foul-smelling rabble, as he called the common public. He detested airplanes and airports, preferring to travel by boat and bringing his beautiful 1955 Rolls-Royce Silver Dawn with him, driven by his chauffeur, Hugo Mulholland.

Leaving the old section of Amiens, Mulholland turned the car onto a small narrow road and continued for a mile before stopping at an iron gate mounted between high, vine-covered stone walls. He pressed a button on a communications box and spoke into the receiver. No voice answered, but the gate slowly began to swing open. Hugo followed a gravel drive that circled around the front of a large French country house.

He slipped from behind the wheel and held the door open as Perlmutter heaved his great bulk from the backseat and walked with the heavy use of a cane up the steps to the front door. A few moments after he pulled the bell chain, a tall, thin man with a narrow, handsome face below a thick, brushed-back mane of white hair pulled open the door, its glass panes etched with sailing ships. He stared at Perlmutter through soft blue eyes and bowed gracefully as he extended his hand.

"Monsieur Perlmutter, I am Paul Hereoux."

"Dr. Hereoux," said Perlmutter, enveloping Hereoux's slim hand with his great fleshy paw. "It is indeed an honor to finally meet the esteemed president of the Society of Jules Verne."

"The honor is mine, to have such a distinguished historian in Mr. Verne's home."

"And a lovely home it is."

Hereoux showed Perlmutter down a long hall into a large library containing more than ten thousand books. "Here is everything Jules Verne wrote and everything ever written about him until his death. All the later works about him are in another room."

Perlmutter acted impressed. Though the size of the library was extraordinary, it was still less than a third the size of Perlmutter's own maritime history collection. He walked over to a section where binders held manuscripts, but he did not reach out and touch one.

"His unpublished material?"

"You're quite astute. Yes, those are manuscripts he either did not finish or did not believe worthy of publishing." Hereoux motioned to a big, overstuffed couch in front of a large picture window overlooking a lush garden. "Won't you please sit down? May I get you coffee or tea?"

"Coffee would be fine."

Hereoux gave instructions over an intercom and then sat down across from Perlmutter. "Now then, St. Julien. May I call you by your Christian name?"

"Please do. Though we've only met face-to-face moments ago, we've known each other for a long time."

"Tell me, how can I help your research?"

Perlmutter spun his cane around in front of his spread knees. "I would like to dig into Verne's research on Captain Nemo and the *Nautilus*."

"You mean, of course, *Twenty Thousand Leagues under the Sea*."

"No, Captain Nemo and his submarine."

"Nemo and his submarine were Verne's greatest creations."

"Suppose they were not merely creations?"

Hereoux looked at him. "I fear I don't understand."

"I have a friend who thinks that Verne did not create Nemo from scratch. He suspects Verne used a real-life model."

Hereoux's expression remained constant, but Perlmutter detected a slight twitch in the blue eyes. "I'm afraid I can't help you with that theory."

"Can't or won't?" Perlmutter asked. It bordered on an insult, but he offered a patronizing smile to go along with it.

A hint of displeasure crossed Hereoux's face. "You're not the only one who has come here with such an outlandish proposal."

"Ridiculous? Yes, but intriguing nonetheless."

"How can I help you, old friend?"

"Allow me to search through these archives."

Hereoux relaxed as if he'd been dealt a straight flush. "Please, consider the library yours."

"One more request. May I have my chauffeur assist me? I can't climb ladders anymore to reach books on the higher shelves."

"Of course. I'm sure he can be trusted. But you must be responsible for any inconveniences."

A nice way of saying damage or theft of the books and manuscripts, Perlmutter thought. "That goes without saying, Paul. I promise that we'll be very careful."

"Then I will leave you to it. If you have any questions, I'll be in my office upstairs."

"There is one question."

"Yes?"

"Who categorized the books on the shelves?"

Hereoux smiled. "Why, Mr. Verne. Every book and manuscript and file was set exactly where he left it when he died. Of course, many have come to research, such as you, and I instruct everyone that all material must be returned exactly as they found it."

"Most interesting," said Perlmutter. "Everything in its place for ninety-eight years. That's something to think about."

As soon as Hereoux closed the library door, Mulholland looked at Perlmutter through thoughtful, circumspect eyes. "Did you notice the reaction when you insinuated that Nemo and the *Nautilus* actually existed?"

"Yes, Dr. Hereoux did seem put off balance. I can only wonder what, if anything, he's been hiding."

Perlmutter's chauffeur, Hugo Mulholland, was a dour fellow, who gazed from sad eyes under a bald head. "Have you figured out yet where you wish to start?" he asked. "You've been sitting and staring at the books for the past hour without pulling any from the shelves."

"Patience, Hugo," Perlmutter replied softly. "What we're searching for does not lie in an obvious spot, or other researchers would have discovered it long ago."

"From what I've read about him, Verne was a complicated man."

"Not complicated, or necessarily brilliant, but he had an imaginative mind. He was the founding father of the science-fiction story, you know. He invented it."

"What about H. G. Wells?"

"He didn't write *The Time Machine* until thirty years after Verne wrote *Five Weeks in a Balloon.*" Perlmutter shifted on the couch and continued studying the bookshelves. For a man his age, he had an amazing ten/fifteen eyesight. Optometrists marveled at his vision. From the center of the room, he could read almost every book title on its spine, unless it was too faded or set in tiny type. His gaze did not linger on the books or the unpublished manuscripts. His interest lay more in the wide range of notebooks.

"So you think Verne had a concept on which to base *Twenty Thousand Leagues under the Sea,*" said Mulholland, helping himself to a cup of coffee Hereoux had personally carried into the library earlier.

"Verne loved the sea. He was raised in the seaport of Nantes, and ran away as a hand on a small sailing ship, but his father beat him to port on a steamer and took him home. His brother, Paul, was in the French Navy and Verne was an avid sailor. After he became successful, he owned several yachts and sailed all the seas around Europe. When he was young, he wrote about a voyage he took on the largest ocean liner of her time, the *Great Eastern.* I have a nagging feeling that something happened on that voyage that inspired Verne to write *Twenty Thousand Leagues.*"

"If a Nemo truly existed in the eighteen-sixties, where did he get the scientific knowledge to build a submarine a hundred years ahead of its time?"

"That's what I want to find out. Somehow Dr. Elmore Egan knew the story. Where he got it is a mystery."

"Is it known what happened to Captain Nemo?" queried Mulholland.

"Verne wrote a book called *The Mysterious Island* six years after *Twenty Thousand Leagues* was published. In *Mysterious Island*, a group of castaways settle on a deserted island and are harassed by pirates. A mysterious unseen benefactor leaves food and supplies for the settlers. He also kills the crew of pirates who attack the settlement. Near the end, the settlers are led to a tunnel leading to a flooded cavern inside the heart of the island's volcano. They find the *Nautilus* and Captain Nemo, who is dying. He warns them the volcano is about to erupt. They escape in time, as the island destroys itself, burying Captain Nemo and his fabulous creation for eternity."

"Strange that Verne took so long to write closure on the story."

Perlmutter shrugged. "Who can say what was on his mind, unless he didn't receive news of the death of the real Nemo until years later."

Hugo turned in a three-hundred-and-sixty-degree circle, gazing at the thousands of books. "So which needle in the haystack holds the key?"

"We can eliminate the books. Anything that's been published has been open for everyone to see and read. And we can skip the manuscripts. They've undoubtedly already been gleaned by anyone who collects Verne lore. Which brings us to his notebooks. Again, they've all been studied and pored over by Verne researchers."

"So where does that leave us?" asked Mulholland.

"Where nobody else looked," Perlmutter said thoughtfully.

"Which is . . . ?"

"Jules Verne was not the kind of man to hide secrets in an obvious place. Like most good writers of fiction, he had a perverse and devious mind. Where would you hide something you didn't want people to find for a hundred years in a library, my old friend?"

"Sounds to me like you've eliminated every piece of paper with the printed or written word on it."

"Exactly!" Perlmutter boomed. "A hiding place that is not part of the books and bookshelves."

"Like a secret compartment in the fireplace," said Mulholland, studying the stones around the mantel. "That would be more permanent."

"You underestimate Verne. He had a superior imaginative mind. Secret fireplace niches were all the rage in mystery stories."

"A piece of furniture or a picture on the wall?"

"Furniture and pictures are not permanent. They can be moved or replaced. Think of something that remains constant."

Mulholland thought a moment. Then his dour face brightened slightly and he looked down. "The floor!"

"Pull up the rugs and throw them on the sofa," instructed Perlmutter. "Carefully examine the seams between the boards. Look for small notches on the ends where they have been pried up before."

Mulholland was on his hands and knees for nearly half an hour, scrutinizing every board laid in the floor. Then suddenly he looked up, grinned and pulled a dime from his pocket. He slipped it between the ends of two boards and pried one up.

"Eureka!" he exclaimed excitedly.

Enthused enough to swivel his great body down on the floor, Perlmutter lay sideways and looked into the slot beneath the board. There was a leather pouch inside. He carefully took it between a thumb and forefinger and gently lifted it out. Then, with no small assistance by Mulholland, he rose to his feet and sank into the sofa again.

Almost reverently, he untied a small velvet cord from around the pouch and opened it. He removed a notebook not much larger than a small stack of postcards but three inches thick. He blew the dust off the cover and read aloud, translating the French wording engraved on the leather jacket.

"Investigation of the ingenious Captain Amherst."

Very slowly Perlmutter began reading the words written in a precise handwriting less than an eighth of an inch high. A master of six languages, he had no problem in comprehending Verne's narrative about the adventures of a British scientific mastermind by the name of Captain Cameron Amherst.

Though his eyes read the words, his mind conjured up the images of this extraordinary man whom Verne had known and whose life he chronicled. Two hours later, he closed the notebook, and leaned heavily back in the sofa with the expression of a man who has just proposed to the woman he loved and been accepted.

"Find anything of interest?" asked Mulholland, curious. "Something that no one else knows?"

"Did you notice the ribbon around the pouch?"

Mulholland nodded. "Couldn't be more than ten or twelve years old? If Verne was the last to handle the pouch, the ribbon would have rotted away long ago."

"Which leads to the conclusion that Dr.

Hereoux learned Verne's secret a long time ago."

"What secret is that?"

Perlmutter stared off into space for several seconds. When he spoke, his voice was soft and faint, as if the words came from a distance. "Pitt was right."

Then he closed his eyes, gave a long sigh and promptly dozed off.

54

Eight hours into the congressional committee hearing, Curtis Merlin Zale was staring frequently at his watch and fidgeting nervously in his chair. He was not the supremely confident man who had faced Congresswoman Smith and her committee members earlier. The smug grin on his face was also gone, replaced by lips tensed and pressed tightly together.

Word from Omo Kanai and late-breaking reports of a disaster in New York should have reached the hearing room hours earlier.

Congressman William August from Oklahoma was in the midst of questioning Zale about the rising prices charged by the oil company refineries when Sandra Delage, wearing a tailored business dress, approached Curtis from behind and laid a paper on his desk. He excused himself before answering August and scanned the paper's contents. His eyes suddenly widened and he looked up at Delage. Her face was as grim as a mortician's. He placed his hand over his microphone and asked several hushed questions, which she answered in a voice too low for anyone sitting nearby to hear. Then she turned and left the proceedings.

Zale was not a man easily shaken by defeat, but at this moment he looked like Napoleon after Waterloo. "I'm sorry," he murmured to August. "Could you repeat the question?"

Loren was tired. Late afternoon had become early evening, but she was not about to let Zale leave the committee hearings, not yet. Her aides had kept her informed on the operation to stop the *Pacific Trojan* and the fact that no demolition charges had been found. Not until two hours later was she alerted to the mission to stop the *Mongol Invader*. She had heard nothing from Pitt or Sandecker since two o'clock, and had fought a nagging fear during the following four hours.

Her anxiety was made worse by a cold anger directed at Zale, who resolutely fired back calculated answers to their questions without hesitation or claims of faulty memory. To the reporters covering the hearings, it looked as if he was in perfect control and steering the proceedings to fit his own agenda.

Loren knew Zale was tiring, too, and she forced patience on herself. She was waiting, like a lioness in ambush, for the right moment to strike with the damaging information given by Sally Morse. She pulled the papers containing the questions and accusations she had prepared from her briefcase and waited patiently until Congressman August had finished his line of questioning.

At that moment, she noticed the faces in the audience suddenly stare behind her. Whispers began circulating throughout the chamber. Then a hand touched her shoulder. She turned and found herself gazing up incredulously into the face of Dirk Pitt. He was dressed in dirty jeans and a wrinkled sweatshirt. He looked exhausted, as if he had just climbed a mountain. His hair was a tangled mess and his face sported a three-day growth of black stubble. A security guard was clutching his arm, trying to drag him from the chamber, but he pulled the guard along with him like a stubborn Saint Bernard.

"Dirk!" she whispered. "What are you doing here?"

He didn't look at her as he answered, but stared with a smug grin at Zale and spoke in a voice that carried across the room through her microphone. "We stopped the Liquid

Natural Gas tanker from blowing up New York Harbor. The ship now rests on the bottom of the sea. Please inform Mr. Zale that his entire Viper team went down with the ship and it is now safe for Ms. Sally Morse, the CEO of Yukon Oil, to testify before your committee without fear of reprisal."

Then Pitt, in what might have looked like an accidental motion, lightly brushed his hand against Loren's auburn hair and exited the chamber.

A vast load was suddenly lifted from Loren's shoulders. She said, "Ladies and Gentlemen, it is getting late and if there is no objection, I would like to adjourn this hearing until nine o'clock tomorrow, when I will call an important witness to testify who will reveal the truth behind Mr. Zale's criminal activities —"

"Rather strong words, don't you think?" interrupted Congressman Sturgis. "We have seen or heard nothing here that shows evidence of any criminal activity."

"You will tomorrow," Loren said evenly, staring at Sturgis with a look of sheer triumph, "when Ms. Morse will supply the names of everyone in Washington and across the rest of the country who has accepted bribes from Mr. Curtis Merlin Zale. I promise you, the trail of graft and corruption, the depth of the money trail into offshore bank accounts, will stun the government to its core and shock the public as no scandal ever has in the past."

"What has this Sally Morse got to do with Mr. Zale?" asked Sturgis, realizing too late he was skating on thin ice.

"She was a former member of the Cerberus inner council. She kept a written record of meetings, payoffs and crimes. There are many names on the list you should find familiar."

The ice cracked and parted, and Sturgis fell through. He abruptly rose and left the chamber without another word, as Loren banged her gavel and adjourned the proceedings until the following day.

The gallery went mad. Reporters from the major news media surged around Zale and rushed after Loren, but Pitt was waiting at the door and hustled her through the noisy mob of newspeople who were shouting questions and trying to block their path. With his arm around her waist, he managed to steer her through the gauntlet and down the steps of the Capitol into a NUMA car waiting at the curb. Giordino stood by the car with the doors open.

Curtis Merlin Zale sat at the table, inundated by a sea of journalists and flashing cameras, like a man lost in the abyss of a nightmare.

Finally, he rose unsteadily to his feet and

fought his way through the turmoil. With the help of Capitol police, he made it to the safety of his limousine. His chauffeur drove him to the mansion that housed the Washington headquarters of Cerberus and then watched as Zale walked like an elderly senior citizen through the lobby and entered the elevator to his luxurious office.

No man was more isolated from reality. He had no close friends, no family still living. Omo Kanai, perhaps the only man to whom Zale could relate, was dead. Zale was alone in a world where his was a household name.

As he sat there behind his desk and stared out the window into the courtyard below, he weighed his future and found it ominously dark. It was inevitable that he would end up in federal prison, regardless of how long he fought to stay free. When the members of the Cerberus cartel turned against him to save themselves, the finest, most expensive criminal trial lawyers in the country would be fighting a battle lost before it had even begun. Their testimony alone was enough to ensure his execution.

His wealth would surely be taken away by an avalanche of lawsuits, federal as well as civil. His loyal team of Vipers was no more. They were lying deep in the silt of New York's outer bay. They no longer stood ready to eliminate those who would testify against him.

He could never escape, never hide anywhere in the world. A man of his stature was too easy for investigators to track down, whether he fled to the Sahara Desert or to a lonely island in the middle of the ocean.

The people who had died because of his greed came back to haunt him now, not as wraiths or hideous ghosts, but like a parade of ordinary people thrown on a screen by a projector. In the end, he had lost his great gamble. He saw no avenue leading to a refuge. The decision was not difficult.

He rose from behind his desk, walked to a bar and poured himself a shot of expensive, fifty-year-old-aged whiskey and sipped it as he returned to his desk and opened a side drawer. He picked up what looked like a small antique snuffbox. There were two pills inside that he had saved in the unlikely event he would be incapacitated from an accident or suffered from a debilitating disease. He took a final drink of the whiskey, placed the pills under his tongue and relaxed in the big leather executive chair.

They found Curtis Merlin Zale dead the next morning, his desk clean of papers. There was no final note expressing shame or regret.

55

Giordino pulled the car to a stop in front of the NUMA building. Pitt stepped to the sidewalk, then turned and leaned in the window and said to Loren, "It won't take long for an army of reporters and television cameras to surround your town house in Alexandria. I think it best that Al takes you to the hangar, at least for tonight. You can bunk with the other ladies until your hearings continue tomorrow. By then, your staff can work out a security team for you."

She leaned out and kissed him lightly on the lips. "Thank you," she said softly.

He smiled and waved as Giordino pulled the car from the curb into traffic.

Pitt went directly to Sandecker's office, where he found the admiral and Rudi Gunn waiting for him. Sandecker was back in one of his good moods, puffing contentedly on one of his big personally wrapped cigars. He stepped over and shook Pitt's hand vigorously. "Great job, great job," he repeated. "Brilliant concept, using a spar with underwater explosives contained in magnetic canisters. You blew half the stern off the ship without endangering the propane tanks."

"We were lucky it worked," said Pitt modestly.

Gunn also shook Pitt's hand. "You left us with quite a mess to clean up."

"It could have been worse."

"We're already working out contracts with salvage companies to remove the ship. Don't want it to be a menace to navigation," said Gunn.

"What about the propane?"

"The tops of the tanks are only thirty feet below the surface," explained Sandecker. "The divers shouldn't have a problem hooking up pipes and pumps to other LNG tankers to remove the gas."

"The Coast Guard has already set buoys around the wreck, and stationed a lightship as a warning to incoming and outgoing ship traffic," Gunn added.

Sandecker moved back behind his desk and blew a large cloud of blue smoke toward the ceiling. "How did Loren's hearing go?"

"Not good for Curtis Merlin Zale."

The admiral's face took on a contented

look. "Do I hear the sound of a jail door closing?"

Pitt's lips raised in a slight grin. "I believe that after he's convicted and sentenced, Curtis Merlin Zale will spend the rest of his days on death row."

Gunn nodded. "A fitting conclusion for a man who murdered hundreds of innocent people in the name of money and power."

"It won't be the last time we'll see the likes of Zale," said Pitt morbidly. "It's only a matter of time before another sociopath comes along."

"You'd better go on home and get some rest," said Sandecker charitably. "Then take a few days off for your research project on Elmore Egan."

"Which reminds me," Gunn said, "Hiram Yaeger wants to see you."

Pitt went down to the computer floor of NUMA and found Yaeger sitting in a small storeroom, staring at Egan's leather briefcase. He looked up as Pitt entered, held up his hand and pointed to the interior of the open case.

"Good timing. It should begin filling with oil in another thirty seconds."

"You have a timetable?" inquired Pitt.

"The fill goes in sequence. Every inflow takes place precisely fourteen hours after the last one."

"Any idea why it's always fourteen hours?"

"Max is working on it," answered Yaeger, closing a heavy, steel door that looked like one on a bank vault. "That's why I wanted you in the storeroom. It's a secure area with steel walls for the protection of important data in the event of fire. Radio waves, microwaves, sound, light — nothing can penetrate these walls."

"And it still fills with oil?"

"Watch and see." Yaeger studied his watch, then began to count down with his index finger. "Now!" he exclaimed.

Before Pitt's eyes, the interior of Egan's leather case began filling with oil as if poured by an unseen hand. "It has to be some kind of trick."

"No trick," said Yaeger, closing the lid.

"But how?"

"Max and I finally found the answer. Egan's case is a receiver."

"I'm drawing a blank," said Pitt, confused.

Yaeger opened the heavy steel door and led the way back to his sophisticated computer system. Max stood on her stage and smiled at their arrival. "Hello, Dirk. I missed you."

Pitt laughed. "I would have brought flowers, but you can't hold them."

"It's no fun not having substance, let me tell you."

"Max," said Yaeger, "tell Dirk what we've discovered about Dr. Egan's leather case."

"The solution took me less than an hour, once I put my circuit boards on the problem." Max gazed at Pitt as though she had feelings toward him. "Did Hiram tell you the case is a receiver?"

"Yes, but what kind of a receiver?"

"Quantum teleportation."

Pitt stared at Max. "That's not possible. Teleportation is beyond the realm of current physics."

"That's what Hiram and I thought when we began our analysis. But it's a fact. The oil that appears in the case is originally placed in a chamber somewhere that measures every atom and molecule. The oil is then altered to a quantum state that is sent and reconstructed in the receiving unit, down to the exact number of atoms and molecules, according to the measurements from the sending chamber. I have, of course, way oversimplified the process. What still mystifies me is how the oil can be sent through solid objects, and with the speed of light. I hope I can find the answer with time."

"Do you know what you're saying?" said Pitt, totally incredulous.

"Indeed we do," said Max confidently. "Though it presents an incredible scientific breakthrough, don't get your hopes up.

There is no way a human could be teleported anytime in the future. Even if it were possible to send and receive a person thousands of miles away and then re-create his body, we wouldn't be able to teleport his mind and the data he has accumulated in a lifetime. He would step out of the receiving chamber with the brain pattern of a newborn baby. Oil, on the other hand, is made up of liquid hydrocarbons and other minerals. Compared with a human, its molecular makeup is far less complicated."

Pitt sat down, trying desperately to put the pieces together. "It seems fantastic that Dr. Egan created a revolutionary dynamic engine in almost the same time span that he designed a working teleporter."

"The man was a genius," said Max. "No doubt about it. What makes him even more extraordinary is that he did it without an army of assistants or a huge government-sponsored laboratory."

"That's true," Pitt agreed. "He did it alone in a hidden lab . . . the location of which we've yet to ferret out."

"I hope you find it," said Yaeger. "The significance of Egan's discovery has mind-boggling possibilities. Substances with basic molecular structures, such as oil, coal, iron or copper ore, and a great variety of other minerals, could be transported without the use of ships, trains and trucks. His teleportation system can rewrite the entire world of product transportation."

Pitt considered the immense potential for a few moments before staring at Max. "Tell me, Max, do you have enough data from Dr. Egan's case to re-create a teleporter device?"

Max shook her wraithlike head sadly. "No, I'm sorry to say. I do not have enough input to place me in the ballpark. Though I have Dr. Egan's receiving chamber as a model, the primary part of the system lies with the sending unit. I could work on the problem for years and not find a solution."

Yaeger laid a hand on Pitt's shoulder. "I wish Max and I could have given you a more detailed picture."

"You both did a remarkable job, and I'm grateful," said Pitt sincerely. "Now it's my turn to supply the answers."

Pitt stopped by his office before heading to the hangar to clear his desk, read his mail and answer voice messages. After an hour, he found himself fighting to stay awake, so he decided to call it a day. At that moment, his phone rang.

"Hello."

"Dirk!" thundered St. Julien Perlmutter's voice. "I'm glad I caught you."

"St. Julien. Where are you?"

"In Amiens, France. Dr. Hereoux has

782

graciously allowed me to remain in Jules Verne's house and work through the night studying a notebook Hugo and I found hidden by Verne almost a hundred years ago."

"Did it supply you with answers?" asked Pitt, his curiosity kindled.

"You were on the right track. Captain Nemo truly existed, except his true name was Cameron Amherst. He was a captain in the Royal Navy."

"Not Dakar the Indian prince?"

"No," replied Perlmutter. "Apparently, Verne had a hatred against the British and changed Cameron's name and native country from England to India."

"What was *his* story?"

"Amherst came from a wealthy family of shipbuilders and shipowners. He joined the Royal Navy and rose rapidly through the ranks, becoming a captain at age twenty-nine. Born in eighteen thirty and blessed with a brilliant mind, he was a child prodigy and became an engineering genius. He constantly came up with all sorts of inventive designs for ships and their propulsion systems. Unfortunately, he was a bit of a firebrand. When the old mossbacks in the admiralty refused to consider his proposals, he went to the newspapers and vilified them as ignorant men afraid of the future. He was then unceremoniously kicked out of the

Navy for insubordination."

"Much like Billy Mitchell eighty years later."

"A fair comparison." Perlmutter continued, "Verne met Amherst on a voyage across the Atlantic on the passenger liner *Great Eastern*. It was Amherst who regaled Verne with stories of his desire to build an underwater vessel capable of going anywhere beneath the oceans. He drew designs on Verne's notebook paper and described in detail the revolutionary propulsion system he had devised to power his radical submarine. Needless to say, Verne was enthralled. He kept up heavy correspondence with Amherst for four years. Then suddenly, the letters stopped coming. Verne went on to write imaginative tales and became famous, and put Amherst from his mind.

"Verne loved the sea, as you know, and he owned several yachts, which he sailed around Europe. It was on one of these voyages off Denmark that a great whalelike vessel rose out of the sea and drifted alongside Verne's sailboat. A stunned Verne, along with his son, Michel, who'd accompanied him, watched as Captain Amherst rose from a forward hatch tower and hailed him, inviting the writer to come aboard. Leaving his boat in Michel's command, Verne went aboard Amherst's astounding underwater vessel."

"So the *Nautilus did* exist."

Perlmutter nodded almost reverently on his end of the phone. "Verne learned that Amherst had secretly built his submarine in a great underwater cavern beneath the cliffs under his family estate in Scotland. When the vessel was completed and had successfully passed its trials, Amherst put together a crew of professional seamen who were unmarried and not bound to families. He then sailed the seas for thirty years."

"How long was Verne on board?" asked Pitt.

"Verne ordered his son to sail the yacht back to port and wait in the hotel there. He was flattered that his old friend had sought him out. He stayed on board the *Nautilus*, which was the actual name given the sub by Amherst, for nearly two weeks."

"Not two years, like the people in the novel?"

"It was more than ample time for Verne to study every inch of the vessel, which he exactingly recorded in his book, with a few writer's liberties here and there. A few years later, he produced *Twenty Thousand Leagues under the Sea*."

"What finally happened to Amherst?"

"According to an account in Verne's notebook, a mysterious messenger came to his house in 1895 and gave him a letter from Amherst. Most of the captain's crew had died and he had intended to return to his ancestral home in Scotland, but it had been destroyed in a fire that killed his remaining relatives. In addition, the cavern in the cliffs where he had built the *Nautilus* had suffered a cave-in, so there wasn't even that to return to."

"So he sailed to the Mysterious Island?"

"No," stated Perlmutter. "Verne made that up so the final resting place of Amherst and his *Nautilus* would not be found. Not, at least, for a long, long time. The letter went on to say that Amherst had found a similar underwater cavern on the Hudson River in New York, which would serve as the tomb for him and the *Nautilus*."

Pitt stiffened, unable to suppress a shout of euphoria. "The Hudson River?"

"That's what was written in the notebook."

"St. Julien."

"Yes."

"I love you to death."

Perlmutter gave out with a chuckle. "My dear boy, with my colossal body, you could never get near enough to do that."

56

The early-morning mist hung poised over the blue water of the river just as it had nearly a thousand years ago when the Norsemen arrived. Visibility was less than a hundred yards, and the fleet of small sailing yachts and powerboats that usually crowded the river on most summer Sundays had yet to leave their docks. The mist was like the touch of a young woman, soft and gentle, as it curled around the little boat that cruised along the shore beneath the rocky palisades. She was not a graceful craft, nor did her bow and stern rise into the mist with intricately carved dragons like those that had come so many centuries before. She was a twenty-six-foot NUMA work boat, efficient, functional and designed for a close-to-shore survey.

The speed was kept to a meticulous four knots as it dragged the long, narrow, yellow sensor below the water in its wake. Signals from the sensor were sent into the recording unit of the side-scan sonar, and Giordino stood and stared intently at the colored three-dimensional display that revealed the bottom of the river and the submerged rock at the base of the palisades. There was no beach, only a brief bit of sand and rock that quickly dropped off again once it reached the water.

Kelly stood at the helm, steering cautiously and keeping her sapphire blue eyes darting between the shoreline to her left and the waters ahead, respectful and wary of any underwater rocks that might carve up the bottom of the boat. The small craft seemed to be barely crawling through the water. The throttle of the big Yamaha 250-horsepower outboard motor on the stern was barely set a notch above idle.

She wore only basic makeup, and her honey maple hair was braided down her back, the mist building on the woven strands, droplets glistening like pearls. Her brief shorts were white, accented by a sea-foam green sleeveless sweater worn under a lightweight jersey cotton jacket. Her feet, nicely shaped, were inserted into open sandals whose color matched her sweater. The long, sculptured legs were spread with feet firmly planted on the deck to compensate for any roll caused by the wake of a passing boat unseen in the mist.

As focused as he was on the sonar recording, Giordino could not resist an occasional quick glance at Kelly's firmly encased stern. Pitt did not have the opportunity. He was comfortably laid back in a lawn chair plopped on the bow of the survey boat. Not one to put up a front to impress anyone, he often carried his favorite lawn chair and a thick soft pad on expeditions such as this one, when he saw no reason to stand for hours at a stretch. He reached down and raised a cup with a flared base for stability and sipped at the black coffee inside. Then he resumed peering at the palisades through wide-angle binoculars whose lenses were ground for detailed close viewing.

Except for sections where the ridges of volcanic rock rose in sheer vertical formation, the steep slopes were covered with brush and small trees. Part of the Newark Basin rift system that had become inactive during the Jurassic Age, the palisades contained characteristic sedimentary sandstones and mud rocks, which had a reddish-brown color and were used to build the brownstone homes and town houses of New York City. The steeper escarpments were composed of igneous rock that was highly resistant to erosion, giving it a great natural beauty.

"Another two hundred yards before we pass beneath Dad's farm," announced Kelly.

"Any readings, Al?" Pitt asked through the windshield that was propped open.

"Rocks and silt," Giordino answered briefly. "Silt and rocks."

"Keep an eye out for any indication of a rock slide."

"You think the entrance to the cavern might have been sealed by nature?"

"I'm guessing it was by man."

"If Cameron took his sub inside the cliffs, there must have been an underwater cavity."

Pitt talked without lowering the glasses. "The question is whether it still exists."

"You'd think sport divers would have stumbled onto it by now," said Kelly.

"It could only happen by chance. There are no wrecks to dive on near here and there are better spots in the river to spearfish."

"One hundred yards," warned Kelly.

Pitt aimed the glasses at the top of the cliff three hundred and fifty feet above and saw the roofs of Egan's house and study rising over the edge. He leaned forward in anticipation and carefully studied the face of the palisade. "I see signs of a fall," he said, pointing at the scattered mass of rock that had slid and tumbled down the side of the steep cliff.

Giordino took a swift glance out his side window to see what Pitt was pointing toward and then quickly refocused on the images on the recording paper. "Nothing yet," he reported.

"Steer another twenty feet from shore," Pitt ordered Kelly. "That will give the sonar a better angle to read the slope underwater."

Kelly looked at the instrument dial on the fathometer. "The bottom drops off steeply before sloping toward the middle of the river."

"Nothing yet," Giordino said quietly. "The rock appears all crammed together."

"I have something," said Pitt almost casually.

Giordino looked up. "Like what?"

"I have what looks like man-made markings in the rock."

Kelly looked up at the cliff. "Like inscriptions?"

"No," replied Pitt. "More like marks from chisels."

"No cave or tunnel from the sonar," Giordino droned.

Pitt came around the side of the cabin and jumped down on the work deck. "Let's pull in the sensor and anchor the boat just offshore."

"You think we should go dive before finding a target?" asked Giordino.

Pitt leaned back and stared up the steep palisade. "We're directly below Dr. Egan's study. If there's a hidden cavern, it has to be around here. We'll have an easier time sighting it beneath the surface by eye."

Kelly expertly turned the boat in a tight circle and shut down the throttle as Pitt pulled in the sensor and dropped the anchor. Then she moved it slowly in reverse in the direction of the river current until the flukes dug into the bottom. Then she switched off the ignition and shook the droplets of moisture from her long braided mane. "Is this where you wish to park?" she inquired with a cute smile.

"Perfect," Pitt complimented her.

"May I come, too? I got my certification in the Bahamas."

"Let us go first. If we find something, I'll surface and wave you in."

It was summer, and the Hudson River water was a brisk seventy-two degrees. Pitt opted for a neoprene quarter-inch wet suit with pads on the knees and elbows. A weight belt with light weights to counteract the buoyancy of the wet suit was clamped around his waist. He pulled on a pair of gloves, his fins and hood before slicking the inside lens of his mask and pulling the straps over his head, setting the mask atop his head with the snorkel dangling. Because he would be diving in no more than ten feet, he did not wear a buoyancy compensator, preferring more freedom and ease of mobility for moving in and around the rocks.

"We'll free-dive first and check out the landscape before we use the tanks."

Giordino nodded silently and lowered the stepladder over the stern. Instead of falling backward over the side, he dropped down three rungs of the ladder, then stepped off into the water. Pitt swung his legs over the bulwark and slipped in with the barest hint of a splash.

The water was as transparent as glass for thirty feet before it faded into a gloom turned green with clouds of minuscule algae. It was also cold to the flesh. Pitt was warm-blooded and preferred his water temperature to be in the low eighties. If God had meant for humans to be fish, he thought, He'd have given us a body temperature of sixty degrees instead of ninety-eight-point-six.

Pitt hyperventilated and curled forward, lifting his legs and using their weight to push him downward in an effortless dive. The great jagged rocks were massed together like pieces of an ill-fitting jigsaw puzzle. Many weighed several tons, while others were no larger than a child's Radio Flyer wagon. He made sure the flukes of the anchor were securely dug into the sandy bottom before surfacing for air.

The current pulled at Pitt and Giordino, and they used their hands as anchors, clutching the rocks and pulling their bodies over the moss-coated surfaces, thankful they had had the foresight to wear gloves to protect their fingertips from the sharp edges. They soon realized they were not in the right area, because this part of the slope disappeared toward the center of the river too gradually.

They surfaced for air and decided to split the search. Pitt would head up and Giordino would follow the rocky shore downriver. Pitt gazed at the sky to get his bearings on the buildings sitting near the crest. He could just make out the top of the chimney of the house. He swam against the current, parallel to Egan's house and study four hundred feet above.

The mist was clearing and the sun was beginning to sparkle the water, casting dappled and shimmering light across the slime-coated rocks. Pitt saw few fish larger than his little finger. They darted around him curiously without the slightest show of fear, somehow knowing that this weird lumbering creature was far too slow to catch them. He wiggled a finger at them, but they spiraled around it as if it were a maypole. He continued lazily kicking his fins while floating on the surface and breathing slowly through his snorkel, as he watched the craggy bottom pass beneath.

Then suddenly, he swam over an open stretch free of the rocks. The bottom was now smooth and flat with a channel cut through the rubble. He judged it dropped off thirty feet before he swam across to the other side, where the jumbled rocks appeared again. Returning across the gap, he measured the width at roughly forty feet. The channel beckoned toward the shore where the rock slide had fallen into the water. He sucked a cubic foot of air into his lungs before holding his breath and diving down to look for an opening through the jagged fall of rock. The boulders, one overcropping the other, looked cold and somber as if there was something diabolic about them, almost as though they held a secret they were reluctant to reveal.

Weeds swayed in the current like the long fingers of a ballet dancer. He found a ledge free of growth that had strange chiseled markings in the hard surface. His heart leaped two beats when he recognized one as the crude carving of a dog. His lungs felt squeezed, and he surfaced for another breath of air. Then he dived again, swimming and sometimes using his hands to pull himself around the rocks.

He watched as a ten-inch smallmouth bass swam from under a large overhanging slab of stone. It saw Pitt's shadow and quickly disappeared. He angled down and chased after it under the ledge. A dark tunnel appeared through the rocks and beckoned him. The skin on the nape of his neck tingled. Another breath on the surface and he entered the opening cautiously. Once inside and free of the glare outside, he could see that the burrow flared out ten feet ahead. That was as far as he decided to go. Expelling the last of his air, he returned to the surface.

Al had climbed back on the boat, having found nothing of interest. Kelly was sitting on top of the cabin, her feet on the deck of the bow staring in Pitt's direction. He waved both arms and yelled.

"I found a way inside!"

Kelly and Giordino needed no further urging. In less than three minutes, they were stroking against the current beside him. Pitt did not remove the mouthpiece of his snorkel for further conversation. Excitedly, he motioned for them to follow him. They paused to fill their lungs, and then Giordino and Kelly trailed behind Pitt's fins through the jumbled mass of stone debris.

They swam through the narrow section of the tunnel, their fins brushing against the sides and disturbing the growth into a green diaphanous cloud. Finally, just when Kelly was beginning to fear that she only had a few seconds left before opening her mouth and taking in a mouthful of water, the cavity fanned out and she gripped Pitt's left ankle, using his momentum to propel her to the surface.

Their heads came free of the water in unison. They spit out the mouthpieces of their snorkels, raised the dive masks over their heads and found themselves in an immense cavern whose roof towered two hundred feet above their heads. They stared in complete surprise, without fully comprehending what they had discovered.

Pitt gazed up in wonder at the head of a serpent with bared fangs that was staring down at him.

57

The gracefully curved serpent head, intricately carved with mouth agape, stared sightlessly at the water flowing into the cavern, as if searching for a distant shore. On an enormous ledge four feet above the water's edge, six open wooden boats, held upright by their keels and wedged by wooden cradles, sat side by side, stern to bow. The serpent rose on the bow post of the largest boat nearest the rim of the ledge.

The boats were built entirely of oak, the largest stretching more than sixty feet in length. The sun's reflection coming through the water in the tunnel cast feathery ribbons of light against the elegantly shaped hulls. From their view in the water, the divers could look up at the keels and the broad, symmetrically arched hulls with their clinker-built, overlapping strake planking that was still held together with rusting iron rivets. Below the rack where shields had once been stored, oars still protruded through small round ports. Now gripped by ghostly hands, they seemed poised, waiting for a command to row. It seemed inconceivable that such aesthetically elegant hull lines could have been designed and built a thousand years in the past.

"They're Viking," Kelly murmured in astonished awe. "They've been here all the time and nobody knew."

"Your father knew," said Pitt. "He knew from the Viking inscriptions that they had settled on the palisades above the Hudson River, which led him to the discovery of the tunnel leading down to the cavern from above."

"They're well preserved," Giordino observed, casting an admiring eye over the Viking ships. "Despite the dampness, I see little signs of rot."

Pitt pointed up at the masts that were still standing with their furled red-and-white coarse woolen sails, then at the vaulted roof of the cavern high above their heads. "They left them stepped because of the cavern's lofty ceiling."

"They look as if all you had to do is drop them in the water, raise the sails and go," Kelly whispered in breathless wonder.

"Let's take a closer look," Pitt said.

After removing their fins, face masks and

weight belts, they climbed a rock-chiseled stairway to the top of the ledge and mounted the boarding ramps that ran from the rock to the upper strake of the largest ship. The ramps were sound and obviously put there by Dr. Egan.

The light inside the cavern was dim, but they recognized the objects scattered on the floorboards. What looked like a body was wrapped in a burial shroud. On each side were smaller bundles in burial shrouds. Around the bodies, a treasure trove of artifacts had been literally dumped in scattered disarray. There were gilt-bronzed figures of saints, a stack of illuminated manuscripts in Gospel Latin and reliquary boxes filled with coins and silver chalices, most likely all stolen from monasteries during raids on England and Ireland. Amber necklaces, gold and silver brooches, elaborate silver-and-bronze necklaces and bracelets lay in piles inside elaborately carved wooden boxes. Bronze dishes and incense burners from the Orient, along with furniture, textiles and linen, and a beautifully carved sled for the chief to be towed on in winter snow, were also lying about.

"My guess is this is Bjarne Sigvatson," said Pitt.

Kelly looked sadly at the two smaller bundles. "They must be his children."

"He must have been quite a warrior to

have accumulated this much wealth," Giordino muttered, gazing raptly at the treasures.

"From reading Dad's research notebooks," said Kelly, "I had the impression important chieftains were sent to Valhalla after a glorious death, along with all their worldly goods and chattels, which included their horses, other animals and their servants. He should also have his battle-ax, sword and shield. I see none of these."

"The burial was a rush job," agreed Giordino.

Pitt motioned toward the boarding ramp. "Let's have a look at the other boats."

To Kelly's horror, the adjacent boats were strewn with bones intermingled with broken and shattered household goods. Few skeletons were intact. Most looked as though they had been hacked to pieces.

Pitt knelt and studied a skull with a jagged gash in the top of the cranium. "There must have been a terrible massacre."

"Could they have fought among themselves?"

"I don't think so," said Giordino. He removed an arrow that was embedded between the ribs of one pile of bones and held it up. "This says Indians."

"The sagas suggested that Sigvatson and his people sailed away from Greenland and were never heard of again," said Pitt, trying to imagine a face on the skull. "It also lends credibility to the legend Dr. Wednesday told of the Indians slaughtering all the Vikings in the settlement."

"This proves it was no myth," Giordino said quietly.

Kelly looked at Pitt. "Then the Norse settlement . . ."

"Was located on your father's farm," Pitt finished. "He found artifacts and was influenced to launch his research project."

Kelly wrung her hands mournfully. "But why did he keep it a secret? Why didn't he call in archaeologists to conduct excavations? Why not show the world that Vikings had arrived in what is now New York and begun a colony?"

"Your father was a brilliant man," said Giordino. "In his mind he must have had a good reason for the secrecy. He definitely didn't want an army of archaeologists and reporters invading his privacy during his experiments."

Thirty minutes later, while Kelly and Giordino examined the rest of the Viking ships — not an easy undertaking in the dim light of the cavern — Pitt began wandering around the ledge. In the gloom he spotted a stairway hacked into the rock that led up into a tunnel. He climbed the first four steps with his hand trailing along one wall for support, when his fingers met with something that felt like an electrical switch. He touched it lightly and determined that the lever swung clockwise. Curious, he turned the lever until it clicked.

Suddenly, the entire cavern was illuminated by bright fluorescent lights set into the rock walls.

"Cool," Kelly uttered in surprise. "Now we can see what we're doing."

Pitt walked over to where she and Giordino were searching through one of the boats. "I know another reason why your father kept this place a secret," he said slowly, deliberately.

Kelly seemed only mildly interested, but Giordino stared at him. He'd known Pitt too long not to recognize when he was about to spring a revelation. Then he saw the direction in which Pitt's eyes were aimed and he turned and did the same.

A long, cylindrical iron vessel was moored to a dock along the far side of the cavern. The hull was covered with a thin coating of rust. The only noticeable protrusion was a small hatch tower set several feet aft of the forward bow. The vessel had not been visible in the darkened cavern interior until Pitt had turned on the lights.

"What in God's name is that?" Kelly muttered.

"That," said Pitt, with a note of triumph in his voice, "is the *Nautilus*."

★ ★ ★

Their astonishment at standing on a dock that had been built by Dr. Elmore Egan and staring down at the legendary and fabled submarine was equal to what they'd felt with the discovery of the Viking ships. To suddenly find a marvel of nineteenth-century engineering that everybody had thought was fiction was like a dream turned real.

At the foot of the dock, rising along the rim of the rock ledge, was a pile of stones stacked in the shape of a sarcophagus. A wooden plaque with carved letters revealed it as the final resting place of the submarine's creator:

*Here lie the mortal remains of
Captain Cameron Amherst.
Made famous by the writings of Jules Verne
as the immortal Captain Nemo.
May those who someday discover his tomb
honor him with the respect he deserves.*

"My esteem of your father continues to grow," Pitt said to Kelly. "He was a man to envy."

"Knowing Dad built this monument with his own hands makes me proud."

Giordino, who'd lagged behind after exploring a side cave, approached the dock. "I found another answer to the mystery that'd been bothering me."

Pitt looked at him. "Which mystery?"

"If Dr. Egan had a hidden laboratory, where was the source of his electrical energy? I found it in a side cave. There are three portable generating units in there, connected to enough batteries to power a small town." He pointed down at the dock and the series of electrical cables running along the edge and through the hatch of the submarine. "Ten to one he used the interior for his laboratory."

"Now that I see the *Nautilus* close up," said Kelly, "it's much bigger than I imagined."

"She hardly looks like the Disney version," Giordino mused. "Her outer hull is simple and functional."

Pitt nodded in agreement. The top of the hull rose but three feet from the water, giving a bare hint of her mass beneath. "I estimate her length at about two hundred and fifty feet, with a twenty-five-foot beam, larger than Verne described. She's close to the dimensions of the first Navy submarine with advanced hydrodynamic design that was launched in 1953."

"The *Albacore*," replied Giordino. "I saw her sailing down the York River about ten years ago. You're right. There is a resemblance."

Giordino walked over to an electrical panel mounted above the dock beside a gangplank leading to the submarine's deck next to the hatch tower. He pressed a pair of switches. The interior of the vessel was instantly bathed in light that beamed up through a series of ports along the roof and through larger view ports seen below in the water.

Pitt turned to Kelly and motioned down the open hatch tower. "Ladies first."

She placed her hands against her chest as if to slow her pounding heart. She wanted to see where her father had worked all those years, to see the inside of the famous vessel, but she found it difficult to take the first step. It seemed to her that she was entering a house of ghosts. Finally, with great force of will, she entered the hatch and climbed down the ladder.

The entry compartment was small. She waited until Pitt and Giordino joined her. In front of them was a door that looked like it belonged on a house more than in a submarine. Pitt turned the latch, opened it and stepped over the threshold.

Silently, they walked through an ornately furnished dining hall fifteen feet in length centered on a teak wood table for ten with beautifully carved standing dolphins for legs. At the far end was another door that led into a library, whose shelves Pitt guessed contained more than five thousand books. He studied the titles on the spines. One side held books on engineering and science. The opposite shelves were stacked with original editions of the classics. He picked one that been written by Jules Verne and opened it. The title page had been inscribed by Verne to "the greatest mind in the universe." He slipped it back carefully in its place on the shelf and continued the exploration.

The next compartment was quite large, stretching more than thirty feet. This area, Pitt was certain, was the grand saloon that Verne had described as filled with art treasures and ancient artifacts Cameron had gleaned from under the sea. But the saloon was no longer a museum and gallery. Elmore Egan had transformed it into a workshop and a chemistry laboratory. The room, twelve feet wide, was filled with counters holding a maze of chemical lab apparatus, a spacious workshop with compact machinery, including a lathe and a drill press, and three different computer stations with an array of printers and scanners. Only the organ was still there, having been too massive for Elmore to move. The instrument on which Amherst had played works from the great composers was a masterpiece of craftsmanship with beautifully finished wood and brass pipes.

Kelly walked over to the counter littered with chemistry equipment and tenderly touched the beakers and test tubes lying about in disorder, assembling and stacking them neatly in racks and on shelves. She lingered in the laboratory, soaking up her father's presence while Pitt and Giordino moved on, passing through a long corridor and into a watertight bulkhead before entering the next compartment. This section of the *Nautilus* had once served as Captain Amherst's private cabin. Egan had converted it into his think tank. Plans, blueprints and drawings, along with a hundred notebooks, were stacked in every square inch of space around a large drafting table where Egan had worked out his designs.

"So this is where one great man lived, and another great man created," Giordino commented philosophically.

"Let's keep going," said Pitt. "I want to see where he built his teleportation sending chamber."

They walked through another watertight bulkhead and into a compartment that had once held the submarine's air tanks. These had been removed by Egan to make room for his teleportation instruments and equipment. There were two panels with dials and switches, a computer desk and an enclosed chamber that contained the sending station.

Pitt smiled when he saw a fifty-five-gallon drum marked Super Slick sitting in the chamber. It was connected to a timing device and a series of tubes, which were themselves connected to a round receptacle on the floor. "Now we know where the oil comes from that keeps filling up Egan's leather case."

"I wonder how it all works," said Giordino, examining the sending station.

"It will take someone smarter than me to figure it out."

"It's amazing that it actually works."

"As crude and elementary as it appears, you're looking at a scientific achievement that will forever alter the transportation of the future."

Pitt stepped over to the instrument panel where the timing device was mounted. He saw that the sequence was set at fourteen hours. He reset it to ten.

"What are you doing?" asked Giordino curiously.

The edges of his lips lifted in a sneaky grin. "I'm sending a message to Hiram Yaeger and Max."

Having gone as far as they could go toward the bow, Pitt and Giordino retraced their steps to the main saloon. Kelly was sitting in a chair, looking for all the world as if she were in the midst of an out-of-body experience.

Pitt squeezed her shoulder tenderly. "We're heading toward the engine room. Would you like to come along?"

She brushed her cheek against his hand.

"Did you find anything interesting?"

"Your father's teleportation compartment."

"Then he actually created and built a device that can send objects through space."

"He did."

Lost in euphoria, she rose from the chair, and quietly followed the two men as they made their way aft.

Once on the other side of the dining hall and the entry compartment, they passed through a galley that made Kelly cringe. Food containers were cluttered around the countertops, dirty dishes and utensils were green with mold in a large sink, and large baskets of trash and garbage in plastic bags were stacked in a heap in one corner of the galley.

"Your father had many qualities," observed Pitt, "but neatness wasn't one of them."

"He had other things on his mind," Kelly said lovingly. "It's a pity he didn't take me into his confidence. I could have acted as his secretary and housekeeper."

They went through the next opening into the crew's quarters. What they saw here was the most mind-boggling of all.

Here is where Elmore had stored the treasures that had once adorned the main saloon and library. The number of canvases would have filled two rooms of the Metropolitan Museum of Art. Leonardo da Vinci, Titian, Raphael, Rembrandt, Vermeer, Rubens and thirty others were stacked in rows. Sculptures from antiquity, in bronze and marble, stood in closets and individual crew's cabins. And then there were the treasures that Amherst had salvaged from ancient shipwrecks: piles of gold and silver bars, boxes filled to overflowing with coins and gemstones. The value of the collection was beyond their comprehension, beyond their wildest appraisal.

"I feel like Ali Baba after he discovered the forty thieves' cave of riches," said Pitt in a hushed voice.

Kelly was equally astounded. "I never dreamed anything like this existed."

Giordino took a handful of gold coins and let them sift through his fingers. "If there was ever a question as to how Dr. Elmore financed his experiments, what we see here tells it all."

They spent nearly an hour combing through the great hoard before carrying on with their tour. After walking through another watertight bulkhead, they found themselves in the *Nautilus*'s engine room. This was the most expansive section of the ship, measuring sixty feet in length by twenty feet in width.

The maze of pipes, tanks and strange-looking mechanisms that Pitt and Giordino recognized as electrical generating equipment had to be a plumber's nightmare. A huge gear system with meshing steel teeth dominated the aft end of the room. While Kelly wandered about, not nearly as fascinated by the machinery as the men, she came to a high podium-like table without a chair that held a large leatherbound book. She opened it and studied the old-fashioned scroll handwriting in brown ink. The book proved to be the chief engineer's log. The last entry was dated June 10, 1901, and read . . .

Closed down the engine for the final time. Will keep the generators operating for power until my demise. The Nautilus *that has served me so faithfully for forty years will now serve as my tomb. This is my last entry.*

It was signed, Cameron Amherst.

Meanwhile, Pitt and Giordino were poring over the massive engine with its distinctive nineteenth-century fittings, valves and unfamiliar mechanisms, many of them cast and polished in brass.

Pitt crawled under and around the great engine, inspecting it from every angle. Finally, he stood and scratched the stubble on his chin. "I've researched hundreds of marine engines in hundreds of different ships, including old steamships, but I've never seen anything that matches this layout."

Giordino, who had been examining the manufacturers' plaques bolted on different parts of the machinery, said, "The power plant did not come from one manufacturer. Amherst must have commissioned thirty different marine engine machinists throughout Europe and America to build this thing before assembling it with his own crew."

"That's how he managed to construct the *Nautilus* in secrecy."

"What do you make of the design?"

"My best guess is that it's a combination of massive electrical energy and a rudimentary form of magnetohydrodynamics."

"So Amherst created the concept a hundred and forty years before it was rediscovered."

"He didn't have the technology to run the seawater through a magnetic core kept at absolute zero by liquid helium — that wouldn't be produced commercially for another sixty years — so he used a kind of sodium converter. It wasn't nearly as efficient, but good enough for his purposes. Amherst had to compensate by relying on massive electrical energy to produce enough generating current to turn the propeller at an efficient rate of speed."

"Then it would seem likely that Egan

used Amherst's engine as a base for his own designs."

"It must have proven an inspiration for him."

"A phenomenal piece of work," said Giordino, appreciating the ingenuity behind the huge engine. "Especially when you realize that it propelled the *Nautilus* into every corner of the undersea world for forty years."

Kelly approached, carrying the engine-room log. She looked as if she were staring at a ghost. "If we're finished in here for now, I'd like to find the passage Dad must have discovered to get back and forth between here and the house above."

Pitt nodded and glanced at Giordino. "We should contact the admiral and report what we've found here."

"I'm sure he'd like to know," Giordino agreed.

Five minutes, no more, was all it took to climb through the passage leading up to the top of the palisades. Pitt felt a strange sensation, knowing the Vikings had passed this same way a thousand years earlier. He could almost hear their voices and touch their presence.

Josh Thomas was sitting in Egan's study, reading a chemical analysis journal, when he froze in fright. The rug in the center of the room suddenly rose from the floor as if a ghost were inside and then flew aside. A trapdoor beneath swung open and Pitt's head popped up like a jack-in-the-box.

"Sorry to intrude," said Pitt with a cheery smile. "But I just happened to be passing by."

Part Six

GHOST FROM THE PAST

58

AUGUST 16, 2003
WASHINGTON, D.C.

Pitt roused himself out of bed, slipped into a robe and helped himself to a cup of coffee brewed by Sally Morse. He wanted to remain in bed for most of the morning, but Sally and Kelly were leaving. After testifying before Loren's congressional committee and giving depositions to the Justice Department, Sally was warmly thanked by a grateful president and released to fly home and resume her duties as chairwoman of Yukon Oil, until her presence was required for additional testimony.

When Pitt swayed sleepy-eyed into the kitchen, Sally was happily humming and unloading the dishwasher. "I never thought I'd hear myself saying this, but I'm going to miss having you and Kelly underfoot."

Sally laughed cheerfully. "That's only because you'll have to go back to fixing your own meals, cleaning the dishes, making your bed and doing your laundry."

"I can't deny I enjoyed it."

She looked becoming in a taupe, silk mélange cowl-neck sweater and brown micro-suede jeans. Her ash blond hair hung loose and flowing. "You should find yourself a good woman to take care of you."

"Loren is the only one who'd have me, but she's too busy playing politics." Pitt sat down behind the breakfast table, which he'd salvaged from an old steamship in the Great Lakes, and sipped his coffee. "What about you? Too busy running an oil company to find a good man?"

"No," she said slowly. "I'm a widow. My husband and I built Yukon Oil together. When he died in a plane crash, I took over. Since then, most men act intimidated when they're around me."

"The price lady CEOs have to pay. But don't worry. You'll get lucky before the year is out."

"I didn't know you can read the future," she said blithely.

"The Great Dirk Pitt sees all, knows all, and I see a tall, dark handsome man of equal status and wealth sweeping you off to Tahiti."

"I can't wait."

Kelly breezed into the kitchen, wearing an ivory-knit, wool, low-cut sleeveless sweater and blue cotton shorts. "I'm almost sorry to leave this museum to man's folly," she quipped.

"You'll get a statement in the mail," Pitt said dourly. "Which reminds me, I'd better make a count of the towels before you girls fly off into the blue."

"My thanks to Sally," said Kelly, zipping up her travel bag. "She was kind enough to offer me a lift in her private jet to the airfield near Dad's farm."

"You ready?" asked Sally.

"What are your plans?" Pitt asked, rising from his chair.

"I'm setting up a philanthropic foundation in Dad's name. Then I plan on donating the paintings and other art treasures to a select list of museums."

"Good for you," Sally complimented her.

"And the hoard of silver and gold?"

"Some of it goes to build and finance the Elmore Egan Science Laboratory, which will be run by Josh Thomas, who plans to recruit the finest young minds in the country to come on board. Most of the rest will go to charities. There is, of course, a share waiting for you and Al."

Pitt shook his head and waved his hands. "Please, not me. I'm comfortable. Al might accept a new Ferrari, but I prefer you put whatever you had earmarked for us to better use."

"I'm beginning to see what Loren said

about you," said Sally, impressed.

"Oh, what was that?"

"That you are an honest man."

"There are times like this when I hate myself."

Pitt carried their luggage down to the limo that was waiting to carry them to Sally's plane at a nearby executive airport.

Sally stepped over to Pitt, hugged him and kissed his cheek. "Good-bye, Dirk Pitt. It was a privilege knowing you."

"Good-bye, Sally. I hope you find that guy waiting out there."

Kelly kissed him full on the mouth. "When will I see you again?"

"Not for a while. Admiral Sandecker intends to keep me busy and out of mischief for a long time."

He stood there for a moment, waving, until the limo turned toward the airport entry gate. Then he slowly closed the hangar door, walked up to his apartment and went back to bed.

When Loren stopped by to spend the weekend with Pitt, she found him leaning under the hood of the 1938 green Packard town car. She looked tired after another long day of hearings into the Zale scandal, which had brought the entire government to a screeching halt. She looked stunning in a black, form-fitting business suit. "Hi, big man. What are you up to?"

"These old carburetors were built to use leaded gas. The new unleaded variety has all sorts of weird chemicals that eat hell out of the guts inside. Whenever I drive the old cars, I have to overhaul the carburetors or they gum up."

"What would you like for dinner?"

"Sure you don't want to dine out?"

"The news media is in a feeding frenzy over the scandal. I'm still considered fair game. The woman who does my hair drove me here in her husband's pickup truck, with me sitting on the floor."

"How lucky you are to be so popular."

Loren made a sour face. "How about pasta with spinach and prosciutto?"

"It's a date."

She called down to him an hour later that dinner was ready. After he cleaned up, he entered the kitchen and found Loren wearing nothing but a silk smoking jacket that she had given Pitt for Christmas but which he never wore, protesting that it made him look like a phony gigolo. He peered into the pot of boiling pasta.

"It has a nice aroma for pure pasta."

"It should. I poured half a bottle of Chardonnay into it."

"Then we don't require predinner cocktails."

They enjoyed the casual dinner, trading

sarcasms and little jabs between them. It was a regular routine between two people of equal wit and intellect. Pitt and Loren contradicted the old maxim that opposites attract. They were as similar in their likes and dislikes as two people could be.

"Are your hearings about over?" he asked.

"Tuesday is the final day. From then on, the Justice Department takes the high road. My job is done."

"You were lucky Sally walked through the door."

Loren nodded as she held up a glass of the Chardonnay. "If not for her, Zale would still be walking the earth and causing mayhem and murder. His suicide solved a multitude of problems."

"What does Justice have in store for his cronies in crime?"

"The Cerberus cartel members will be indicted. Every agent in the Justice Department is working overtime to build cases against the thousands of bureaucrats and elected politicians who were known to have taken bribes. The consequences of this scandal will be felt for a long time."

"Hopefully, it will discourage others from going off the deep end for money."

"A huge task force is out there now, tracking down the offshore investments and bank accounts of the guilty parties, as provided by Hiram Yaeger."

Pitt stared into his wine as he swirled the contents around in the glass. "So where do *we* go from here?"

She touched his hand lightly with her fingers. "We go on as before."

"You in Congress and me under the sea," he said slowly.

A soft look came into her violet eyes. "I believe it was meant to be that way."

"So much for my illusion of becoming a grandfather."

She pulled her hand away. "It hasn't been easy competing with a ghost."

"Summer?" He said the name as if he were seeing something far in the distance.

"You've never quite gotten over her."

"I thought I did, once."

"Maeve."

"When Summer was lost in the sea and Maeve died in my arms, it left an emptiness inside me." He shook away the memories like a dog shaking away water. "I'm too sentimental for my own good." He came around the table and kissed her lightly on the lips. "I have a lovely, wonderful woman and don't appreciate her the way I should."

At that tender moment, Pitt's door buzzer sounded. His brow raised and he turned and peered into the monitor of the video security camera mounted inconspicuously outside. The image of a young man and young woman filled the screen. They were standing at the door beside a pile of luggage.

"Looks like they've come to stay," Loren said sardonically.

"I wonder who they are?"

Loren held Pitt's hand from pressing the button to the intercom. "I left my purse sitting on the fender of the Packard. I'll run down, pick it up and get rid of them."

"I wonder what they'll think when they see you looking like that," he said, pointing a finger at the smoking jacket that barely covered her body.

"I'll just peek around the door."

Pitt relaxed and finished the pasta. He was just taking a final sip of wine when Loren's voice came over the intercom.

"Dirk, I think you should come down."

There was something in the tone of her voice that struck him as peculiar, almost as if she was hesitant to speak. He dropped down the spiral staircase and walked past his collector cars to the entrance door of the hangar. Loren was standing partially hidden behind the three-quarters-open door, talking to the young couple.

They both looked to be in their early twenties. There was a distinct presence about the man. His hair was black and wavy, and he was a good inch taller than Pitt. Their build and weight seemed nearly identical. The eyes were also a mesmeric opaline green. He glanced at Loren, who stood and stared at the young couple, spellbound. He gazed more deeply at the man's face and stiffened. It was as if he was looking into a magic mirror that reflected himself when he was twenty-five years younger.

He forced his attention from the man to the woman, and a strange tingling sensation coursed through his body and his heart increased its beat. She was quite beautiful, tall and lithe with long, flaming red hair. She stared back at Pitt through pearl gray eyes. Memories came flooding back, and he had to grasp the door frame to keep his knees from sagging.

"Mr. Pitt." The young man spoke in a deep voice. It was a statement, not a question.

"I'm Pitt."

Loren shivered as the young man smiled a smile that she had seen so often on Pitt's lips.

"My sister and I have waited a long time to meet you. Twenty-three years, to be exact."

"Now that you've found me, how can I help you?" Pitt asked, as if afraid of the answer.

"Mother was right. We do look alike."

"Your mother?"

"Her name was Summer Moran. Our

grandfather was Frederick Moran."

Pitt felt as if a vise were crushing his heart. He barely got it out. "She and her father died in an underwater earthquake off Hawaii many years ago."

The young woman shook her head. "Mother survived, but she was critically injured. Her legs and back were crushed and her face badly disfigured. She never walked again and was confined to bed for the rest of her life."

"I can't, no, I won't believe it." The words came as if they were spoken through a veil. "I lost her in the sea when she swam back to save her father."

"Believe me, sir," said the young lady, "it's true. After she was badly injured by an undersea rockfall, Mother was saved by my grandfather's men, who carried her to the surface where they were soon rescued by an island fishing boat. She was rushed to a hospital in Honolulu, where she hovered between life and death for nearly a month. Unconscious most of the time, she was unable to tell the doctors and nurses who she was. Finally, over a year later, when she had recovered enough to be released, she returned to her family home on the island of Kauai, where she resided until her death. Fortunately, Grandfather left her a substantial estate, and she received wonderful care from a staff of housekeepers and nurses."

"Were you and your brother born before her injuries?" asked Loren, clutching the smoking jacket around her body.

The woman shook her head. "She gave birth to us in the hospital a week shy of nine months later."

"You're twins?" Loren gasped, stunned at the difference in looks between them.

The young woman smiled. "We're fraternal. It isn't unusual for nonidentical twins to differ. My brother looks like my father. I took after my mother."

"She never tried to contact me?" Pitt asked grievously.

"Mother was sure that if you had known, you would have rushed to her side. She didn't wish you to see her pitifully broken body and disfigurement. She wanted you to remember her as she was."

Undeserved guilt and utter confusion swept over Pitt. "God, if I had only known." The memories of Hawaii came flooding back. Summer had been a breathtakingly gorgeous woman, and she still haunted his dreams.

"It's not your fault," said Loren, squeezing his arm. "She felt she had a good reason for keeping the secret."

"If she's still alive, where is she?" Pitt demanded. "I want to know."

"Mother died last month," answered the young man. "She was in very poor health near the end. She was buried on a hill over-looking the ocean. She willed herself to live until my sister and I graduated from college. Only then did she tell us about you. Her last wish was that we meet."

"And why was that?" Pitt asked, though he was sure of the answer.

"I was named after Mother," said the young woman. "My name is Summer, too."

The man smiled. "She named me after my father. My name is also Dirk Pitt."

Discovering that Summer, broken in body, had borne him a son and daughter, and then raised them without his knowledge all these years, tore at his heart. He was dev-astated and jubilant at the same time.

Pitt gathered himself together and stepped forward. He circled his arms around their shoulders and embraced them. "You must forgive me. Suddenly discov-ering that I have two lovely grown children comes as no small surprise."

"You don't know how happy we are to fi-nally find you, Father," said Summer, her voice on the verge of a sob.

Tears came to everyone's eyes. Both chil-dren cried openly. Loren buried her head in her hands. Pitt's eyes watered like over-flowing wells.

He took them both by the hand and pulled them into the hangar. Then he stepped back and smiled broadly. "I prefer you call me Dad. We don't stand on formality around here, especially now that you've come to my home."

"You don't mind if we stay here?" asked Summer innocently.

"Is there a dome on the Capitol?" He helped them with their luggage and led them inside. He pointed at the big Pullman car with the letters MANHATTAN LIMITED painted in gold on the side. "You have your choice of four lavishly appointed staterooms. As soon as you settle in, come upstairs. We have a lot of catching up to do."

"Where did you go to school?" asked Loren.

"Summer received her master's from the Scripps Institute of Oceanography. I received mine in marine engineering from the New York Maritime College."

"I suspect your mother had something to do with your curricula," said Pitt.

"Yes," replied Summer. "She inspired us to go into ocean science."

"A wise woman, your mother." Pitt knew full well that Summer had prepared her children to eventually work with their father.

The young people stopped and stared in astonishment at the collection of classic cars and aircraft in the hangar. "Are these all yours?" asked Summer.

"For the moment." Pitt laughed. "But I

think I can safely say that someday they'll belong to the two of you."

Dirk gazed wonderingly at a big orange-and-brown car. "Is this a Duesenberg?" he asked quietly.

"Are you familiar with old cars?"

"I've loved old automobiles since I was a little boy. My first car was a 1940 Ford convertible."

"A chip off the old block," said Loren, wiping her tears.

Now Pitt was really touched by his newly found offspring. "Ever drive a Duesenberg?"

"Oh, no, never."

Pitt put his arm around his son and said proudly, "You will, my boy. You will."